I0586741

Journey of Betrayals

John H Gray

The story of one man's conflicted life as he struggles with life's temptations and his religious background.

ISBN 978-0-9952387-2-5

Acknowledgments

Writing this book would not have been possible without the assistance of many friends and family.

I especially thank my wife Bobbie for her patience and encouragement. At times I know I bored her terribly as I sat writing or on the Internet researching a topic, or just drifting off and visualizing the story.

I thank Michele Thorne for her never ending support and assistance in reading through the manuscript and offering comments and suggestions. To Bernard Walsh in New Zealand a special thank you for your generous support. To Ingrid Coolen in the Netherlands I thank for her insight into life in Holland during WWII and for proof reading the story. To my good friend Errol Gray (no relative) an appreciation for his ongoing support throughout the project. Paul Ledoux, Sam Barber, Kevin and Karen Slater, Andre Thibert, Jacek and Regina Czapiewski and my other supporters. If I have omitted mentioning you it is my error for which I apologize.

I must also acknowledge the patient support I received from Winston the Himalayan cat and Alfie the King Charles Cavalier dog as they sat either side of me during the writing process.

Prologue

Boca Catalina, Aruba, Dutch West Indies

Wizened and deeply tanned from years of exposure to the elements, Hans stood toward the back of the multimillion dollar catamaran. He scanned the water, keeping a vigilant eye on his "cares". The tourists, each of whom had gladly parted with $50 in order to sail the miserable 15 minutes up the coast of Aruba and drink the cheap liquor provided by the company. "All of this in the name of having fun", he thought. He was anchored no more than a few hundred yards from the old wreck of the Antilla, the scuttled German World War II freighter. He watched as they snorkeled and drifted over the rusting remains of the old sunken ship that lay on her side. In their minds, each was probably thinking of some romantic or dramatic scene, he surmised. In reality, he was sick of visiting the wreck site. The events and history of this ship had reached him in real life in ways he preferred to forget.

Looking out over the still and turquoise waters of the Caribbean, he wondered if things could have worked out differently. It was over 25 years since he had experienced his lover's deceit that was so deep it had totally derailed him and destroyed his well established and privileged life. Unable to accept the rejection and loss, he had made reckless and irreversible changes. Gone was the lifestyle of carefree living without any consequences. Gone was the Porsche. Gone was the beautiful home in Munich, which he had inherited and was decorated with antiques and priceless art. Gone too were his ties to his family and siblings. Gone too was his beautiful Greetje, a woman of incredible beauty and wit. All that mattered to him after that was his escape to the Caribbean in order to erase and forget this tragedy.

Since abandoning all of his friends, interests and passions, and after moving to Aruba, his life had further spiraled downward. He had rented a cheap unit in a rundown working class apartment building, infested with bugs and fortified against crime by welded steel bars on his doors and windows. Hans had hit bottom and hit it very hard indeed, assisted by his addiction to the rum that he drank neat.

As Captain of the tourist catamaran, he was able to float into a surreal world for several hours each day and maintain some self esteem. The tourists looked up to him as a source of history, knowledge and as a part of the rough and tumble life of a Caribbean sailor. He reveled in this. His stories were pure lies and fabrications, yet who was to know the truth.

If they only knew the truth, he thought. He had gambled, lost or drunk his way through whatever little money he had left after arriving from Germany.

Each morning, regardless of rain or oppressive heat from the blistering sun, he walked to his work on the catamaran, a knapsack on his back containing all his personal items. At age 50, he was fighting the ageing process and competing with the young 20- something year olds who also worked the boat. To maintain his self esteem and to prove his prowess to the younger crew, he was constantly prowling each assortment of tourists for the young girl who he estimated would be charmed by his "old mariner" yarns. More often than not, he scored a win. This would generally mean a good night of sex, a meal and drinks and then a good night sleep at one of the ritzy resort hotels, where the young and gullible victim was staying. On the odd occasion, after spinning the yarn of his sad life, his stories would resonate and he would be given some cash by the sympathetic girl. They never learned.

Still, this was only a distraction. He considered his situation and what it could and should have been. On his arrival in Aruba, he had been introduced to Isaac Klassen Jr., a major power and financial player in resort and tourist businesses. Isaac had talked of building up a major water sport, real estate and entertainment empire and had asked Hans to be a part of it.

Thinking back over the years, Hans' mind flooded with scenes and emotions. Scenes of past relationships. Scenes of lost opportunities. Scenes of what could have been.

Hans looked over to the shore and clearly saw what would have been his future. His former potential partner was sitting with his beautiful, wealthy wife and family on the silky white sand beach. Hans sighed and sounded the klaxon to summon the tourists back onboard for their return trip. A trip that was complete with the loose women and free booze. Hans vowed to spend yet another night in a luxury suite. He preened and smiled a gracious smile and exuded a dominant presence to the young ladies climbing back on board after their snorkeling adventure. The early afternoon heat seared down on Hans as he stood at the helm and started the short cruise back to the High Rise Hotels of Palm Beach.

He looked back at the white sand covered beach where Isaac Klassen Junior sat with his young wife and family. Hans did not understand why he felt some bond to Isaac. He never would.

Chapter 1

Lancaster Pennsylvania, April 1889

The bitterly cold winds of late spring howled across the still frozen fields. In the small graveyard they stood huddled against the biting wind. The Mennonite farmers and their wives looked on sadly as the two small coffins, hewn from rough pine boards, were lowered into the freshly, but awkwardly dug graves in the frozen earth.

Prayers were said for the twin boys who had been unable to survive the dreaded cholera outbreak that had ravaged the small farming community the past bitter winter.

Isaac looked around at the gathered brethren. Desperation and sadness was reflected in their faces. He moved closer to Inge, his wife until their bodies touched and provided her with some shelter from the incessant wind. Inge turned and looked up at Isaac, tears streaming down her face. This was not the first time they had to attend such a funeral. Isaac attempted a small comforting smile and reached his hands out and took hers in a firm grasp. She continued to weep silently. The pain at the loss or her loved children dug deep into her heart and soul. They had brought so much joy and laughter into her and Isaac's home in the 4 short years of their life.

Issac stepped forward and scooped a handful of loose dirt from the ground in front of him. He scattered the dirt onto the small coffins in the graves and started to pray out loud and was soon joined by the others.

After the prayers he turned and escorted Inge on the short walk back to their buggy, consoling her with kind words. He helped Inge up into the small front seat and reached in and covered her legs and lap with a hand woven coach blanket.

As he started to climb up into the buggy, he turned to see several of the men standing and watching them. Unsure of the reason, Isaac climbed back down and walked over to them. With solemn looks on their faces they greeted Isaac. It was Johannes Schmidt, Isaac's neighboring farmer friend who spoke first.

"Isaac, we must find a way. Too many are sick. We do not have enough crops. We cannot survive if this is to continue"

Isaac looked at them. All were nodding in agreement with Johannes.

Johannes continued, "We are going to prepare a meeting of our community and with the elders. We will try to find a way to improve our lives. We are asking if you will join us and maybe speak of some of the ideas you have mentioned to me."

Isaac had spoken with Johannes at length when they had worked the fields in the fall, harvesting their crops. He had described his dreams of a peaceful life of farming in a hospitable land and living with a happy family.

"My friend, Johannes. When will there be such a meeting? I cannot attend now as we are in a period of mourning for our dear children. I will of course be happy to assist and speak if the brethren wish to have me."

"Isaac, we respect you and understand" Johannes replied. "You must come to my farm when the mourning is over and we will plan"

Isaac nodded and turned and walked back to his buggy and waiting Inge.

They drove the buggy back the short 3 miles from the small Mennonite church to their simple farmstead that had been a source of warmth and joy to them when the boys were alive. Now it seemed a cold and inhospitable place with no meaning.

Isaac and Inge entered and removed their coats and boots. They went into the drafty kitchen and sat.

"Isaac, what are we to do?" asked Inge. My heart is dead and I no longer wish to stay in this hard place. Our God has not been kind to our community and for that there must be a reason. This is no improvement from the horrible conditions we fled in Europe."

Isaac looked at the sad expression on her face. He had never seen her natural beauty so removed.

"Inge, the men are calling a meeting to discuss what can be done. They are asking me to attend and possibly speak of my ideas and thoughts for a better life and land. I will of course do this as soon as the mourning period is over."

The days passed by and a week later, Isaac walked to Johannes farmhouse. Isaac had sought permission from the elders to shorten the normal mourning period due to the seriousness of the situation.

Isaac knocked at the door to the wooden farmhouse. Johannes opened the door and welcomed Isaac in. After removing Isaac's coat, he was ushered into the kitchen. They engaged in small talk but eventually the talk drifted around to the more serious issues the community faced.

After hours of discussion, Johannes agreed that he would have the word of the meeting spread amongst the members of the community. It was agreed that the meeting would need to be held in a large and warm place. Finally, the communal farmers' barn was suggested by Johannes. They agreed on this. Johannes had prepared some wurst and asked Isaac to join him in a simple but filling lunch.

They continued talking and swapping ideas over the lunch.

Finally, Isaac stood and dressed into his thin winter coat for the walk back to his home and Inge.

Isaac felt a surge of satisfaction now that there was a plan to try and resolve the many issues facing him and his fellow Mennonites.

He entered back into his home and embraced Inge. He held her for a long while and then told her of the planned meeting. After they spoke for some time, he noticed that she now seemed calmer than in the previous months.

Chapter 2

In the old communal farmer's barn where the weekly farmer's market was held, Isaac stood amongst the other Mennonite farmers. He listened to the general rumblings and the theme of the conversations. It was early April. The past winter had been particularly hard on the Pennsylvania farmers. The ice and snow storms had stayed well past the normal thaw period. Families had been hit hard with death and diseases, including cholera and a virulent influenza. In order to feed themselves and their families many of the farmers had been forced to sell off livestock at greatly reduced prices, due to the lack of feed they had available and their inability to pay for additional food from other sources. Life here was difficult.

In the barn, the talk was despondent. While the Mennonites had purchased their lands, many were unable to provide for their families or meet the costs of operating their farms. To further worsen the situation, the cost of land purchases was being driven up by the incessant greed of the privileged few who had been granted land by the Federal Government for their war services. The Mennonite farmers were hard working, honest and peace abiding people who wanted no harm and only to work and enjoy their labors.

Having worked and broken in the land from overgrown shrubs, rocky outcrops, weeds and unruly trees, the farmers had a pride and determination. They would not give up. Defeat on the land was unknown to these men. As the discussion continued, it was becoming very clear that the local farms were unable to support and sustain all of the new arrivals. The population had swelled with the arrival of large families from Europe who were seeking a better life and to escape from difficulties in Prussia, Germany and Holland.

An alternative was needed to handle this situation.

Isaac Klassen, the young and progressive man that he was, sought permission to address the gathered crowd of farmers. After several minutes of silence and speculation as to what he could possibly offer, Isaac was granted the floor. Isaac was known as an honest, hard working and fair man. He was widely respected in the community.

He walked up onto a small landing area that was used for the shearing of sheep.

"Brethren" he called out. "We need not all stay and suffer these indignities on our families. While it is good here for some, we cannot expect to continue to just be able to exist and survive, with so many new families joining us. We must look beyond. I have news that I think will solve this problem and offer new hope. I have recently learned of a great land opportunity in Ontario, Canada. The land, which is available for purchase, is fertile with rich soil and is located on a river. This land is at a cost that is at a fraction of the cost of the land here in Pennsylvania. I am also told that amongst the community, there is also a great demand for woodworking artisans to build furnishings for the homes of the new settlers. Many of you are such artisans and whether you move to this place or not, it is a good place to establish and sell your works.

I am forming a group to go forward and explore this land. The area is within several days of horse and buggy from where we are. I am going to prepare a group to go and check this land and opportunity. I am seeking some fine farming men to accompany me. If we find that this is all true, then we shall form a migration to travel and settle these lands. I will send back a report to the elders after I perform my investigation. I will leave in 3 days. If there are those who wish to join me, come forward."

A hush fell throughout the barn. Many had heard about the Ontario lands, but few had accurate information and even fewer wanted to risk everything by   moving to yet another country again.

Isaac stood awaiting questions. Finally, a man who had recently arrived from Germany raised his hand. In a heavily accented voice he called, "I have heard of this place. Are we to be alone? Are there others of our belief there? Will it be a safe place for me and my family?"

Isaac pondered the questions. Finally after some deep thought he responded. "In my findings, I am advised that the people of this area are open and accepting. It is unlikely we will be exposed to the hatred and the prejudices that we are all aware of in our former homelands. This country of Canada and these people are known to accept all peoples from afar"

"But what assurances do we have?" asked one of the older farmers. "I cannot make such a move at my age and be faced with even more burdens"

Isaac responded "I will go and personally check the lands and arrange to meet with businessmen and other farmers. I will find answers and when satisfied, I will return and present what I have found"

Small groups gathered and started conversations amongst themselves. Isaac was left alone. Finally, three of the newer arrivals from Europe approached him. "We have decided to join with you on this mission. If we find that all is correct, then surely we must secure this land for our families. Will it be safe for us to transport our silver coins to make such a purchase?"

Isaac had not expected this. He did not know how to answer. Finally, another two of the young strong farmhands came forward. They agreed to travel and help to protect the small band of adventurers.

Isaac again stood on the small platform and was joined by the others who had decided to make the journey. All spoke briefly to the gathering. Finally, well wishes, blessings and songs erupted in celebration and hope that the findings of the venture would result in a new future for the expanding Mennonite community.

That night, Isaac conferred with Inge, his wife. They discussed the communal meeting and the plan to seek better lands in Canada. Inge worried aloud whether this was the correct action to take. After a long discussion considering the risks and possible the benefits, and after considering the bleak situation in which they were in, Inge accepted the decision to explore the possibility of a better life in Canada. Later that evening and the next day, Inge commenced the preparation of the clothing, food and other items for the trip.

Chapter 3

For the next several days, the community buzzed with excited talk of the brave men who were setting off to the strange and unknown land of Canada in pursuit of finding them a better life.

Isaac and his group worked to ready the horses and the few Russian buggies owned by several of the families. Other members came forward with offers of food, and in some cases, small amounts of money. They entrusted the money to Isaac and asked it to be used to hold land purchases, if indeed it was as good as purported. Isaac was overwhelmed at the total trust placed in him.

Finally, the day for departure arrived. The horses and their attached buggies were lined up in a procession. What seemed like the whole Mennonite community of Lancaster was on hand to witness this pilgrimage and to bestow blessings and good wishes. Small handmade gifts and foods were handed up to the riders.

The small procession proceeded from the Village and followed a winding bullock track into the farm fields.

It was early spring, and while the temperatures were still crisp, Isaac could feel the gentle heat of the sun's rays as they filtered to his face under his wide brimmed traditional hat.

As they wound their way through the farms, other farmers and their wives who were out preparing for the spring seeding ran over to wish them a safe and successful mission. Women passed up fresh baked bread and cake. The men handed over tobacco and sausages which had been prepared using the old traditional methods.

Sitting alongside their husbands in the buggies, the women watched each move with the fear of failure for the mission. No one spoke of such fear, but it was visible in their demeanor.

As the group left the cultivated farmlands, the track rose up a gentle incline. Ahead was a small forest of dense pine and other evergreen trees. The track meandered through this peaceful scene. Isaac was worried about carrying the community members silver coins. He had heard of the unseemly attacks that had happened in this area. He stopped his horse and buggy. He dismounted and walked back to the two young and strong farmhands who had joined the mission. He told them of his concern. After much discussion, one of them decided to move to the lead horse, while the other elected to go to the last buggy and watch the rear. As non violent and peaceful people, these Mennonites were unsure how to deal with such a predicament should it happen.

Isaac led the procession into the thicket of trees and emerged up the incline. A peaceful pall fell over them. The only sounds were the horses snorting and their hooves hitting the drying packed pathway.

Late in the afternoon the light started to drop. Isaac and the other men conferred and agreed that a stop for the night was needed. The horses were tethered to trees and the buggies rolled together. Makeshift tent shelters were erected. A fire was prepared and the women took the food that had been contributed and prepared a meal. After a small religious ceremony of thanks for their safe passage, they all settled to partake of the many different food items.

As total darkness fell, Isaac and Inge sat alongside their buggy talking about their dreams of a new life and the adventure before them. The Northern nights were still cold. They huddled together. Above them, the Northern sky was purple velvet studded with sparkling diamond stars.

 Isaac smiled. "Inge, I have a good feeling about this trip we make for us and our Brethren" Inge smiled and moved closer into his chest, clasping his large hands.

As minutes went by, both Isaac and Inge drifted into a deep sleep.

Chapter 4

The dawn arrived quickly. The speckled sun flickered on her eyelids, caused by the shadows created by the early sun filtering through the branches of the giant ash trees under which they had sheltered.

Inge looked toward the other sleeping travelers. None had awakened.

While vainglory was frowned upon in their religion, Inge had felt it to be one of the most important attributes in maintaining a relationship with her husband and lover. A woman must portray God's design and beauty.

She quietly arose and went down a small embankment and away from the still sleeping group. She took her small brush from her private bag and commenced brushing her long auburn hair. This beautiful hair had long been a controversy back in Lancaster amongst other jealous women and had incensed the elders. As she brushed the long strands and breathed in the cool spring air, she felt a presence behind her. Turning, she saw Isaac, tall and glowing in the early morning sun.

Isaac was smiling and had a glint of mischief on his face. This was a look she knew and loved. "Oh Isaac. We cannot possibly do such a thing here. What if the others are to awake? It will be my shame."

Isaac stepped forward and thrust his strong arm behind her back. "My dearest Inge, how can there possibly be any shame in a love of ours that is so deep and without interference from the outside? It is the most pure of love for there is no one like you"

Inge looked into his long but handsome face. "I know of your love and passion for me. My dearest Isaac, we must wait until we settle in our new lands. All will be perfect then, and maybe we will be blessed with a child"

Isaac stood back and laughed. "My Inge, you are always so correct. Let us awaken the others. Today will be the long day, for we should reach the border with Canada. I will admit to you, but to no one else, that I am a little apprehensive and worried. Are we doing the right thing? Is Canada the right place? There have been so many from the Ukraine who fled south to America from Canada. Are we making some big mistake? There are so many back in Lancaster who are relying on me. I cannot deceive or mislead our Brethren"

"Come, Isaac. You are a good and true believer. It is not within your soul to lead any of our people astray. They believe and trust you. You are a strong and good person. I know the Lord will assist you in this mission"

"Last night you whispered how you knew this mission was blessed. Trust your instincts."

Isaac and Inge walked back to the encampment. Isaac went from man to man gently shaking each awake.

The Old Order Mennonites stood together and entered into daily prayer. Upon completion, the women scattered to arrange foods. Unlike a traditional breakfast on the farm, these meals were prepared from whatever was readily available.

Soon, the group sat at a hastily prepared long table. Blessings were given. Zwiebach was produced from a large cane basket that was passed around to each person. The talk turned to the day ahead. Isaac announced that they were within a day of reaching the invisible Canadian border. On this news, the spirits of the group arose.

Isaac called the men together. He explained the day ahead. It would not be an easy day. Again there had been mounting hostilities between Canada and The United States. Isaac cautioned that when crossing the border the group should not present any bias, but rather state their purpose as farmers in pursuit of better land and opportunity.

With the horses saddled and the covered wagons tethered, the procession to the Canadian border began.

They rode along in the soft sun of a beautiful northern spring day. On the sides of the track, remnants of the past winter were evident. Strips of un-melted snow lay in the ditches and on the shoulders of the fields through which they passed. As they moved further northward there was more snow and they experienced much colder temperatures.

As their little wagon train rose over a small series of inclines, Isaac viewed the river. To the right was a wooden bridge. This was the bridge into Canada. Isaac called to the others to stop. He wanted time to watch and observe the process of travelers going into and out of Canada. He was alarmed at the sight of soldiers at the crossing. Tensions between Canada and The United States had escalated. "Were these the dreaded Loyalist soldiers who hated all Americans?" he worried.

The group watched for hours. Farmers with equipment and goods, families, single men and business types were seemingly crossing without any difficulty.

Isaac made his bold decision. The small procession made its way down to the crossing. A sloppily dressed and rotund official walked up to them. He looked at each of them. "You are Old Order Mennonites. Why are you coming to Canada when so many of your sorts are leaving?"

Isaac dismounted and walked up the man. "Good sir, we have had hard times in Pennsylvania. We know of the lands available in Ontario and come in peace to farm and develop these lands. We are also artisans and will craft furniture and build homes for your new settlers."

The official looked at him and smiled. "Sir, if you think that miserable Colonel Wellington who has the grant of all that land will be sympathetic, then maybe you should turn around and go back. He is a bastard. He will make fodder of you all. He cares not of any religion. To him money is the only God"

Walking, he went off laughing. "Go ahead to your fate, and remember, sometimes death is better. He will take everything from you...including your lives"

Isaac looked back over his shoulder. He perceived this to be a weak man's challenge. The strength of the men who were with him and their morals and tenacity were unknown to these weak and ignorant people.

"We will succeed "Isaac said, though quietly.

Chapter 5

Isaac and his small group drove their wagons into the softly rolling farmlands of Ontario, on their way to the small town of Berlin, Ontario. Berlin was located on the banks of the Grand Bend. Just outside of Berlin there were some of the most fertile lands available for settling. Isaac and his group were, naturally, very excited.

Isaac and the men stopped to ask about overnight accommodation at a local road house. The proprietors welcomed them. Mennonites, after all did not create problems and always paid well.

With formalities settled, the Mennonites were welcomed into the small Inn. They were unsure. Unlike other experiences they had been exposed to, they were welcomed in without comment or criticism. Isaac began to understand and appreciate the differences that existed beyond the invisible border.

Others in the group were not of the same belief as Isaac. There was strong suspicion that things would turn very bad and that religious persecution would again surface, as it had in Old Europe. Many in the group had relatives from Prussia, The Netherlands and Germany where hundreds of years ago persecution for the belief of Mennonite values had resulted in death, starvation and torture. Naturally, there was great caution and fear.

Isaac awoke the next day and spoke with Inge and shared his thoughts and beliefs. If the new settlers were to succeed, then there needed to be very strong relations and communication with the new community they would be joining. Inge and Isaac spoke for many hours and in detail. Finally, it was agreed that once settled, a small gathering should be held to display and sell their goods. It was hoped that this would allay any fears that the other citizens of Berlin may have about the newly arrived Mennonites.

Very few who lived in the small and peaceful communities knew of, or had experienced the deep hostilities and hatred that war brings. That unfortunate event was on the cusp of developing in Berlin, Ontario through the actions of a handful of ill informed and bigoted citizens.

Chapter 6

That Sunday, a religious day of worship and rest, the group stayed in the Inn and performed chores and rested. It was decided to hold a small meeting to plan for the day ahead. A small delegation would visit Colonel Wellington on Monday to discuss purchasing land from his grant. Isaac asked who would be prepared to assist in this. Johannes Schmidt, his neighbor presented himself along with another burly farmer named Emile.

As it was still early in the day, the men decided to ride to the area where the lands were located. They set off shortly after noon and arrived at the area around 1:30pm. The men dismounted and Isaac surveyed the lands in front of him. To his right were huge tracts of rocky and heavily wooded hilly land. Further to his left there were lands full of brush, and small growths of shrub that stretched to the banks of the river.

After sometime, the men decided to attempt to ride down to the river. As they made their slow progress, Johannes called for a halt. He dismounted his steed and started using a small shovel he had brought with him. He started to dig into the gravelly soil. Initially the shovel scrapped into small rocks. Johannes raked these to the side and continued his dig. Within minutes he was digging out dark rich soil. A large smile crossed his face.

"My friends, with this rich soil we will be able to plant many crops. Vegetables, corn, and cultivate an orchard."

Isaac looked back to his right at the heavily forested area. The size of the forest exceeded the open land. He was concerned.

"How are we to support all of our Brethren who wish to settle here" he asked. "There is much land, but much of it cannot be easily farmed"

The burly farmer, Emile, spoke. "Isaac and Johannes, we can clear this land and furthermore that forest will provide us with the lumber we need to build furniture and our cabins. Do not be disheartened by this. It is of value to us. We can clear some of that land and use part of that forest to produce more lumber. We will be indeed fortunate if we can purchase that land and the area beside it."

Isaac thought about this. "Emile, you are correct. We will ask the Colonel for both areas tomorrow."

Johannes went to the saddle bags on his horse and removed some papers. With the help of Isaac, he started drawing a rudimentary map of the forested land and the partially cleared lands. When the map was completed, the men started their ride back to the town.

The ride back was uneventful and the men chatted excitedly about the possibilities that existed, should they be able to purchase the lands.

Chapter 7

That night there was great excitement amongst the group over the news the three had brought back regarding the lands they had seen. Talk bubbled with enthusiasm and plans for a new Mennonite settlement. The talk evolved into details of which livestock to raise and where to purchase it. Isaac had learned there were other small Mennonite settlements within a day's ride of where they planned to settle.

"I believe we will be able to visit the others and trade with them to start our farms" Isaac said.

Soon the plans for the future settlement were taking place.

Isaac turned to Johannes and Emile. "I think I will now sleep as tomorrow we will go and meet the Colonel. We must be on guard and alert in order to make an arrangement that is fair and favorable"

With that, Isaac left the room to retire to his bed.

The morning came quickly. Sun streamed through the Inn's leaded glass windows. The shadows cast by the giant oak trees at the front of the Inn, danced on the walls of the bedroom. It was to be a fine and sunny northern spring day.

Isaac arose, bathed and dressed in the finest of clothes they had brought with them for this occasion. When dressed he descended to the Inn's dining room to meet with Johannes and Emile who were already waiting for him.

They all sat and partook of a simple breakfast of eggs, milk and bread.

At 9:00am Isaac stood and walked into the main foyer of the Inn. The rest of the group were waiting there and wished Isaac, Johannes and Emile luck and offered prayer.

Isaac asked the boy at the desk to have their horses brought from the Inn's stables.

Within minutes, the trio was riding on their way to visit Colonel Wellington.

As they rode through the streets of Berlin, they were amazed at the cleanliness of the town and the brisk pace of business that was already underway at this early hour. Isaac commented to the others on the number of times they had been greeted by strangers in the German language. This surprised them.

After a short while they came to the Offices of Colonel Wellington. They hitched their horses to the post at the front of the office and entered.

A short, obese clerk with eyes like a pigs sat behind a huge desk covered with survey maps and papers. He looked up. "Yes gentlemen, what is your business here?" There was no welcoming smile. In fact, the greeting lacked any enthusiasm and bordered upon annoyance.

Isaac took the lead. "We are here to meet with the Colonel to discuss a land purchase. We understand that we must speak with him since we can no longer purchase through the Government Land Office."

The clerk sighed and looked down at the maps on his desk. "The Colonel is busy today. It is possible you will need to return another time."

"We have travelled a long way to meet the Colonel and are looking at purchasing a large amount of land."

At that the clerk became curious. "How much land?" he asked.

"To start with we believe 60,000 acres will be needed. We have visited the lands and have prepared a map of those lands we are interested in."

At this the clerk started to become flustered. "If you wait I will see when the Colonel will see you"

The trio stood in the clerk's office not speaking. After several minutes, the creaking of the large oak wood door heralded in the clerk and a diminutive man wearing a monocle and dressed in a light grey suit.

The clerk retreated behind his desk.

The Colonel stepped forward to position himself in front of the trio.

"I am Colonel Wellington and I understand you come on business. What exactly is that business and what do you want from me?"

Isaac stepped forward and with a slight bow extended his hand, while at the same time introducing himself and his partners.

"We have travelled here from Lancaster, Pennsylvania in pursuit of establishing a new farming community. We are crop and livestock farmers. Amongst us are also skilled artisans to make furniture and also men who can build new homesteads. In order to do this we are looking to purchase lands in this area."

The Colonel stood quietly. After a long silence he said "I understand you have already chosen some lands. I will be curious to learn what these are" He then turned to the clerk. "Please take the maps to the meeting room and spread them on the table and advise me when your ineffective little self has completed that simple task."

The clerk bunched up papers and maps and scurried off to an anteroom that was located off the main entrance corridor.

The Colonel stood stiff and still and surveyed Isaac and the others. His demeanor was crisp. Every now and then a twitch of his right eye would trigger and to counteract it he would raise his upper lip causing his handlebar mustache to droop on one side while rising on the other.

Isaac sensed that this was going to be a difficult meeting. He glanced to the others. Not a word was spoken.

Finally the clerk emerged, sweating profusely and red-faced. "The room is ready, sirs."

Chapter 8

The Colonel strode ahead of Isaac, Johannes and Emile into the large overbearing meeting room. The walls were paneled with heavy dark wood rising some 15 feet. The ceiling was plastered with relief work and 2 large ostentatious chandeliers lit the room. At the centre of the room was a large oval shaped oak table with a number of leather upholstered chairs. Off to one side of the room was a large credenza covered with various liquor bottles.

Spread out on the table before them were large survey maps.

The Colonel turned sharply from his position at the head of the table. "Sit down." he barked. The trio separated. Isaac sat to the right of the Colonel and Johannes and Emile to the Colonel's left in order to be able to see each other's reactions.

"Obviously you have come to present a business offer to me. Why should I bother to even look at this?"

For several minutes there was a pall of silence. The Colonel got up and walked to the credenza and poured amber colored liquor into a diamond cut crystal glass.

"If I understand it correctly you men do not partake of the finest nectar God has allowed us to devise, so I won't bother to offer you any."

With that he spun and returned to the table.

"Well let's hear what you want."

Isaac glanced at the others.

"Colonel," he started, "We are honest and hardworking farmers who wish to move from the poverty we are experiencing in Pennsylvania and start a better life for our small community here in Berlin"

"I want you to know that I am not particularly fond of your types. I served God and country with exemplary military service for which I was rewarded with this land grant. Now, you people who refuse to participate in the military and protect our country come here wanting to live and get things that you have not stood up for. I am not convinced your community would benefit us here in Berlin."

"Colonel" Isaac replied. "We are peaceful people. We do not seek to harm or create any problems. Historically we have been persecuted. All we are asking is to be able to establish a productive small community that will make a significant contribution to Berlin. We do not ask for anything unless we work for it. We avoid conflict and just wish to live a peaceful and productive life."

"If I relent and consider your proposal, how do I know you can pay? Especially since you are coming from hard depressed times and the poverty in Lancaster? I am not a bank and do not loan money. Don't waste anymore of my time unless you can satisfy my question."

Isaac looked to the others with uncertainty. Johannes nodded his head.

Isaac took that to mean to proceed and discuss that they were able to pay.

"Colonel, we will pay for the purchase in silver coinage, some of which we have brought with us to Berlin"

"I understand you want 60,000 acres? Is that correct?"

"Yes" replied Isaac.

The Colonel arose from his chair and stabbed at the maps on the table.

"And which land?"

Johannes withdrew the rough map he had sketched and passed it to the Colonel, who looked at it intensely.

He looked up at Johannes. "Show me on this map which is the land you wish to purchase."

The trio leaned over and scoured the map. Finally burly Emile spoke.

"It is here at this location where the river bends."

He placed the fingers of both hands on the map to illustrate the area.

The Colonel frowned. In his mind he knew that a good part of the land the trio wished to purchase was forest and not tillable. If he was smart he could unload this less than desirable land to these uneducated farmers.

"Gentlemen, maybe I spoke too harshly. I think it might be possible to help you with this purchase you wish to make. I need to determine a cost for those lands. I remember when the Government Land Office was selling tracts of land they were charging $10 an acre. Since they no longer sell the land and it is sold by private owners, that cost has changed. I believe that $15 an acre is fair at this time. Do we have an agreement?"

Isaac looked at the others. Johannes seemed disturbed.

"Colonel, we need to talk together privately."

"Certainly" the Colonel responded. "I will leave you to talk. Tell my clerk when you are ready." He stood and removed a gold watch on a chain attached to his vest pocket. He looked at it and then he exited the room.

The trio sat down. Johannes spoke first. "Isaac, a lot of that land will be unable to produce enough for us in the beginning. I think he asks too much for it. It will take us years to clear enough for crops and livestock."

Isaac, Johannes and Emile sat for a long while discussing the situation.

Finally, Isaac said "Let us take this to the others in Lancaster and present it. I feel that since we are a community we should all participate. I will advise the Colonel"

Isaac informed the clerk who immediately fetched the Colonel. The Colonel returned with a beaming smile.

"Gentlemen, what have you decided?"

Isaac spoke. "Good Sir, since this involves others in our community, we will return to discuss it with them."

The Colonel stood motionless. His visions of a quick sale and passing off the inferior land were vanishing. He must act before the sale is gone.

"I have looked at the land in question again and I think I can offer a much better price. The price for all 60,000 acres I will sell at $10 an acre. Is this an acceptable amount, Sirs?"

Isaac looked to Johannes and Emile. Johannes nodded.

"Again we must speak privately" said Isaac.

The Colonel smiled, then nodded and left.

The trio huddled.

Johannes was ecstatic. "Isaac, we can prepare some of that land very soon. It is spring and we have the summer and autumn months to complete this. Most of our community can stay in Lancaster as the summer months are gentle and the people can grow enough. It is the winter that causes so much hardship. I propose we pay a small amount to the Colonel and return to Lancaster to speak with the elders."

After much discussion, it was decided. Johannes and Isaac would ride back to Lancaster, but the rest of the group, including Inge, Isaacs's wife would stay. Isaac did not want to risk the return trip with the silver they had originally brought with them.

Isaac again asked the clerk to get the Colonel.

The Colonel re entered the meeting room exuding charm. They all sat and Isaac advised the Colonel of their plan.

"This is excellent" the Colonel responded.

"Today is Monday. Johannes and I will travel and return with the final decision from the elders by Friday. Is that an acceptable deal?" asked Isaac.

The Colonel beamed. "Of course it is. When will you bring the silver?"

Johannes turned to Emile. "This afternoon Emile will bring it to you. Please draw up papers. Upon those papers being correct Emile will deposit some of the silver with you. This will be our deposit on the lands we discussed. Isaac and I will start our ride today and meet with the elders."

Chapter 9

The decision was made. Emile would stay with the rest of the group while Isaac and Johannes rode back to Lancaster to meet the elders and other Mennonite farmers.

The return trip to Lancaster was fast. Upon arrival, Isaac and Johannes were greeted with great excitement. After bathing and a quick meal they arranged a communal meeting that evening in the community hall.

The hall was packed with those eager to hear of the findings of Isaac and the group. Isaac addressed the gathering.

"Brethren, we did indeed see the lands. There are fields that can be easily cultivated but there is also a heavily forested part that will require much effort. There are trees to fell and stumps to pull and large rocks to be removed. We cannot do this work in a few months. It will take years to clear enough land for us to have crops and livestock that will support us all. The soils are fertile and will support all the types of crops we now grow. The forest will yield timbers that we can use for furniture, cabins and to heat our cabins in the winter months."

Questions were shouted from the seated crowd.

"I am going to pass a map that Johannes made and a map the Colonel provided. You will see that this is a large tract of land and ideally located on the river"

The maps were laid out on a small table and were instantly crowded around by the curious.

One of the elders stood to speak and a hush descended in the hall.

"Isaac, what is it you are advising? We should not go? There is not enough usable land? I do not fully understand. Is this a better place than where we are?"

Isaac arose and went to the front to address the gathering.

"I do advise that we purchase this tract. I am telling of the challenges we face. I think we should proceed immediately. We have been able to obtain this tract at a reasonable price that we have discussed with the elders. I suggest that we start our migration in small groups. I call for those who wish to join in the first group to come forward. These men will assist in clearing some of the fields and building the first cabins. After this we will have another group arrive. If we arrive all together it will be a problem. We must go in a number of small parties."

The elders huddled and started to speak amongst themselves. After about 30 minutes, the elders stood and faced the gathering.

"We give our approval and blessings to this plan" said the oldest of the elders.

The hall was filled with excited chatter. Isaac and Johannes went back to the front of the assembled Mennonites.

"Johannes and I will meet with those who wish to be in the first party. We need strong men to start clearing the fields and preparing pasture for livestock. We will also need those who can build cabins. We seek those who will join to bring their wives to provide adequate meals. This will not be an easy life at the start, but the rewards will be great"

A number of the men surged forward, eager to be selected.

For the next several hours Isaac and Johannes sat and spoke with the selected men and women.

"I am to return Friday to complete the arrangement with the Colonel. I will take a group of working men with me and in a week we will send for the women and children"

It was suggested that another meeting be held to plan and prepare for the journey back to Berlin.

The hall emptied very late that night. Groups left chattering and planning. Finally, it seemed that their troubles and difficulties in Lancaster, Pennsylvania were coming to an end.

Chapter 10

With the mortgages and land purchases completed, the next few months saw the steady arrival in Berlin of more families from Lancaster. Fields were cleared and tilled. Some had already been seeded and planted. Work had started on cutting back some of the forest. Livestock was purchased from a neighboring Mennonite community. A sawmill was built to process the timber harvested from the forest.

Life was taking on a semblance of normalcy.

Concerned that they be accepted by the primarily German population, the women prepared a plan. Over the short time they had been there, the Mennonite women from Pennsylvania, who could bake and sew like no one else, had become treasured within the community. Their husbands had proved their worth in breaking some of the most inhospitable lands into the most fertile farms, and in crafting some of the most beautiful furniture to be seen in the county.

The Mennonites were accepted as skilled bakers, farmers and craftsmen. They had become a peaceful and hard working component of the Berlin community. Within the town of Berlin they found merchants who wished to sell the furniture they crafted and to purchase their farm crops.

Inge was concerned that the community of Berlin was still apprehensive of the Mennonites. After all they were different to the rest of the community. Furthermore, some of the older Germans in Berlin remembered the Mennonites from years ago in their native Germany and Prussia.

To allay fears, Inge arranged a bake sale in Berlin Township. In addition to the cakes, pies and many sweet items, the women displayed quilts, clothing and other handmade goods.

As time progressed, the small group dissolved into the community. While they maintained tight ties and attended religious gatherings, the members became a little more distant with each other, each working their own farm.

Chapter 11

For Isaac and Inge the next few years were idyllic. The farm provided them with food and an income. In all, life was good.

Isaac and Johannes' friendship continued to be strong. Johannes had continued to farm next to Isaacs and the two were inseparable often working together on tasks on the farms.

In 1901, Isaac and Inge were blessed with the birth of a son. They named him Jakob. He was an active baby and over time he developed into a strong young man.

When not at Mennonite school, Jakob worked with Isaac on the farm assisting with many tasks. Feeding chickens, baling of the hay, slaughter of the sheep. Jakob never refused to help. In his spare time, Jakob would read and demonstrated that he had a natural talent for musical instruments. He spent hours trying to understand the reading of sheet music and how it varied for different instruments. He practiced the violin and became fascinated with the saxophone, an instrument not widely accepted within his faith.

Isaac and Inge felt blessed that God had bestowed such a good child upon them.

Isaac, Inge and Jakob continued to live a bucolic life on their farm. Neighbors stopped by with gifts of jams, freshly made sausages and homemade garments.

In 1905, four years after Jakob's birth, Johannes and his wife gave birth to a daughter whom they named Anke.

Jakob and Anke became great friends and played for many hours on the farms and also walked together to and from the church school.

Jakob assisted Anke with her home studies and often found ways to explain things that she could not grasp in the school where she was taught by the strict Mennonite teachers of whom she was afraid.

As Jakob and Anke grew in age, so did their like for each other. Anke would hang on the side of the wooden fence watching Jakob and Isaac work the sheep and cattle in the paddocks.

Jakob had finished schooling. It was 1913. Jakob accompanied Isaac into Berlin on the trips to sell produce and perform business at the banks. The town merchants got to know the Klassen family well and respected their honesty and integrity.

Jakob sensed that things were changing with the people of Berlin. A fear and suspicion seemed to be developing. In talks with the merchants, the topic of war was frequently brought up. It was confusing to this young man of 12. Jakob listened to the heated discussions and tried to understand why there were such strong feelings and arguments. In his mind, everyone should be able to be peaceful and happy working with their farms, stores or factories. The discussions of hatred in faraway lands seemed to have no significance here in Berlin. It was all very confusing.

Neither Jakob nor Isaac could foresee the events about to unfold in Europe and how those events would impact their existing or future lives.

Chapter 12

At the early age of 13, Jakob was a strong young man and a respected community member. Fellow Mennonites of his age often visited and sought his advice on many topics from girls through to leaving the community in search of the new world beyond. Jakob would listen attentively to their concerns, desires and dreams. Sometimes he would offer advice but more often than not he entered into discussions aimed at getting his friends to determine their own solutions.

Jakob was greatly liked. The elders saw a future leader and pillar in their community. He was respected in Berlin by the merchants and all those who had dealings with him.

On the farm, Jakob assisted Isaac with all manner of tasks. He learned to butcher sheep, build barns, and the methods of irrigating the fields of vegetables.

It seemed Jakob could do no wrong.

Jakob's natural curiosity was insatiable. He would visit and sit with the oldest Mennonites asking questions of their old countries. He asked questions about Prussia. He asked questions about the persecutions of Mennonites in old Europe. These issues presented him with a dilemma as he could not comprehend how others could be so cruel and ignorant.

It was in these talks that Jakob learned of his own background and the existence of relatives in both Holland and Germany. He was intrigued as to who they were and what they now did in life.

Young Jakob saw a future life of travel and adventure. He started thinking of travelling to Europe and meeting these distant family members.

Life was about to change.

Berlin was becoming more of a distant experience. Jakob witnessed brawls and drunkenness in the streets.

Jakob and Isaac visited Berlin less frequently. On the odd occasion insults were hurled at them by drunks outside the bars. Often these insults referred to Isaac and Jakob as no good Germans, accusing them of stealing their land, jobs, food and women.

A division between the large German population and the British who were loyal to the Dominion of Canada was developing.

Soon the frictions occurred between Isaac and the merchants with whom he had dealt with for many years.

At night, they would sit and discuss the persecutions that had happened in Europe and speculated whether this could happen in Ontario, Canada.

Isaac's strong belief in Canada caused him to convince Jakob that what he witnessed on those trips into Berlin were the actions of a few and that law and order would prevail. He stressed to Jakob that in all his time in Canada he had never been treated badly. Jakob accepted his father's words.

Isaac and Jakob continued to work and improve their farm which had become the model for all of the other Mennonite farmers. When they were not busy with their own farm, they would visit other farmers who they knew needed assistance.

Jakob and Isaac were loved by the other Mennonites. Isaac was seen as a natural leader. He was someone who had saved them from the difficulties of those hard days back in Lancaster, Pennsylvania.

Jakob started to assume more of the responsibilities at the farm as age crept up on Isaac. He would often get together a group of other young men to assist him with baling hay and other heavy duties while insisting that Isaac rest and leave the heavy work to the younger farmers.

Chapter 13

July 28th, 1914. Fate was to intervene. Germany declares war on Serbia and follows quickly with the declaration of war on Russia and then on August 4th, 1914 Britain declares war on Germany.

Berlin, Ontario is not immune to far off battles in Europe which start to claim millions of lives.

In the town of Berlin, Ontario, elected officials, military officers past and present, business leaders and citizens begin dialogue that quickly escalates into a fear and paranoia.

In 1915, The Dominion of Canada pledges 250,000 men to King George V in an effort to present an image of loyalty to the rest of the Commonwealth. Berlin's leaders decide to mount a major military recruitment to enlist 35000 soldiers from the local area and send these men to Europe to show Canada's support for Britain.

The recruitment efforts are poorly conceived and executed. Gangs of "soldiers" grab young unsuspecting men from streets in the evenings, forcing them into military service. Those young men with either religious convictions or health issues are mocked, belittled and set upon. All of this headed up and supported by an illogical and pugilistic recruiting sergeant. The behavior is condoned by senior military officers and the local constabulary. Berlin would show its loyal commitment and deliver the soldiers it had pledged to Britain.

With the poor enforcement of any disciplinary action against the unruly and illegal acts, the atmosphere in Berlin deteriorated as military goons performed more and more vile acts. The statue of

Germany's Kaiser Wilhelm is torn down and thrown into the river after being dragged through the streets by drunken rioting soldiers. They smash into the German Concordia Club and destroy furniture, cutlery, paintings and other German artifacts. They finally leave dragging and then burning the German flag.

Hysteria reaches uncontrollable levels in Berlin. There are riots. At the behest of some poorly informed officials it is determined that a referendum must be held to change the name of Berlin to something that shows the population is against Germany and the war. After many debates and struggles a name is chosen. The name change of Berlin to Kitchener is rejected by the Ontario Provincial Government. The fight continues until finally, a delegation to the Federal Government of Canada is made and consent is given after years of argument and many friendships lost.

Against this backdrop of misguided patriotic events, the mostly German population lives in fear. The Postmaster of Canada intercepts and prohibits delivery of any mail to Germany and confiscates mail from anyone that is considered sympathetic to the German cause, whether true or false. Paranoia sweeps the town. Friends become enemies. Everyone is suspicious.

At no time do the leaders or elected officials attempt to quell the situation.

In the Mennonite community there is concern. Farmers and their families are harassed. Explanations that the Mennonites are pacifists and refuse weapons of war are rejected. Some Mennonites are attacked and injured in unprovoked attacks.

Isaac and Jakob are concerned and watch the events from a distance. History appears to be repeating itself.

Chapter 14

Klassen Farm, 1917

With the impact of the war surrounding them, Jakob and Isaac continue to farm their land and assist others. Jakob is concerned as Isaac's health is starting to deteriorate and he is no longer able to assist with even the menial tasks on the farm.

Jakob spends long days on the farm, often starting before sunrise and returning to the old farmhouse in early dusk, exhausted by the day's work.

For the next 2 years, Jakob continues to work the farm alone and perform all the hard tasks. At times he is joined by others when the larger tasks need to be done.

Jakob has been observing that some of the buildings need replacement before the coming winter. That night he discusses his concerns with Isaac and Inge.

"If we are to shelter the livestock and their feed this winter we will need to repair the barns and rebuild the smaller sheds. I don't think the structures will survive the ice and snow storms"

Isaac nodded his head in agreement.

"Will the others work with us? It is too much work for you Jakob."

"I believe that our friends will help me" said Jakob. "I would like to start this immediately as summer will soon end. I will visit the mill tomorrow to ask for enough wood to allow the repairs and building."

Isaac smiled. He thought back to the heavily wooded lands they had first seen upon their arrival. Now he knew their value.

Chapter 15

Jakob arose to a beautiful late summer morning. After breakfast with Isaac and Inge, he started off for the mill. Along the way he stopped on occasion to speak with his neighboring farmers.

"Good day to you, Jakob Klassen. What brings you to these parts?" called the old farmer who was known for his skills with horses.

Jakob waved back to him.

"Good day, Jan. I make this trip to arrange for timbers to repair and rebuild some of our farm buildings before the snows come. Several are in bad need of repair."

The farmer Jan straightened up from the work he was performing on a horse's hoof. He looked at Jakob for a long, quiet minute.

"Jakob, how is the health of Isaac? Can he do such work with you?"

"I will start alone and do what work I can. I fear that Isaac cannot help anymore"

Jan pushed his wide brimmed hat toward the back of his head, showing his strong weathered face.

"Jakob, I will speak to our neighboring farmers, many who are young and strong and have benefitted over the years from the sacrifices and guidance of Isaac. When the lumbers are brought to your farm the men will form work parties .We will do this work the way we did when we first settled these lands."

Jakob started to resist.

"Jan. We are not requesting help."

"Jakob, it will be this way. Our community must assist now. Isaac and Inge have helped so many to settle and build new lives here. We will not allow this work to be done without our help. Later today I will ride to visit Isaac. We will speak of the work"

With this, Jan turned back to the horse and bent down to reach the hoof he had been working on.

Jakob knew it was impossible to dissuade Jan from his plan.

"I will return in early afternoon. I will be there to speak with you and Isaac."

With that Jakob continued his ride toward the mill.

After arriving at the mill, he was greeted by several workers who knew him and Isaac. He detailed his needs. After some discussion, it was decided one of the mill hands would return with Jakob to determine the lumber required to do the job. He would also stay and participate in the planning of the work.

Jakob was pleased to have the company on the ride back to the farm.

As they were approaching Johannes' farm, Anke, who was working in the front vegetable garden waved them to stop.

Jakob pulled his horse to a halt and dismounted.

"Anke", he shouted. "Is there a problem here? Your actions seem that it is urgent."

"No. I have some news to share with you. I am going to be leaving our community to go and study to become a nurse. I will help those who return from that horrid war in Europe with injuries. It will be a long time before I return. I will come back for festivities and special times with my family."

"Anke, I am happy for you and sad that you will go away. We have been such good friends. It will not be the same when you are gone. I will miss you. I know you will do well in your studies. When do you leave? Where will you go to study and receive your training?"

"I leave in one week for Winnipeg. There are many Mennonites there and I will stay with a family. I will start to work at the Hospital in Winnipeg and train there. I am excited to go."

Chapter 16

Over the next week crews from various farms visited with Jakob and Isaac to assist with the construction. Working from sunrise until dusk, the new barn was quickly built using the techniques and traditional Mennonite methods.

With the new construction completed, attention was turned to the repair of the existing farm sheds.

Each day Inge was assisted by the women in preparing soups and traditional foods for the men. Each evening the men and the women would gather to discuss the next day and share in a simple but hearty meal.

Within two weeks the work was complete. Summer was drawing to an end. Dusk arrived earlier and in the evenings there was a marked coolness in the air. Soon wood fires were lit in open hearths and in the small wood burning stoves to heat the simple farmhouses.

As Old Order Mennonites, the Klassens did not have electricity in the farmhouse, but relied on oil lamps and candles made by the local women.

Jakob would leave the farmhouse in the early evening and walk to the barn to check the cattle and sheep who had been brought in from the pastures. After a quick walk to each building, Jakob returned to the farmhouse and prepared for bed.

He lay in his bed in the small room at the back of the farmhouse. Isaac and Inge were in the adjacent room. Jakob started to drift into a sleep that had been fuelled by the long hours and heavy work on the farm, preparing for winter.

As he lay there he heard the sound of horses being ridden hard. He was curious. Why would any of the local farmers be riding at this time and why a large group of them. Jakob jumped from his bed. There must be a disaster of some type. He quickly dressed and ran to the front yard, prepared to offer help with whatever crisis was happening.

What Jakob observed caused him to freeze on the spot. These were not his fellow farmers riding to his farm with such speed and fury. He squinted in the dark and made out the riders as members of the notorious 118 Battalion. These were not soldiers of discipline or high morals as Jakob had learned on his trips into Berlin where he sold the farm produce and furniture handcrafted by Isaac.

These were sloppy, drunken and ignorant louts, who used their uniform and rank to beat and terrify other young men who were not in the military. In addition, they used their positions to abuse store owners and demand free goods, food and drink.

While their behavior defied all military standards, it was tolerated by the police and local politicians who feared that any action against them would adversely impact the recruiting efforts of the 118 Battalion. After all, a commitment had been made to send local troops to assist in fighting the war.

The 118 Battalion had a reputation that was both terrible and feared.

These were the same soldiers who had sacked and destroyed the German Concordia Club, smashed the furniture, shredded and destroyed the German flag and removed the statue of Kaiser Wilhelm and dragged it through the streets while smashing at it with sticks and wooden clubs.

While these ugly events unfolded nightly, the local authorities looked the other way.

Jakob was scared and given his Mennonite religious beliefs could not understand this behavior. He thought back to his times with the Elders and the talks they had about persecution in the Old Europe. Could it now be happening here in Canada? Jakob recalled the anti-German insults and curses hurled at Isaac and himself when they took their produce to Berlin or the Market.

As he stood at the farm gate, the horses galloped by and toward the farm barns. Several of the horses were brought to an abrupt halt and the soldiers loudly dismounted, shouting and swearing. The remainder of the group rode to the rear of the barn.

Jakob ran back into the farmhouse to waken Isaac and Inge. He heard a major crash and more shouting and cursing. He quickly entered the room where Isaac and Inge were soundly sleeping.

"Father, wake up." He shouted. "We have problems. The soldiers are at our barn. I fear they mean to do us harm."

Isaac arose slowly, mustering all the energy he could. Age was defying his previous virulent energies. Jakob grabbed a coat from the rack in the hallway and draped it around Isaac. Together they went out to the front yard.

Standing there at the gate they witnessed the soldiers stumbling, laughing and some urinating against the barn.

Isaac stood quietly and observed. After a few minutes he quietly said to Jakob,

"My son, do not try to stop these men. They have no morals or conscience. Our religion forbids us from taking up weapons and acting in rage. We must act in peace, but I see that these men are drunk and behaving this way because of their drunkenness. You will not be able to speak to them or have them stop. They will attack you. We came to this land with very little and we will survive in spite of them."

As they watched the soldiers smashing the farm machinery and instruments, they heard a shuffling to their right. Coming to them out of the darkness was Johannes, their neighbor.

As Johannes approached them, Jakob and Isaac noticed tears running down his cheeks.

"They have shot and killed my precious horses. They came to my house looking for my daughter. It is good fortune that Anke has gone to visit the school where she will study. Isaac, are the bad times returning?"

As they stood together, Jakob pointed to the inside of the barn. Flames were flickering where the bales of hay were stored. Soon the flames spread and the crackle of rapidly burning wood erupted. The sounds and cries of the panicked animals in the barn filled the air. There was no saving the barn or animals from the ferocious fire that was burning.

Isaac stood looking at the devastation of his life's work. He turned to Johannes.

"Are the others to be attacked? We have no way to travel to warn them. Our buggy has been destroyed as well."

Suddenly some of the soldiers ran to the horses and started to ride off leaving a scene of total destruction behind. A remaining few stood drinking whiskey from bottles laughing and slapping each other's backs.

A large heavy man attempted several times to mount his horse and fell. Cursing he picked up a wooden plank and beat the horse. Finally he was able to climb on to the horse in the most awkward manner. As he started to ride off he became aware of Jakob, Isaac and Johannes standing at the gate of the farmhouse. He turned his horse toward them and rode up to within a few feet of them.

"We'll soon be rid of all you dirty rotten Krauts. All of you fucking German sympathizers, the whole fucking lot of you. Look at you all, too dammed afraid to stand up and fight. You won't even protect your own property. So tell me reverends, where's your great God now. I didn't see him coming to help. See, it doesn't help you men or the women to dress in those stupid clothes and say you do it for God. Ha, this is the only real God." he slurred, raising a half empty whiskey bottle.

He threw the bottle at Jakob, who walked over picked it up and went to the side of the horse and handed it back up to the drunken soldier.

"Please sir. Can you go and leave us. We mean no harm to you or anyone. We simply wish to farm, make our furniture and arts and live a peaceful existence."

"Ah, you cowardly piece of shit. Go on. Hide behind that religious big hat and those suspenders. Pretend to farm so you can stay at home with Mummy and not help this country in its war. A bunch of cowards, the lot of you."

With a scowl on his face the drunken rider threw the whiskey bottle at the farmhouse and then reined his horse around and rode back to the few remaining soldiers.

More bottles were taken from the saddle bags. More drinking and shouting of profanities went on until, tired of this scene, the soldiers slowly started to ride off to their next prey.

Flames flickered and dark plumes of smoke drifted into the sky. The Klassens barns and farm had been thoroughly sacked.

Chapter 17

Isaac, Jakob and Johannes stood quietly and looked at the smoldering destruction in disbelief.

Isaac was the first to speak.

"I am being punished. I am cursed. It was I who recommended this settlement. Now we will all be subjected to the hostilities of these poor misinformed men whose visions are not clear. The wars are not here. Why are they pursuing those wars and hatreds here in Berlin. We have no involvement with them. How can we make them understand?"

Johannes drew a long breath and then replied.

"Isaac, you cannot blame this upon yourself. These men are poorly informed and acting upon the information that is given to them by others who wish to create this atmosphere of evil. It is my belief that much of this information is wrong and is spread on purpose by those who do not want us here. Our lands are now some of the most fertile and produce the finest crops. I know that they have become the envy of some. In particular, it is a desire of the Colonel Wellington to have us sell these lands back to him. It is said he regrets the decision he made to sell to us. This I have heard when I am in the town selling at the market."

Jakob listened intently. Again he began to question his belief in religion and humanity. He wondered why they could not take up arms and fight to protect themselves.

Isaac shook his head and stared down at the ground.

"Our life here has been good. We left Lancaster in the belief we could achieve this better life. We have labored hard and helped each other in building this community. We cannot let events like this just happen. We must approach the authorities in Berlin and ask their help."

Johannes smiled.

"Isaac, you are always seeking to make things right. I cannot share your belief that these authorities will help us. They have nothing to gain by helping us. They are also the men who were elected by those who would like to see us leave. Isaac, I advise you to be patient. These hostilities in Europe cannot last forever. We must visit with the other neighboring Mennonite communities and discuss the best way of protecting ourselves."

"Johannes, you speak wisely. I am getting old. It is late and dark. Tonight you will stay with us and in the morning we will discuss."

The three men turned away from the smoking remains of the barns and walked slowly back to Isaac's farmhouse. Upon entering, Inge greeted them. Her face displayed a gentle understanding, but the grief of what had happened penetrated the veneer.

Inge spoke quietly

"I have made some warm milk for you. Please sit and let us be calm. We will pray and then sleep. Tomorrow we will face new challenges, but we will start again. All is not lost. We still have fertile lands, good neighbors and our health."

With heads bowed Isaac lead them through a small prayer asking forgiveness for those who had wrought destruction on his and

Johannes' farms and sought guidance for the awkward days ahead.

Sleep did not come easily to any of them that night.

Jakob lay awake. He was disturbed. In his mind he kept questioning why the Mennonites were now being subjected to this treatment again. He recalled discussions with older members in the community and their stories of past horrors. He wondered if these things happened to members of other religions and also to those who had no religion or were atheists. His mind raced. He could not answer his own questions and he had no one to turn to.

It was then that Jakob resolved that he would never allow this to happen to him. It was the beginning of the changes in Jakob's life.

Chapter 18

Dawn broke. Jakob arose before the others and went out to the still smoldering remains. He walked around and surveyed the scene with disgust. Not one of the farm animals had survived the inferno.

Jakob resolved to take charge of the situation. He sat on an old stump that they used for splitting firewood. He buried himself deep in thought. He sat for what seemed hours before he was joined by Johannes. Johannes looked grim.

" Jakob" he said. "Good morning. I just sat with Isaac and Inge for morning breakfast. He is not well. I fear that this attack on his property has had a far deeper effect on Isaac than we realized."

Jakob nodded his head. He had seen the deterioration in Isaac over the last few months. It was obvious that he would not be able to rebuild the farm to its former self.

Jakob looked directly at Johannes. "I will be leaving shortly to visit the other farms. I would be happy if you could stay with Isaac and Inge until my return. I will pack some food and drink and leave soon. I am concerned about our neighbors," he said, pointing to small wisps of smoke arising on the horizon over the wheat fields. "I must find out what the situation is and try to get us help."

Johannes nodded. "I will accompany you when you leave. We will stop at my home to gather some supplies. I will have my wife return with me to stay with Inge and help with Isaac."

Jakob and Johannes walked back to the farmhouse where Isaac and Inge were still seated at the small wooden table. An untouched bowl of food sat in front of Isaac.

Isaacs face was drawn and lacked its normal color. Jakob immediately knew that Isaac was suffering a major problem.

The nearest doctor was within at least a few hours ride. Jakob hastened the process of gathering some food items and drink. He turned to Isaac and Inge. "I am going for help. Johannes will return to be with you. First, he will go to his home and bring his wife and some items back here. I will continue on by foot. Hopefully someone will pass by with cart and buggy and I will be able to catch a ride."

Soon Johannes and his wife returned to the farmhouse to help Inge. Jakob and Johannes bid farewell and started their trek to get assistance. Shortly before mid-day, they reached Johannes farm. While the buildings remained intact, swarms of flies hovered over the corpses of the dead horses and cattle which were now starting to bloat in the sun.

"Come in." said Johannes. "You must take a drink of water before you leave."

Jakob thanked him and after a quick drink returned to the worn path out to the main track that lead to the road into Berlin. As he walked toward Berlin he saw the cause of the smoke he had seen earlier. The community's small Church Hall had been burned to the ground. Anger swelled inside him. Being unable to do anything, he continued his walk but at a faster pace.

Shortly after passing the Church, he heard the distinctive clatter of hooves behind him. He turned to see a man from another community approaching in a covered wagon. He waved him to stop. This was not a person that Jakob knew. Jakob walked up to the wagon and introduced himself.

The man driving the wagon was dressed in somber clothing and appeared very solemn. Jakob relayed the events of the night and explained his need to travel toward Berlin to seek the assistance of the Doctor for Isaac. The man nodded.

" I am Julius van Loon. I am travelling to Berlin. Last night our small village was also set upon. There were casualties. You are welcome to sit up front with me if you can accept that I am transporting the bodies of those killed in the chaos of last night."

Jakob was stunned. He wondered how bad the attacks had been and how many farms were sacked. Jakob accepted the offer. He climbed up. Throughout the journey little was said.

They rode on to the outskirts of Berlin and stopped at the Doctors residence. Jakob strode to the door and knocked loudly. There was no response. He waited and knocked again. Still there was no response. Anxious, Jakob walked around to the back of the stone cottage. As he did so, he noticed an older grey haired woman hanging clothing to dry.

"Madam" he called loudly.

The woman turned to Jakob and looked at him intently.

"Yes. What is your business?"

"I need to see the Doctor. It is an emergency and the man who drove me also requires help."

Jakob explained the events of the night before and the need for assistance with the dead in the wagon.

"The Doctor is at Church. He will return soon. You may sit here and wait" she said gesturing to a small bench in the garden. Your driver may join you. I will return in a moment with some cool drinks."

With that she scurried off into a small red door at the rear of the house.

Jakob and Julius sat quietly. Soon voices were heard at the front of the property. The Doctor, his wife and 2 children had returned. Shortly after entering the house, the Doctor emerged with a worried expression on his face.

He sat and listened to their stories, occasionally interrupting with the odd question. When he was satisfied, he spoke.

"There is nothing that can be done for the deceased in your wagon, my dear Julius. We will bring them in for identification and preparation for burial. We must do this quickly as I wish to leave and assist the father of Jakob. Jakob and I will return to his farmhouse using two of my fastest horses. Do you have the strength to do this Jakob?"

Jakob smiled, nodded and went to assist in removing the dead from the wagon.

As soon as the task was completed, he and the Doctor walked over to the stables. Inside the stables were some of the finest horses that Jakob had ever laid eyes on. The Doctor walked down an aisle between the penned horses. At the end of the row there were two pens containing large black stallions.

The Doctor turned to Jakob. "Do you think you can handle such a horse?" he asked.

"I have been on many horses since I was just a small boy" Jakob replied.

The Doctor fetched bridles and saddles from hooks on the stable wall and placed them on the stallions. While he was doing this Jakob was aware of the stallion looking directly at him as if the horse was trying to understand who he was and why this was happening.

When the horses were saddled the Doctor passed a set of reins to Jakob. The Doctor led the first horse from the stable and beckoned Jakob to follow.

They mounted the horses and trotted out to the roadway. After leaving the edge of the town, the Doctor called to Jakob to speed up the horse. Soon both were galloping toward Isaacs' farm.

In the late afternoon the Doctor and Jakob arrived at the farm and dismounted. They entered the farmhouse and found Johannes and Inge sitting with Isaac, while Johannes' wife was preparing a simple meal. Introductions were made.

The Doctor asked for privacy to examine Isaac. Isaac slowly arose and motioned to the Doctor to follow him to the small bedroom at the front of the house.

Soon the Doctor returned to the small kitchen. He sat at the small wooden table with the rest.

"Isaac's condition is not good. I fear last night's disaster was too much for him. He has suffered a heart attack. I have given medicines to him that will force him to rest and sleep. He must not be disturbed and it is certain that he will never be able to work again. He is too fragile for me to take him to our hospital. He is going to need a lot of special care. I will instruct you on the medicines and foods he will need to recover."

Jakob looked around at the others and saw the sadness and grief on their faces. Again he questioned the existence of a God and if there was indeed a God then why things like this happened. He knew of the teaching of God's will. It made no sense to him. What was the purpose to work hard and honestly all one's life and then have this happen? He felt himself drifting even further away from the beliefs that had been ingrained in him. He realized his conflict in accepting these beliefs and reconciling them with the events of life.

The Doctor stood. "There is nothing more I can do here today, so I will now depart." He looked at Jakob and spoke to him "Jakob, you are to keep the horse tonight. Tomorrow please come to see me. I will have medicines ready for you to return and treat Isaac."

Jakob walked with the Doctor to where the horses were grazing. Once they were alone he stopped and asked the Doctor "How bad is Isaac?"

The Doctor looked down and idly kicked a small stone to the side of the pathway.

"Jakob, I suggest you prepare for his death. His heart is barely working. I will do all I can, but he is very weak. Come tomorrow and I will have the medicines."

The Doctor mounted his fine stallion and slowly rode off. Jakob's bitterness swelled. He battled to control his emotions. Finally he returned to the others.

"While Isaac recovers, I will be repairing the farm with help from the other farmers. I will operate the farm. We will buy new livestock and try to return to our normal lives" Jakob announced, but deep inside he knew that this would only be for a short while.

Chapter 19

The next day Jakob rode back to the Doctors residence. Isaac had rested peacefully during the night.

Jakob walked up to the front door of the Doctors residence and knocked.

"Come in, Jakob" called the Doctor. "The medicines are ready. How is the patient?"

"I checked him this morning before I left. He was sleeping but looked very pale. The skin of his face was white. Normally he looks tanned from working the fields with me."

The Doctor nodded. "This is my concern. I fear that his blood circulation is so poor. His heart is failing. These medicines may relieve the problem. It is urgent he receive these soon. Please return now and quickly."

"Doctor, what about your horse? I cannot afford to buy such a magnificent animal" Jakob stated.

"The Doctor smiled. "Jakob, until you recover your farm he is yours to use. Go now. It is important that no more time be wasted."

Jakob thanked the Doctor and rode back to the farm at a fast pace. By mid afternoon he had arrived back safely. The medicines were given to Isaac who seemed livelier than he had that morning. Jakob was relieved.

That night Jakob sat with Inge and discussed their predicament. Without the barns and with their farm animals dead, they would be reliant upon the other farmers. Jakob was worried about this situation. Winter was fast approaching.

With his ailing father and aging mother, Jakob was concerned. The rebuilding of the farm would need to be done quickly and he began to doubt his abilities. He would need lots of assistance to build the new barns. He worried about the cost of replacing the livestock. He was unsure if the past summers harvest would provide enough income.

Jakob was resolute. He would not give up, as that is exactly what the drunken louts had wanted. He would fight back and win the only way he knew how. He would defeat them by restoring the farm and its operation.

Inge was distraught. Her beloved Isaac was ill and the farm destroyed. Jakob looked at her as she lamented the situation.

"My dearest mother," he started, "We will recover from this. We have faced formidable challenges before. We can overcome this setback. I have already spoken to several neighbors. They have offered to spread the word of our misfortune amongst the others. "

"Jakob, you cannot do all this alone" Inge responded.

"I will not be alone in doing this. Tomorrow Johannes and I will start planning."

Chapter 20

The morning's sunrise was spectacular. Jakob awoke to the golden rays glistening on an early frost. The frost crystals sparkled in the sun. Jakob arose feeling good. He quietly walked to Isaac's room. Isaac was still sleeping, his chest heaving as he breathed in his sleep. Jakob observed that some color had returned to Isaacs face. He was relieved. Feeling invigorated, even with all the problems he had to manage, Jakob slipped out of the house and started his walk to Johannes's farm.

As he walked along in the cool morning air, Jakob observed 2 riders approaching from a distance. His initial reaction was one of concern given the recent events. As the riders came closer, Jakob recognized them as merchants from Berlin with whom both he and Isaac had dealt with since their arrival from Lancaster.

"Greetings, Jakob" they called. "We have learned of your troubles from the Doctor in town and have come to offer our assistance. You and Isaac have been good and loyal to us over the years. We need to know how we can help you in these troubled times."

"I am on my way to visit with Johannes, our good neighbor. We are about to discuss a plan to rebuild our farms and livestock. If you are interested please join me."

The riders dismounted their steeds and walked beside Jakob the rest of the distance to Johannes farm. At the farm they tethered their horses at his barn and followed Jakob to the small farmhouse. Johannes met them at the door and welcomed them. Introductions were made.

The small group sat in the kitchen where Johannes had a large pot of steaming coffee brewing. Within minutes the talk turned to the attacks that had taken place. The merchants expressed their sorrow and dismay at the events occurring in Berlin and at the hysteria that had erupted since the illogical commitment to recruit so many soldiers to meet the political pledge to England. They discussed the massive loss of life. Millions were falling in a war that seemed to have little relevance to Canada and many other nations.

This talk got Jakob thinking again about the Mennonite beliefs. On one hand, he understood and appreciated the religion's position on peace. On the other hand he saw the need to protect one's self and property. He was conflicted. All this talk of war and destruction was further fuelling his doubts.

Soon the talk turned to rebuilding the farms. Jakob and Johannes learned that there had been several other farms that had been sacked that same night.

The merchants put forward their plan for the assistance they could offer. They had known Johannes, Isaac and Jakob for years and all dealings had been honest and all parties had been satisfied with them.

The older Merchant spoke. "Gentlemen, we have known and dealt with you for years. You have never let us down or deceived us. We need your produce even more. This war is making it difficult to procure goods. We therefore spoke with other store owners and have a proposal for you. We would like to pay a deposit in advance on the next year's crops. We will pay 25% of the sum that we paid for this past years yield. It is our pleasure to do this. We ask that you execute a simple agreement that summarizes this. There will not be any harsh penalties."

Johannes and Jakob looked at each other with amazement. No one had ever offered support like this. They asked many questions about the arrangement. Finally, an agreement was produced and both Johannes and Jakob examined it and then signed. Upon signing the younger merchant reached into his jacket and removed a large envelope of cash which he handed to Jakob. Johannes estimated the cash required to replace his livestock. This represented a small amount compared to the costs that Jakob faced in restoring the farm. Jakob handed cash to Johannes and placed the remainder of the monies in his vest pocket.

With the financial formalities over, the merchants stood to leave. Johannes offered a small prayer for the safe return.

Jakob and Johannes returned to the house and started planning their mutual recoveries. Johannes was going to immediately visit the neighboring communities to replace his slaughtered livestock. In addition, he committed to buy livestock for Jakob.

They continued to talk until early evening and by then had a strong plan of recovery worked out. Johannes would provide shelter for any livestock purchased until Jakob's farm and barns were rebuilt.

Jakob had devised a plan that would allow him to purchase materials over the winter months and commence building in the early spring. He would assist Johannes over the winter with the cattle and sheep.

With the plans established, Jakob returned home to advise Isaac and Inge of what would be happening. Inge took Jakob's hand and squeezed it, smiling and soon her eyes filled with tears. "How could we have been so lucky to have blessed with such a good son" she wondered. Isaac sat at the table and nodded with a small smile.

Hopefully, their life would return to normal. Life's plans, however, called for a different turn of events.

Chapter 21

Klassen Farm, 1918

Throughout the winter months Jakob assisted Johannes with farming tasks. He distributed feed to the cattle and mucked out the barns. Johannes was appreciative of the help.

The winter was unusually mild. Spring arrived early and Jakob was able to start on the construction projects much earlier than he had planned. Again, farmhands and laborers from adjacent farms volunteered their help.

Weeks went by and the first of the three barns were completed. Jakob and Johannes drove the cattle that Johannes had been keeping for Jakob down to the new barn, along with feedstock.

The appearances of normalcy returned. Each day saw progress. Jakob found himself contented and again absorbed into operating the farm. For the first time in a long while he was content.

Within a couple of months the remaining farm buildings were rebuilt. Inge was proud of her men and the work performed. In appreciation, she arranged for the neighboring Mennonite women to prepare a large feast to thank the workers who had assisted Jakob in the task.

With the war in Europe ending, talk drifted to the events that had occurred in Europe. It seemed everyone had been exposed to the horrors which were witnessed with the return of local boys who had gone to fight in the war. These were neighbors and friends who had been exposed to mustard gas, blinded or wounded by shrapnel. Others received word of the death of friends. It was a sober and somber discussion.

Again, Jakob wondered at why there were constant wars and the position of the Mennonites against war and the taking up of arms to protect ones property. The conflicting thoughts and values were once again running wild in his mind.

Chapter 22

Klassen Farm, 1920

For the next 2 years, life at the Klassen farm was quiet and settled. Jakob worked the farm and assisted his neighbor Johannes with some of the heavier tasks.

Isaac would come and sit and watch the cutting of hay, the harvesting of the crops and the mustering of the livestock. His health prevented him from actively participating, even though he wished that he could.

Life was good again.

Sunday on the Klassen farm was a day of rest and religious observance. This particular Sunday, Jakob took out the fishing pole he had made as a boy and some meat to use as bait.

"I am going down to the river to see if I can catch us some fine fish for tonight's dinner" he called.

"Jakob, please wait. I wish to accompany you," Isaac called from the kitchen.

" Isaac, are you up to the walk? It is through the tall grasses to the river bank. Are you sure you have the strength to walk there and back?" asked Inge

"My dearest. If I did not have this strength and desire, I would not suggest that I go. I will go with Jakob. It has been a long time since I visited the river."

Jakob smiled and gave a slight chuckle. This was the Isaac he remembered.

Together they started their walk to the river bank and to the bend in the river with the rock shelf. There were small rapids at that point and that is where the fishing was best. They walked through the tall reedy grasses that grew to a height taller than them. Jakob parted the grasses with his arms and Isaac followed closely behind.

As they moved through the grasses, there was the sound of a shot fired from a shotgun. Isaac cried out in pain and fell to the ground. Jakob spun around to see Isaac on the ground with blood spurting from his neck. Jakob dropped to his knees and placed his hand on Isaacs's neck. He could not find any pulse. He looked into Isaacs eyes. They were open and stared blankly ahead.

Isaac was dead. His death had been instant. His weak heart and poor blood circulation had already weakened him. He could not have withstood the injury.

Within minutes, 2 young boys crashed onto the scene. Jakob arose. His anger was at boiling point. He looked at the boys who were holding an old shotgun. He estimated their ages to be around 14.

"You have killed my father" he thundered. "What the hell do you think you were doing?"

The oldest boy stammered a reply. "Sir, we saw the grasses moving and thought it was a pheasant. We are sorry."

The younger boy started to weep.

"Were you never taught not to shoot unless you were sure of the target? You will come with me now" he commanded. He had not seen these boys before.

Jakob removed his jacket and threw it at the older boy who clumsily caught it. He then bent down and gently picked up Isaac. He raised him over his shoulder. He was surprised at Isaac's light weight. He started to walk back to the farmhouse with the boys scared and following him.

Upon approaching, Inge ran from the front yard where she had been working in her small vegetable garden. She ran as fast as she could for her age and stumbled when she reached Jakob.

"I am sorry, Isaac is dead. There was a horrible shooting accident" Jakob said in a choked voice.

Inge screamed out and dropped to the ground. Tears poured from her eyes.

"My dearest Isaac. You have given so much too so many of our brethren. What will I do without you? How will I be able to live and continue the life we built?" she sobbed.

Jakob continued to the farmhouse and entered the front door. He went to the room Isaac and Inge slept in and laid Isaac on the bed. Next Jakob went and filled a small basin with water. He returned and wiped away the blood that had saturated Isaac's neck and face.

Inge entered and fell upon her knees praying. Jakob joined her. After 10 minutes he stood and walked out to where the two boys stood waiting.

He looked at them sternly. "You will walk with me to my neighbor Johannes's farmhouse. There you will wait while I ride and seek the assistance of the local constabulary. "

The boys were nervous. Jakob reached and took the shotgun from the oldest boy.

"I will take this and place it in my house."

A few minutes later the three started their walk to Johannes's farmhouse.

As they approached the farm, they noticed Johannes repairing a fence. He waved at them and stopped. He looked at Jakob and then at the boys.

"Who are these boys and why are they with you? "Johannes asked.

Jakob walked up to Johannes and in an old Dutch dialect used by the Mennonites told Johannes of Isaac's death. Johannes' face went white. His eyes took in the boys.

"Who are these boys? Where do they come from?" Johannes asked

Jakob replied, "I am leaving them with you while I go and report this to the authorities. I will need to take one of your fastest horses."

"Jakob, you may indeed take my finest horse. I will await your return."

Jakob knew the horse well. He went into the barn and saddled up the horse and started off on a fast ride to Kitchener.

Chapter 23

Jakob rode hard and fast. He passed by others who waved to him in greeting. He barely acknowledged them. It was early afternoon on Sunday when he pulled his horse into the hitching post at the local constabulary. The front door was closed but not locked. Jakob entered. He recognized the constable sitting behind the large oak desk as one who had attended the farm after the attack.

The constable looked up from the papers he was working on. He frowned upon recognizing Jakob then stood and approached the counter where Jakob stood.

"Good afternoon. What brings you here good man. I hope there is no more trouble at your homestead with those soldiers."

"No sir. We have had a serious accident and my father Isaac is dead. I need your assistance."

Jakob relayed the earlier events of the day. The constable stood and thought for a while.

"I will need to come immediately. First I must have my junior constable come here to replace me. I will send a messenger to summon him. I will also need to contact the Doctor and take him with me to confirm all of this."

With this, he called a young boy from the rear of the station. He gave instructions to the boy to hurry and to tell the junior constable to come immediately.

Jakob started to excuse himself and advised the constable he would see him back at the farm as riding in any form of car was prohibited in his religion. The constable grudgingly agreed. Jakob ran to the hitching post and untied the horse and started his journey back to the farm. On the way the constable passed him.

Upon arriving back at the farm, Jakob observed the constable speaking to Inge, who had changed into traditional mourning clothes. Jakob approached. The constable asked to see Isaac. Jakob ushered the constable and the Doctor into the front bedroom where Isaac lay.

The Doctor pulled back the sheets and examined Isaac. After a few minutes the Doctor turned to the constable and pronounced Isaac as formally dead with a gunshot wound to the neck.

The constable nodded and asked Jakob to escort him to Johannes's farm so he could question the boys. Jakob agreed and left with him.

At Johannes's farmhouse, the two boys sat quietly. The constable entered and immediately expressed shock.

"I know these boys. They are the sons of our most prominent businessman, the famous butcher and sausage maker for the town and neighboring districts. These are good boys. I cannot find it in my mind why they would do anything malicious."

Jakob spoke." Good sir. I understand that they meant no harm and this was not an intentional act. I need for you and the Doctor to handle those tasks that the Government requires so that we can proceed quickly with the funeral preparations in accordance with our Mennonite custom."

The constable looked back at Jakob.

"Please tell me what you refer too" he said.

"In our religion, the members of our community who know the deceased Isaac will visit in the next day or two. We will prepare a simple handmade casket for his burial here on our property within three days. We will have no eulogies; instead the elders will express their respect for Isaac and what he contributed to the community throughout his life.

We will conduct his service at the newly built church after which we will bury Isaac here on our farm in a dedicated area. We will ask our fellow farmers and friends to form a procession with their horses and buggies to take Isaac to the church from our humble home. When the ceremony is complete we will return to bury Isaac in the grave which I, Johannes and fellow farmers will have prepared. We ask you to tell the merchants and others who knew Isaac through his days of trading in Kitchener not to send or bring flowers as our religion does not allow for this."

The constable nodded his agreement.

Chapter 24

Monday morning. The first mourners started arriving to visit Isaac and pay their respects. It was obvious that Isaac was a respected and well liked man. There was a constant procession to the farmhouse. People who the Klassens had not seen for years since the original settlement arrived to pay their respects.

Inge remained steadfast. Jakob was concerned for her. She had endured so much over the past few years and now this.

Details of the simple funeral were provided to those who needed the information.

Jakob was shocked at the number of families who offered their carriages and buggies for the funeral procession. While he knew that Isaac was a leader and popular in the community, he never expected this outpouring.

Throughout Monday, more visitors came to the farmhouse.

Jakob excused himself and quietly left. He needed to decide on the best location to prepare a burial plot. He walked to the barn and again sat on the old tree stump that he and Isaac used to split firewood. As he sat there, Johannes walked up.

"Jakob, what is it you are thinking?"

Jakob explained to Johannes that he could not decide a location best suited for the burial. Johannes recalled the many mornings that he and Isaac had sat and looked to the east to watch the sunrise while milking the cows. He pointed to a small knoll that faced east.

"Jakob" he said, "Isaac always believed that when the sun rose for a new day that there would be new miracles and life. I know he loved that particular place on his land. I suggest he be placed there."

Jakob stood and entered the barn. He returned with a spade and shovel and went to hand dig a grave which was the Mennonite custom.

Chapter 25

Tuesday. Jakob arose and dressed in his formal Mennonite clothing for the solemn service. He waited in the kitchen for Inge. While waiting he prepared a simple breakfast of eggs, bread and coffee.

Inge joined him and together they sat in silence. Finally Inge spoke.

"Jakob, when I met Isaac we were full of dreams. Our life was not easy, however, I never heard him complain. He always looked for a way to try and make things right. You are so fortunate to have his blood. I am sure you too will continue to be a good man. We did experience some very bad times in Lancaster and previously Isaac's family in Germany and Holland had suffered tremendously. Isaac had the vision and the drive to leave and try to start our new lives in Lancaster and then here in Canada. We are lucky to have had such a fine man as husband and as a father to you. I am sure Isaac would wish for you to carry on his values and tradition."

While encouraged by her kind words, Jakob still had the unsettling thoughts about religion and life. He could not tell her this or discuss it with anyone in the community. He listened to her words but wondered why she and Isaac never discussed the family relatives in Europe. Any attempt he made was always met with silence or a change in the topic. This had bothered him for years.

As they sat having their breakfast, there was a rapid knock at the door. Jakob frowned. He arose and went to the front door. Upon opening the door he was shocked, for there was Johannes's daughter Anke.

"Anke, you are welcome. I am so surprised to see you. Please come in."

Anke walked into the house and Jakob took her coat and hung it on the hooks near the front door.

"Come Anke, we are having a simple breakfast."

"I cannot join you until I pay my respects and prayers for Isaac."

Jakob escorted her to the front parlor where Isaac had been moved for visitors wishing to visit. He left her and in doing so whispered "Please join us when you finish."

A short while later Anke joined Inge and Jakob in the kitchen. Jakob quickly stood to pour her a coffee. He looked at her. During her absence she had developed into a handsome woman. He was mesmerized. "How could this be happening?" he wondered. "Especially on today when we need to pay respect."

"I want to tell you that I was always fond of Isaac and the knowledge he shared with our family. You are fortunate to have had such a great man in your lives"

Jakob searched for a reply and was shocked to find he could not respond. Finally Inge spoke

 "You are kind to come and share those words."

Jakob continued to look at Anke. She was no longer the little ragamuffin he had played with in the fields and who had swung on the farm gate, much to Isaac's feigned annoyance.

Finally there was another knock at the door. Upon opening the door, Jakob was greeted by two of the community's most senior elders and a bishop. He bowed and ushered them into the house.

"It is time for us to prepare for the funeral procession. The carriages and buggies of our fellow members are arriving and we must be ready."

Jakob lead the trio into the front parlor and the final preparations were completed.

There was another knock at the door. Several large men entered to remove the simple casket and place it on the carriage for the journey to the church.

Jakob took Inge's arm and assisted her to the waiting buggy at the head of the procession.

The procession wound its way from the Klassen farmhouse down the beaten track to the road that lead to the recently rebuilt church. Along the route farmhands stood on the side of the road, removing their hats and bowing their heads in respect.

Chapter 26

The church service was simple and lasted for just over an hour. There were no eulogies. Members stood and made brief statements in which Isaac was remembered for his contributions to the community.

With the service over, Isaac's body was returned to the farm. Jakob, Johannes and several others carried the casket up to the freshly dug grave. Prayers were recited as the casket was slowly lowered by ropes to its final place of rest.

Inge kneeled and took a handful of loose dirt. She bent forward to scatter the dirt onto the coffin as it was being lowered. Suddenly she lurched forward and fell into the grave. Inge landed on the coffin in a humped position. The men lowering the coffin were jerked forward by the sudden increase in the weight. They pulled back on the ropes. As if it was a reincarnation, the coffin's edge resurfaced over the edge of the grave with Inge mounted on top. The small group looked on in horror. From the rear of the group, Anke rushed forward.

"Please. Let me to her. I am a trained nurse."

Anke knelt on the loose soil where the coffin was now placed. She reached across to feel for Inge's pulse. There was none. Inge too had moved on.

Anke turned to the sea of faces looking anxiously at her. "I am sorry, Inge has passed."

Anke stood and then turned and walked toward Jakob. She reached for his arm.

"Jakob, I am sorry this has happened like this. I know Inge loved Isaac very much. I believe his death was probably too much for her to bear and the difficult thought of going on alone."

For the first time ever, Anke observed that Jakob was blinking back tears. In all the years she had known him, growing up together on the farm, walking to school and playing with the other children; she had never seen him cry.

She placed her arm through his and started to lead him away from the gravesite and back to the farmhouse. As she did so she nodded to the clergy who had attended for Isaac's burial. They turned and joined Anke and Jakob.

Several of the men walked to their buggies and took blankets into which they placed Inge's inert body and carried her into the farmhouse where she was placed in the front parlor.

Several of the women tended to her at rest. The men spoke and then returned to the grave for Isaac's burial.

Jakob huddled with the clergy who had attended to officiate over Isaac's burial. Plans were hastily made to perform another service the next day.

After the burial service for Isaac, Jakob and the men returned to the farmhouse where freshly baked foods had been placed out for those who wished to participate in celebrating the passing of Isaac and pay their respects to Inge.

Jakob saw Anke sitting alone at the back of the kitchen. He walked over to her.

"Anke, it is so good to see you have come back here to live. What will you do here?"

Anke looked up and smiled. "Jakob, I will be staying for one week and then I must return as I am to enter into examinations for the nursing studies I have just completed. If I pass these examinations I will be sent to the big hospital in Toronto."

"Anke, is that what you want? You will be in the presence of many sick and suffering. It must not be pleasant for you. Why don't you return to the farm with Johannes. He is getting older and he and his wife could surely use your help."

"Jakob, I have always wanted to help people. After training for nursing, I realized how much I enjoy it and what it means to me."

"I wish you would consider it and stay."

"At this time I cannot, Jakob."

With this, Anke stood and walked to where two members of the clergy were talking. She approached them smiling and started into a conversation. Every so often she glanced in Jakob's direction.

People started leaving the Klassen home as the afternoon wore on.

Anke crossed the parlor room to bid farewell to Jakob. She took his hands in hers and held them for what seemed the longest time. Jakob was at a loss.

"Anke, I wish to thank you for attending today. It means a great deal to me."

"Thank you. I must leave now to return to the farmhouse. I will come tomorrow for the service for Inge and visit with you after."

Anke walked to the door and Jakob assisted her with her coat. She turned and smiled.

"Jakob, all this will pass. We do not always understand the ways that are chosen for us."

Members of the local congregation gathered at the church the next day for yet another Klassen funeral. After the church service, members returned to the Klassen farm where Inge was to be buried in a small grave alongside Isaac.

Unlike the reception for Isaac, most members of the congregation drifted off to their homes after offering support to Jakob.

Chapter 27

1925

The next five years progressed uneventfully for Jakob. He stayed at the farm and with the help of hired farmhands kept the farm operating. The farm was producing a record number of crops and Jakob's livestock became award winning cattle at the local rural farm shows.

Through those years however, Jakob still thought about his ancestral past. He yearned to know more of the history that had driven Isaac and Inge to migrate to North America. He wanted to know more about his ancestors and existing relatives in Holland and Germany. The curiosity gnawed at him night and day. Whenever an opportunity presented itself Jakob would sit with the remaining elders and glean as much information as possible. With time passing, the memories of the elders were fading. During the most recent talk, Jakob was taken by surprise.

"Jakob Klassen," one of the oldest men called to him. "I am in possession of some valued material from the old country. I believe it is of importance to you. Isaac had entrusted this to me. I was to keep it until he passed. Now I must pass it to you."

Jakob looked and saw the old man was holding a yellowed sheaf of papers.

"These are records of the families that lived in our communities in Europe and who remained there after we left for America. Many will now be dead, but the children who were documented should still be alive. Jakob, I ask that you be very careful with this information. There are records and information contained in these papers that some do not want known."

Jakob frowned. He could not imagine why this would be.

"Sir, I thank you for this. I will be careful and use the information for my personal reasons."

Jakob took the bundle of papers that were tied together with a faded blue ribbon.

That night, Jakob sat at the kitchen table alone. He gently untied the ribbon which was tearing as he did so. By the light of the oil lamp on the table, he cautiously separated the first layers of parchment. They were dry and flaky. He was worried about either tearing or destroying one.

After laying the first page out on the table, Jakob scanned the document using light from the lamp. Recorded in a neatly written ink script was a long list of names. Jakob read down the list. He did not recognize any of the names. All were in German. Hours passed by like minutes. Very late that evening Jakob retired to his room. He lay thinking how both the farmhouse and his life seemed empty now that he was alone since the deaths of Isaac and Inge. He finally drifted off into a restless sleep, his mind racing with the names and places detailed in the old papers.

The morning arrived. He heard the sounds of the farmhands moving the cattle to a different pasture. Today he would not work the farm. Instead Jakob would visit with Johannes's and assist him with some heavy work.

Jakob arose, dressed and started the walk to Johannes farm. He called to one of the hired farmhands to come and work with him.

They entered through the front gates of the farm and made their way to the little farmhouse. Johannes was at the door awaiting them.

"Before we work we will have coffee," he said.

As they sat on the front porch sipping the coffee, Jakob became aware of a shuffling sound in the house. He turned and stared down the hallway that separated the front area from the kitchen. To his surprise, Anke was working in the kitchen.

"Anke has finished her studies and work and now returns to us. We are happy to have her return."

"I must go and speak with her."

Jakob turned and hurried to the kitchen where Anke stood dressed in traditional Mennonite clothing with a large white apron.

"I am pleased you are home, Anke. I believe your presence will be a big help to Johannes. He is in good health, but age is evident."

Anke smiled and thanked him. With this she left the room to wash some clothing and prepare for other household tasks.

Jakob watched her leave and realized how much he had missed her during her absence. He wondered what horrible things she had seen and experienced while treating the soldiers who had returned from the battlefields of Europe. He sensed that Anke held secrets that would never be shared.

Jakob returned to join Johannes and the farmhand. They discussed the repair work that needed to be done to the fencing and barn. After more coffee and with a plan in hand they set off to their labors.

As they worked in the fields replacing fence posts, the sun beat down on them mercilessly. Shortly before noon, Anke walked into the field carrying a large wicker basket of some sweet baked goods, some ham and freshly made fruit juices. The men were hot and famished. They sat, ate and talked. When finished, Anke left and the men resumed repairing the fences.

At the end of a long day, Jakob and the farmhand returned to Jakob's farm. The farmhand asked for lodging that night as the trip to his rented room near the town was a long walk and he was fatigued.

Jakob obliged and soon he too retired.

Early in the morning, Jakob was awakened by a series of soft knocking sounds. He jumped from his bed and went to the door. Anke was standing there with a basket of fresh farm eggs and freshly baked bread.

"I have come with a breakfast for you. The work you did yesterday must have made you tired and hungry. I will prepare the foods for you."

With that she went to the kitchen and commenced preparation of a breakfast.

Chapter 28

Anke and Jakob sat and talked for several hours. Jakob was in no hurry to leave the farmhouse that morning. He found Anke's company to be very comforting after the recent deaths of Isaac and Inge. He was surprised to find this comfort and the things that they had in common.

Jakob wanted to discuss his conflicted feelings about religion and the life he had witnessed. He pondered this for some while and finally decided against introducing something that may upset Anke. She was very devoted to religion and the Mennonite beliefs. He did not want to create a problem in their friendship. He wondered whether he should discuss the old lists of the Mennonites who were either in Europe or had immigrated to North America. He felt the need to share his thoughts and ideas with someone who could relate to his feelings.

Jakob looked across the table at Anke and asked " Anke, I must ask you this. When you were training and later nursing, you saw many badly wounded soldiers who had returned from Europe. Did this make you question the existence of a God and did it cause you to wonder about the pacifist beliefs we hold as Mennonites?"

Anke raised her head and looked directly into his eyes. "Jakob, you ask a strange question of me. You know that our family are devout and practice our religion without any doubts. Why are you asking this? What I saw and what I was able to do for those soldiers only strengthened my resolve and beliefs. Jakob, is there something wrong that makes you ask me such a question?"

"No Anke. I sometimes wonder if we are wrong."

"Jakob, I must now return to Johannes. I had promised to sew clothing today and it is starting to get late in the morning. Tomorrow Johannes and I will travel into town. We have handmade quilts and some furniture we wish to sell. If you wish to join us we would welcome you. Do you have any produce to take into the market?"

"I must go to speak with the Doctor and complete some paperwork. I would be happy to accompany you and Johannes."

"We will leave very early. Come to our house and we will all partake of a breakfast and prayers."

"I will be with you for breakfast and to assist in loading your buggy."

Anke reached to take the plates from in front of Jakob. She gathered them together and took them to the copper washtub which she had filled with water. She placed the dishes and pots from breakfast into water and started to scrub them. Jakob stood up from the table and crossed over to assist her.

She looked at Jakob and said "Jakob, I can see from your looks and the questions you ask that you are troubled. Is it something you would like to speak of?"

Jakob fell quiet for some time. "Anke, I am searching in my mind for the reasons that these bad things are happening again. Our ancestors in Europe suffered badly. Why have these things arisen again? I do not understand. It is making me question my faith and strength."

"Oh, Jakob. You were always the one in Church School who asked the difficult questions and yet often you had all the answers.

Think back to those days. Do not let these thoughts take over your mind. You are a good person and I understand that to have the values that you have then you must question many things in life."

Anke walked to the door and picked up her coat. She then proceeded to open the door to leave.

"Jakob, I must go. I will not be able to complete my tasks for the trip tomorrow if I stay here any later."

Jakob smiled and escorted her out to the farm gate.

Chapter 29

Jakob settled into a quiet life. He worked the farm, attended at church and established friendships with the merchants with whom he dealt.

He had studied the papers he had been handed and the lists of names of the Mennonites who had migrated and the names of the families in Holland and Germany who had remained behind. He was unable to find any names that linked the Klassen family to any location in Europe. He was frustrated as he knew from Isaac that there were still relatives in Holland and Germany who had chosen not to emigrate and had decided to take their chances in Europe.

Jakob's friendship with Anke had changed. Jakob now knew that he wished to take Anke to be his wife.

It was two years after Anke had returned to the farm that Jakob made his decision. In accordance with the Mennonite custom, Jakob visited the Deacon of the church to advise him that he wished to marry Anke. The Deacon would then visit the father and family of the intended bride and relay the request for marriage.

Though conflicted in his beliefs, Jakob still adhered to the old customs out of respect for the community.

Early the next morning Jakob was awakened by sharp knocking at the front door and his name being called. He opened the door to find Johannes and Anke standing there. Johannes was smiling and rushed to Jakob with his hands extended.

"Jakob, you have made Anke and I happy. Finally we will be family. I am sure that this is what Isaac and Inge would have wished and blessed. You must come to our home and we will plan. Can you come tonight?"

Jakob looked at Anke who was glowing with happiness.

"I will visit and bring some fresh meats that we have recently slaughtered."

Johannes was so excited that Jakob thought he had become younger in looks.

"Johannes, I would like to spend some time alone with Anke so we can discuss marriage and our plans."

Johannes removed his large brimmed hat and backed away with a slight bow to Jakob. "Yes. I will now leave you two. You have lightened my heart."

Anke walked beside Jakob as they started down to the orchard at the rear of the farmhouse. Jakob stopped and asked if Anke wanted some refreshments. He then went into the farmhouse and reemerged with a large pitcher of juice and some glasses. He and Anke sat on some old wooden chairs in the orchard.

"Jakob, you have surprised me. I have wanted this for so long and patiently waited, hoping you would want to marry me. We will have a good life together. We will be blessed."

Jakob looked closely at her. She was radiant. He was indeed lucky to have such a good friend who would now be his partner in life.

"Anke, we must plan quickly. As you know, marriages in our religion happen within weeks of receiving the approval of the father. I will visit this evening and discuss all the details with your family. We will have a small but nice service at the church."

Anke stayed throughout the day. She assisted Jakob to clean in the house. In the late afternoon, he wrapped the fresh meats and placed them in a large straw basket. Shortly before sunset, Anke and Jakob set off to walk to Johannes' farmhouse.

That night there was great excitement and laughter. Jakob smiled yet was still fighting back the conflicted beliefs. If Anke or Johannes knew of these Jakob was sure the wedding would not happen.

Chapter 30

The news of Jakob and Anke's wedding spread quickly through the small community. Soon neighbors starting visiting and many questions were asked and blessings given.

In the community this was seen as a tribute to Isaac and Inge and also to Johannes, as they were the founders of the settlement. Hopes, feelings and sentiments were openly expressed to Jakob and Anke for a long and happy marriage.

The next two weeks passed rapidly until the wedding day.

The wedding ceremony was held in Johannes's home in the late morning. There was much noise making and singing as was the tradition of the Old Mennonite Order.

Jakob stood to speak. "Dear friends and good neighbors. We thank you for joining Anke and I in the celebration of our marriage. I am happy to say that we will be staying and continuing our farm and will be here as your friends and members of our small Mennonite Conference. Over the years with Isaac, I had the opportunity to meet with you all. I hope we can continue in his manner and I can do the good deeds he did for everyone. I wish that he and Inge were here today to join with all of us in this happy occasion."

The festivities continued with some dancing and more singing from the men.

As the late afternoon sun began to set and the early dusk arrived, the guests started to bid their farewells and proceed to their horse drawn carriages.

Soon Jakob and Anke were alone as a married couple. This was the very first time they had ever been totally alone.

Jakob walked across the floor of the parlor and reached out to Anke. He looked deeply into her eyes and her radiant glow. It was obvious that Anke was extremely happy with the events that had presented themselves in her life. She had always loved Jakob but could never display this or tell anyone for fear of reprimand in the Church.

Jakob wrapped his long arms around Anke and held her very close to him. Anke trembled. Although Anke had seen and experienced many things during her days as a nurse, nothing had prepared her for this. She started to think back to her days at Church school and the teachings of love, marriage and commitment. Deep inside she was scared. Very scared.

Jakob sensed her feelings.

"Tonight my dear Anke, we will sleep together as man and wife for the first time. Please I ask you, do not be scared. Anything that happens will be with God's blessing."

Anke nodded. A large tear rolled down her cheek. She now realized that whatever relationship she had previously had with Jakob was now over.

"Jakob, I love you dearly. I do not wish to be a bad wife on the night of our marriage. I am scared and need to have you comfort me."

"My dearest Anke, I do not wish to see you in distress like this. In time we will make love and all will be correct."

Anke looked up at him. "Jakob, when we played as children, I often wondered if we would be husband and wife. I also thought many times of you holding and kissing me. I said nothing to any of my friends for fear of a public shaming in the Church."

Jakob released her from his embrace. He looked at her and started to laugh.

"Anke, the attraction we have felt for each other over all the years cannot be influenced by a few. My love for you has grown deeper. Please accept my love. We will go on to the days ahead and become the best of lovers."

Chapter 31

Jakob took Anke's arm and guided them to his bedroom. They embraced and shared a kiss of passion. "Anke. I promise that we will have a good and fulfilling life."

Anke hugged Jakob and held him closer and laid her head against his chest.

"Jakob, I have always believed in you and have watched the many things you have done for many of our friends in our community. You are a good person."

Jakob sat down on the bed and beckoned Anke to sit with him.

"Tomorrow I must leave early to be with the farmhands as they prepare to take some of the livestock to auction. I am sad to have to leave you so early."

Jakob reached around and pulled Anke toward him. She did not resist.

They fell back onto the bed. Soon they were entwined in kisses and reaching for each other.

Jakob fumbled with the thin cloth ribbons that held Anke's dress in place. Anke stood and disrobed and then fell back onto the bed with Jakob. Jakob admired her beautiful body. As they lay on the bed, Jakob and Anke started to sexually explore each other's body. Jakob heaved himself up and removed the heavy shirt and work overalls.

Jakob cupped his hand under Anke's full breast and kissed her neck. Anke shuddered and placed her hands behind his neck and pulled him tight. Jakob continued to kiss her breasts and then proceeded to kiss her arms and stomach. Anke writhed in pleasure. As their passion increased, Anke reached for him. Jakob continued to massage her breasts and body. Even though his hands were calloused and hardened from working in the fields, his touch while caressing Anke's body surprised her with how gentle his touch was.

Their passion continued as they found each other. Neither could talk.

Anke found herself aroused and responding in ways that she had never thought possible.

As Jakob continued to pleasure Anke, she reached for him. She started to stroke his penis. Eventually, as was inevitable, Jakob ejaculated. She felt his warm sperm oozing through her fingers and realized that this could have been another life in the form of a baby she had always dreamed of. Excited, Anke rolled toward Jakob and straddled her leg over him. She raised herself on to him and then took him and placed him inside of her.

They continued lovemaking for what seemed the longest time.

Exhausted, Anke lay her head down on Jakob's shoulder and they both fell into a deep and satisfying sleep.

Before the dawn broke, Anke slid from the bed. She reflected on their night of love. She had never experienced the emotion and feeling that she now felt.

Anke smiled. She had no regrets. Now she understood God's wish and the purpose of man and woman and the institution of marriage in their church.

Anke slowly dressed in her traditional clothes as the wedding was over and the special dresses would now be put away for a future occasion.

After dressing, Anke went to the kitchen to prepare a breakfast for Jakob and the men before they rounded up the livestock for the auction.

In the kitchen, she smiled and felt a great calm knowing she had married the one person she loved and had found this happiness.

It was dark outside, but as she prepared the breakfast dawn started to break. She looked out across the fields at the clear sky and the bright orange hued sun arising. Today would be a beautiful day.

She heard the shuffling of Jakob's boots on the pine floors and turned to see Jakob standing at the kitchen entrance smiling.

Chapter 32

Jakob and Anke settled into a quiet and peaceful life. The farm continued to prosper. Anke became involved in various events with the women of the Mennonite community. She attended sales in the town where they sold baked goods, quilts and other handmade items. In addition to these activities, Anke offered her nursing skills to the elderly and sick in their community.

Three years passed by without incident. Anke found a quiet contentment. She was happy with this life. She was near her parents and also living a fulfilled life on the farm and within the community.

Jakob's continued curiosity and conflict in his beliefs grew. He perused the lists of the names each night of those who had stayed in Europe. Eventually, he started sending letters to those he could identify as relatives of the farmers he knew in the community. He obtained addresses from those relatives.

Unfortunately for Jakob, most of the letters were returned to him unopened as the addressee could not be found. Jakob was not to be deterred. He continued to write and seek information on his relatives and ancestors.

As he and Anke sat one evening talking, Anke looked at him. "Jakob, over the last year you have become different. You do not participate with the men at the church. You do not travel into town but have the farmhands take our produce to market. You have changed. You seem withdrawn. You used to be happy, but now you are quiet and seem sad. It troubles me to see you like this. Please tell me what the problem is. The farm is doing well, we have good neighbors and yet you seem so distracted in our life. What is wrong? Please share your troubles with me."

Jakob sat quietly for a long time not saying a word. Finally he stood and walked to the small wooden desk in the parlor from which he took a small binder in which the yellowing lists of names were kept. He returned and sat across from Anke.

"Anke, I will share with you the reason for my troubled thoughts. In the years before we married, I became conflicted in my thoughts about many things in life. I did not understand the need for the war in Europe, or why in our local town the people turned against each other. I was particularly upset when our farms were attacked and I disagreed with the pacifist position we had to accept because of our religion. After those attacks Isaac's health deteriorated. We did nothing to protect ourselves. At that point I felt the start of a real anger growing in me. I wanted to fight those men who attacked our farms. Later, when those two boys shot and killed Isaac the same anger and fury burst inside of me. For years I have questioned the teaching of our religion regarding these matters. It has reached a point where I am finding myself lost and unable to accept our religious beliefs any longer. I feel trapped and unsure what I should do. There is no one I can discuss this with. In addition, I continue to be obsessed with finding those of my ancestors and relatives who stayed behind in Holland and Germany. I cannot explain this but I believe there is a strong reason for this desire to find them."

Anke reached across and laid her hand gently on his shoulder. She had never seen Jakob so distressed.

"Jakob, we must find a solution to this. Your internal conflict is destroying you. We should seek assistance from the elders as I am sure others have also had these thoughts and have needed guidance and assistance."

Jakob shook his head. "This would bring great shame on me. I cannot do such a thing. Instead I have some recent information that I will share with you as my wife. I received some letters back from several of the names on the lists to whom I wrote."

He handed the yellowed lists to Anke. She stared at them. "What are these?' she asked.

Jakob explained what they contained and how they came to be in his possession. Anke looked at him in disbelief.

"All these years and you never told me? Jakob, why were you afraid to share these with me. I would have been interested and helped. I remember as children when we walked to school you talked about other family and how one day you hoped to find them. That was many years ago. Have you been carrying these thoughts that long?"

"My dear Anke. It is actually a lot worse now. I have watched as many new inventions have been developed. I cannot accept that we as Mennonites cannot choose and use some of the modern developments. I do not find them sinful or against our fundamental beliefs. I fear that I am drifting further away from our community. I believe that in the future we will be forced to accept these new ways. The children of our community have already questioned why we cannot have simple things like electricity in our homes. Anke, the times have changed and I need to change as well. That means I will continue to search for relatives and question the church's stance on all these new developments. We cannot stay behind in time. We must adapt and change."

Anke frowned. "Jakob, I do not fully understand what you are saying or what you will do."

Jakob took a recently received letter and handed it to Anke. "I believe you should read this and then we will talk further."

Anke moved to the old oil lamp so she could read the letter. Upon opening it she was bewildered. "Jakob, this is written in an old German that I cannot understand."

Jakob took the letter from her shaking hand and started to read the contents to her. When he finished he walked over to the desk and removed a small book.

"Anke, all these years I knew there was a reason for my thinking about the relatives who remained. This letter confirms my thoughts. It finally answers my question. I have finally found a relative in Holland. He has offered to assist me to locate the others. While I am happy to learn of this, it deepens my conflict. I have a plan."

With that Jakob opened the small book he had retrieved from the desk. The book was a schedule of ship sailings from Montreal to Europe.

"Anke, I have decided we must go on such a voyage to meet these relatives of ours."

Anke was at a loss for words. She took the schedule from Jakob.

"Jakob, where did you get this?"

"On my last trip to the market I stopped at the Canadian Pacific office. I asked about travelling to Holland and was advised to travel by rail to Montreal and then board the Canadian Pacific Ship *"The Empress of Britain"* which sails to Le Havre after stopping at Southampton in England. I have thought for a long time about this. We have saved considerable money. I can lease out the farm and we will take a trip away from here."

Anke looked at him. Her eyes were moist with tears. How could she have missed seeing his torment throughout the years. She realized that she now faced a dilemma. Should she agree to go or stay alone if Jakob decided to leave on this trip. After thinking about the situation for a while she spoke.

"Jakob, I will consider accompanying you on this trip but you must agree that we meet the elders and discuss your concerns and the reasons to make this trip."

Jakob started to object but then realized that he would need to do such a thing in order to lease out his farm and be granted the permissions to travel.

"Anke, please set up such a meeting. We will go together and meet the elders."

Chapter 33

Anke arranged for her and Jakob to meet with the church elders the following Sunday after the service. They met in the attached house of the church Deacon. Some freshly baked cake and tea was brought into the room by an assistant to the Deacon.

They sat and chatted for a while and then Anke introduced the need for the meeting. The group fell totally silent as she explained the mental conflict that Jakob was experiencing with both his religious belief and the strong need to seek out his ancestors and relatives. When she finished the room remained silent.

Jakob addressed the elders. "Sirs, I would do nothing to disgrace our congregation which is why we are here to seek your permission and guidance. Since I was a young boy I have tried to understand many things in life. One of those was to understand why other members of our family remained in Europe, yet Isaac travelled with Inge to America. Isaac would never answer my questions. I know that there are relatives there and I must visit."

The elders nodded their agreement.

"Jakob, how will you make this journey? As you know we Mennonites only use horse and buggy and to undertake a trip like this you will need the blessing of our Bishop. Tell us of how you intend to travel and how long you will be away from here."

Jakob turned and faced the group. Anke sat at his side.

"I will travel by train from Kitchener to Montreal. We will stay in a modest hotel and the next day we will board the ship which will take us to Europe. I will arrange the train trip so we will not need to stay more than one night in Montreal. We will stay on the ship until it reaches Le Havre in France. We will then take the train trip to Amsterdam from Paris where I will meet with a relative of my neighboring farmer. He will assist us with accommodation before we visit the villages in which we believe our ancestors are. I do not know how long we will stay in Europe, but I expect more than six months."

The senior elder looked at Jakob and asked "Jakob, a trip like this will mean that you and Anke will be exposed to many temptations and things that as Mennonites we shun. Given your failing belief in our principles, how will you be able to avoid these temptations?"

"I will have my devout wife Anke with me. I know she will provide me the strength to avoid such things."

The elder continued. "What arrangements will be made for the farm? We have some new members joining us from America. They are looking to farm here. Will you lease to them while you are gone?"

"Have they farmed before? I need to lease to someone with farming experience in both livestock and crops."

"Yes Jakob. They have the experience. We will arrange for them to visit with you in the coming week. Now please leave us to discuss this matter. You may wait in the room outside. If you wish more refreshments we will have them brought to you."

Anke and Jakob left the meeting. They sat in the adjacent room for what seemed eternity. Finally, the assistant to the Deacon entered and ushered them back into the elders.

Jakob looked at the faces of the elders. They were somber.

117

The senior elder addressed Jakob and Anke.

"Jakob, we have many concerns about your making this trip. I am sure you are aware of the discussion of a new war in Europe. The clouds of war are already gathering. The rise of Adolf Hitler in Germany has already created major problems. His stated ideology has many worried. We believe your timing is wrong. It would be better for you to wait until the situation in Germany is better understood. We are also distressed to hear of your questioning our ways and doctrine. I fear that the temptations of the outside world will prove too much for you to resist given your faltering belief. We cannot grant you our approval. We will discuss this further with the Bishop."

Anke spoke. "Gentlemen, I have known Jakob since we were children growing up next to each other on the farm. While he has doubts, he has never done anything to shame himself or our religion. He has had to deal with tragic events at a young age. He has provided assistance to many who sought his help. Jakob is a man of strength and character. I implore you to grant him approval to make this trip. I will be with him and be there to guide him in his decisions. As you all know, I have already travelled while nursing. I did not succumb to the temptations of the outside world. I returned with my faith and values intact. I am sure I will be able to keep Jakob from straying into these temptations."

The senior elder looked to the others. "We will further discuss. Please leave us again."

Anke and Jakob returned to the adjacent room. As they sat they could hear the murmur of the elder's voices. Time went by. After about an hour they were ushered back into the meeting.

"We have reconsidered. It is our decision to grant you our approval on the condition that you both commit to uphold tradition and continue with daily prayer and observe our customs when possible."

Jakob smiled and thanked the elders. He and Anke stood, bowed and made their exit.

During the ride back to the farm Jakob was the happiest that Anke had seen him in a long time.

Chapter 34

The next few days passed by quickly. Jakob prepared a shipment of produce to be taken to the market in Kitchener at the week's end. Throughout the week he had spoken excitedly to Anke and her father Johannes about making the trip. Johannes was worried.

As Jakob and the farmhands were leaving for the market, they passed by Johannes's farm. Johannes was standing outside of the farm gate. He walked forward to the horse drawn wagon on which Jakob and the farmhands sat.

"Jakob, I am very concerned that you are making this trip to Europe at this time. Our fellow Mennonites are receiving information from Europe that since Adolf Hitler came into power, terrible things are rumored to be happening. Jewish Doctors have had their licenses revoked. Jews have had drivers licenses cancelled. There are reports of many Jews being taken to labor camps. Jakob, the very situation that Isaac and others feared is starting again. I implore you not to go at such a dangerous time. I am worried for Anke and you. It is not safe for you, especially as Mennonites. You will be the target of abuse."

Jakob responded to Johannes. "During the last war with Germany, The Netherlands was neutral. The Germans promised not to attack or invade The Netherlands and this is where Anke and I will be staying. We will be safe."

Johannes was getting old and did not have the energy to dispute this with Jakob. He abruptly turned away and started walking back to his home.

Jakob watched as the stooped figure slowly made his way back along the gently inclined pathway. Jakob wondered whether he should go after Johannes and comfort him. He was aware there were risks associated with the trip but considered them to be minor. He resolved to visit Johannes when returning from the market.

The ride into the market was without incident. Along the way they passed by neighboring farmers, some of who signaled Jakob to stop.

Several neighbors from Germany had heard of Jakob's planned trip. They spoke to Jakob of their concerns about the trip and advised him to wait some time as the situation in Germany seemed to be worsening. No one knew what the other countries would do. They spoke of the fears arising from Germany's massive rearming in 1934. They saw no need for this unless Hitler had plans to invade other countries or declare a war.

All who spoke to Jakob advised him to stay.

Jakob again spoke of The Netherlands former neutrality and that they would be safe in neutral Holland.

The other farmers disagreed with him, but Jakob was not to be dissuaded.

Finally, after a long discussion with the farmers, they continued into the market. Jakob's customers were waiting for the arrival of the fresh produce. Greetings were shouted and Jakob waved his acknowledgement. The farmhands started to fill the stalls with vegetables. As they did, Jakob advised them he had some business to attend to. He walked off in the direction of the Canadian Pacific railway station and office.

He entered the station and was greeted by a porter.

"Good morning, sir. Can I assist you?"

Jakob smiled and asked where he could obtain information on ships to Europe. The porter directed him to a glass paned door at the end of a narrow corridor. Painted on the door were the words "Canadian Pacific Steamships". Jakob walked to door and loudly knocked. Soon a young man wearing a dark suit and white shirt with a bowtie opened the door to Jakob.

"Can I help you?" he asked.

Jakob replied "I am looking to reserve a trip for my wife and I to Europe."

"Come in please. I can certainly make those arrangements," the well groomed young man replied.

Jakob entered the office. The young man gestured to sit at an oak table in the centre of the office.

When they were both seated, Jakob introduced himself. He then went on to discuss the trip he planned to make with Anke. The young man listened. When Jakob was finished he left the table and went to a display rack containing many brochures. He removed several and gave them to Jakob.

"These contain information on our ships. This is a schedule of the dates the ships sail and information on the ports they stop at. There is also a fare schedule. When will you wish to reserve?"

Jakob thought about this. "I will need to speak with my wife and we will return in a few days from now."

The young man nodded. "Please remember that you will need a Government issued passport in order to book and undertake this travel."

Jakob had completely overlooked this.

"I will need to obtain passports for my wife and I. It will be after that I will book. Thank you for your help and the information."

Jakob gathered the brochures together and was escorted to the door.

"It will be a pleasure to make those bookings for you and your wife."

Jakob left the station and walked back to the market where the farmhands were actively selling the produce from the stalls which were almost empty. As he walked to the stalls, the Doctor who had attended to Isaac saw him and called to Jakob.

"How are you and what is happening at the farm?"

Jakob informed the Doctor of his marriage, the farm and his plans for Europe.

"Don't go." the Doctor said and turned away.

Chapter 35

Jakob stopped at Johannes's farm when returning from the market. He told the farmhands to continue on and then walked the front door of the farmhouse. He knocked loudly. Johannes slowly opened the door and welcomed Jakob into the house.

After they were seated in the kitchen where Johannes had set out some foods, he finally spoke.

"Jakob, you are not doing the right thing. Too many speak of the danger of travelling to Europe. There are many fleeing now for fear of what will happen. This man Hitler is not a man of his word. I fear the worst. He is stating the intentions of the Nazi party to become a master race. He speaks of the 1000 year Third Reich. This man will cause many problems. I beg you to delay going on this trip. Anke is my only daughter and you are like a son to me. I could not bear the loss of either of you. There is also my age and that of my wife. We are old and very soon we will no longer be able to operate the farm. I have already spoken to the elders of our Mennonite conference about transferring the farm to you and Anke. They have agreed. Please, Jakob, consider my plea to stay until it is clear what is happening in Europe."

"Johannes. Today I obtained information on travelling to Holland. We will need to obtain documents and also the ship only sails in the spring months. We will be here for a while longer. I promise we will not leave if war in Europe appears imminent."

Johannes smiled. "For this I thank you dearly."

Jakob excused himself and left to walk back to his farm. Upon arriving back at his home he relayed his conversation with Johannes to Anke.

"Jakob, please tell me this is a promise you will definitely keep."

Jakob nodded his agreement.

After they had eaten their dinner, Jakob sat with Anke and discussed the visit to the Canadian Pacific office. He placed the brochures on the table. Both he and Anke read them in detail.

"Anke, we will need to visit the offices of the Government to apply for our passports. We should do this soon. I would like for us to do this in the next week. We will spend a day in Kitchener and visit with our friends there as well."

Anke, who managed their financial affairs, took some paper and a pencil to calculate the cost of the trip. When finished she advised Jakob that they had adequate funds to make the trip and to cover a long stay in Holland.

As it was early in the night, Jakob started writing letters in response to the contacts he had developed in Europe. These were the names on the lists who had written back. He wrote to them all to tell them of his plans and ask for advice on accommodation. The evening wore on. It was late when Jakob decided to go to bed. Anke had already retired for the night.

Jakob quietly slipped into the bed. Anke was not asleep. She turned onto her back and looked at the dark presence of Jakob.

"Nothing is going to stop you from making this trip. I fear you do not think correctly. We have a good life here. Why must you sacrifice all we have built together and undertake this mission?"

Jakob reiterated the promise he had earlier made to Johannes.

"If I believe that there is danger and a high risk to us, we will not go."

Jakob reached out and took her hand.

"Anke, I will do nothing that would put you in danger."

Anke smiled and curled herself into his body.

Little did they know of the events that were yet to occur?

Chapter 36

With the late autumn weather setting in, Anke and Jakob were busy preparing for the winter ahead. Crops were harvested and the stock feeds required for over wintering of the livestock were stored in the barns.

Jakob received a visit from the church Deacon late one afternoon while he was returning to the farmhouse from the lower fields near the river.

"Jakob." The Deacon called to him. "I wish to speak with you. Can we sit together in your home?"

Jakob was exhausted from the day's work. "Yes, of course," he responded.

They walked together to the house making small talk along the way. When inside the house, Anke directed them to sit in the parlor.

The Deacon started. "Jakob, you recall the discussion with the elders in which you expressed your desire to lease your farm while you make your travels in Europe? The family looking to settle on a farm has arrived. Will you still lease your farm?"

"Deacon, there have been some changes since we had the discussion with the elders. Our good neighbor, Johannes who is my wife's father has started the transfer of his farm to us. This means we will have the two farms that we will wish to join together as one large farm. Will this change the family's interest in the lease arrangement?"

The Deacon thought about this development and then spoke. "I do not think that this will change anything. The father has three grown sons who are also farm workers. I think this will work well for them. We need to establish a time for us all to sit and make arrangements. With your permission I would like to invite them to visit here at the farm. I will attend along with one of our elders. When will be a good time for this visit?"

"Good sir, we would wish to leave for Europe before the winter months arrive. Arrange this soon please."

"I will do so and later we will gather at the community church after to complete the arrangements should the farm and the conditions be satisfactory to the family. They arrived only days ago and are resting from a difficult trip during which they encountered an attack on them. This happened before they crossed into Canada."

Jakob thought back to the attacks on the farm and the tumultuous situations that had arisen between citizens of former Berlin, Ontario, over war and religions.

"Deacon, go ahead. I am sure we will find a mutual agreement amongst us all. We are reasonable people and I would like to make an arrangement so we can complete our plans for this trip."

The Deacon arose and extended his hand to Jakob. "I will send a message advising when we will visit."

After several days went by, Jakob received that message. The visit was to be the next day.

That night Jakob and Anke sat and spoke of the future arrangements. Months had passed since his promise to Johannes and Anke that if the situation in Europe had deteriorated he would not go there. In reality there had not been any published reports of further actions in Germany that placed Holland in any increased danger.

"Anke, we now have our passports and necessary travel documentation. We will be able to book our trip if this lease arrangement is completed."

Anke was still not sure. Johannes was getting old and frail. She worried about leaving him and she still had serious doubts about the venture that Jakob planned. Still, he was her husband to obey.

"Jakob, we will speak after the family visits and a decision on the lease is made. It is foolishness to continue to speak further at this time as we cannot make plans."

Chapter 37

Jakob and Anke were visited by the Deacon, an elder and the family who had recently arrived in their community from America. Jakob was impressed by the man's knowledge of farming and livestock management. After several hours it was decided to meet at the church the next day to conclude an arrangement for the lease.

Jakob was ecstatic.

"Anke, tomorrow we will visit the Canadian Pacific Office in Kitchener after our meeting at the church. We will book our trip. I am so happy that this moment has arrived."

Anke acknowledged his desire, though had serious and lingering doubts as to the wisdom of making the trip or leasing the farms. "Yes, Jakob but we must set a time for us to return. Can we agree to return home in six months?"

Jakob thought about this. "Yes, I think six months will be time enough for me to locate relatives and visit."

Anke arose and went to the bedroom. Shortly thereafter, Jakob joined her. Within minutes Jakob had fallen into a deep sleep. Anke lay awake beside him uncertain and scared of the future. After a number of hours had passed by, Anke fell into a restless sleep. She was truly worried. Johannes had contacted some of his old family in Holland and had been assured that Anke and Jakob would be welcome to stay with them in their modest home in Amsterdam. This was of some relief to Anke. At least she would be among family, even if they were distant and she had never met them before.

Anke woke and arose early. She quietly left the bedroom and proceeded to the kitchen where she prepared some tea for herself. She sat quietly in deep thought. She wondered how Jakob could have changed the way he had over the past years.

She worried about the changes in Jakob. The changes were not good. He had become consumed in his desire to visit Europe and hunt for his ancestral relatives. She could not understand why he wished to do this and believed that no good could be gained from this.

She sat alone for hours. The more she thought, the more depressed she found herself becoming. She had agreed to accompany Jakob and it was too late to change this. No matter what argument she presented to herself she realized there was no way out. She was committed to the trip.

Anke looked out at the early soft dawn with its pink clouds. She looked across to the barns where the horses stood in the paddock grazing. Next to the barn were the larger paddocks where the cattle stood huddled awaiting the early morning milking. Anke realized how much she was going to miss the farm which had become her security and home.

Just prior to the sunrise, Jakob entered the kitchen. Anke greeted him with a forced smile.

"Jakob, I will prepare you a breakfast before you leave to join the boys with the milking."

"Anke, I will return after the milking and change into clothing for a visit to town. Today we will go and book our tickets and then visit

131

some of our friends in Kitchener. I will not be long at the barn. I will return as soon as I can. If you are ready we will leave almost immediately. I will have the farmhands prepare our horse and buggy for the trip."

Upon finishing breakfast Jakob left the farmhouse for the short walk to the barn. When he was gone, Anke cried inconsolably. She realized that she should be happy to be embarking upon a new adventure and experience a new country and its customs. She could not erase the thoughts from her mind that this trip was fated. She returned to the bedroom and knelt and prayed for a long while. Finally she dressed and awaited Jakob's return.

Jakob returned after several hours and changed his clothes for the trip to town.

Chapter 38

Anke and Jakob were escorted to their horse and buggy. It had been prepared by the farmhands for their trip into town. Anke was helped onto the front seat. Jakob climbed himself up and took the reins.

Dressed in their appropriate attire for business and visiting they rode away from the farm. As they approached their neighbor's farm, Anke reached out and held Jakob's arm which was controlling the horses bridle.

"Jakob, please stop and wait. I must go in and visit Johannes. He is getting old and I worry so much about him. I need to see him before we make our arrangements."

Jakob swung himself down from the buggy and went around to the side to assist Anke.

"I will never stand between you and your wishes with your family. I have known them since I was a little boy. They have been there for me every time I needed assistance. We became one family a long time ago. Let us go visit."

During the visit, Jakob told Johannes of the decision that had been made regarding the trip to Europe. Johannes again begged Jakob to reconsider.

After spending time discussing the lease of the farmlands and the expectations of the visits they would make during their European trip, Anke and Jakob excused themselves to complete their trip to Kitchener.

They left Johannes's farm and rode toward the dirt roadway that lead to Kitchener. Anke was quiet and did not speak to Jakob even if to answer a question. Jakob thought of this and realized that the trip was a major disruption in Anke's life. He vowed to make things right. After all, Anke was his life's love.

They rode on in silence, passing by farmer friends whom Jakob had dealt with. Many waved and some came to their fences to briefly extend greetings. In the community there was great disagreement about the trip Anke and Jakob were planning. Very few understood Jakob's reasoning or desire to go back to Europe where in past generations the Mennonites had suffered. Even though many were in disagreement, they did not express this. Everybody was hoping for a safe and rewarding trip for Jakob and Anke.

Once on the dirt road, Jakob was at ease. The morning was cool. It was early autumn. Jakob took great delight in pointing out the subtle changes of the seasons to Anke. The giant maples that studded the sides of the road were starting to display the bright yellows before the frosts that would render them a brilliant red. He pointed to the wheat fields yet to be harvested. The husks had turned to a creamy yellow.

As they continued Jakob found a great contentment in the land and the events unfolding before him. Finally his dream of establishing contact with the old ancestors was materializing.

Throughout the journey into town Anke spoke very little. She could not bring herself to accept the idea of leaving the land and the friends with whom she had grown up.

Jakob was so enraptured with all that lay before him that he did not sense or see the anguish that Anke was experiencing. He was focused on only one thing.

They continued their journey in silence. Anke started praying that Jakob would reconsider the trip and the perils that were possible, but in her mind she knew he could not be stopped. The possibility of Divine intervention was not real.

As they continued their ride they passed other farmers returning from the town. Many called their greetings and some stopped to wish Jakob a good and safe journey to Europe.

Through all of this Anke was gracious and courteous. She wished blessings on all.

Chapter 39

They arrived in town shortly after 10:00am. Jakob drove the horse and buggy to the Canadian Pacific station and offices. He climbed down from his seat and went around the front of the buggy and assisted Anke down from the high seat. Together they walked through the railway station to the office that Jakob had previously visited. Jakob knocked loudly on the door. They waited for minutes. Finally, the door was opened.

The young man in his perfect 3 piece suit, white shirt and orange bow tie greeted them. He looked at Jakob.

"Please do come in. It is a pleasure to welcome you back Sir. What can I do to be of assistance? But first, let me introduce myself. I am Horace Winthrop, senior booking clerk for Canadian Pacific. I understand that you are interested in travelling with us to France."

Jakob and Anke were shown the same oak desk that Jakob had sat at for his earlier visit.

"Thank you" Jakob said.

"You must have had a long ride in from your farming area. Let me have some tea or light refreshment brought to us." He rang a small bell on the side of his desk. An assistant appeared and was given instructions. Within minutes a tray arrived with fresh tea and a pitcher of juice.

"Now, what have you decided for your trip to France and beyond?" he asked.

Jakob awkwardly withdrew some papers from the pocket inside his jacket. "I have looked at these very carefully and I am uncertain. As you can gather we are Mennonites and do not seek luxury or to use the modern inventions. We do not require many of the luxuries that are in the pamphlets you provided me. We are looking modest means to take us to our families in Holland and Germany. "

"Sir, I do understand however it is my duty to offer all options to you. This is my job. Please understand."

Jakob smiled after the young man spoke and expressed his loyalty to the company.

"Horace, I have looked at the information you provided and we have made a decision. Our decision is to leave from the port of Montreal to Le Havre in France on the November sailing."

"That is excellent Sir. On which of our ships are you planning to travel?"

"We will travel upon the *Empress of Britain II.*" This seems to be a safe and beautiful ship."

Horace the shipping clerk sat back in his chair.

"Sir, you could not have chosen a finer vessel. The *Empress of Britain II*" is the largest ship in our fleet and one of the most luxurious. When I immigrated to Canada with my family this was the very ship I travelled on. You will be very satisfied. Now we need to address the details in order to book both you and your fine wife for this crossing. Have you decided upon the class in which you wish to travel? There are enormous differences between the three classes."

Jakob responded. "As we are of the Mennonite faith, we live simply and without many of the things that others enjoy."

"Sir, the journey to cross the Atlantic will take five days with an additional day to take you to Le Havre in France. I am sure you will want those days to pass in comfort and for you and your wife and to be able to use some of the fine facilities on the ship."

"We are simple farmers just wanting to travel in search of family. We do not need many of the luxuries I am sure are offered on this fine ship." Jakob responded.

"Sir, it is my duty to present each class to you so you can make a correct decision.

There is "Cabin Class" This is our finest. You will have your own cabin and access to the lounges and also to the fine foods prepared and served in the exclusive dining room. We have "Tourist Class" as well. This class offers a smaller and less opulent cabin. Dining is in a separate dining room. The menu offers less choice than Cabin Class. Then we have "Third Class". This class has the most cabins and passengers. There is less privacy and dining is held in a common dining room. Due to the large number of Third Class passengers, dining is served at different times. The costs for each class differ greatly. The fee to Le Havre from Montreal for Cabin Class is $445, the cost of Tourist Class is $258 and finally Third Class is $180. These prices are for a return voyage and include your meals and entertainment. Which class would you prefer?"

Jakob turned and spoke to Anke. "Five days is a long time to endure discomfort. I propose we book the Tourist Class."

Anke frowned at him. "No Jakob. I am sure that the Third Class accommodation will be suitable and probably better than some rooms in which we have had to sleep in the past. Please, Horace can you describe the cabin?"

Horace laid a diagram on the table that showed the ships layout.

"There are two areas for the Third Class berths. One at the aft and one area lower near the engine room. I recommend you book a berth in the rear as it is quieter and a little more private. There is a specific cabin I will recommend. It contains two galvanized iron beds, seats, a table and a folding lavatory. There are only a few of these particular cabins. I can book one for you."

Jakob accepted the recommendation. "Horace, how many passengers will be on the ship for the crossing?"

"The ship is capable of accommodating 1200 passengers. The Cabin and Tourist Classes hold 400 passengers and the Third Class holds 800. Shall we proceed to book?"

Jakob reached inside his jacket and withdrew an envelope containing the money for the fare.

"Sir, in addition to the fare there are some small amounts you are required to pay. There is a Canadian wharfage fee of $1.00 for each of you and a fee for baggage. The baggage fee is $1.50 for your 1st bag and $2.00 for the 2nd bag. These fees are for the handling and storage of the bags by our Baggage master. He will arrange for your bags to be loaded onto the ship, stored and upon arrival in Le Havre he will have them sent onto Paris where they will be inspected and cleared by French Customs."

Jakob removed money from the envelope and counted out the amount calculated by Horace. Horace wrote a receipt to which he attached an official stamped document. He then produced a shipping schedule with the dates of the sailings from Montreal. He placed the schedule in front of Jakob and Anke.

After several minutes Jakob and Anke spoke with each other and selected a date in November.

Horace immediately processed the bookings and handed Jakob a pouch containing their tickets.

Horace continued. "Now we need to address how you will travel to Montreal. I am pleased to inform you that since you are travelling to Montreal to board a Canadian Pacific ship that your rail fare is free. I suggest we reserve you a sleeper on the overnight train to Montreal. You will arrive rested in Montreal and our staff will be able to transport your baggage to the ship which sails late in the afternoon."

Jakob could not have been any happier. Anke's veiled expression hid the true feelings she had. She was nervous and scared.

With the business finished, Jakob turned to Anke and took her hand.

"Come, my dear we will go and visit our friends here in town. We will celebrate the beginning of our journey."

Chapter 40

During the days leading up to their departure, many members of their congregation came to visit and extend wishes and blessings upon them. Several of the men gave Jakob handwritten notes containing names and addresses of members of their families who had stayed behind in Holland and Germany. They requested Jakob to try and visit. Jakob responded that he would try his utmost to do so.

Finally the day arrived. Two of the farmhands loaded their luggage onto the buggy and one climbed on to drive the buggy into the station at Kitchener.

It was late afternoon and the sun cast long shadows across the fields that were now empty as the harvests had been completed. A small group had gathered to wish them farewell. Amongst them was Johannes. Though smiling and appearing to be happy for Jakob and Anke, he was sad and fearful for the couple. His belief in the dangers that lurked in the form of the Nazis in Germany still remained. Johannes knew more about the situation in Germany than many of the others. He received frequent letters from his relatives in Europe. The letters described the rise of the Communist Party and the political upheaval that was happening in Germany.

At the station, the station master collected their tickets and inspected their ship boarding documents. He then summoned a porter who took their luggage to the baggage car.

Anke and Jakob were then escorted onboard and shown their cabin. After the porter left, Jakob looked in amazement at the décor and fittings in their compartment. There were light switches, electrical outlets and many features which were frowned upon in his religion. These he knew, would be a great temptation.

After a short delay, they heard the station master's whistle and then the sound of the engine building up steam. There was a sudden lurch as the train started to pull away from the station. Within minutes they were gliding through the gently undulating landscape. They sat quietly watching the countryside slide by. As the train headed eastward, the sky darkened and the night fell quickly.

There was a soft knock on the compartments door. Jakob opened the door.

"Sir, it is time for you to visit the dining car for your dinner. Would you like me to accompany you there?"

"Yes. Please wait while my wife and I gather certain of our possessions."

"Certainly, sir. Please do not worry about the safety of items in your compartment. I will lock it when we leave and reopen it after you have dined."

Anke and Jakob walked along a narrow corridor until they reached the dining car. Jakob was in awe of the dining car. There were large framed pictures of trains in scenic settings and the carriage was furnished with quality tables and seating. He had not expected this. They were shown to a booth at the centre of the car and seated. A waiter arrived and handed them a folded menu that featured a train steaming through Kicking Horse Pass in The Canadian Rockies.

Anke and Jakob read the menu which contained many items. Finally the waiter returned to explain the items listed and to answer any of their questions. He handed them slips which were the meal checks as verbal orders were not accepted.

Anke ordered The Pacific Coast broiled fish. Fish was a rarity for them on the farm. Jakob looked over the menu again and finally wrote his order for 2 grilled lamb chops, hashed browned potatoes, scrambled egg and an order of hot rolls.

When they had eaten, Jakob ordered a pot of Cocoa.

With their meal complete they requested assistance from the porter to accompany them back to the carriage and unlock their door.

Anke and Jakob prayed together for a while and then prepared for bed. The beds were small fold out sleepers. They were both exhausted and sleep came quickly.

The train made steady progress through the night and in the early morning they were passing by the uniquely styled farmhouses of rural Quebec. Jakob was fascinated. He dressed and when Anke was also dressed they said their Morning Prayer service. Jakob had promised the clergy he would continue to practice during the trip and Anke was making sure he kept that commitment.

Again there was a knock at the door. Jakob answered it to a different porter who smiled and advised them that their breakfast setting was waiting. They walked back down the narrow corridor to the dining car. The tables had been set differently for breakfast. Anke wrote an order for an omelet and Jakob wrote an order for ham with 2 fried eggs and toast. They followed this with a pot of tea.

As they made their way back from the dining car, the porter spoke. "We will be pulling into the Montreal Station in 45 minutes. I understand you will be transferring to the port to board our magnificent ocean liner, *"The Empress of Britain II."* I hope that one day soon I will be able to take a voyage on her with my wife."

As they sat looking out of the window, the suburbs of Montreal flew by. Bells rang at level crossings. As they progressed into the City of Montreal, the landmark buildings and sites appeared. Jakob and Anke looked out in amazement at the City.

The train finally pulled into the station. Again the porter came to their cabin. "I am to assist you to the transportation that will take you to the port where your ship is docked."

Jakob and Anke gathered up the possessions they had taken into the compartment with them.

"Your baggage will be transferred to the ship for you. That is a service we pride ourselves on."

They walked along the long platform and up a flight of wide stairs to the street above. A black Ford car was at the curb. The porter walked to the front and signaled the driver who immediately opened his door and came to Anke and Jakob.

"May I please see your tickets for the ship?" After verifying their identity, the dates on the tickets and the luggage slips for the baggage master, he opened the rear door of the car for them to climb in.

Jakob was uncertain. He had never been in a car before. These too were frowned upon by the Old Order Mennonites. Anke proceeded and entered the car. She extended her hand to Jakob to assist him.

They drove to the docks. Upon arrival the driver stopped at a guarded entrance and spoke to the guard and presented Jakob and Anke's papers and tickets. They were waved in and drove a short distance to where *"The Empress of Britain II"* was docked.

Jakob gasped at the size and grandeur of the ship. He stepped out of the car and stood looking at the ship. It was over 8 stories high. The hull was a clean glistening white and the 3 funnels of the ship were painted in a unique orange. Jakob, looked at the length of the ship. He estimated it to be at least 800 feet in length.

The driver of the car came up to him with Anke. "Sir, I will now assist you to board at the gangway. Please follow me."

They set off on the short walk. At the gangway they were welcomed and again asked for their tickets and passports. After a brief introduction they were assigned a crew member to escort them to their cabin.

They descended several levels and finally the crew member turned right and started walking toward the bow of the ship. Jakob was amazed at the structure of the ship. The cabin was the last one they came to after walking the polished floor of the hallway. The crewman opened their door and checked that all pillows and linens were present. He demonstrated the use of the lavatory and other features of the cabin then left.

Anke and Jakob sat on the wooden chairs in the cabin. Anke spoke first. "Jakob let us rest for a while and then we will walk and learn the layout of the ship." Jakob pointed to the guide they had been handed upon boarding. There were plans showing the various sections of the ship and the location of lounges, dining rooms and other service areas.

They lay on the beds and rested for the next couple of hours. Anke drifted into a deep sleep.

Chapter 41

At 1:30pm Anke awoke. She freshened herself and then she and Jakob left the cabin and retraced their way back to the stairway. At the stairway a ship's officer dressed in white and wearing a cap was assisting some passengers. Jakob waited until he was finished and then approached him.

"Good afternoon. Can you direct us to the dining area where we can have some lunch?"

The officer looked at his watch. "You must hurry as the lunch sitting is closing. I am going in that direction so you can walk with me."

The dining room was large. Individual tables were arranged throughout the room. Many were now empty and the staff were clearing away dishes. Anke and Jakob were greeted by the maitre'd and shown to a table. Soon a waiter arrived and listed the items available for a late lunch.

Anke ordered a Cobb salad and Jakob ordered poached salmon. They drank the fresh fruit juices that were in glass jugs at the centre of the table. After they finished their lunch they returned to their cabin.

The weather was a fine but cool autumn day. The sun shone brightly but the air was cool and a slight wind was blowing. Anke and Jakob retrieved their coats and found their way to the ship's deck.

At 2:30pm the ship's massive horns sounded. Three separate blasts sounded.

Jakob and Anke stood on deck watching as the mooring ropes were released and the ship started to slowly edge back from the wharf. At the stern of the ship was a tug boat helping to turn the ship. Another tug was at the bow and pulled the ship forward after it had completed the turn. The Empress increased power. Black smoke poured from the 3 funnels. The ship started its cruise up the St Lawrence toward the Atlantic Ocean.

Jakob stood at the railing and slid his hand around Anke's waist.

"Our adventure has really begun. We will see and experience new things that would never have been possible had we stayed in Kitchener. I wish to locate the families of my relatives, but I am also looking forward to experiencing new foods and the customs of the people in the countries we will visit."

Anke turned to him. "Jakob, do not forget the promise you made to the elders. You promised to abide by the teachings of our faith. Please do not forget that promise. I see the many temptations around us and your natural curiosity."

Jakob continued looking across the river at the shores as the ship continued to pick up speed. They stood on the deck for a while and then went back into the ship and sat in the rear lounge. Before long they were approached by a drink waiter offering wines and liquor. Jakob thanked him and requested a large pot of hot tea.

Anke and Jakob sat and watched the other passengers for the next hour.

Time slipped by quickly. There was a rush of passengers from the lounge as the sun was setting. Anke and Jakob stood, put on their coats and exited to the deck to see what the excitement was about.

They looked west to the shore. The ship was gliding by Quebec City and there high on the hill was The Chateau Frontenac highlighted by a golden sunset behind it.

The Empress sounded several short blasts from its horn.

They stayed on deck until the magnificent sight faded from view.

The ship continued up the St. Lawrence and passed the Gaspe in the evening on its way out to the vast Atlantic Ocean.

Anke silently thought "Good bye my dear Canada."

Chapter 42

The crossing of the Atlantic was uneventful. Anke and Jakob passed their time in the ship's massive library. Jakob discovered an atlas containing many maps of countries of the world. He discovered maps of Holland and Germany that were in great detail. Jakob obtained some paper and stencils from the ship's librarian and painstakingly copied the maps. He paid particular attention to the names of the villages and towns and entered them onto to his carefully drawn maps with great care. Jakob believed these would be invaluable to him in his endeavor to find the families.

When not sitting in the lounge or library, Jakob and Anke sat for hours listening to the music that emanated from the ship's ballroom. Jakob's love for music swelled as they listened to the beautiful strands of music that drifted from the ballroom. They sat on the outer deck wrapped in their winter coats. They had never heard such encompassing music. Jakob was enthralled.

On the second night of the crossing Jakob and Anke sat out on the deck. The sounds of the ship's orchestra drifted up from the ballroom.

"Anke, I am so in love with you. These things that we experience on the ship show me how much I love you. We needed to make this trip for each other. We have been married and love each other but needed to experience a change together that would make us appreciate the life we have."

Anke sat and thought. "Jakob you are correct. Our life on the farm was nice, but we were becoming distant from each other."

They returned to their cabin

Jakob took Anke into his arms. He removed her clothing and fell back onto the small bed. Anke reached up and placed her arms around Jakob's strong neck. She pulled herself into a position where it allowed Jakob to easily penetrate her with

his engorged and erect penis. Through their passionate lovemaking Anke wondered if it was God's wish that after years of marriage they had not conceived a child. She had earlier wondered if she was pregnant. Did this maybe account for her frequent moods and nervousness, she wondered.

She loved him and accepted the failures she sometimes witnessed.

The next days were uneventful. The weather had turned cooler and the skies were a continual dull grey. They passed the time by reading one of the many books in the ship's library.

They had slept soundly and on the fourth morning were awakened by the loud blasts of the ships horn. Jakob washed and dressed quickly.

"I will go on deck and see what has happened." As he prepared to leave the cabin the low and constant sound of the ship's engines changed. "Anke we are arriving. Dress and come to the deck. I will wait for you there."

Jakob hurried to the deck where fellow passengers were lining the deck railing. Even though the weather was grey and a steady drizzle of rain was falling, there was great excitement. They had arrived at the docks of Southampton, England.

Soon Anke joined Jakob. They stood and looked on amazed at the size of the docks and the number of surrounding buildings. In particular, Jakob found the huge shipside cranes that were on rail tracks to be fascinating.

As they stood taking in the sights, several tug boats arrived alongside the Empress. Ropes were tossed from the ship and soon the ship was being nudged and towed to the wharf where it would dock and passengers discharged.

Jakob and Anke had decided against leaving the ship as it was destined to sail later that day. They returned to the ships dining room for breakfast. There were significantly less passengers dining.

After a leisurely breakfast, they went back on deck and watched the flow of passengers leaving the ship via the gangway. On the dock were various officials in uniforms. As they stood watching, the cranes started to load cargo and goods onto the ship for the short voyage to France or for the return trip to Canada.

Jakob was intrigued to see cars being driven onto large rope nets. These nets were then gently raised by crane. When the load was evenly balanced the crane lifted the car and swung it to the forward hatch where it was then lowered into the hold below. This procedure was repeated several times.

As they watched this loading of the cars there was a very loud drone from in the harbor behind the ship. Jakob and Anke turned to observe a seaplane accelerating down the harbor for takeoff. They were in awe at all the activity in the port.

"I have never heard of such a thing. A plane that can land and then take off from the water."

Standing beside them was an older crew member. He turned and spoke to Jakob.

"Yes. That is what they call a flying boat. That particular plane is a Sunderland. It is a very fine machine. They even fly that model around the world to places like Australia and New Zealand. It is very popular for those who can afford such a thing. They take the passengers out to the plane on that launch there." He said, pointing to a white launch with a mahogany top that was approaching a long walkway that extended into the ocean.

Jakob stood in silence. He marveled at all the machinery and equipment that was in use. He watched the different forms of transportation and again wondered why his religion resisted such progress when it would have made the lives of the community much easier. Again, his doubts were deepening.

Jakob and Anke returned to their cabin as the fine wet drizzle had turned into heavy and gusting rain.

"Anke it seems that winter has already arrived here in England. It is different to the start of our winter at home. In some ways this rain and wind seems colder. What will we experience in Holland?"

"Jakob, I packed our winter clothing so I am sure we will be fine. Surely Holland will not be colder the Canada."

They stayed in their cabin until lunch hour and then returned to the dining room. There were more passengers at the lunch setting than they had encountered at the breakfast.

Jakob listened carefully to the new passengers conversations. They all spoke with a strange and funny accent.

153

While eating the ships horn sound three long loud bursts. They were departing for the short crossing to Le Havre.

"Anke within hours we will be in France and so much closer to our destination. Tomorrow we will travel on to Paris to collect our baggage and continue by rail to Amsterdam where we will be met by a family member of the Deacon of our church in Kitchener. He has provided me with many details of how this young man looks. He speaks English, Dutch and German. I understand we will spend a day or two with him and his family before he guides us to your relative's home. I feel as if all this is a dream."

After completing their meal and talking at length about the days and months ahead, Anke and Jakob headed back to the deck. The rains had stopped yet a cool wind continued to blow. Jakob was anxious to watch as England slid behind them and the lights of Le Havre illuminated the sky as they approached the French port.

Chapter 43

The next morning, Anke and Jakob awoke, dressed and left their cabin for a light breakfast onboard before leaving for the railway station.

After breakfast, they walked out onto the deck and observed the huge dockside cranes offloading the passengers' luggage in large rope nets. The luggage was then loaded onto an open truck to be taken to the rail station where it was to be loaded onto the Paris bound train for clearance by French Customs. They watched as the crew, in conjunction with the dock workers, secured a gangway for the passengers to disembark. On the middle deck several of the ships' officers stood at the entrance to the gangway to bid farewell and to offer any assistance that was required. Anke and Jakob returned to their cabin and packed their personal items into the small leather suitcase they had bought for the trip and exited the cabin to descend the gangway into France.

At the entrance to the gangway, the 1st Officer came forward and shook Jakob's hand.

"I hope your voyage with us was pleasant. I wish you and your wife good and safe travels in Europe"

They descended the gangway and as they stepped onto French soil were immediately met by a French Official.

"Bonjour. Welcome to France. May I please see your passports and travel papers. Where are you headed?"

Jakob handed over their passports and travel documents.

"We are travelling through France and Belgium to Amsterdam. We will be travelling today by train."

The French Official scanned their documents and handed them back to Jakob.

"All is in order. You may proceed. Enjoy your short stay in Le Havre."

"Sir, can you direct us to the Gare du Havre? I am told it is a short distance and we can walk there from the docks here."

The Official laughed loudly.

" Monsieur, the Gare du Havre is 2.5km from here. It will be a long walk."

Jakob thought back to the farm and the long walks that both he and Anke made to school and to visit the other farms. Jakob considered that this walk would be good for them after they had been somewhat inactive on the voyage from Canada.

Jakob thanked the Official and started off in the direction that had been provided to him.

The morning air was cool and crisp. As they walked slowly toward the station, Jakob was amazed at the busy pace of life. There were passengers walking, bikes, and cars with loud horns blowing and the occasional truck rumbling by.

After an hour they reached their destination. During their walk Anke had stopped to look into the windows of different stores they passed. She was in awe of the many different fashion stores and jewelers. This was so different to anything she had previously seen.

The station was bustling with people. Some were arriving, others waiting to greet family and friends and more were at the counters purchasing tickets. In the entrance there was a uniformed man. Jakob approached him and asked directions in order to purchase their tickets to Amsterdam.

Jakob was directed to a booth at the far end of the station. Across from the booth there was a small seating area for passengers waiting to be served. He and Anke sat patiently until the young family at the counter was finished making their purchases.

Jakob approached the counter.

"Yes. Where will you be travelling to?" asked the clerk

He was wearing a jacket with the words "French National Railway" embroidered onto the breast pocket.

"My wife and I wish to purchase tickets to Paris and onto Amsterdam. Can you assist us with this or must we purchase other tickets at the border?"

"No. I can sell you the ongoing ticket. You will need to change trains in Paris for the onward trip to Amsterdam. You will need to travel from Le Havre to Paris, arriving at Gare St Lazare. You will need to connect to the train for Amsterdam. The train to Amsterdam leaves from another station, Gare du Noord. It is a distance and you will need to take a taxi. May I suggest you take the late morning train to Paris. This will give you time to have your luggage cleared by Customs and released for shipping onto Amsterdam. The distance to Paris is 228Km and the trip takes almost 3 hours. If you wish, I can sell you tickets for the overnight train to Amsterdam. That is an 8 hour journey. "

Jakob turned to Anke.

"Are you tired and wishing to rest or should we book the trip as this man recommends?"

"Jakob, if we do not travel directly to Amsterdam then we will need to find lodgings for the night. I am not so tired and feel we should travel to our destination as quickly as we can."

Jakob nodded in agreement and proceeded to purchase the tickets.

"May I suggest that you use the waiting room lounge to rest and refresh. I should also advise that there is a small café within 5 minutes walking from the station. There you can purchase coffees from many different parts of the world. The café is famous for its croissants and pastries. I strongly recommend this."

Jakob thanked the man. They visited the lounge to freshen up and discuss the day ahead.

"Jakob, now that we have our travel information, I will send a telegram to my relatives in Amsterdam. I will advise them of our arrival time and the train information. I am most anxious to meet Wilhelm Schneer and his family. Wilhelm is Johannes' younger brother and my Uncle. His wife is Julia. We have written to each other many times over the years. When I was away nursing at the Hospital, Julia wrote many letters of encouragement."

"Yes. That is a good idea. There is a French Post Office counter I saw. You can send telegrams from there. I will accompany you there and after we will find the café that the ticket man told us of."

They walked from the waiting room lounge across the large marble floored foyer to the French Post Office counter.

Anke hand wrote out the message and passed it to the clerk who counted the words and requested payment in Francs. Anke looked panicked as she had no French currency. Jakob smiled and reached into his coat pocket and withdrew several French banknotes.

After sending the telegram, Jakob and Anke approached the station attendant and requested storage for their case. With this done, they left the station for the short walk to the café.

Upon entering the café they were greeted with a warm wave of air laced with the aromas of fresh coffee and freshly baked goods.

Anke had not realized her hunger until then. Jakob walked down the glass counters under which were displayed trays of different delicacies. They were seated at a corner table looking out to the street. The waiter took their orders for coffee and asked which pastries they would like to choose.

They were confused.

"Can you recommend some pastries? We have never seen so many different types."

The waiter threw his left arm forward in a display of annoyance and checked his watch.

"I will select some pastries appropriate for this time of morning."

The waiter marched off to the serving counter and moments later returned with a silver multi tiered plate containing an assortment of pastries.

Anke reached and took a Millefeulle. Jakob took a chocolate croissant. They sat silently enjoying the treats.

After 30 minutes, they paid the waiter and thanked him for his assistance in selecting the delicious pastries.

Anke and Jakob then left the café and strolled back to the station where they retrieved their case.

There was a large blackboard near the ticket counter. Written in thick white chalk were the departure times for the various trains. Upon checking this, Jakob saw the information for their train's departure and the platform information.

They walked to the platform and presented their tickets to the conductor standing at the end of the last carriage on the train. He directed them to the second carriage behind the engine.

"Please enjoy your trip to Gare Saint-Lazarre in Paris."

They climbed aboard and settled into their selected seats for the trip to Paris.

Chapter 44

Three sharp whistle bursts signaled all passengers were onboard and the train was ready.

Loud hissing of steam and a heavy chugging commenced followed by a long blast from the trains whistle. The carriage shuddered and then lurched forward as the train slowly picked up speed. A rhythmic pattern developed as the wheels clicked over the joints in the rails. It soon became a constant and soothing sound to the passengers.

Jakob was excited. He stared from the carriage window as the train slipped away from Le Havre and started its south east trip into France and toward Paris. Jakob had purchased a map of France and laid it out on the seat beside him to follow the train's progress. Soon the buildings of Le Havre thinned and the landscape quickly became one of pastoral scenes and dairy farms. Jakob viewed these with great interest. The farms and their structures were very different to those he had left in Ontario.

Anke sat across from Jakob and watched him with curiosity. She wondered what drove this man to have such a desire to travel and seek out these relatives.

They settled into the trip in silence. Anke closed her eyes and fell into a light sleep. Jakob continued to observe the countryside that slipped by.

Jakob was in awe of the landscape and could barely contain his excitement when the train started to cross the Barentin Viaduct. He looked out at the 100 foot drop to the river passing beneath the Viaduct. He marveled at the brick construction of the Viaduct.

For Jakob the adventure was unfolding as he had imagined during those long nights on the farm in Ontario.

Anke awoke as the trains motion changed as it slowed to a stop at Gare de Rouen-Rive-Droite. Several new passengers boarded and settled in their carriage. Jakob frowned and leant forward to Anke. In a low voice he whispered

"Anke, there are many soldiers on the station platform. They seem to be guarding the station as they are not boarding the train. This is a concern."

Anke looked and saw the soldiers.

"Jakob, we were warned of the unsettled times in Europe. Now you are seeing it."

Jakob frowned. The soldiers were all carrying weapons, yet there was no unrest in France. He looked at Anke.

"Anke, we are to be safe. Holland has always been a neutral country. The Germans consider the Dutch to be racially aligned with them. I am sure we will be safe in Holland."

Anke was not convinced. Slowly the train pulled away from the station. Anke too was surprised by the number of French soldiers on the platform. One of the new passengers observed her looking at the scene. He spoke

"France has increased its military in order to protect its borders. Do not be afraid. This is a plan to protect France from the actions of Hitler that are being carried out in other neighboring countries."

Anke smiled at the man and simply nodded. Shortly thereafter, the train conductor entered the carriage calling for tickets to inspect.

The trip proceeded in silence. Soon the train was slowing to stop and pickup more passengers at Gare de Mantes la Jolie. Again there were a large number of armed soldiers on the platform. At this station only a couple of people boarded. After a brief stop the train started rolling toward its final destination...Paris.

The gently rolling hills and pastures slowly receded and more houses and buildings appeared as the train rushed on toward Paris through the suburbs.

The conductor re-appeared calling "Paris arrival in 10 minutes"

Jakob and Anke started preparing for their arrival.

Chapter 45

The train pulled into the St Lazare station in the early afternoon. Anke and Jakob took their small brown leather case and left the train. They stepped down onto the platform of the cavernous building that housed the station. All around people were walking quickly in all directions. Again Jakob saw the many soldiers sauntering along the platforms. Anke was nervous.

"Jakob, I am scared. I do not like to see all these soldiers. There is a reason they are here. I believe the French are expecting trouble. Before we proceed further I earnestly implore you to let us go back to our peaceful farms in Canada. This is an ill omen. It is not too late for us to return. I fear for our safety. Holland is next to Germany and could be attacked. Hitler has already entered other countries. Please, let us return."

Jakob stopped walking and looked at the drawn look on Anke's face.

"Anke, you worry for nothing. In the newspaper on the train there was an article on the treaty that Hitler signed in September of this year with Chamberlain from Britain, Mussolini and Ciano from Italy, and Daladier from France. This happened in September. The newspaper showed a photograph of Chamberlain announcing this great situation in Britain and pronouncing that there will be no war. It seems that the troubles in Europe are in the German territories. No force was used when Hitler took these territories. My dear Anke we will be safe in Holland."

"Jakob, I do not share your vision. I witnessed the horrors of Germany's last war. This is a foolish plan of yours. Again I ask you to please take us back. There will be no benefits from this trip."

"Anke we will go on to Holland. I promise you that we will leave if the situation appears to put our safety at risk."

Anke looked down to the ground. Tears splashed down her cheeks and landed on the dirt encrusted paving of the platform. Anke could not understand why she was becoming so emotional. Previously she would have cautiously accepted Jakob's promises. These emotions had her confused.

Oblivious to the extent of Anke's anguish, Jakob continued. He stopped and asked a station attendant for direction to the Customs Hall so they could clear their luggage onto Amsterdam.

At the far end of the station they found the Customs Hall where a large sign displaying the word "Douane" was prominently displayed. Jakob and Anke entered and were greeted by a uniformed agent.

"Bonjour. How can I assist you? Have you luggage to be cleared?"

Jakob handed the agent the baggage tickets that had been issued in Le Havre. The agent took them and walked past several piles of neatly stacked suitcases and trunks. He turned and went to the rear of the last pile and withdrew the two large cases belonging to Jakob and Anke. He placed them on a cart and rolled them to a long flat table for inspection.

"What is the purpose of your visit?"

"Sir, we are just passing through France to Holland to visit relatives. We are religious people and wish to visit with relatives and learn of our ancestors."

The French Customs agent looked at Jakob with a shocked expression.

"Are you not aware of the troubles here in Europe? You must be insane. Hitler has already started removing the privileges of Jews. Of what religion are you that you think you will escape this fate?"

"We are Old Order Mennonites. We are a peaceful people and wish no harm to anyone."

"I wish you a safe passage. Please open your cases for me."

Jakob placed the cases on the table and opened the latches. The agent looked into the cases at the neatly folded clothing. He lifted the clothing to look beneath it. Satisfied he told Jakob to close the cases as they were cleared.

"Mr. Klassen, I will have your cases transported for loading onto Etoile du Nord or as the English call it The Star of the North."

Chapter 46

Jakob was hungry. It had been hours since they ate in Le Havre. With the Customs formalities completed, they walked from the station to a local restaurant. The weather was cold and the skies grey and overcast. While there were some tables and chairs set up on the sidewalk, they elected to eat inside the restaurant.

Upon entering they were quickly met by the Maitre'd and shown to a table at the front window looking out onto the narrow street. There was a constant procession of passersby.

A smartly uniformed waiter came to the table and offered wine. Jakob was tempted but Anke quickly declined and requested sparkling water and coffees for them both. The waiter provided a hand written menu.

"I strongly recommend the very nice special luncheon we have today. It is Coq au Vin"

Jakob looked puzzled and Anke frowned.

"May I ask what that is?"

The waiter gave a mouth watering description of the chicken dish and Jakob placed an order of the meal for them both.

Fresh crusty breads were delivered to the table and shortly thereafter the Coq au Vin was presented.

Jakob and Anke were starved. They sampled the food.

Jakob looked over at Anke.

"This food must be from God. How can they make a chicken taste like this?"

Anke smiled a faint smile.

"Jakob, please consider my wish. I want to go back to Canada. While all this is interesting, I am uncomfortable and very scared."

"Anke, look around. You will see that people are doing normal things. Shopping, eating here, talking and laughing outside on the street. You are worrying too much."

"Jakob, all is not right. See all the soldiers. They are there for a reason. I also find the weather and city grey. This is not a happy place right now. We should leave while we are able to."

"Anke, we will go onto to Holland and there we will make that decision. We will be with your relatives and I am sure they will tell us of the real situation between Germany and Holland."

"Do you promise? Will you place your hand on our bible and promise me? Please Jakob as I cannot continue on this trip knowing that such danger exists all around us."

Jakob reached his hand over the table and took her hand and held it for the longest time and then answered.

"Anke we have known each other for many years. I would never allow us to go where we would be harmed. Please. I promise that we will return to Canada if we find the situation bad."

She sat and thought about his statement. It was true that they had both experienced good and bad events in their lives. He had seen the sacking of the farm and she had dealt with the hideous injuries and broken bodies of the men who returned from the previous war.

"I will go on with you. If we find that Holland is unsettled by all this upheaval then we will leave and go back."

They finished their meal in silence.

After paying the bill they walked arm in arm and took a taxi to the Gare du Noord station for their overnight trip.

Chapter 47

The taxi stopped a short distance from the main entrance to the station. Anke and Jakob walked through the misty drizzle toward Gare du Noord. They were walking slowly and taking in the sights and sounds of Paris. As they were approaching the entrance to the station, Anke was pushed from behind. She stumbled and fell. As she was falling, a hand wearing a black leather glove grabbed the small purse she was carrying. Anke crashed heavily to the ground. She cried out.

"Jakob, our papers are in that purse."

Jakob was seething. Again the conflict he felt arose in him. Why did his religion preach pacifism and prevent him from attacking this thief. Within seconds Jakob ran after the thief who was running at a pace much slower than Jakob's. It was easy for Jakob to keep him in view as he was wearing a strange blue beret and wore a dark rain jacket. People walking on the sidewalk looked on in bewilderment. Jakob was calling out to stop the thief.

As the thief turned the corner, two uniformed soldiers were approaching from the other direction. Realizing what was happening they tackled the thief.

Jakob arrived seconds later. One of the soldiers snatched off the beret the thief was wearing and which had hidden his features. He was a young man with an olive complexion.

"Wait here. I will bring the Gendarme from the station to deal with this" the taller of the two soldiers said and started walking back to the station entrance.

"I must return to my wife" a distraught Jakob said.

The tall soldier nodded his head and handed the purse to Jakob.

"Then we will take this scoundrel to the Gendarme at the station."

They started the walk back. Jakob ran ahead of them anxious to return to Anke.

A group had gathered around Anke who was still on the ground. Jakob ran to her.

"Anke. Are you hurt? Is anything broken?"

Jakob looked at Anke. She had a large gash on her chin. Blood was pouring from the wound and mixed with dirty water from the pavement that had splashed up onto her face.

"We must take you inside. I will get some medical supplies and tend to you."

A Gendarme approached. On seeing Anke's condition he announced he would get an ambulance.

Jakob stood and looked at him.

"No sir. We cannot accept that. We are Old Order Mennonites and shun hospitals and doctors of the Government. Tell me where I can buy bandages and ointment."

"In the station there is a small store that sells basic medicines and bandages. If you insist on rejecting help from a doctor, then I will assist you to take your wife into the station where she can rest and tidy up in the waiting lounge."

They lifted Anke to her feet and very slowly walked the short distance to the station entrance. Anke was unable to walk down the stairs. Jakob and the Gendarme supported her back and legs and carried her. Once inside they sat her on a bench and rested.

As they sat there, another Gendarme walked toward them. He spoke rapidly in French to the Gendarme who was assisting them. He then turned to Jakob and Anke.

"I am sorry that this has happened to you here in Paris. The person who did this is not French. He is from Morocco. It is a problem for us here. These young men come to Paris and when they are unable to find work they start to steal, break in to buildings and commit other crimes. He will be charged and deported back to Morocco. Did you check to see if all your things are in the purse?"

Jakob opened the purse and checked the contents.

"Yes. It seems everything is there."

While the discussion was taking place, blood continued to run down Anke's neck staining her clothes and pooling beside her on the seat.

"I must go and get bandages now. She is losing a lot of blood."

The Gendarme advised Jakob to get professional assistance. Again Jakob refused.

Anke had turned pale and it appeared she would faint. A distinguished gentleman wearing a bowler hat stopped and looked at them. He walked up to Anke and put down his leather case on the ground beside her. He spoke quickly to the Gendarmes.

"I am a Doctor. My office is close by. This lady requires treatment and possibly stitches. That wound is deep. It needs to be properly cleaned as it will become infected from all that dirt. I strongly advise this woman get treatment now."

The older Gendarme spoke to Jakob and advised him again to do this. He then spoke to the younger Gendarme in French. The younger man nodded his head in agreement.

The Doctor waited while they spoke. Finally Jakob agreed to accompany Anke to the Doctor's office.

"We were to travel to Amsterdam tonight. What do you advise us?" asked Jakob

"First we will check your wife over to ensure there are no other injuries." replied the Doctor.

The Gendarmes stood talking together. Finally the younger one spoke to Jakob.

"We assume you have luggage that is waiting to be placed in the baggage car of the Etoile du Nord. Your wife's clothes are spoilt. If you provide me with your baggage tickets we will have the bags removed so your wife can dress in clean clothes for the trip you will make."

Jakob was amazed at the help they were receiving. He had been told that people of Paris were arrogant and not very friendly.

He took the baggage claim tickets from the purse and handed them to the Gendarmes.

The younger Gendarme took them.

"Go with your wife and Doctor. I will be at the station and will wait for your return. I will have your bags ready for you."

They assisted Anke to her feet and the Gendarmes carried her up the stairs. Once on the pavement she was able to shuffle her feet and move slowly. Jakob and the Doctor supported her and walked beside her.

"I should introduce myself. I am Dr Hugo Porrier. I am a family Doctor. I am concerned that there may be more than just the wound on the face. Your wife should be able to walk. I suspect she has received an injury to her hip. We will examine her thoroughly and find out."

Jakob looked concerned.

"If that is the case then we will not travel tonight."

They reached the doctor's office which fronted onto the street. There was a large green door with polished brass fittings. At the front was a narrow garden enclosed by a black wrought iron fence. From the outside the building was neat and beautifully maintained.

They entered and the Doctor immediately took Anke to an examination room. He called to his nurse assistant who arrived within seconds.

"This lady was assaulted. She is badly cut on the face and is having difficulty walking. Please assist her in putting on a gown so I can examine her hip area."

The Doctor left the room and closed the door quietly behind him.

"You look exhausted. Can I offer you some of our superb coffee while you wait? The examination will not take long."

Jakob accepted the offer and was soon drinking a dark Italian coffee. The Doctor had returned to the examination room.

His nurse went in and out of the room several times carrying different bandages and pieces of equipment.

After 30 minutes, the Doctor opened the door and beckoned Jakob to enter the room. Anke lay on a bed asleep and covered with a light green sheet. The Doctor motioned to Jakob to come to the side of the bed. He then lifted the sheet and exposed the hip. There was an ugly purple bruise and a mild laceration. He indicated the door and he and Jakob silently left the room.

"Your wife is in shock. I advise you not to travel tonight. If you wish she can stay here tonight in the infirmary. I have nurses here 24 hours as there are some other patients who need to stay overnight. I can arrange a place for you to stay overnight which is close to here. You can stay here as long as you want. Your wife has been mildly sedated and will probably sleep for many hours."

Jakob thought about the predicament. He realized that it was impossible to travel that night.

"You are correct. We cannot travel. I must go and retrieve some clothing from our luggage at the station. I must also send a telegram to Anke's relatives in Amsterdam to advise them we will not arrive as planned."

"Your wife will be safe here. I will be in my upstairs office. Go and when you return we will make arrangements for you to spend the evening. Tomorrow morning we will reassess the situation. I believe your wife will experience less pain and be able to walk easier."

Jakob thanked the Doctor and left to walk back to the station. He felt miserable that he had put Anke into such a predicament.

Chapter 48

Jakob entered the station and looked for the Gendarme. Not immediately seeing him, he walked to the baggage area. There talking with several of the baggage handlers was the young Gendarme. Jakob walked up to him.

"These gentlemen have placed your baggage over there away from the other bags. You can take what you need and then they will hold them for you until they receive updated information on your travel plans."

Jakob thanked them and proceeded to the area where their bags were stacked. He first removed the little brown suitcase they had used during their trip from Le Havre to Paris. Next he opened the larger cases. He removed the contents of the small case and placed them into one of the larger cases. He then searched through both of the larger cases and removed some clothing for Anke and himself. As the temperatures were getting colder he also took a heavy coat for each of them. After packing the items into the small case, Jakob returned to speak with the Gendarme.

"Thank you for all your help. I must now go and send a telegram to our relatives in Holland to tell them about this incident and the change in our plans."

"It has been a pleasure to serve you. I am sorry you have experienced this unpleasantness here in Paris. You can be assured that the person who did this will be severely punished."

Jakob shook hands with him and walked back to the French Post Office where he sent another telegram to Anke's relatives.

He strolled back to the Doctors deep in reflection. Maybe Anke was right and they should return to Canada. He soon dismissed this thought and his mind again drifted to the conflict between the things he was now experiencing in life and the teachings of his religion. He thought about the work the Doctor had done. Why were his brethren so against Hospitals and Medical services that the Government oversaw and provided?

He entered the Doctors office and was greeted by the nurse who had assisted the Doctor in treating Anke. She forced a smile and asked him to wait in the Doctor's office. When he was seated, the nurse left to get the Doctor.

A few minutes later, the Doctor entered. The suit jacket, vest and tie were gone. He was dressed casually. He went behind the large desk and sat down. He was frowning. His demeanor had changed.

"Jakob, I have to share some bad news with you. Did you not know that Anke was pregnant? You should not have been travelling so much with her. The assault that was made on her while she was tired, weak and pregnant has caused her serious problems. She has lost the baby. Shortly after you left for the station she miscarried. I am truly sorry. The baby was premature by many months and could not survive."

Jakob sat in stunned silence. How could he have been so short sighted and stupid.

"Is Anke going to be alright?"

"Yes. She is still sedated. She will sleep through the night and we will be watching her carefully. I suggest you wait 2 days before continuing your journey."

Jakob nodded.

"Given this recent development I have an offer to make you. Upstairs in my private quarters I do have extra sleeping quarters. For a small payment, less than a hotel or pension, I will have beds made up for you. Would you like to have this arrangement?"

"That is most kind. I must also pay you for the medical help you have given."

"I am dedicated to assisting those in need. For the lodging and medical treatment I will ask $25 American." Jakob reached into his breast pocket and withdrew his wallet and counted out $25 for the Doctor.

"Can I now go and see Anke?"

"I will have the nurse assist you. I am sending Anke's clothing to the laundry which is on the next street. There was a lot of blood that seeped through and the garments need to be professionally cleaned. We can probably get them back late tomorrow afternoon."

The Doctor arose.

"Again I am truly sorry for all that has happened to you and your wife here in Paris. This has been a most unfortunate series of nasty incidents."

Jakob left the room and was escorted to Anke by the nurse.

Anke was conscious and smiled a weak smile.

"Anke, did you know you were with child?"

"Jakob I wasn't sure. I believed I was but wanted to wait a few more weeks before speaking to you of this. I am so sorry. I thought I might be and this is the reason I wished to return to

Canada. Jakob, I am scared for everything. Please let us go back. There are too many bad things here and what is happening in the countries around Holland is evil. Please see it. You seem not to recognize the danger."

"Anke, you are tired. Sleep and we will discuss all this in the morning."

Jakob bent and kissed her on the cheek of her badly bruised face.

The nurse took his arm and gently steered him to the door.

Chapter 49

That night Jakob lay awake for hours thinking of the most recent incidents that had occurred. He finally fell into a restless sleep in the early hours of the morning. He awoke to the aroma of coffee and foods cooking. He arose and dressed. After freshening up, Jakob descended the stairs. At the reception desk there was a different nurse.

"Good morning, Mr. Jakob."

"How is my wife Anke?"

"We have been watching her closely. She is fine. She is still sleeping. I suggest we do not wake her yet."

Jakob agreed and returned to his room. After some time he returned to the nurse.

"Your wife is awake. We will go and see her."

Jakob and the nurse entered the small room. Anke was sitting propped up by several pillows.

Jakob took her hand. Tears welled in her eyes.

"My dear Jakob, I should have told you I thought I might be pregnant. I was not sure and I was scared you would be angry as it would have made our trip impossible. I am sorry."

"Anke, do not make an apology. It is I who was stupid. I should have been more understanding and asked why you had such reluctance to the trip. I have done much thinking. I will return later and we can talk. For now please rest. All will be fine."

"No Jakob. I fear that God is punishing us. We have left our community. We have travelled in boat and train and car. All these are not allowed in our religion. We have disobeyed. Now we are being punished."

Jakob felt embarrassed and lost. He did not believe that they were being punished, but rather they were identified as people who were not sophisticated and in a large city where it was easy to be taken advantage of.

"Anke, please rest. When I return later today we can talk. I have given much thought into returning to our farm."

Jakob left the room. The nurse smiled and left with him.

"It is not unusual for a woman to feel such guilt after such a loss. Give her some time. All will be correct soon."

Jakob went to his room and selected a winter coat. He dressed for a long walk in Paris. He had a lot of thinking ahead. He walked and walked, admiring the architecture of the buildings and watching the people who scurried about their business. Finally after several hours Jakob started back to the Doctors.

Upon entering he was greeted by the nurse who had originally helped with Anke.

"Mr. Jakob. Anke is asking for you. Can you come with me now to see her?"

Jakob and the nurse entered the room. Anke was awake and immediately smiled as they entered. The nurse turned to Jakob.

"I will leave you alone now with your wife. Please call me if anything is required."

Jakob sat on an old white chair beside the bed.

"Anke. I have done a lot of thinking. We have come a long way from our farm. Holland is but a few hours from here. Please let us go to Holland. After we met the relatives we shall return to Canada. I suggest we return to the farms in April. It is only a few months from now and we will be back at our farms in time for spring planting. You will meet Johannes' brother and you have family in Holland. I promise that we will not stay longer."

Anke looked at him and again smiled.

"If you promise we can leave and be back in time to assist with the spring planting, then yes, we will complete the trip to Holland. I am relying on your promise. When will we continue?"

Jakob advised her of the Doctor's recommendation and told her of the laundering of her clothing.

"We shall leave tomorrow afternoon if you are rested and able to travel."

"Please advise my relatives of when we will. Send them another telegram."

Jakob laughed.

"They will know me well at the French Post Office at the station."

Anke too started to laugh. Finally it seemed that their relationship was returning to normal.

Chapter 50

Jakob left Anke to rest. He put on his coat and started his walk back to the station in order to change their tickets to Amsterdam. As he entered the station he saw the young Gendarme standing near the counter and giving directions to a young couple. He saw Jakob, waved and started across to him.

"Jakob. How is your wife Anke ? Has she recovered enough for you both to continue your trip?"

Jakob recalled the events of the past day and the loss of their child. The Gendarme was shocked.

"Sacre Bleu. I shall see to it that this is reported to the head of the prefect. The person who did this to Anke will now be most severely punished."

Jakob was about to respond that they forgave him and that they were pacifists and did not seek revenge or punishment for the Moroccan. He did not. The actions of this person had affected three lives. Regardless of his beliefs, Jakob disregarded them.

"I will accompany you to the ticket counter in case you experience difficulties exchanging those tickets. We French can sometimes be a bit difficult."

Jakob smiled and thanked him.

At the ticket counter, the Gendarme spoke rapidly to the clerk in French. Finally there was a pause.

The Gendarme advised Jakob that there was a late morning train that would get them to Amsterdam in the early evening. Jakob agreed and the new tickets were issued.

Jakob and the Gendarme then went to the baggage office and advised the same men who he had dealt with previously of the changes. The baggage was retagged and set aside for tomorrow morning's train.

With the changes completed, Jakob entered the French Post Office kiosk. The clerk smiled and waved to Jakob. He turned and went to a rack of tiny compartments and removed a yellow paper.

"Jakob Klassen. You have a return telegram from Amsterdam. I believe it is from the people to whom you have been sending messages."

Jakob took the telegram and read it. Julia had sent her greetings and expressed concern about the assault on Anke.

Jakob drafted a reply. He advised that Anke was recovering and included the train information for the arrival in Amsterdam.

Jakob returned to the Doctors and was surprised to see Anke was out of bed and sitting with the nurse at the reception desk.

"Jakob, I am feeling so much better. Were you able to change our tickets? When will we now leave? Did you send a telegram?'

Jakob took Anke by the arm and gently sat her down on a chaise lounge at the wall beside the desk. He told her of the new arrangements.

"Jakob , you have made me feel better about the trip. Knowing that we can return to Canada for the spring encourages me. I am much happier."

Jakob looked at the clock behind the desk. It was late afternoon. He had not eaten that day and was hungry.

"Anke ,do you feel well enough to accompany me to a small Bistro I passed when I left you for the station? It is not far."

"Yes, Jakob. The medicines they gave me have made me hungry and very thirsty. We shall go and eat an early dinner. I will sleep early as tomorrow will be a difficult and exhausting day for me."

Chapter 51

Anke and Jakob left the Doctors to walk the short distance to the Bistro. Even though they were dressed in their winter coats, the -13 degree temperature and wind penetrated their clothing.

Anke laughed.

"Jakob, this reminds me of back at the farm when we walked on those cold days"

Jakob was happy to see his Anke returning to a good and pleasant mood.

They arrived at the Bistro some 10 minutes after leaving the house. Upon entering the Bistro a warm atmosphere greeted them. The Maître d greeted them as they walked in the large glass door. The Bistro was filled with warmth and delicious aromas.

They were seated next to an open fireplace with logs crackling and embers glowing.

Anke looked across the table at Jakob.

"Jakob, this is perfect. I know that we are of different minds about this trip. Paris has not been good to me. Tonight I feel so much better. Maybe I have worried too much."

"Anke, I have given you my promise. We will spend time in Amsterdam. I will search for the relatives and after meet them, we will return to the farm."

"Jakob, you have always been a good man and a man of principles. I know you must do this. You have spoken of this for years. Let us complete the trip to Amsterdam. There, you can complete your search and then we will return."

Jakob quietly sat and thought about the list of names he had been given and the letters he had written. Suddenly he was now confronted with establishing contact with the names on those papers he had been given back in Canada

As they sat enjoying the atmosphere of the Bistro, a short and jolly waiter came to their table.

"Good evening. I see you are not French. Can I assist you in ordering the best foods we prepare?"

Anke looked at the waiter

"That is very kind. What do you recommend to us?"

The waiter stood and thought for a moment.

For you Madam, I recommend Parmentier Cream Soup followed by our delicious Lobster Newburgh and for you Sir I recommend the Lentil soup followed by the Beef Bourguignon. For your dessert we shall serve Profiteroles stuffed with fresh custard and whipped cream and drizzled with molten dark chocolate. You will not be disappointed."

Jakob looked at Anke for approval.

"Yes. That sounds like a beautiful meal."

The waiter left and returned with some sparkling water.

Jakob and Anke were happy. Finally there was some pleasantry and enjoyment.

Their conversation drifted to the train trip to Amsterdam. Jakob told Anke of the departure times and the stops the train would make.

"Jakob, when we arrive in Amsterdam how will we find our way to my Uncle's house?"

"I have checked and there is a tram that goes close to the area that they live in. We will take this tram."

As they sat talking, the waiter reappeared with another helper and set down their meals. Anke was in awe at the presentation and the food. She was very happy.

"Tomorrow Jakob we will be in Holland. Our journey is almost complete."

Chapter 52

In the morning, Jakob and Anke bid farewell the Doctor and staff. They commenced their short walk to the station. The streets were busy with office workers scurrying to work and storekeepers opening their businesses for the day. Like the previous day, the weather was cold with an ashen grey sky. The cold wind had dropped and they found the walk refreshing. Soon they were at the station.

As they walked down the stairs to the platform area, Jakob heard his name called. He turned to see the young Gendarme walking quickly towards them.

"Bonjour. Good morning. I hope the last couple of days have been good for you. Paris can be a wonderful place. It is most unfortunate that you experienced the actions of this one person."

Anke smiled.

"Yes. We have been able to see a nice side of Paris life. Last evening we went to the Bistro Jules and enjoyed the most pleasant evening."

"Madam. That was an excellent choice. Bistro Jules is one of our best in this area. I too frequent it with my wife. It is one of our favorites. I hope you will again one day return and enjoy Paris some more. Come in the spring. The city wakes up and comes alive. There is music on the streets, artists selling their paintings, sidewalk cafes. There is a lot to see and enjoy. Here, I will write down my address and should you return we will meet again and it will be my pleasure to show you Paris from a Parisian's view."

He withdrew his police notebook and quickly scribbled his information.

"Now I must go and patrol the platform. There is a particular workers train that comes through from Germany. There is concern there will be trouble."

Anke was confused.

"Adolf Hitler has started equipping unemployed Germans with uniforms and jobs in the Military. There is so much conflict developing in Germany. I worry as we have family there. I hope that they too will leave soon. It is not good there."

Anke looked at Jakob and was about to speak. Jakob raised his hand in a gesture to silence her.

The young Gendarme shook their hands and walked off in the opposite direction away from their train's platform.

They walked to the platform to board the "Etoile du Nord" luxury train to Amsterdam via Brussels. Anke stopped to purchase a couple of books from the little newsstand. The books were in French. There were no English books. Anke smiled and thought to herself that this would make her practice the French she had learned at school.

Upon reaching the train, the conductor inspected their tickets and requested to see their passports.

After the formalities were completed, they were directed to their carriage. Jakob assisted Anke up the steps and into the carriage. They looked at the interior of the carriage in awe. It was luxurious and tastefully decorated with large plush seating. Jakob found their seats. He was delighted that these seats were next to a large panoramic window. He placed their small suitcase into the luggage rack and they settled in for the 7 hour trip to Amsterdam.

The shrill blast of the station masters whistle signaled all passengers were aboard and the train was ready for departure.

The train sounded its loud horn and with a shudder the train pulled away from Gare du Noord.

Within a few minutes the train had accelerated to a high speed and already the suburbs of Paris were slipping away.

Chapter 53

Jakob sat contently watching the French countryside slip by the window. He remained fascinated at the farms and their structures as they passed by.

"How could French farming be so different to that in Canada" he wondered.

Anke sat quietly reading her book. Shortly before noon she put down her book and asked Jakob

"Jakob, are you not concerned with all the troubles in Germany that we are hearing about?" "Anke, we have discussed this many times. Hitler has given agreements to bordering countries. The issues seem to be just within Germany. Yes it worries me when I hear about his attitude towards Jews. I have not heard a single problem with our Mennonite religion. I can only assume that we are safe from his actions."

Anke fell quiet and stared from the train window. While she had heard Jakob's words and his promise, she did not believe all would be safe.

A boy dressed in uniform came through the carriage announcing that the dining car was commencing luncheon service. He handed menus to the passengers as he walked by them.

Jakob assisted Anke to her feet and together they walked down the aisle and crossed from carriage to carriage until they reached the dining car. They were ushered to a table at the rear of the car.

Anke selected the chicken vol au vent and Jakob ordered a Belgian carbonnade. An order of Pain Francais was delivered with their food.

Jakob and Anke were quickly developing a liking for these fine European cuisines.

A waiter approached and offered wine. Again Jakob was tempted but Anke declined and ordered sparkling water.

They ate in silence. Jakob looked around. The dining car was full. At the entrance a few passengers were standing and awaiting seating.

When they finished their meals, they returned to their seats. The countryside was flying by as the train was travelling at considerable speed.

Almost 2 hours after the luncheon the train started to slow. The conductor walked into the carriage.

"We are approaching the border with Belgium. Please have your passports and travel papers ready for inspection."

There was a squealing of brakes and the train ground to a halt. Soon officials entered the carriage and performed a quick inspection of the passengers and their passports.

After a 30 minute stop, the train started onto Brussels.

Anke returned to her reading and Jakob perused a French newspaper he had found. The arrival at Brussels station happened sooner than they had expected.

The stop in Brussels was to be brief. Anke and Jakob remained onboard. Several new passengers boarded and entered their carriage. Smiles and greetings were exchanged.

Jakob listened with interest to the Dutch being spoken. While he understood the Dutch it was extremely different to the old Pennsylvania Dutch that he had been taught while growing up in Kitchener. Jakob struck up conversation with a scholarly looking gentleman. He was a teacher. They talked and shared words together, often laughing about how the word and pronunciation had been changed by those who had gone to North America.

Anke joined in the conversation.

"Sir, where do you live in Holland?"

"I live in The Hague."

"This is our first trip to Holland. In fact this is our first trip anywhere outside of Canada. May I please ask you a question? We have heard from several others during our trip of the troubles in Germany and the possible danger to Holland."

"I do not believe that will happen. During the last war Holland maintained its neutrality. If war was to break out, Holland will again declare herself a neutral country. We are not aggressive people and present no threat to Adolf Hitler or the German people. We do not have a large army though we do protect our canals and land with soldiers patrolling. In Holland recently there has been a lot of political activity. There has been an active communist party that has been recruiting. A Dutch Nazi Party has been formed and other smaller political factions have arisen. Most Dutch are busy working hard to earn money and have less interest in these groups."

Jakob smiled.

"Anke, this is what I have been saying. We will be safe in Holland."

The conversation drifted to questions about life in Canada and what had gone wrong in the United States with the Mennonite settlements that caused some to migrate to Canada.

By now a small attentive group was listening to the conversation.

Jakob recalled his past and told the story to an enraptured audience. Soon questions were being asked. It seemed many were interested in leaving Holland for either Canada or The United States.

Jakob spoke of the past troubles in Berlin, Ontario. He also spoke of the vast rich agricultural lands and of his and Anke's farms.

The small group asked questions about politics, health and life in Canada. Jakob and Anke provided honest answers.

Anke was curious. Why would these people wish to leave The Netherlands.

Chapter 54

The conductor reappeared in the carriage and was surprised to see the group huddled together in conversation.

"Is everything in order? Is there a problem here?

"No" Jakob responded. "Everything is fine. We are discussing our home in Canada."

"We are at the Dutch border. Again you will need to present your passports and travel documents.

Again officials entered the carriage to examine the passengers' papers. One of the officials took Anke and Jakob's passports.

"What is the purpose of your visit?"

"We are here to visit family relatives from the past." Jakob responded.

The official smiled. "Welcome to The Netherlands"

The officials completed the inspection and the train continued on to Amsterdam.

The late afternoon was quickly becoming dark during the early winter days. Jakob returned to watch the country pass by but with the fading light found it difficult. The lights from small houses started to flicker by.

The conductor re entered. "Amsterdam in 10 minutes"

Jakob and Anke started to gather up their possessions and pack them back into the small suitcase.

"Finally. After all the planning we are here in Amsterdam."

The train slowed to a crawl and inched into the station and eventually ground to a halt.

Passengers stood and started putting on their winter coats and then made their way to the exit

Jakob assisted Anke down onto the platform. They started walking to the stairway at the end of the platform. Standing at the bottom of the staircase was a tall man holding a small board with their names hand written on it. Anke rushed forward.

"I am Anke and this is Jakob my husband."

"Welcome, I am Aaron, the son of Julia and Wilhelm. I am here to greet you and assist you. I will accompany you back to our home. First we must get you baggage from the station here."

They walked to the baggage room. Anke was excitedly talking with Aaron who had great difficulty keeping up with her many questions. Aaron laughed.

"We will have plenty of time to answer all those questions, Anke. We will have many questions for you and Jakob as well."

They retrieved their luggage. In all it was only 2 larger suitcases. Aaron carried a case in each hand. He was large and strong.

"We live 30 minutes from here. We will take the tram to the stop near our house. We can board the tram here at the station."

Aaron carried the suitcases up the stairs to street level. They crossed the street to a tram waiting area in the middle of the street. It was dark and cold. They stood waiting from the tram. Eventually the electric tram rattled into sight. Aaron signaled the driver and pointed to the suitcases. The tram came to a noisy halt. Aaron told Jakob to go onto the tram first. He then passed up the cases to Jakob who placed them behind the driver. Aaron climbed up into the tram and produced some guilders to pay for their fares. Jakob objected.

"You are relatives and in our country now. You are our guests."

They settled into the narrow seats. Jakob sat with Anke and Aaron sat across the narrow isle alone. The tram rattled along through Amsterdam. It passed canals and areas in which there were multi story homes. Both Anke and Jakob were overwhelmed at the opulence of the homes.

The tram turned into a narrow one way street. At the end of the street it screeched to a halt.

"We are now at my home," Aaron said aloud.

"Let us gather the bags and go meet my parents. They have been excited all day. A traditional Mennonite celebratory meal has been prepared in your honor. Come, we shall now walk to the home."

Chapter 55

The three walked from where the tram had stopped to a laneway that ran off from the main street. Aaron turned and walked to the second house. Jakob and Anke looked at the house. It was a narrow 3 storey home. The front door was at street level. They started up the short front path and were not even at the door before the front door flew open. Standing in the doorway were her aunt and uncle...Julia and Wilhelm.

Anke gasped in astonishment. Wilhelm was a younger image of her father, Johannes. He stretched out his arms to her and hugged her.

"Welcome to our simple home. We are pleased to have you visit."

Introductions were made. Julia was fussing over taking their coats and getting them into the house. She took their luggage and set it in the front room.

"Aaron. Please show Anke and Jakob their room. You will find everything you will need for your stay in the room I hope."

Aaron guided them up a flight of stairs to a large room that had windows overlooking the street. The room was warm and inviting. There was a soft ambiance and feel to the room. There was a large bed to one side of the room on which there was a brightly colored quilt that had obviously been made by Julia. Anke was happy.

Aaron spoke. "I will leave you to freshen up from your travels. When you are ready we have prepared a traditional meal that we will all sit together and partake of."

Aaron left to fetch their luggage. When the luggage was in the room, Aaron left them to settle in.

Anke and Jakob bathed and changed into fresh clothing. After 30 minutes they went down the narrow staircase to join the Schneer family in celebration of meeting their relatives.

Julia had prepared a large wooden table and set places for each of them.

"Is there any help I can give you?" Anke asked.

"You can come into my kitchen and help to bring in the foods."

Anke followed Julia out to the kitchen in the rear of the house. The aromas were over powering. Anke realized her hunger.

Julia started removing dishes from the wood burning oven. There was a large tureen of Chicken Borscht Soup, Freshly baked Rye Bread, a Cabbage Casserole, and a large platter of Pork and Sauerkraut. For dessert there was a tray laden with Sugar Cakes .

Anke was amazed at the selection and quantity of food.

Jakob and Anke sat a prayed with the family.

As they started to eat Wilhelm stood.

"We must toast this happy event. I will get us some Mennonite wine."

He left the table and proceeded back to the kitchen where the sounds of glasses being removed from the cupboard could be heard.

Anke looked to Jakob and frowned.

"Julia, we were taught that all alcohol in any form is evil. We will need to say no to Wilhelm's kind offer."

Julia, Wilhelm and Aaron roared in laughter.

Anke and Jakob looked at them as if they had all gone quite mad.

Wilhelm walked around the table and placed a wine glass in front of each of them. Jakob and Anke were becoming anxious. Were Julia and Wilhelm still good practicing Mennonites they wondered?

Wilhelm walked around the table pouring the reddish orange drink into the glasses.

"Anke. Wilhelm told you that this was Mennonite wine. We make it ourselves here. It is grape juice with lemon juice, orange juice, ginger ale and sugar and water. There is no alcohol. Oh, you needed to have seen your faces when Wilhelm announced we would toast with wine. You will soon learn that my dear husband likes to play many tricks. We have been married together for 35 years and he still manages to trick me. At our church functions he is always joking and making our community laugh. These days that is a good thing."

Wilhelm stood at the head of the table. He raised his glass and started the toast.

"Dear Lord, thank you for safely delivering Jakob and my niece Anke to our home. Bless this feast that we have before us. Anke, my dear and you Jakob, welcome. May your stay with us be good and enjoyable."

Jakob arose.

"We are lucky to be here in such good company. Anke and I thank you for this feast and the opportunity to stay with you."

They sat and ate. Conversation drifted back and forth across the table. Wilhelm asked Anke about life in Canada and about his brother Johannes. Much small talk ensued.

"Tomorrow when you are rested we will speak in detail of family and Jakob's quest to find his relatives. You are welcome to stay with us until Jakob completes his mission."

Julia spoke

"Anke, it is Dutch Christmas starting with Sinterklass next week on December 5th.. You will enjoy seeing how the Dutch celebrate it differently from others. The children put out their shoes for Sinterklass and his assistant Black Pete and their white horse to place gifts in. It is a nice tradition the Dutch have. We will celebrate, but in Mennonite tradition. We will prepare some sweet foods and exchange only simple gifts and sing some of our songs. We will invite members of our congregation and the children will sing in the Capella style that we have been taught over many years. We will also prepare Roll Kuchen for our guests."

Anke smiled and a look of relief flooded her face. Finally she had some family life again. She had missed this since they departed Canada.

"It will be interesting for us and I will want to help you and learn of the foods."

"I will invite some of the other women and we will all cook together. It seems we each have a unique and different recipe depending where we came from. Many of the families in our congregation migrated here from Russia. You will learn about many cabbage dishes. It seems the Babushkas learned to use cabbage to make many things."

Anke winced. She hated cabbage.

With the meal finished Julia, Aaron and Anke cleared off the table and went to clean the dishes and kitchen.

Jakob and Wilhelm retired to a room with comfortable seating and sat to talk.

"Jakob. I have had letters from Johannes. He is worried and concerned for the safety of Anke and you. I have written back to him and assured him you will be safe here with us in Holland. Tomorrow you must show me the list of names and the locations of those families. I refer to the list you were given in Canada. I am aware you have attempted to write many of them. Some I have known well. Be careful. Some do not want to be found after the troubles they had before settling here. You must be sensitive to their wishes."

"Wilhelm, I will never cause any problem or try to interfere. If certain families wish to be left alone, then I promise this."

Wilhelm nodded. "You must be very careful and respect those wishes fervently."

Chapter 56

After breakfast the next morning Julia and Anke donned their winter coats and covered their heads with their little bonnets. Julia picked up a large cane basket.

"Wilhelm, I am going to the market with Anke to purchase foods for our dinner. We will return later this morning."

Julia and Anke left the house and were immediately hit by the chill of the winter air.

In the house, Jakob and Wilhelm sat at the kitchen table. Wilhelm scoured the list of names that Jakob had handed him on the old yellowed paper he had brought from Canada. Wilhelm was quiet. He took a pencil and wrote some notes. After an hour or so he put the list down.

"Jakob, this is not going to be an easy task for you. These people you wish to visit are in different areas that are widely separated. You do not have the knowledge of the Netherlands to find many of these places. Most are remote farming areas without the service of train or tram. To meet all these people could take you months. This is not a simple undertaking."

Jakob thought about this and then responded

"Wilhelm, we have the time. I have promised Anke that we will return to our farm in time for the spring seeding. That will be in April."

Wilhelm buried his face into his hands and thought.

"Jakob, why is it so important for you to find these relatives? Are you sure that they will want to see you. You have written many and yet have had only a few write back."

"When I spoke with Isaac and Inge they were extremely closed about the reasons why they left Europe. I have never been able to understand why we were the only ones to migrate to North America and all the other family members stayed here. I need to find the truth."

"Sometimes it is better to not know."

Wilhelm pondered the task that was facing Jakob.

"I have an idea. I will speak with Aaron about this. We still own our farm near Leiden. We have leased farm to another family who are devout in our faith. At the farm we still have horses and several buggies. I will speak to Aaron and ask if he will accompany you on the trips. I believe this is the only way you will be able to visit some of those locations. Leiden is within an easy distance from here and you will be able to travel there by a bus. When Aaron returns we will discuss all this. When will you start your visits?"

"I am thinking the start of January. Anke will want to enjoy the Christmas here with your family and friends. She has had a difficult time of recent."

Jakob told Wilhelm of the misadventures in Paris. Wilhelm listened intently.

"You must allow her to rest and gain strength. Will she go on these visits?"

"I am thinking that she will go with me to those who are close. I will make the longer trips alone."

The morning wore on and finally Julia and Anke returned. They entered the house noisily chattering and laughing. Wilhelm looked at Jakob.

"I can sense that this visit to my home is good for both Julia and Anke."

Anke's and Julia's laughter and talk continued in the kitchen as they stored the foods they had purchased at the market. Shortly thereafter pans and pots clanked as they prepared a lunch.

Wilhelm and Jakob joined them in the kitchen.

"I have looked at the places that Jakob wishes to visit. It will take a number of trips into the country. I am hoping Aaron will travel with him in one of our buggies. Some of the locations are very remote."

Anke looked concerned. Wilhelm noticed her worried look.

"Anke, do not worry. The country where the farms are located is safe to travel. My concern is that Jakob find these relatives and that they have not moved to different places in the Netherlands."

Chapter 57

It was late afternoon when Aaron returned. He walked into the house and proceeded to the kitchen where he poured a large glass of water. He seemed forlorn. Julia and Anke exchanged glances.

Aaron walked through to where Jakob and Wilhelm sat talking. They had the list of names laid out on a low table in front of them. Wilhelm looked up at Aaron.

"Welcome back Aaron. You do not seem happy. Is there a problem?"

Aaron looked at them both. He turned to look back at the kitchen and moved further into the room.

"I do not wish to scare either mother Julia or cousin Anke so I will speak quietly. This afternoon at the store, old man van Grimsven told us of the trip he had made to Germany in this past November. He described the horrible events that the Nazis are performing. He discussed what the Germans called "kristallnacht". He tells of looting of Jewish stores, burning of synagogues and books and many other atrocities. He described mass arrests of people and the deportation of these people to camps. I fear that we in The Netherlands are blind. It will only be a matter of time before Hitler decides to make us part of his envisaged Aryan Third Reich. We should be prepared. I worry that even though Hitler says he will not invade us, he will. He is not a man of his word. The events in our neighboring countries are witness to this."

Aaron sighed and sat down heavily.

"My son we are pacifists and cannot become involved physically in any fight. There are other ways we can assist if what you predict happens. In the meanwhile we will be careful and observant of events around us."

Aaron nodded. I do understand father."

"In the meanwhile, there is something that Jakob and I would like to speak about with you."

Aaron glanced at the papers on the table and frowned.

"Aaron this is an old list of names of family. They are Klassens. The list was given to Jakob in Canada. It contains the names and locations where these families were known to be living some years ago. Jakob has written many and had some responses. He wishes to visit these relatives. The locations are spread out and in the country. I fear that without knowledge of the locations, he will never find them. We are wondering if you would go with him. Take one of our buggies from the farm. It will be necessary as these locations are remote."

Aaron sat and thought about this for some while.

Jakob spoke "I am thinking of starting the visits in early January."

"I have a job and I also assist the van Grimsvens' with their store. I cannot be away for a long period. They are elderly and need my help. I will think about your request. How long will you stay in The Netherlands?"

Jakob repeated the information he had given to Wilhelm.

As they sat in silence Julia and Anke came in carrying a plate of freshly baked pastries.

"These were fresh at the bakery this morning. I could not resist" Julia said.

The plate was passed around and small talk ensued. There was talk of the upcoming gathering of members of their congregation for the Christmas celebration. Eventually the talk drifted to a series of questions about Jakob's mission to visit the families.

Aaron spoke. "I have looked at the places you wish to visit. Here is my idea. If you agree, we can travel to them on weekends when I am not needed at the store. This means it will take longer to see them all, but that I will do for you."

Chapter 58

For the next few days, Julia and Anke busied themselves preparing for Christmas. The weather was particularly cold for December in Amsterdam. Jakob spent hours looking at maps and trying to learn about the areas in which the relatives were located. He was concerned that the grey and cold of The Netherlands may impede their progress. Finally, he selected a family that was located close to Wilhelm's farm at Leiden. He discussed this with Aaron and they agreed to make a visit during the first week of January.

Christmas day came. The first visitors to the Schneer home started arriving in the late morning. By mid-afternoon there was a large gathering. Laughter and loud talk filled the house. Julia and Anke had prepared many foods and arranged a large table with the treats. Many of the women had brought pies, cakes and other delicacies.

Jakob and Anke were introduced to other members of the tight Mennonite community to which the Schneers belonged. Many were curious about Canada. Anke spent many hours describing her farm life and the time she spent studying nursing. She spoke of the experience of nursing the returning soldiers from World War 1. She explained how she had been young and that it was her belief that she was doing God's work by tending to those who had been injured.

The Mennonite men were gathered and discussing Jakob's plans to visit the families. Contact had been lost with many of them over the years. Many of the men cautioned that this could be both difficult and dangerous.

As the afternoon grew late, the mothers of the young children gathered them together for them to sing and entertain. After several songs were sung they were joined by some of the men.

Anke was happy. This was a life she could understand and appreciate. She watched Jakob as he spoke with the men. Though sociable and engaging, she detected that he was hiding his impatience. It was obvious that the impending visits were paramount in his mind and desire.

As the darkness enveloped the streets, the guests started to leave. When the home was empty and Julia and Anke had tidied up, she approached Jakob.

"Jakob you do not seem happy. I sense that you wish to go and start visiting. Why can you not relax and enjoy this season and our visit here?"

"Anke I am unfamiliar with this sort of life. I have always worked the farm. We never had days when we stopped and read and entertained. I need to be active. I feel wrong when I sit and talk or walk with Wilhelm. I was taught that in life I was to work and not be idle. My wait to start the visits in January is hard on me."

"Jakob you are worrying me. I have seen changes in you since we left the farm. I do not see those changes as good or wholesome. I fear that what we have experienced has changed you. It is not a single thing but I believe many things. On the farm we lived in the traditional ways. Since we left we have used electricity, eaten foods that were self-indulgent, travelled by automobile and you have tried alcohol. I have watched you enjoy these and many other vices that we are prohibited to partake of by the Elders. Jakob it seems that again you are losing the faith that we were taught. Remember the meetings with the Elders before we left? You made promises but I think they are far from your mind now."

"Anke we are in a different country and the customs here are unlike those back at the farm. Here in Europe our faith has had to adapt to change."

"Jakob that is not the difference I speak of. It is what I see you doing and becoming. You are changing. It is more than adapting. It seems you have replaced your beliefs with acceptance of these differences. You no longer pray intently or try to keep our ways. Please think about what I have said and examine your ways."

"Anke, I still have my beliefs. I do not wish to offend your family. When we are travelling or visiting our relatives and living in their homes we must be appropriate."

"Jakob you give me an excuse, not a truthful reason."

Chapter 59

Jakob lay awake that night thinking of Anke's comments. As he reflected upon them, he realized that he was changing. The conflict between his desires, religion and lifestyle was greater than ever. He thought back to the days at the farm. In his mind the image of the attack and sacking of the farm by the soldiers kept recurring. He also thought of Isaac and the impact the destruction had upon him. He continued to reflect on the past. The more he thought of the events that he had witnessed they caused him further doubt. He knew that if the Elders were to learn of the things which he and Anke had done, that they would be immediately excommunicated.

As he lay there he wondered if being excommunicated would be all that bad a thing for him. Anke would be horrified. He tried to bring order to his mixed and conflicted thoughts.

After several hours passed, Jakob fell into a deep sleep.

When they all awoke in the morning, the skies over Amsterdam were a leaden grey and the temperature bitterly cold. Julia called Anke to join her in the kitchen to prepare a breakfast.

"Today I will teach you a Dutch recipe. We will make pannenkoeken. These are Dutch pancakes and one of Wilhelm's favorite breakfasts. We will use apple on the pancake and pour some homemade treacle on it for sweetness."

Anke watched as the mixture was prepared and the large pancakes cooked. Julia placed them on individual plates and Anke took them to the dining table where Jakob and Wilhelm were sitting and discussing Wilhelm's farm.

Julia joined them at the table. Anke spoke "I will pray before we enjoy this meal."

She started to softly pray and the others joined in.

They ate in silence enjoying both the pancakes and the dark coffee with cream.

After the breakfast was over and the table cleared, Aaron left and returned within minutes with a large map of the Netherlands. He laid the map out on the table.

"Jakob can you please give me the list with the names and locations of the farms. Please tell me which ones wrote back to you and know of your plans to visit."

Jakob pushed away from the table and climbed the stairs to their room. He retrieved the list and joined Aaron and Wilhelm again. They sat at the table for hours. Finally Aaron spoke.

"I have been able to prepare a plan. We will be able to travel the distances from Leiden to these locations. It will take us several months to visit all of them. Some places we need to visit will require us to stay overnight at an Inn. It may be that the relatives we visit will offer us a night stay. I am concerned Jakob. The weather here in The Netherlands is not always friendly in January and February. We may experience delay and interruption of our travel."

Anke had joined the group and had been sitting quietly and listening. Finally she spoke

"We must return to Canada in time for the spring plantings. Jakob if the delays become too great then you will not be able to visit all who are on that list. We have made agreements and must honor those."

Wilhelm and Aaron both looked toward Jakob. It was obvious to them that Anke was not fully committed to this plan.

Wilhelm sat and thought.

"Anke, Jakob I have an idea. These people you wish to visit are relatives. It is possible that they come here for business or to the markets. I wish for you to write and invite them to visit here if they are coming to the city. We can accept them here at our house. This will make it easier for you to meet with them."

Jakob thanked Wilhelm and stood to leave the room. Anke followed. They went up to their room.

"Jakob I am tired of this whole matter. You must see that others are cautioning you that this is a bad idea you have."

Chapter 60

Throughout the morning Anke and Jakob sat at the kitchen table writing letters to the names on the list. In the early afternoon Jakob took the letters and walked out to wait for a passing tram. An old tram rattled into sight. It stopped and several passengers got off. Jakob ran to the rear of the tram where a small mailbox was mounted for those who wished to mail letters but could not get to a mailbox. Jakob thought this was a smart and efficient service that the Dutch had devised. The tram rattled away down the narrow street.

Back at the house, Wilhelm and Aaron were engaged in an intense discussion. Seeing Jakob entering the house the conversation stopped. It was obvious that there was a disagreement regarding the planned travel and use of the horse and buggy.

The weather continued to be bleak all afternoon. Julia sat with Anke quilting and talking. Jakob was bored. He stood and advised everyone that he was going for a long walk. He dressed in his winter coat, gloves and a heavy scarf. He placed his large black Mennonite hat on his head and left the house.

His walk took him along canals and into a small district studded with storefronts and several cafes and bars. As he slowly walked along he became aware of the sound of jazz emanating from one of the bars. He stopped and peered in the windows. There at the rear of the dimly lit bar was an instrumental group. Jakob hesitated before deciding to go in. He removed his hat and seated himself close to the musical group. He sat fascinated at the beautiful sounds that each instrument produced.

A tall slender Dutchman wearing a stripped apron approached.

"I recommend our finest ale which we brew here from the finest ingredients."

Jakob nodded. The downward spiral was starting. In complete disregard for the promises he had made to Anke and the Elders, Jakob was defying the customs and his faith.

"Yes. I will take a mug."

The Tall Dutchman went behind the bar and soon returned with a large glass mug with the name "Van den Heuvel" etched on the glass.

Jakob handed over several guilders.

The ale started to have effect on him. Jakob was unaccustomed to such a strong drink. He finished the drink quickly and ordered yet another. By the end of several more drinks the musical group had stopped playing. Jakob went over to where they were sitting. He introduced himself and became engaged in a discussion about music. He told them of how he had once played saxophone in Canada. They talked and talked. Finally Jakob was invited to try the tenor saxophone.

Jakob looked around the bar. There were very few patrons so he decided he would join in with the group. They played a basic tune. Jakob took the sax and started wailing along with the group. They were amazed. Jakob displayed a natural ability to quickly pickup on the tune and play in time and beat with them.

Hours passed by. Jakob looked out at the dark night that had descended. He thanked the group and dressed to leave. As he was leaving one of the members called out to him to wait.

"Jakob. You added a lot to our music. You have a distinctive style. Will you come back tomorrow? We play here every day. We can pay you only a small amount."

Jakob thought about this. He was bored being at the house waiting to travel. His conflict arose in his mind. Was this just a temptation or was he really discarding his beliefs.

"Yes I will return and play. I have enjoyed this afternoon. I will be here tomorrow."

Chapter 61

Upon returning to the house, Jakob found that dinner had already been served. Wilhelm and Julia sat in the large front room. Neither Aaron nor Anke were with them.

Jakob removed his winter coat and called a greeting to them. He received a look of disapproval from Wilhelm. Julia got up and excused herself.

"I cannot but believe you have been in a place of temptation. You smell of cigarettes and drink. You are disappointing everyone. I will forgive you this one time but if this happens again you must leave my house. You have betrayed us all."

Jakob stood in front of Wilhelm who was glaring at him.

"I did drink. I was drawn to the music they were playing at the small café. I played with instruments in Canada. I have a love of music. I have agreed to play with a group for a couple of hours each weekend. Wilhelm I need to do something. I cannot sit and be idle. I have always been active. I promise you that I will not drink when I return there to play the music. I promise this."

"Jakob your promises to all of us mean nothing now. You are deceitful and betraying us as a family and destroying your marriage. Is nothing sacred to you anymore? I will not tolerate this. You must make a decision that is correct. What will your decision be? If you continue, I will ask you to leave this house tonight. I will not accommodate sinners under our roof. You must decide this alone and now. Anke is in another room and does not wish to see you. You have lost your way."

Jakob was torn and ashamed. His thoughts were of the farm and all the members of the Mennonite community with whom he had grown up.

"Wilhelm it is true that I have strayed away from our strict doctrine. I do not wish to bring disrepute to Anke or your household. I will seek forgiveness and repent for my selfish actions.

"Jakob if you are being honest we will go and meet with clergy here in Amsterdam in the morning. I know them well. We will not need an appointment. I will ask Anke to join with us. You must be serious in this commitment and understand that you may not be forgiven. You have strayed several times. The Elders may decide you are unworthy of our practice and that you are unable to resist the life outside our congregation. I cannot predict what will befall you."

"Wilhelm it is hard to understand why we shun certain developments that would make our lives and health better. I do understand that there are many temptations that could lead to my downfall. Why do we not accept electricity to light our homes back in Canada and yet here in Holland you use it? Why can we not use a car? There are many observations I have made of things that would assist us in many ways. We could improve the quality of produce on our farms. I don't understand and am in such a conflict."

"Tomorrow we will explain all this to the Elders. Understand that here in Europe our customs have changed. I am sure they will be patient and understand you."

Jakob thanked Wilhelm and ascended the stairs to the room he and Anke had been using. He entered the room and was alone.

Anke was not there. He felt a wave of loneliness creep over him. He was tempted to return downstairs and ask Wilhelm to ask Anke to return to him in the room.

As he stood deciding this there was a slight knock on the door. The door opened and Anke walked in.

"Jakob this behavior must stop. I understand from my uncle that tomorrow we will visit the church Elders and seek answers and forgiveness for the actions you have performed. Since this is so I will return here tonight. Please give serious thought to our situation."

Chapter 62

Dressed for the cold morning, Jakob, Anke and Wilhelm left to take a tram to the church. 45 minutes later they entered the rectory where they were greeted by an elderly housekeeper who showed them into a waiting area.

A tall distinguished man joined them within minutes. Pleasantries were exchanged and introductions made. Soon, three other men entered. They all sat. It was obvious that Wilhelm had much respect from the Elders.

Wilhelm explained the situation in detail. Anke sat with her head bowed. She was embarrassed. When Wilhelm was finished the tall Elder called upon Jakob to explain.

Jakob launched into a detailed description of the events in his life that had lead him to the conflict between his religion and his views. The Elders sat in total silence until he was finished.

The tall Elder spoke.

"Jakob we all face challenges and temptations every day. It is a strong and true believer who can summon the strength to resist. I believe I speak for us all when I say we can understand. Some of the past events have surely tested you. Not all of us have had those experiences. You must personally decide what you want. Our beliefs are there to assist and guide us in difficult times."

Jakob replied. "I am confused. I do not wish to leave our faith but I question many things every day. This makes me unhappy with my life."

"Then I think that my fellow Elders and I need to speak in private. Wilhelm you will join us."

The Elders stood and with Wilhelm they left the room. Jakob and Anke sat alone. They felt awkward and uncomfortable. Some 30 minutes later the Elders returned. Each had a serious and stony expression on their face.

They sat in a semi circle facing Jakob and Anke.

"We have discussed all you have told us. We understand your turmoil. We have arrived at a decision. Today we will write to your congregation in Kitchener and advise them of your behavior and your ongoing concerns. It is not up to us to decide upon your excommunication or whether you stay within the faith. The Elders of your church will decide this. In the meantime please pray and repent for your digressions. We will summon you when we receive a reply."

Several weeks went by. January 1939 saw milder temperatures arrive. Jakob was eager to commence his travels. Given his recent problems he decided to defer to Aaron and Wilhelm's decisions.

During the last week of January Wilhelm received a visit from the assistant to the Deacon of the church. They were requested to attend at 11:00am the next day to hear the decision of the Elders in Canada.

Jakob, Anke and Wilhelm set off in the morning for the meeting. Again, upon arrival they were ushered into the same waiting room by the same assistant. They waited for what seemed the longest time. Finally they were escorted to the meeting room where the Elders sat seated. A table with 2 chairs had been set up in front of the semi circle of chairs upon which the Elders sat. Anke and Jakob were directed to sit at the table. Finally the tall Elder arose.

"We have heard back from your congregation's Deacon. They met and discussed the situation. We are asked to advise you of their decision and the reasons for the decisions."

Jakob shifted uncomfortably in his wooden chair.

The tall Elder continued. Here is the written response that I am required to deliver to you.

"Jakob Klassen you have strayed from the teachings and practice of our church. We have offered you many opportunities to reform yet you continue and refuse to cooperate with the church. You have remained stubborn and unyielding to the Ordnung and the council of elders. You now face excommunication. Because of your circumstances we will allow you to continue to attend services however you will not receive communion. We consider some of your behavior and actions to be those of a deviant and until you repent you are to be considered outside of our fold. Upon return to Canada we will meet again to discuss whether you can be accepted back into the church. Until then you will be shunned by members of our congregation."

Anke gasped and sobbed aloud. The mantle of shame would also be worn by her. She was his wife. Together they would suffer.

The Elders stood one by one and left the room. There was no further conversation.

Jakob turned to Wilhelm. "I must finish here in Holland and return to Canada and resolve this issue for Anke's and my sake. The ruling is too harsh."

"Jakob you had been warned many times. I do not understand why you do not listen and act on those warnings."

They gathered up their coats and belongings and proceeded to the tram for the ride back to the house. Upon their arrival Aaron called to Jakob. "There is a letter for you from one of those on the list."

Jakob eagerly took the letter and ripped it open. It was written in a script that he could not understand. He handed the letter to Wilhelm who scanned it.

"It is from a cousin of Isaac. He knew Isaac before he and Inge left for America. He says he is coming to Amsterdam in 3 days. He will visit with us here."

After the bad news of the morning this came as a relief to Jakob.

Wilhelm asked Jakob to join him for a private talk. "Jakob I am concerned for you. I believe you are a good and smart person. My brother Johannes speaks fondly of you. I understand you have faced challenges in life and these have caused you to doubt many things. I will try to help you. I know that it will not be easy when you return to Canada. I have been told of the fine advice you shared with other young people when you were younger. You do have principles. Right now they are confused by your views on life. It is my wish to help you through this period of difficulty. You can be a strong person and do right."

Jakob was at a loss. He had not expected Wilhelm to be kind and understanding. He thought the visit to the church and the decision would have turned Wilhelm against him.

"I must live my life Wilhelm. There is a spirit inside me that is adventurous and causes me to challenge certain beliefs. I do not see that any harm can be done."

Wilhelm took Jakob's hand and shook it hard. "We understand each other. I will not stop you with your passion for music. Go and play with your friends at the café but please do not continue to partake of alcohol."

Jakob was relieved. He swore that he would do better from this day on.

When they were done talking Wilhelm called Julia and Anke to join them.

"Jakob and I have spoken. We have an agreement. Jakob will stay here with us. He is going to continue to play music with his friends and will not drink alcohol. I will assist this troubled young man to find his way back to our religion and beliefs. He is not a bad person. He just needs support and help."

Anke spoke. "Wilhelm we thank you for making this offer to help Jakob. He needs someone to guide him. He has experienced many bad incidents since the deaths of Isaac and Inge. He is not a weak man. He just needs someone to talk with."

Julia re-entered the room."It has been a difficult day. Let us join together in a prayer to help us move beyond this. Then we shall eat a late lunch that I have prepared while you were at the church."

They knelled on the bare wooden boards and prayed. As they were finishing, Aaron arrived home. He was excited.

"Wilhelm, Jakob I have good news for you. I spoke with Henk, the farmer who has leased our farm. He needs labor for the farm. He has offered to give Jakob work at the farm and free lodging at the farm house. This is good. Jakob will have something to do and it will make leaving for our travels much easier."

"Jakob you will no longer be bored. You will experience Dutch farming," Wilhelm laughed.

The days slowly dragged by. Jakob was eager to receive the visiting relative. Late on the third day there was a knock at Wilhelm's door. Aaron opened the door and greeted the relative. He was alone. The very tall man entered the house. Jakob walked up to him, introduced himself and shook his hand vigorously.

Aaron suggested they use the parlor where they would be alone. Jakob took the relative's coat and they settled into the chairs in the parlor. Within minutes Anke joined them. Jakob introduced his wife.

Anke offered to make either a tea or coffee. She left to make coffee and when it was ready she returned to the parlor.

"Jakob, my name is Augustus. I farm in the south. The work is hard but I enjoy it. We have a large dairy farm. It keeps us very busy. Today I had business here. Now, please tell me about Isaac and Inge and life in Canada. I knew Isaac when he was a boy. That was many years ago. He was older than me then."

Jakob and Anke spent the next hour discussing their life and families. Augustus looked at the clock in the parlor.

"I must leave shortly. I have more friends to visit. Jakob, for your sake I suggest you do not pursue some of the family. I mean those ones who did not reply to your letters. There is a reason for this and no one will want to discuss this with you. I am sorry but it is best that this be left silent. I have only heard rumor of what happened and I will not discuss a rumor."

Jakob and Anke quietly accepted the older man's comments. He arose from the chair and thanked Jakob and Anke for their kindness and dressed in his winter clothes for his next visit.

Jakob and Anke returned to the parlor and discussed the mysterious comments that Augustus had made. Jakob's curiosity was running wild.

Chapter 63

February arrived. The temperatures climbed from the cold of the previous month. At the farm Jakob worked preparing for the spring weather ahead. He assisted in maintenance of equipment, feeding the livestock and other general tasks.

Every morning at 4:30am Jakob and Henk would walk to the nearest barn where they would do the daily milking by hand. Jakob found this a calming and satisfying time. He was alone and his concentration was on the milking and the animals. When finished they would return to the house for a large breakfast and discuss the work ahead of them for that day.

Jakob was on his way to the plow shed when he observed Aaron riding toward him. It was a Saturday so Jakob was not surprised.

"Jakob I come with news for you. We have received letters of reply from more of those to whom you wrote. Come we will go inside and you can read them."

Jakob and Aaron entered the house and removed their winter work coats and boots before going to the kitchen. Jakob poured them both large coffees and poured in the fresh cream he had skimmed from the vats that morning after the milking was completed. He sat at the table with Aaron.

Aaron placed 6 envelopes on the table. With his hand shaking slightly Jakob picked them up and opened each one carefully.

He read each in silence. When he was finished he looked at Aaron and smiled.

"Aaron we have been invited to meet with 2 of the families at their farms. The replies are friendly. 1 other wished to meet us at Wilhelm's house when they are next in Amsterdam. The others do not wish to meet. This troubles me and I am not sure why this is so. Here are the letters from the families who want us to visit. Are the locations far away?"

Aaron looked at the letters.

"One is very close to here. The other is across The Netherlands and very close to the border with Germany. That visit we will need to plan. The distance means we will need to stay a night somewhere."

"Aaron when should we make these trips?"

"Jakob I suggest we visit in the next 2 weeks. The weather has been good so far. For the trip to the border we should plan early March as you and Anke must also prepare for your return to Canada in time for spring planting."

Jakob was happy. He finally would have the contact he so eagerly desired. He would soon be able to learn of the events that lead to Isaac and Inge leaving Europe for North America.

"I will write to each family. Please take the letters and mail them. I will tell them of our plan and the dates on which we will arrive."

Jakob left to get paper and envelopes. He sat and wrote quick replies. He handed the completed letters to Aaron.

"Please mail them upon your return. How shall we plan for the trip to the family near the border?"

"Jakob I will seek information for a place to stay overnight near the family's home. I have contacts that can help us with this. Now I must return. Wilhelm has not been well this past week and I need to be there to assist Julia. Anke is well and wants to visit with you. I think next weekend we will visit."

"I miss Anke and to have her come here and experience the farm for several days would mean a lot. Can you arrive next Friday and return to Amsterdam late on Sunday?"

Aaron thought about this. "Yes I am not working at Van Grimsven's on Friday. We will make the trip. "

Jakob wished blessings for a safe return trip and offered a prayer for Wilhelm's recovery and Aaron's safe return to the home in Amsterdam.

Chapter 64

The following week the days went by slowly. Jakob was eager to see Anke. They had been apart for weeks now. Jakob worked around the farm. With the warmer temperatures he was able to work outside repairing fences and gates. Each night he would sit with Henk and his family. They prayed and ate together. After meals Henk and Jakob would sit and talk of the differences in farming between The Netherlands and Canada.

As the week drew to an end, the family excitedly prepared for Anke's arrival. The room was cleaned and prepared. A new quilt for the bed was provided and fresh cakes and cookies were baked.

On Friday shortly before noon, Aaron and Anke arrived. Jakob hugged Anke and with his arm wrapped around her waist they went into the house where the family was gathered to greet Anke. She was delighted and spent some time speaking to each of the children. Finally Henk returned from the barns. He looked at Anke and smiled. "Welcome to our humble little home. Please sit. You and Aaron must be hungry from your trip. We will prepare some cake and refreshments."

After a while Jakob took the bag containing Anke's effects up to the room. Anke excused herself and joined him.

"Jakob you seem to be happy. This makes me pleased. Are you enjoying the farm?"

"Anke I am. I did not realize the need I have to do this work. Henk is a good man to work with. How is Wilhelm? Aaron told us he has not been well."

Anke looked at Jakob. "I saw illness like Wilhelm's when I was nursing. I am very concerned for him. He appears to have consumption. Recovery from it is rare. It can spread to others. He has to be isolated. He is a strong man and that may help him. The doctors have visited and he will be given a new medicine."

"Anke I am concerned. I shall return with you. It is time now for me to arrange our tickets for the return to Canada."

Anke could barely contain herself. She did a little hop and smiled profusely.

"Jakob , do you really mean this? I have waited to hear you say this. I miss my home. I cannot wait to return to our friends. I know we will have to overcome the excommunication. It is my belief that our community will accept you back. They are all good people. They know the work that you and Isaac did and the advice you gave many when you were younger. They do not forget those things. We will be accepted back."

Anke and Jakob spent the weekend talking with the family and walking on the farm. Jakob had spoken of his need to return to Amsterdam to look after arrangements and that he would return by the following weekend.

On Sunday, Aaron, Anke and Jakob set off for the short trip back to Amsterdam.

Upon arrival, Jakob noticed a musty smell to the house. He mentioned this to Anke. With illness in the house they needed to get clean air in the house. Jakob found Julia sitting stoically in her kitchen.

"This is what God wants. It is his will if Wilhelm is to get better or die and go to him."

Jakob reached out and embraced Julia.

"Wilhelm is a good and righteous man. He is strong. We will pray for recovery. "

Anke changed from her travelling clothes to a traditional apron and skirt.

"Julia you have taught me a lot. I will cook for this evening. You can join me."

The late afternoon was taken up with the sounds of cooking and occasional laughter as Julia and Anke worked in the kitchen.

As Aaron and Jakob sat in the living room the doctors arrived to visit Wilhelm. Aaron ushered them to his room. Wilhelm lay in his bed, his breathing was labored and wheezing.

The doctors requested privacy. After a lengthy period they returned to Aaron and Jakob. Upon hearing the doctors in the living room, Julia and Anke joined them.

"We have made an extensive examination of Wilhelm. The new medicine has prevented his condition from worsening. He still has serious days ahead of him. We will return at this time tomorrow for another examination."

Aaron escorted the doctors to the front door. He thanked them and confirmed he would greet them the next day.

Chapter 65

"Jakob please come to our room. We must speak."

Anke started up the narrow and creaking stairs. At the second floor landing she opened the dark brown door. She and Jakob walked into the dimly lit room. Jakob sat on the edge of the iron bed on which there was a kapok mattress. Anke sat on a wooden pine chair that Aaron had made as a boy.

Anke spoke. "Jakob, I know I have been impatient and wanting us to return but now things are different. I must stay and help Julia now that Wilhelm has been taken ill. Julia has been like a mother to me. She is elderly and needs help. Aaron is here but must work to make money for the family. Please do not be upset with me. I know you had a strong desire to meet the relatives of Isaac. It does not seem your plans will be a success. The relative who visited here was polite but unable to share information with you. It is my belief that they do not want to discuss the past. Please end this important mission of yours. You and Aaron must now visit the 2 families you mailed. I will stay and help at the house. I believe we must delay our return. Tomorrow we will hear the doctors' findings."

"Anke I am content here. I am happy to work at the farm and assist Henk. I am learning many new things. I will be able to share these with our farming neighbors back home. If we are to delay our return I am not unhappy. It is already March and soon spring will be here in Holland as well."

Anke stood and walked to him. They embraced. Anke bent and kissed Jakob's forehead. Jakob reached up and caressed her breasts. Soon they engaged in long and passionate love making.

"Anke you are as pretty and passionate as the days we first married."

"Jakob I am happy to see that you are more the man I married and without the impatience and aggravation."

"I have enjoyed meeting and living with this family. I have enjoyed the different experience dealing with the Dutch with whom we trade. I will never forget our time here."

After they rested Anke and Jakob went to the kitchen. Anke put on the large white apron and started to prepare some foods. Julia came in to assist her with the potatoes and other vegetables. Aaron appeared with a fresh chicken.

Quietly they all worked to prepare the dinner. Finally Aaron spoke.

"Anke what are the doctors saying about father? You trained as a nurse. What are we to expect?"

"Aaron it has been some years since I was a nursing. Many changes have happened with treatments and medicines. I cannot answer your question. We must wait until the doctors' return tomorrow and learn from them."

Julia turned and seemed to sense a change in Anke.

"Anke what is wrong? Are you thinking of leaving? You are still welcome to stay in our home. We will manage even with Wilhelm ill."

"No Julia. I have spoken with Jakob. We are going to change our plans for the return to Canada. I will stay and help you. Jakob will continue to assist Henk at the farm. Aaron and Jakob will complete their visits. I insist we do this. I am trained as a nurse and can offer that assistance to you. You and Wilhelm have been kind and generous to Jakob and I. We will not leave you at this time when you have these circumstances to deal with."

Julia bowed her head slightly in agreement. "You are kind. I will need your help. You and Jakob are welcome to stay here. "

They sat and ate the supper. Jakob spoke of his days at the farm. Anke chattered about the new meals and baking she had learned from Julia. Every so often, Aaron would leave and visit Wilhelm.

"How is he?" Anke asked when he returned.

"He is sleeping. His breathing seems better. There is no wheezing as there was before. We will pray now and place his future with God."

Chapter 66

Anke awoke early to a bright sunrise. The skies had cleared of the dull leaden clouds that had hung over Amsterdam for the past weeks. She felt invigorated. Carefully she descended the stairs and started some coffee on the stove. She then went to check on Wilhelm. He was awake but looked drawn and tired.

"Wilhelm I will get you a juice to drink."

Wilhelm raised his hand slightly and appeared to nod. Anke returned to the kitchen and found some bottled orange. She poured a glass and returned to Wilhelm. She held the glass to his lips. He clumsily sipped at the juice. After a few gulps he slunk back onto the pillow. Anke sensed his exhaustion and hurriedly left him to rest.

The others arrived at the table and Anke served up a breakfast of ham, eggs, bread and coffee.

It was late in the morning when the doctors arrived. Aaron again ushered them to Wilhelm where he left them.

They could hear the murmured voices of the doctors discussing Wilhelm's condition. The doctors came down the stairs and into the kitchen.

"We have examined Wilhelm and I am pleased to report that his condition is improved. He is not well yet. It will be weeks before he is able to regain his strength and be out of bed for most of the day. For now we will visit every third day. If his condition seems worse you must contact us immediately. Anke, you are a trained nurse we understand. May we speak with you in private about the care he needs."

Anke was advised of the symptoms to watch for and the treatments and food to give Wilhelm. She hastily made notes and tucked them into her apron's pocket.

When the doctors left and the breakfast utensils were washed, Anke asked Jakob to accompany her on a walk.

They walked to the marketplace. Anke purchased foods for the evening meal. She was excited when she saw the early spring flowers at some of the street stalls. Jakob stopped and bought her bunches of freshly cut hyacinth in a myriad of bright colors, some daffodils and several shoots of forsythia.

They continued their walk for several hours. They walked by canals and watched people cycling, walking and just sitting on the narrow benches along the walkways.

"Anke this weekend I will return to the farm to assist Henk. As spring is almost here there is a lot of work to be done. Aaron and I will go and visit a family the next weekend. Aaron thinks we should visit with the last family in April when the temperatures are a lot warmer. It is the furthest we will travel. The farm is close to the German border. The trip will take us two days. I trust Wilhelm will be well by then and then we can return to our home in Canada."

"We will know in days if Wilhelm will recover. His illness is serious and has taken many lives. He is better with the new medicine but needs a lot of care. This will require a lot from me over the next weeks. Please go and finish with your visits and work at the farm. I have contributions to make here."

"I will wait another 2 days and assist at the house. I believe we will know if Wilhelm's condition improves during these days."

"This morning I took him juice. I saw the improvement already. I am hopeful."

They continued their walk back to the house in silence. Upon entering Julia came to the door.

"Jakob there are people here to see you. They are more of your family relatives. They changed their minds and decided to visit us here. Please use the living room. Anke and I will leave you to your talk."

Jakob was stunned. He entered the room and found an older man and woman dressed in peasant style dress. The man stood. He was also as tall as the other relative who had visited them earlier.

"Greetings. I am Jakob Klassen, son of Isaac and Inge Klassen of Kitchener, Ontario, Canada."

Jakob extended his hand to the man. The old man took his hand to shake. It was hard and calloused from hard work.

"We are related. I am the cousin of Isaac. I was a young boy when he left for America. We are in Amsterdam to sell this year's spring crops. I wanted to meet you. Tell me about Isaac and America."

Jakob was disturbed. Did they not know of Isaac and Inge's deaths. Why did they think he was from America?

Jakob sat and started talking. Questions were asked. It quickly became obvious that very little was known about the Klassens and their life. Jakob talked for hours. When he stopped he started asking questions of the family heritage and the reasons that lead to Isaac and Inge migrating to America. At this point the visiting relatives became anxious and evasive. Sensing a problem, Jakob changed the conversation and asked the questions in a gentle manner. Again he was met with resistance. Finally the old man stood.

"We must leave now before it is too dark for us to travel. God bless. We are pleased to have met you. I am sorry that Isaac and Inge had troubles. We have also had many troubles here with war and sickness. I give you our address. Please write."

The old couple shuffled toward the door. Jakob assisted them with their winter clothing.

After they left Jakob sat and told Anke of the meeting. That he was unable to learn any important information troubled him. This made him even more curious.

"Anke there is some strong reason that some do not wish to meet and others won't talk. These were Isaac's family. I must find the reason."

Chapter 67

The next weeks slipped by. Jakob worked at the farm and Anke assisted Julia with the home and nursing Wilhelm. Anke was happy. The winter months were fading. On their daily trips to the market Julia and Anke would stop at the flower seller's carts and buy beautiful bouquets for the home. They would also stop at carts of the street sellers and sample pickled herring, cheese and other delights.

Slowly Wilhelm's health grew stronger. Soon Wilhelm was making jokes and asking to be released from his bed.

The doctors visited and pronounced Wilhelm cured but needing a less active role in the family. Wilhelm attempted to raise himself from the bed when given the doctors findings. He fell back onto the bed due to his weakness. Anke went and took his hand.

"Wilhelm. This is good but now you must move slowly. You have been very ill. Please listen to my advice as a nurse. I am sure we will get you back to the life you enjoyed. You must not try to do things you could before this illness. It will take time for you to get stronger."

Anke assisted Wilhelm from his bed. She wrapped him in a loose blanket.

"Anke I want to go and see my home and Julia. I will go with you to the kitchen. I will sit and watch as you and Julia make this my home. I am so blessed to have you here to support me and Julia."

Cautiously Anke helped Wilhelm to his feet and assisted him with walking to the kitchen where Julia was making borscht. Upon entering Julia crossed the room and hugged Wilhelm.

"My prayers have been answered. I thank God for your recovery. I have prepared delicious borscht. This will be good for you. You will eat and then return to your bed. You are still weak. I will hear no other words about this."

Anke smiled to herself. Their love for each other was obvious.

The next morning Anke arose, dressed and went down to the kitchen. Wilhelm was sitting at the end of the long pine table. He chuckled when Anke entered and he saw the look of disapproval on her face.

"Anke I was sick. Not dead. Now I need some good coffee and a breakfast of your pancakes. After that I will relax and then go for a small walk. I plan to visit my farm soon. I need to get some strength to do that."

"Wilhelm you must not go about things so fast. You have been very ill. It will take time until you have the strength to leave here and take that trip."

Wilhelm looked at her and chuckled. "Get me some of that Mennonite wine."

Anke walked to him and threw her arms around him.

"Oh, Wilhelm. You are such strong person. I will go and wake Julia. She has not slept well since you became sick. This will make her happy."

After several minutes, Julia joined them. Anke was preparing the ingredients for the pancakes.

"Anke you have learned a lot while here. I will sit here with Wilhelm and watch you make the pancakes this morning."

"Yes Julia. I have learned many things while here. I will never forget this time I have spent with you and Wilhelm. You both have been so kind to Jakob and me."

As they sat and started the Morning Prayer, Aaron joined them. When the prayer was complete and the food served Aaron spoke.

"I have been contacted by the family near the German border that Jakob wishes to visit. They have asked us to visit this weekend. I am not busy at the store. I will go to the farm and on Friday we will start the trip. This will be the last visit we will make. Spring is here and it will be a nice ride through the farms and flower fields. I am looking forward to it. We will be gone for three days and return here late Sunday."

Chapter 68

Aaron and Jakob left the farm early on Friday morning. They travelled through the countryside and watched farmers preparing for spring. Jakob watched as a farmer plowed his fields behind two large and strong draft horses. It brought back memories of the farm in Canada and of the days he would assist Isaac with the plowing. For the first time on the trip, Jakob felt a twinge of homesickness. He quickly dismissed the feeling.

They travelled on for hours and mid afternoon they stopped at a café in a little village. After a meal of soup and some sandwiches they continued. It grew dark quite early as summer had not yet arrived. After several more hours they entered another village. Aaron dismounted and went into a store that seemed to sell everything.

"Good afternoon sir. We are travelling and need somewhere to sleep this evening. Can you advise us if there is a hotel or lodging where we can rent for a night?"

The storekeeper stood and pinched his chin while he thought. Finally he spoke.

"Go beyond the Mill and travel another kilometer. You will see a farm house with several buildings behind it. Go there and ask for Mrs. De Groot. She does rent out rooms to travelers such as you. I caution you that she will not tolerate smoking, drinking or noise."

"Sir we are Mennonites and do not partake of alcohol or tobacco. We need to leave early tomorrow to complete our travels. Thank you for the help."

They reached the farmhouse after another 30 minutes. Aaron stopped the horse and buggy and went to the front door. He rapped on the door. It was opened by a large woman with a beaming smile.

"Good evening. We are travelling to the border and require a room to sleep this evening. We will leave early in the morning. We do not need food. We need a place to wash and then sleep."

The woman looked closely at him.

"Tell the other one to come. Let me see him."

Aaron walked back to the buggy and called to Jakob to come and meet the woman.

After introducing themselves they briefly described the purpose of their trip. Mrs. de Groot smiled and asked them in.

"I have a room with two mattresses I can let you have tonight. I will charge you five florin. Come and I will show you the room."

Aaron and Jakob climbed the creaking stairs to the second floor. Mrs. de Groot opened the door of a large room. On each side of the room were mattresses on the floor and an old oak chair under the front window. A small oil lamp sat on a bureau near the chair.

"This room is fine for us." Aaron said. He removed a wallet and removed the money to pay the woman.

"I am heating fresh milk to have before I sleep. Would you men like some? I am sure you must be tired and hungry after riding all day."

"That is most kind. Yes we will have milk with you. First we will bring in our bag from the buggy and tether the horse. I will return."

Aaron left and Jakob followed the woman. She showed him into a dark parlor with two oil lamps burning. Within minutes Aaron returned with the little baggage they had brought with them.

"I believe we will reach the family tomorrow morning. It has been a ride without difficulties"

"Aaron it is much easier ride here than we have in Canada. We have hills and turns and streams to cross. Here the land is flat and easy to travel."

Mrs. de Groot returned with a tray containing three large cups of steaming milk. She asked them the purpose of their trip. Jakob spoke and told her of his curiosity and the travels to Holland from Canada. He spoke for a long while without any interruption. Finally Mrs. De Groot asked the name of the family they were visiting near the border. Jakob pulled out the list of names and showed it to her. She studied it and sat back staring of into the distance.

"I know that family. When I was young we lived close to them. They are a deeply religious and hard working people. Do you speak both Dutch and German? Many on the border speak only German. It would help you."

Jakob responded "Yes I do speak some German."

"If you leave early in the morning you will be at their farm by noon. Now I must finish and retire for the night. Is there anything more I can get you?"

Jakob and Aaron thanked her and left to prepare for the night's sleep. They were soon both in a dead sleep.

Chapter 69

As Jakob and Aaron were preparing to leave that morning, Mrs. de Groot knocked on their door.

"Boys I have made a small package of food for you to take with you. There are no more cafes between here and your destination. It is just simple food of sausage and sandwiches."

Jakob thanked her for her kindness and reached into his pocket for money to pay her for the food.

"No. I will not accept your money. Go now and be safe on your trip. Remember you will be very close to Germany and there are many bad things happening there. You must be careful."

"But this is The Netherlands" Jakob replied.

"Some Germans do not recognize the border or the differences between our countries. You must be careful. The area to which you go has seen some problems from Hitler's Nazi soldiers."

"We will be very careful," Aaron responded.

They exchanged farewells and as they were pulling away Mrs. de Groot called to them

"Please stop and visit when you return from the visit. I will be interested to hear of your visit with the family."

Jakob and Aaron waved and drove away on the loosely graveled road. It was a lonely trip. There were no farmers working in fields and they did not encounter any other travelers. After almost 2 hours, Aaron tapped Jakob on the shoulder to awaken Jakob who had been sleeping. He pointed to a speck in the distance that was approaching them. Soon it became distinguishable.

Within minutes a 1930's BMW motorbike with an attached sidecar skidded to a halt in front of their horse scattering the loose gravel. The driver wore a German Army uniform and had a rifle slung over his shoulder. Another soldier sat on the rear seat behind him, also with a rifle over his shoulder. In the sidecar was a black uniformed SS officer. They sat stationary and in silence for a good minute. The SS officer climbed from the sidecar and walked to Aaron's side of the buggy.

"Greetings, Dutchman. Where are you going?"

Jakob and Aaron looked past the SS officer and saw the soldier on the rear of the bike had removed the rifle from his shoulder and was holding it in a firing position.

"We are going to visit relatives. I do not understand why you are here or asking these questions. You are in The Netherlands and this is Dutch soil. You have crossed our border."

"Helmut, did you cross the border? Did you make a mistake? Are we lost? There are no checkpoints. If we are in The Netherlands then we are here in error. I thought we were still in Germany" he sarcastically said to the driver.

The soldiers on the bike laughed.

The SS officer stared at Aaron and then turned his look to Jakob. He stood looking at Jakob who was wearing his wide brimmed Mennonite hat and farm clothes.

"I demand to know what you have in that buggy."

"We have our clothing. That is all."

The SS officer turned and ordered the soldier on the rear of the bike to search the buggy.

Again Aaron protested.

"I suggest you remain quiet. We will be finished soon. What is the name of the relatives you are visiting?"

Jakob spoke in Dutch. "The name is Loonstra"

The SS officer turned to Aaron. "Tell him to address me in German."

"He is Fries and has had little education. He cannot speak German. He lives on the north coast. Very few people there speak or know German. He told you the relatives we are visiting are called Loonstra."

The soldier completed looking through the buggy and whispered something to the SS officer who nodded. Together they turned and walked back to the motorbike. The driver started the bike and they continued in the direction Jakob and Aaron had come from.

"Jakob I fear something is wrong. They are not heading back toward the border but further away from it. Their behavior is strange. Let us proceed quickly now. We are close to the farm."

Aaron sped the horse along the rough track. After 30 minutes they encountered freshly plowed fields. Off in the distance was a white and green farm house with large grain silos.

"Jakob that is the Loonstra farm. We are here."

They turned off the track and went through a gate onto a dirt path that led to the front of the house. As they approached a young man dressed in traditional Mennonite clothing started to walk towards them. He waved.

Within minutes Aaron stopped the buggy in front of the nearest barn. They dismounted. Aaron stayed back. Jakob jumped down from the buggy and went to the young man.

"I am Jakob Klassen from Canada."

"I am your nephew Pieter Loonstra. We have been anxiously awaiting your arrival. Come let me take you into meet our family."

As they walked slowly toward the house, Jakob noticed the young man casting furtive looks around at the fields and the other barns. He seemed nervous.

"This is turning out to be a strange morning" thought Jakob.

Chapter 70

The Loonstra family was waiting for Jakob and Aaron. Introductions were made. The farm house was large with huge windows that overlooked the front of the farm, the barns and the utility sheds. Jakob was impressed.

Lars Loonstra invited Jakob and Aaron to sit while refreshments were fetched. They sat and Jakob talked about Canada, Isaac and Jakob's quest to learn more of the family and relatives. Lars listened intently. When Jakob had finished Lars spoke. He described the days years ago when Isaac was still in Europe. He spoke of the hardships for many who had left Prussia for Germany and Holland. He spoke of the sicknesses that had plagued them and the hard times many encountered.

"Is this why Isaac left for America?" Jakob asked.

Lars looked at him and paused for a long while before answering.

"Since he was a small boy, Isaac spoke of travelling to the new world and an easy life with a beautiful wife and a large farm of his own. It was his dream and no one could change his mind. The Klassen family lived near here in a small hamlet. One day we found that Isaac had left for America. We were never told why he left so quickly and without a ceremony. The Klassen families were strong members in the church."

Jakob was perplexed. He did not understand. All the relatives avoided his direct questions. Something sinister must be hidden. It was no coincidence that all of them were evasive in their answers. He tried again.

"Lars I have never been able to learn of the past. It seems that no one wishes to help me. I do not wish to create trouble but I have this strong desire to find out about the past and the Klassen families."

"After Isaac left for America, the Klassen families moved from the district. Some travelled to the south of Holland and some completely disappeared. We do not know where they settled or even if any are still alive today. There has been war and other upheavals in Europe. Many have lost contact. Come, let us get you and Aaron settled for your stay with us and then we will have supper."

Jakob and Aaron stopped to talk at the buggy.

"Aaron I do not believe I am being told the truth. Everyone I have spoken with has a similar story. It is if they agreed on what to say before I arrived here."

Back inside the house Jakob and Aaron freshened up and changed clothes for the dinner.

Lars and his wife, Greta had sat in the parlor waiting for their return.

"We will wait and our daughter and her husband will soon join us. Pieter has gone to bring them to meet you. You will then have met the whole of the Loonstra family. Tomorrow we will take you around the farm and into the market."

Pieter entered with a tall blonde woman and a dark haired muscular man.

"Jakob this is my Anna and her husband Leopold. They own the farm behind us. It borders with Germany."

Jakob and Aaron shook hands with Leopold. Talk returned to the trip from Canada and about Canada. Eventually Jakob asked about being a neighbor with Germany. Leopold looked at Lars and the talk fell silent. Jakob was embarrassed.

"Come Greta and I have prepared a dinner to welcome you."

The men left the parlor and were seated at the large table in a dining room off the kitchen. Large platters of pork, beef and lamb were laid on the table. Fresh breads, juices and milk were placed in the centre.

Before the meal Lars lead them all in a prayer of thanks and blessed the food.

Jakob's conflict arose again. He wondered how they could be so pious but at the same time be deceptive in answering his questions to the long sought out question of his ancestry and the secrets they knew.

Chapter 71

Around the table there was a lot of chatter. Lars and Leopold discussed the upcoming crop season while the women spoke of social gatherings with other church ladies. Pieter spoke little. Every now and then Leopold would ask Jakob questions about farming in Canada. Eventually Lars asked him to tell them all of the trip from Canada and the events along the way.

Jakob spoke of the crossing of the Atlantic and their experiences in Paris. The table fell silent as the group listened.

As they continued to eat and talk, Pieter left the table and headed to the kitchen. Jakob frowned and watched him depart. He thought no more of it and returned to the discussion.

Lars enquired about the health of Wilhelm. Having heard of the Paris adventure he also asked whether Anke was fine. Greta was concerned and asked several questions. Jakob assured them that Anke had been given excellent treatment and was fine.

"Now you that know us we expect you to return for a stay with your bride. We wish to meet her."

As Jakob turned to speak to Lars he noticed Pieter outside through one of the large windows. He was on his way to the nearest barn and was carrying a white box. Jakob watched him enter the barn. Minutes later he emerged without the white box. Jakob said nothing. Pieter rejoined them and sat at his place at the table. Again Jakob observed the furtive glances passed from

Pieter to Leopold and Lars. Jakob now knew that something else was taking place.

He excused himself from the table.

"If you will excuse me I feel a little ill and tired after the last two days travel. I will go for a short walk."

Aaron looked at him. "I will join you."

"No. I will just walk a little by myself. I need to think and breathe some fresh air."

Jakob took his jacket and walked out of the house. He circled the house looking around for anything strange. Finally he walked to the barn that Pieter had entered only a few minutes earlier. The barn was old and musty. It smelled strongly of the animals that had been kept in it over the winter months. The rough hewn walls were hung with various farm implements. Jakob looked up at the rafters. Some steel meat hooks hung from them along with coils of rope and fencing wire.

"A typical barn" he thought.

He looked around for the white box he had seen Pieter carrying. The light conditions were poor by good enough to illuminate a box that size. He looked up at the rafters again. There was a storage area but no stairs or ladder. This was strange.

Jakob returned to the house and joined the others.

"Are you feeling any better?" asked Lars.

"Yes"

As he sat drinking a sweet black coffee he was aware that Pieter was watching him surreptitiously.

Later he asked Lars where they could leave there horse and buggy. Lars advised them to take the buggy to the barn and leave the horse in the paddock next to the house. Jakob motioned to Aaron to join him. Once outside he told Aaron what he had seen and how Pieter's actions were not normal.

"Jakob we are all sworn to be truthful. We will go now and speak with Lars and Leopold. I too feel that something is not right here."

As they entered the parlor, Lars and Leopold who were deep in talk immediately stopped.

"Thank you. We have placed the buggy in the barn and put the horse in the paddock next to the house. There is something that we would like to speak of. Since we arrived we have noticed things. Pieter is watching us and seems distracted. I saw him taking a white box to the barn. It is nowhere to be found. When we are present people are acting differently. Are we unwelcome here?"

Pieter hung his head. Lars and Leopold exchanged looks. Leopold spoke.

"Jakob and Aaron. You must understand that these are times of great uncertainty. Our neighbor Germany is creating unrest in countries other than The Netherlands. They do not respect agreements that have been made. They have started persecuting Jews and others. Children are being sent away on the kindertransportes to England. The Nazi's are imposing a life that is not correct or normal. They are right next to us. We fear that we could be next."

Jakob and Aaron listened. After some minutes Jakob recalled the events earlier that day with the SS officer and soldiers. A look of panic showed on their faces but none more so than on Pieter's.

Leopold spoke. "This is not good news. For them to cross the border armed and in the company of an SS officer is indeed serious. We, the Dutch Mennonites are committed to helping Jewish families and those who the Germans are mistreating. Many of the people you have visited are committed to this cause. Our church in The Netherlands supports this action."

Pieter's hands were slightly shaking.

"What is here for them?" Jakob asked.

"I wish we could tell you all. It is best you do not know as the Germans have many ways to make people give away secrets."

"That is a decision we will make. You can trust us completely."

Lars and Leopold huddled together.

"Pieter take Jakob and Aaron to the kitchen. We must speak privately."

Pieter left them and returned to Leopold and Lars. Soon Pieter returned.

"Please come back to the room. Lars wishes to speak to you."

When they were all seated Lars spoke. "I must have your complete agreement that anything we discuss will never leave this house or be told to anyone."

Jakob and Aaron agreed.

"We told you that we Dutch Mennonites are committed to assisting those fleeing the Nazis. We are part of a group helping shelter these souls. Jakob what you saw was Pieter taking food to some who are hiding in our barn. They are scared for their lives. Leopold and I believe that the SS patrol you saw earlier is looking for them. They are Leopold's neighbors on the German side. It is the family Rosenberg. They keep a small farm as a hobby. He is Professor Julius Rosenberg. He is a Professor of Political Science at the University of Utrecht. He has spoken out against Hitler and the Fascist regime. The Germans are pursuing him. Pieter is very upset. He had planned to marry the Professor's adopted daughter. She is not Jewish and is from one of the orphanages that closed. The professor is hidden in the barn with his wife and 2 daughters. We hope to assist them escape to Amsterdam and on to England. This is a brilliant man and the Germans must never capture him. They will imprison and possibly execute him without any trial."

Jakob and Aaron listened in silence.
" I have an idea. On Sunday we will start our trip back to Leiden.
We can take the family in our buggy. It will be dangerous."

"Jakob, that is indeed a kind offer. Tomorrow I will go to the border where cars and trucks cross. There are Dutch soldiers there. One of the soldiers is a friend I grew up with. I will ask if they will escort you for a distance from this border. Pieter check outside. If it is safe then please go to the Professor and tell him of this."

Pieter sauntered out of the house and pretended to be looking after Aaron's horse. All the while he was alert and watching for hidden eyes. When he considered it safe he went to the barn. Before entering he looked around again.

"Professor Julius" he called. "I have news for you. I will come up to the loft. Please stay hidden. If I am caught I can tell them a tale of retrieving a tool from there."

There, partially covered under the straw bales were the Professor, his wife and his two daughters aged twelve and nineteen. Pieter crawled in beside them.

"We have relatives visiting. Tomorrow they will return by horse and buggy to Leiden and then to Amsterdam. Leopold is arranging for Dutch soldiers to accompany them part of the way. You must be ready early in the morning. They are going to take you in their buggy. Please be ready. The buggy is here in the barn. We will get you in there and hidden while it is in the barn."

The Professor stared at Pieter.

"Why are they taking this risk? We are a wanted Jewish family. If we are caught we will all be taken back to Germany and maybe executed. You will all be punished I am sure."

"We made a commitment and we will keep it. I will also marry your daughter when it is safe."

The Professor laughed a small laugh. "You young people. You are our hope"

"Tomorrow at sunrise Jakob and Aaron will leave. I will pray for your safe deliverance."

Pieter crawled down and left the barn. As he did so he saw a flash of light near the dirt track that ran to the farm house from the road. Someone on a bike was there and watching the farm. Pieter walked back to the barn. He called to the Professor to warn him. He then took a large bundle of hay and went to fed Aaron's horse.

He hoped this would disguise the reason for his visit to the barn. He looked back to the road. There was no one there.

Pieter entered the house. He ran to the parlor and up to Lars bedroom. He shook him awake.

"We are being watched. There was someone on the dirt track by the road. I don't think they saw anything. We must warn Jakob and Aaron.

They all gathered in the large front room. The oil lamps were extinguished and they watched from the large windows. They sat for over an hour looking for any movement or light. When satisfied the person was gone they retired for the night.

Chapter 72

They awoke to a pale and watery dawn. A fine misty rain was falling. Jakob and Aaron stood looking from the parlor windows while drinking their coffee.

Aaron spoke. "This weather will make the trip slow. Maybe we should wait and see if it improves. I will not wish to delay too long."

Jakob replied"Leopold has already left to speak to the soldiers at the Border near Enschede. I am expecting he will return with company. Accompany me for a short walk. I am concerned that we may encounter problems. I am going to walk to the end of the track to the area where Pieter thought he saw someone."

Jakob and Aaron took their jackets and left the farmhouse for the walk to the road. As they walked along Jakob noticed something lying in the grass off the side of the track. He stopped and walked into the grass to inspect it. He bent down and picked up. It was a wet and crumpled piece of a German newspaper. Jakob carefully unfolded it. He looked at the date. It was from the previous day. Now there was no doubt in his mind that someone had been there watching the house. He folded the paper and put it in his breast pocket. They continued their walk to the road. It was deserted.

When walking back, they stopped at the point where they had found the paper. Jakob looked toward the barn. He could clearly make out the open entranceway into the barn and also the front of the farmhouse. If the person spying on the house had been there for a while it was more than possible Pieter's trip to the barn with the food had been observed. This caused a serious concern to Jakob.

They returned to the house and were speaking with Pieter when Leopold arrived with two Dutch soldiers on horseback. The soldiers were armed. Leopold entered the house. The soldiers followed, removing their helmets as they entered.

Jakob told Leopold and the soldiers of their find beside the track and took out the paper for the soldiers to examine.

"It is best you leave immediately. The soldiers will accompany you until you are far from the border. I need to do work in the fields today. I will go to the barn pretending I need equipment and will advise the Professor to get his family into the buggy. Pieter you will accompany me. You will assist in concealing the family and then come with me. We will take equipment to repair the gate to the road. We will be able to see if Jakob and Aaron get followed. If this happens I will take our fastest horse and ride to warn them."

Quick introductions were made. The soldiers left and went to their horses. Aaron fetched his horse from the paddock. He took the horse to the barn to couple it to the buggy. With the family hidden in the buggy it was considerably heavier. He looked in. The family could not be seen. Pieter had done an excellent job in concealing them.

Jakob walked back to the house. He and Aaron profusely thanked Greta for the hospitality and then they returned to start their journey.

As they were preparing to leave, one of the Dutch soldiers called him.

"Jakob. We will ride a way behind you. If we are too close it will look obvious that we are guarding you and the buggy. This will only arouse suspicions. We will not be far behind but close enough to assist should you be accosted."

They started their journey in the cold misty rain. On the road Jakob turned to look for the soldiers. They were nowhere to be seen. He wondered if they were behind them. He increased their travelling speed. All around them remained quiet.

After about an hour the rain stopped and the mist dissipated. Jakob again looked back and again there was no sign of the soldiers.

They continued their ride until they reached the home of Mrs. de Groot.

"We will stop here. I will speak to Mrs. de Groot and ask if she can provide a meal. I think we are now a safe distance from the Border."

Jakob climbed down from the buggy and knocked at the door. Mrs. de Groot answered. She beamed a smile upon seeing it was Jakob.

"Quickly. Come in. After you left we had a German patrol here. They were nasty. It is wrong for them to be here. I have sent a message to our Guard."

Jakob explained the situation and inquired whether it was possible to stop for a meal as he did not want to do that in any of the Villages. Mrs. de Groot thought about his request for a few minutes.

"Yes it is possible. Please ask the family to come immediately."

Jakob returned to the horse and buggy. He called into the rear of the buggy.

"We are stopping here for a meal. You must go to the house without delay."

There was shuffling and boxes and items started moving in the buggy. Aaron was at the front to assist them down. This was the first time Jakob and Aaron had seen the family. Aaron took the youngest girl and swung her down to the ground. She let out an excited squeal. He laughed.

When they were safely in the house Jakob and Aaron introduced themselves to the Professor. He was a slight man with thin brown hair and a moustache. He wore thick glasses with a heavy black frame.

"I do not know how to thank you for this help. We were doomed if we had stayed in Germany. Leopold had said you are taking us to Amsterdam. I have a suggestion. Will we pass by Utrecht? I have friends there. He also teaches at the University there. We are very close friends. I am sure we will be able to stay with them until we can arrange an onward trip to England."

"Yes we will pass close to Utrecht as I am taking Jakob to the area near Leiden. It will not be a problem to stop there."

The Professor looked relieved. He went to his wife and spoke with her and explained the plan. When he finished she looked across at Jakob and Aaron and smiled.

Mrs. de Groot prepared a large tureen of soup, some cuts of cold meats and fresh breads. The family ate. When they were finished the Professor approached her.

"I wish to pay you for this fine meal."

"No. You must keep your money to help you with the future travels you need to make in order to take your family to safety. I am good friends with the Loonstra family. We look after each other's interests."

"That is very kind of you. I hope one day we can help you. I wish that we will be able to visit again but under different circumstances."

With the meal finished and everyone more relaxed, Jakob, Aaron and the family climbed back into the buggy to continue the trip. It was decided that having to disguise their presence was no longer required.

The weather had changed. A warm sun and gentle breeze greeted them as they travelled on toward Utrecht.

They rode along in silence. The professor came and sat with Jakob and Aaron.

"In Utrecht I will direct you to our friend's home. It is an easy location to reach. I do not know how we can ever repay you for this kindness. We had to leave Germany in a hurry. All of our possessions are still there. It was Leopold who found out the German patrols were looking for us. I owe him our family's lives."

"Professor. I have witnessed many things in my life that made no sense." Jakob said. He then described to the Professor the events he had witnessed in the last war and the hostilities that had arisen in the former Berlin, Ontario.

The Professor was quiet for several minutes. "We humans need to find a way to live together. Nothing will ever be achieved by wars and feuds over religion and money."

They continued to make small talk until they reached the outskirts of Utrecht.

The Professor gave directions to their friend's home. He jumped down from the buggy and knocked at their door. It was opened by a middle aged serious looking man who beamed when he recognized the Professor.

The Professor entered into an animated conversation. The man who answered the door cast glances at the buggy. He went inside and returned with his wife. She ran to the buggy.

"Thank you. Thank you." She cried to Aaron and Jakob.

"Rosenbergs. You are welcome to stay. Please come with me."

The family took what meager possessions they had and proceeded to the house.

After final words Jakob and Aaron continued on to Leiden. They arrived very late that evening at the farm. Aaron spent the night before continuing back to Amsterdam in the morning.

Chapter 73

Weeks passed by. Jakob assisted Henk at the farm. Anke immersed herself in food shopping and helping Julia. Wilhelm's recovery had progressed well.

In late May, Jakob returned from the farm to spend time with Anke.

"Anke it is time for me to make the arrangements for our return home. I shall go this week to the travel company and make the plans."

Anke sat quietly and finally said "Jakob let us go for a walk to the park nearby. We can talk there."

They walked the few minutes to the park and sat on a long bench. There were some ducks swimming in the murky waters of the pond. Large willow like trees swayed in the gentle breeze. They sat and watched as cyclists rode by and others strolled along arm in arm.

"Jakob I have something I wish to talk about. While you have been working at the farm I have been able to think about many things without the influence of you or others. Do not be offended by what I am going to say.

I have thought about you a lot. I understand now, more than ever, your feelings and conflict. Living here in the city has exposed me to many new things and a different way of life. I understand how you see this life and why you question the teachings of our church.

I have come to appreciate life here in Amsterdam. The life we lived back at the farm in Ontario was for a time in the past. New ways of doing things will be introduced and our faith will need to adapt.

I see nothing shameful about living a life that uses these changes."

Jakob stared at her. "I am surprised. I never believed I would ever hear that from you. Anke, we must return and look after our farming business."

"No Jakob. Not too soon. I have never enjoyed my life like this. I love Julia and Wilhelm. I like to shop for the foods and to walk the canals and to look at all the different flowers. This is a heaven to me. Please can we stay a little longer? It is too late for any spring planting. It is now the growing season. We will return in time for the fall harvesting. I will be happy if you agree."

Jakob thought about Anke's sudden change.

"I will speak to Henk. I am sure I can stay and help with the farm. It is a place and work I am happy with. Yes, we will stay. I will go to the travel company and plan our return trip for the fall."

Anke jumped to her feet. "Jakob I am so happy you agree"

Jakob stood and they leisurely walked to the small café where he had played his music. They sat outside on the sidewalk and ordered coffee. As they were chatting and taking delight in the late morning sun, one of the musicians that Jakob had played with joined them.

"Greetings, Jakob."

"Greetings, Richard. This is my wife Anke. We are making plans for the summer. We will be staying until autumn."

"Jakob I am pleased to hear this. Would you return and play with us. Many of the customers have asked if you will be returning to play with us. Now that it is summer we are only playing on the weekends."

Jakob looked to Anke. She laughed. "Jakob I know this is a passion. Go and play with them."

Jakob invited Richard to sit with them and together they decided upon the plans for Jakob playing.

Jakob and Anke walked back to the house relaxed and happy. Upon returning Anke scuttled off to find Julia. Jakob realized that this was something that had been discussed with Julia long before this morning. Julia quickly walked to him.

"I am so pleased you and Anke have agreed to stay for the summer. Summer in Amsterdam is beautiful. You will both enjoy everything the city offers during the summer months."

"I will need to speak with Henk. He must agree that I am needed at the farm or I will need to seek other jobs."

"I will speak with Wilhelm. He still owns the farm and I know we will find work for you. Maybe we can find work for you closer to our home here."

"Yes. Now that I have completed the visits I no longer need to stay at the farm near Leiden."

Chapter 74

The summer months arrived. Anke and Jakob were content with their life in Amsterdam. Through his many contacts, Wilhelm found a job for Jakob organizing shipments of food abroad. The job was not far from their home. On the weekends Jakob would play his saxophone with the group at the café. Life was relaxed.

Jakob visited the travel company. He took the documents that had been issued in Canada along with their passports and other identity documents that showed their legitimacy as residents in Canada. The clerk at the travel company looked at the documents.

"All appears to be in order. I will check on the dates for the sailings from France to Canada. I should advise you that there have been many who wish to travel to Canada or America to flee what is happening now in certain countries here in Europe. It may be impossible to obtain travel on the dates you request."

"We are able to travel on other dates. We wish to return by the end of August."

The clerk took some large books containing the shipping schedules from a bookshelf behind him. He opened them to August, 1939.

"There is a ship that leaves for Halifax on August 9th. From there you will need to purchase rail tickets. I can check for a berth on the ship should you so desire."

"Yes, please check and if you can make the reservations."

The clerk spent time on the phone calling different offices. Half an hour passed by.

"May I suggest you return after the lunch hour? This will take some time. It seems that most of the sailings are heavily booked. I am awaiting a call from our agent in France."

Jakob agreed and left to find somewhere to eat a light lunch. After an hour he returned to the travel company's office. The clerk was all smiles.

"Yes I was able to secure those dates for your trip. Now we will complete the arrangements and you will make the payment."

Jakob returned early afternoon to the house and shared the information regarding the upcoming travel plans for their return home.

As the days passed, Anke learned more cooking skills from Julia. Soon Anke was preparing most of the meals for the family.

One afternoon, Anke was at home cooking while Aaron was in the parlor reading.

There was a knock at the door. Aaron went to the door. Anke could hear the murmur of voices but was unable to hear the conversation. After 5 minutes Aaron entered the kitchen.

"That was a strange visit. The young man would not identify himself. He handed me this letter. He said it is an urgent matter for Jakob. "

Anke took the letter. It had no identifying information and Jakob's full name was written in heavy black in a cursive script.

"This is indeed strange. We will wait for Jakob to return and he will open it."

Late in the afternoon Jakob came home. He was greeted by Aaron who advised him of the letter. Jakob was curious.

Jakob went to Anke. She had placed the letter in her apron pocket. She removed the letter and handed it to Jakob. He sat at the table and opened it. He gasped out loud. His hands started shaking.

"Jakob what is it? Is something wrong?" She watched as his eyes welled with tears.

Chapter 75

Anke and Aaron stood looking at Jakob in total silence. After some time Anke spoke again.

"Jakob you worry me. What is in that letter? Who is it from? Is it bad news?"

"Anke, for all my life I have believed there were more in my family. Now I have the proof. Here, you may read this."

Jakob handed the letter to Anke. Aaron moved to her side to read with her.

99 Fredrickstrasse

Munich

Greetings Jakob Klassen

Firstly let me introduce myself. I am Josef Klassen, the brother of your father. I have learned of your visits to several families and the questions you have been asking. I would very much enjoy a visit with you and to assist you in your pursuit.

There are some details I will be able to share with you. I was born several years after Isaac departed for America so my knowledge is based on what I heard from my elderly parents. There was another brother who was a year older than Isaac. He died a number of years ago.

It would be a pleasure to meet Isaac's son. At the time you receive this letter I will be in New York City on business. I will return to Munich on August 22nd. I strongly advise you not to visit me in

Germany. There has been unrest and it is not safe. The Nazis are treating foreigners and others in horrible ways. I propose we meet when I am on one of my trips to New York. I travel there several times each year, though I am not sure for how much longer. I am an old man now and tire easily.

Please send me your address in Canada and I will contact you to make arrangements for a visit.

Kind regards

Josef Klassen

Anke set the letter down on the table. She could sense the impact this had on Jakob.

"Jakob this is good news. You were correct. There were other family members. It will be our duty to welcome Josef to our home in Canada. You must be happy now. Your trip has proven to be correct."

"Anke I am concerned. In the letter Josef states he is old. I must speak with him before anything happens to him. I will go to Germany to see him."

Both Aaron and Anke shouted their objections simultaneously.

"No Jakob. You have been told many times that it is not safe for you to travel to Germany, especially as a Mennonite. Hitler's thugs are arresting and persecuting those of different faiths." Anke replied. "We have tickets to return to Canada. We will be back in Canada before Josef returns to Munich. We cannot contact him while he is in New York as we do not know where he is. We must allow him to visit at a future time when he is in

America. It is a short trip from New York City to our farm in Canada."

"Tomorrow I will go and change the dates for our trip. I have waited many years to discover I have family. This is too important for me. I cannot leave here now I have this knowledge."

Aaron spoke. "Jakob do not go. Your decision is not of good judgment. It is a decision of emotion. When we visited the Loonstra family you observed how the Germans are behaving and the fear of the people. The Rosenbergs left all their possessions and the life they lived behind them and fled. Jakob you cannot go on such a dangerous trip. What will Anke do? Will she go with you?"

"No Aaron. I will not go to Germany."

Jakob persisted. "I will go. My mind is made up. I know the danger. I will dress in clothing other than our traditional wear. I will visit at the end of August and return early September. We will then leave immediately for our return trip. I will go back to Canada with my thoughts and mind at ease. This is what we came here to find, Anke. I cannot leave now I have this knowledge."

Aaron scowled and left to speak with Wilhelm of this development.

Aaron walked outside to the rear of the house where there was a small stable. There was a sweet smell in the air. The tall grasses swayed as the gentle winds caressed them.

At the entrance to the stable, Wilhelm was attending to a horses hoof. He had a hammer and was replacing a shoe. He stopped when he saw Aaron approaching.

"Son is something wrong? Your look betrays you. What has happened? Is someone hurt? You do not seem happy. You are a normally happy. What is wrong?"

Aaron and Wilhelm sat on stools made from sawn off tree trunks. Aaron relayed the content of Josef's letter and Jakob's reckless plan to travel to visit Josef in Germany.

Wilhelm sat quietly not speaking. He stared into the distance. When he spoke it was harsh.

"Jakob must learn. There are things he should leave alone. This will bring trouble. There are reasons no one wants to talk about the past with him. Is he not realizing any of this? Josef is no good. The family did not accept him easily. I have met him. Jakob must be prevented from going to see him. He abandoned the faith as a young man. He has a bad reputation. This is indeed a very bad development. He cannot rely on Josef to help him if he encounters trouble in Germany. Josef is a selfish man. He cares only about himself. I believe the reason he wants contact with Jakob is selfish. Maybe he is thinking of being able to stay with them in Canada in the event of a war. It is possible that Josef realizes that Anke and Jakob have no children and wants the farm should something happen to them. This is an evil man. We cannot allow this trip. I will go and speak to Jakob alone. We must not let Anke know of all this. I fear that Jakob and Anke are moving further apart. I see many things. I pretend not to notice. Anke is our family. We must do everything to protect her. I do not understand how Jakob is unable to see these things. He had good parents. It is possible he has the same bad spirit lurking in him as Josef. I will try to stop this but I think it will be impossible. Jakob has spent years of effort and excessive money in pursuing this.

Aaron please return to the house and tell Jakob I wish to see him alone. Stay and comfort Anke."

Chapter 76

Wilhelm sat talking to Jakob for hours trying to dissuade him from making the trip. He did not reveal the information he had pertaining to Josef. He was concerned that if he discussed Josef then this may further fuel Jakob's plan. It was apparent that Jakob's resolve to travel to Germany was final.

Wilhelm was angry. Because of his deep faith and commitment he could not let that anger control him. He stopped speaking and looked at Jakob. The expression on Jakob's face was blank. He was too occupied with new thoughts since the letter had arrived. It was almost as if he had heard nothing Wilhelm had said.

Wilhelm returned to the stable and lifted the horse's hoof to continue his work. Jakob left to return to the house.

That evening as they sat for prayer and dinner there was a pall of silence at the table. No one spoke. Anke excused herself and ran to their room in tears. Wilhelm looked at Julia and shook his head. After some time Julia left the table and, as a ruse, took some plates to the kitchen and then quickly proceeded to Anke. She knocked and entered the room. Anke was kneeling beside the bed with her head buried into the sheet.

"Anke it seems Jakob will not be convinced that it is wrong to make this trip. He is stubborn. We can only hope and pray that he goes safely and returns in time for you to return to the farm in Canada."

"Julia, my grief is much deeper than just the trip. I have lost trust. Jakob has ignored so many warnings. We have been excommunicated from our congregation. He has changed to a person I do not know anymore. I have failed as a wife. I tried to obey and support us. I feel empty inside. Our life is too hard. Jakob has made it hard. It is not the farming or money. It is Jakob's persistent pursuit of this hunt for relatives. He has become obsessed with it. He doesn't see the damage that has resulted. What am I to do now? I have lost a child, ignored Johannes in his aging, and foregone the observance of the rules of the church. I am in trouble. I can no longer do these things."

"Let him go on this trip. You will stay safely with us. We shall seek guidance from the Elders. Wilhelm and I love and respect you. We will help you. It will not be easy. I will speak to Wilhelm when we are alone and tell him of your hurt. I suspect he has already seen it. He is a smart and compassionate man."

Julia left Anke and joined Wilhelm in the parlor. There was an uncomfortable mood in the air. Aaron stood and announced "I will walk outside for a while before sleeping. I need time to think alone."

There were just the three of them left in the parlor. Wilhelm was reading scriptures. Julia continued some broidering. Jakob sat watching them. No one spoke.

Finally Julia put down her work. "Jakob you are making one of the biggest mistakes of your life. You could easily be detained or worse and be killed by the Nazis. You have a beautiful wife who has been loyal and kind to you. Why do you persist with this dream of yours? What will come of it? Surely you now see that there is little to gain by continuing with this foolishness. Please think about this. I ask for all of us. We want happiness for you and Anke. This is causing much unhappiness and sorrow. If you must go to Germany then go alone and return quickly. I do not believe you can subject Anke to any more of this. She is very disturbed. You are her husband and should be ashamed for how you have treated her and brought her to this sad condition. I will pray for you but not with you. You have disappointed my family. Shame is on you, Jakob."

Jakob stood and stormed from the room. He slammed the door as he left the house. He did not return that night.

Chapter 77

Mid-morning the next day Jakob returned to the house. Upon entering Julia confronted him. His clothes smelled strongly of cigarette smoke and there was a strong presence of alcohol. His hair was a mess and his eyes red.

"Jakob you cannot run from the truth. I spoke to you from my heart. We all wish for you to find a peace and live in happiness. You are making your own problems. Come in and have something to eat and drink. We will talk later. Did you sleep? You do not look well. Where did you go?"

"I went to the café to see my friends. We played music all night. I have decided that I am going to Munich. This I must do. Anke can stay with you. Later today I will go to the travel company and make the changes."

"Jakob please think about what this trip has resulted in. The relatives you met have hardly provided you any information. How do you know that Josef in Munich will provide more?"

"I was never told of Isaac having any brothers. There is something in the past that I must find out. Why is everyone withholding this from me?"

"I believe you are being protected from information that may be harmful. The relatives you met are not bad people. I think that they only mean to shelter you from whatever happened in the past. Please leave it alone. Do not change your plans. Return to Canada on the dates you have planned. I am superstitious and believe that to change travel dates can result in tragedy. Do not take my fear lightly."

"Julia those who travel often change plans frequently. Your superstition is not founded on fact."

"We Mennonites are all superstitious. In the bible we can read of happenings and superstition. Do not dismiss this, Jakob."

Jakob finished eating and climbed the stairs to their room. Anke was not there. He had not seen her in the house since his return. He guessed she had gone with Aaron to the market. He washed and put new clothes on for his trip to the travel company.

Upon arriving at the travel company the clerk welcomed him.

"Welcome back. Is everything correct with the details for your passage?"

"Yes. There is a family matter that has arisen. I must go to Germany and need to leave the beginning of September. I will also require a rail ticket to Munich."

The clerk again fetched the books containing the shipping schedules.

"The soonest a ship leaves is September 10th. Shall I change your bookings?"

"Yes that will be fine."

Shortly thereafter Jakob left with a rail ticket and modified dates for the trip home.

At the house Anke had returned from the market with Aaron. They had purchased fresh chicken and a variety of meats. Julia was busy packing the items away. Anke ignored Jakob.

Wilhelm came in the back door of the house. He looked at the scene and walked by to the parlor where he sat down to look at a newspaper that Aaron had bought.

The news contained in the paper alluded to the desperate situation that was roiling through Germany. There was open speculation about the goals of the Nazi regime and their ultimate ambitions.

Wilhelm re-entered the kitchen and thrust the newspaper at Jakob.

"This may make you to seriously listen to the advice you have been given. There is nothing good happening there. How can you ignore all of this?"

Wilhelm had finally let his anger surface. "Anke will stay here."

Chapter 78

Summer was passing. Jakob remained in Amsterdam working at the job Wilhelm had helped him find. Anke continued to enjoy the Dutch way of life. Occasionally she and Jakob would spend time walking and visiting attractions. It was clear that their lives had changed. Anke had lost the enthusiasm she had once possessed.

They sat on the wall of an arched bridge over a canal. Barges of all sizes slowly glided by underneath. It was early afternoon.

"Anke we must speak of my visit to Josef in Munich. I will leave on August 29th. I have purchased a rail ticket. I will return after meeting Josef. I will only stay a few days. We shall then proceed to take our ship to Halifax."

"Jakob, it seems that you will do what you want to do. You have become selfish. I can do nothing to stop you. Go and make this visit. I hope when you return we never speak of this again and that the conflicted beliefs you have are resolved. You are not the kind and caring man I knew and married. You make my life sad. It is the life here in Amsterdam and the people I have met that keep me alive."

"Anke, we will return to the farms and the life we had. I have started to miss the way of life we had there. I will make this final visit. There will be no more."

Anke looked at him. She could no longer tell if he was telling the truth or simply saying something to make her calm. She slid off the rough stone wall and started to head back to the house. Jakob frowned and jumped down.

They walked in silence. On occasion various neighbors Anke had met would pass them by. Brief greetings were exchanged.

That night as they all sat for dinner, Jakob spoke. "I will leave for Munich the day after tomorrow. I will arrive in Munich on the 22nds of August. I will visit Josef for several days and return here. We will leave September 7th to reach our ship in time."

Wilhelm spoke. "Tomorrow evening we will hold a special ceremony. We will invite members of our clergy and pray after which we will partake of a special dinner."

After dinner Jakob went to their room and selected clothing for the trip. As he laid out his clothing Anke entered.

"Jakob are we to be all right? Will we stay married? What will I do if something happens to you in Germany? I am lonely in my thoughts and they are not good thoughts. I implore you again not to go."

Jakob ignored her pleading.

They slept that night in separate beds. Jakob arose very early. He left the house in search of a newspaper. The articles in the paper Wilhelm had thrust at him days earlier had disturbed him but he would not admit that. He found a kiosk selling papers, cigarettes and candies. He paid for the paper and went to a bench where he sat and read. The front page was splashed with a huge photo of hundreds of soldiers marching the streets of Berlin. They were all in uniform with helmets and carrying rifles over their shoulders. This looked like an army preparing for war. Jakob read the article and then folded the paper and threw it into a trash basket. "There is no point in taking it to the house and creating more problems" he thought.

Throughout the day, Jakob attended to a number of errands and that night enjoyed the ceremonial dinner that Wilhelm had organized. He spoke to the Deacon who cautioned him to take care.

When the evening was over, Jakob and Anke retired to their room.

"We will have breakfast together and then I will leave for the station."

Anke did not sleep easily that night. In the morning they were greeted by the family and all ate breakfast together. After breakfast, Jakob took the small case and started to make his way to the main station for the trip to Munich.

Anke watched from the front windows as he walked away into the foggy morning.

Chapter 79

Jakob walked through the swirling misty fog to the main rail station in Amsterdam. There were very few people on the streets. Jakob found this surprising. The occasional truck passed by him belching black diesel fumes into the air. Several women cyclists rode toward him chattering and laughing. The morning felt strange and lonely to him. Maybe Anke and the others were right. Maybe this was a mistake. He pushed those thoughts from his mind.

At the station he handed his tickets to the conductor at the gate to the platforms. The conductor looked at the tickets and smiled.

"Good morning sir. You will be on the Rhinegold. That is a beautiful train for your long trip."

Jakob had not wanted to travel on such a luxurious train but had found that there were few choices, most of which took longer to reach Munich.

The conductor directed him to the platform for the train. Jakob boarded and was shown his seat by the onboard purser. The coach was elaborate. Jakob settled himself into his seat for the almost twelve hour trip.

With the coach still almost empty, the train pulled away from the station. Jakob had bought some newspapers and picked one up to read. After a couple of hours lunch orders were taken. Jakob decided on roasted pork tenderloin.

The lunch was completed and the train started to slow for the German border. The train came to a halt and sat stationary for several minutes. There was a persistent hum in the carriage from the electrics and other equipment.

As Jakob sat silently, a German official accompanied by 2 soldiers and a rail official started checking passenger's papers. They approached Jakob. He handed his passport and tickets to the official. The official examined them and turned to Jakob

"Why are you going to Munich. This is a passport from Canada. What is your business?"

"I am travelling to visit a relative there."

"What is this relative's name? Where does he live in Munich?"

"His name is Herr Josef Klassen. He is the brother of my deceased father. I am travelling to meet him for the first time."

On hearing the name the official turned to one of the soldiers.

"He is fine to travel. I know of Josef Klassen and his work for The Third Reich."

Jakob was startled to hear this. He stayed silent.

The official handed back the papers and continued to the next passenger.

Jakob sat wondering. What could Josef Klassen, a former Mennonite possibly be doing to assist Hitler and his plans for The Third Reich. He sat quietly realizing how little he knew of the situation he was entering into. He put down his newspapers and stared from the window. What was the situation? Why had no one mentioned the existence of Josef or the other brother? What was being so neatly hidden by all these people he had seen?

As he pondered these questions, a stocky man wearing a fedora and wearing a dark blue woolen overcoat entered the carriage. He removed his coat and sat himself down facing Jakob just two seats way.   Jakob looked at him and did not receive any acknowledgment from the man.

The man took out a book from his jacket and started going through the motions of reading. Jakob positioned his newspaper so as to keep a view of the man. It was clear that Jakob was being watched. After a while Jakob got up and walked to one of the coaches equipped with a kitchen where he ordered a coffee. He turned a counter stool to face back at the direction from which he had come. He sat sipping the coffee. Within minutes the man from the coach crashed into the coach. He walked slowly to the counter and ordered a black coffee. Jakob attempted a conversation. The man grunted and turned away.

Upon returning to his seat, Jakob noticed his suitcase had been moved. He opened it. The contents had been disturbed. There was no doubt in Jakob's mind that he was being closely watched.

Within minutes of his return, the man reentered and went to his seat. This time he sat openly watching Jakob. He made no effort to conceal the fact that he was staring at Jakob.

Throughout the trip Jakob was shadowed when he went to use the washroom or to the kitchen car to buy a drink or sandwich. He was nervous. He had done nothing to draw this attention. What was it in mentioning Josef Klassen's name that had started this?

As the train passed the various stations enroute to Munich, Jakob observed the hundreds of uniformed soldiers on the platforms. All were armed. Finally Jakob was experiencing the oppressive atmosphere of Germany in the upheaval he had been warned of.

The man was joined by another in a black uniform and wearing a full length leather coat. They both spoke to each other in low voices all the time glancing in Jakob's direction.

The black uniformed man approached Jakob.

"I am an SS Officer and require your papers. When your visit to Josef Klassen is complete you will receive these back at the Commandants Office in Munich. Please hand them to me immediately."

Jakob started to question the Officer.

"You will hand them to me. We will ask you the questions. Since you are here for a short visit this will not be an inconvenience. You are in Germany and will obey the German laws. Hand me your papers, please. I will not ask again in a polite manner. It is in your interest to co-operate."

Jakob looked toward the other man. He was gone.

The SS Officer took the papers. "Where you are going these will not be needed."

Chapter 80

As Jakob was about to exit the train, the SS Officer reappeared at the coach doorway.

"Jakob Klassen, I will accompany to the home of Josef Klassen. I need to speak to that man."

They walked to the curb where a black military use Mercedes was parked. The driver ran from the front of the car and opened the rear door upon seeing them approach. The SS Officer gave the address to the driver and they sped off in the direction of Josef's house.

Some 10 minutes later they turned onto a street lined with large houses. The driver parked in front of 99 Fredrikstrasse. It was an imposing grandiose home. Jakob and the SS Officer walked up the wide marble stairs to the front door. The Officer rang the brass bell. Shortly thereafter the door was opened by a beautiful young woman dressed in a maid's uniform. Upon opening the door she stared at Jakob with a look of shock.

"We are here to speak with Josef Klassen." The Officer said.

The maid asked them to wait and left to inform Josef of the visitors at the door.

Minutes later the door opened. Jakob gasped. Standing in front of him was his identical but older image. It was not just similar. Everything appeared the same...the nose, forehead, ears, and cheek bones. Josef was also in shock at the younger version of himself standing and facing him.

The SS Officer smirked. "Yes. It is interesting Herr Josef. I have come to remind you of the unfinished business you have with the Party. The timing and urgency require you to complete this business now. As an incentive, we have confiscated this young man's identity and travel documents. They are to be placed with the local commandant here in Munich. Upon completion of your agreement, the documents will be released back to your relative. Until then he is unable to travel from here. We will be watching all his moves. I urge you to finish your business quickly. Certain members are expressing impatience and question your commitment."

Josef looked uneasy. "I have just returned from America. The documents are signed. There is nothing to worry about."

"I shall advise the appropriate people here and in Berlin. Be prepared to produce all the contracts and supporting documents in the next few days. As I advised you, there is no time to waste. Now I will leave you and your relative, Jakob."

The SS Officer turned and walked back to the waiting car. Josef stood and watched as he climbed into the car and it sped away. He shook his head and turned to Jakob.

"So you are Jakob from Canada. I am pleased to meet you. I assume you received my letter then since you are here standing on my doorstep. I had advised you of the dangers here and not to visit me in Munich. You have now seen and experienced the situation. An honest man cannot make a living without them interfering. Come in please. We will sit and talk."

Jakob entered the palatial home. As he did so, the maid took his case and stood by as he removed his coat. She smiled at Jakob and took his coat. Jakob felt something strange as she smiled at him and looked into his eyes. It was a sudden experience of emotion he had not felt before. She smiled and half turned as she walked away with his coat and case. Jakob continued to look after her as she crossed the huge foyer to place his belongings on a bench at the bottom of the large winding staircase. She then left them.

"Jakob you must be tired and hungry after your trip. Did you travel from Amsterdam today?"

"Yes. I took the Rhinegold train. It was a long trip. I was watched and questioned by the soldiers and that Officer."

"We will go into my study and take a drink. I will ask Sabine, the maid to prepare a light meal for you."

He left to speak with the maid. When he returned they walked through the foyer to a room decorated with an oriental carpet and an oak desk on which there were two telephones. Several high backed leather chairs sat to the side of the desk next to a marble fireplace. Josef motioned to Jakob to take a seat. Josef walked to a cabinet with intricate lead glass doors. He opened the doors and removed a bottle with an amber liquid and two balloon shaped glasses.

"Join me in a fine Cognac, Jakob."

"I am Mennonite. I do not drink alcohol."

Josef roared a loud laugh. "Jakob the world is in upheaval. I stopped any of that silly practice and ideas many years ago. When considering all that is happening here in Europe, a small drink is insignificant. I urge you. Forget the ideals and join in with me."

Jakob thought for a minute and then accepted.

"Tell me of the reason for this trip. I have learned from conversations with others that you have been seeking information on Isaac's family and the relatives of the family. Is that correct? Tell me why you need this information and tell me of the life you had with Isaac in Canada."

Jakob started talking. Josef was intrigued. As Jakob talked Josef poured them another Cognac. It wasn't long before Sabine joined them with a platter of sandwiches and meats. She placed the platter on a table in front of their chairs. As she did so she raised her eyes to make direct contact with Jakob's. A barely perceptible smile cracked at the corner of the lips. There was no doubt she found Jakob of interest. Jakob shifted in his chair unsure whether Josef had seen the interaction.

Jakob continued speaking between snacking on the food Sabine had left for them.

Josef finally spoke. "Tomorrow we will have more time to talk. I have information for you that will answer many of your questions. For now, let us finish. You are tired and I must complete some work for the Nazi Party."

Jakob wanted to ask more of Josef's work and involvement with the Nazis but the effect of the Cognac was hitting him hard. He stood and started from the study. Josef called Sabine to assist Jakob to a guest room.

Sabine appeared and took Jakob by the arm and assisted him up two flights of stairs. She opened the door to the room. In the middle of the room was a huge bed with a white duvet. Heavy lace curtains draped the windows.

Sabine went to the bed and turned back the sheets and moved the pillows into a comfortable sleeping position. She turned to Jakob and looked at him for the longest moment. Jakob sat back on the bed.

"Good night Sabine. I will see you in the morning. Sleep well. Tonight I am very tired and I believe tomorrow will be a big day for me."

Sabine smiled but seemed somewhat saddened to be leaving Jakob.

Chapter 81

Jakob awoke to the aroma of foods cooking and coffee brewing. He arose and took a bath. He dressed and joined Josef in the elegantly appointed dining room. Sunlight streamed in through windows that stretched from floor to the ceiling. Josef was pleased to see him.

"Jakob take a seat. Sabine has prepared a magnificent breakfast. I suspect it is in your honor. We have eggs, different kinds of wurst, smoked thick bacon, fresh baked rolls and my favorite Italian coffee. You will eat like a prince this morning. After we eat I shall take you for a brief stroll. We will buy the newspapers and return. I will then sit with you and tell you of all I know of the Klassens and Isaac."

"I would like that. Yes, I see we have a feast here for breakfast. That is good as I did not have a lot of food yesterday during the trip. The Germans who were watching me made it difficult."

Jakob and Josef continued their breakfast making small talk. From time to time Sabine would enter the room. She always looked to Jakob and flashed him a little smile.

Jakob was convinced that Josef had seen this. He asked Josef "How long has Sabine worked for you?"

"I used to employ her family. Her father kept my grounds and garden and also looked after my cars. Sabine's mother was a chef. She worked at one of the finer restaurants here and also assisted me with the house. There has never been a Mrs. Josef Klassen in my life. I have been too busy with my businesses."

Jakob's curiosity increased. "Josef you must tell me what your business is. This house and all you have. It must be expensive. You must have a good business and trade."

"I have been alone and worked hard all my life. These are the rewards."

With the breakfast finished, they put on their coats and started their walk. As they strolled Josef pointed out the various buildings and told Jakob of their history. They passed neighbors who looked at them in astonishment as both Jakob and Josef looked identical...only they were a young version and an older version. The neighbors were uncertain which of the two to greet.

They reached the bookseller on a street corner. Josef purchased three different papers and handed the bearded man several Reich marks. They then started back to the home.

Upon reaching home they went into the study. Josef buried himself in the papers and did not speak. Finally he lifted his head and said to Jakob "I must stay informed of what is happening. As you know, there is military turmoil all around us. I must know what is happening as this affects my businesses."

After an hour or so had passed, Josef put the papers down "Let's have a coffee and some cake. Then we shall speak."

He called Sabine who entered in minutes. He requested some fresh coffee and cake be served to them in the study.

When the tray was brought in Josef spoke to Sabine. "I request that we have no interruptions. Should we have any visitors please ask them to make an appointment for the afternoon."

Josef stood and poured the coffee into large china cups. He sliced pieces of German Plum Cake. "This is one of Sabine's best cakes. I am particularly fond of this cake."

Jakob tried the cake. The sweet and slightly bitter flavors excited his taste buds.

"Josef, this is indeed a delicious treat. You are a lucky man to have Sabine who can bake like this. We have many traditional foods that are delicious, but none like this."

Come and sit. We will now discuss the Klassen family. Remember I was born after Isaac so some of it is what I have been told."

Chapter 82

Jakob settled into the comfortable leather chair and waited. Josef looked at him.

"Are you sure you want to visit the past? There are things left quiet with those who are now dead. How will you use this information? It is the past. You cannot change things nor will this information assist you in life. It is probably best left buried in the past. There is no one alive who could possibly benefit from knowing these things."

"Josef, all my life I have had a premonition that there has been more to our lives than I was told. Whenever I asked Isaac or Inge for stories of their past they would go quiet. Nothing from the past was ever shared with me. I need to know. It does not matter that I cannot use the information. It is personal. It is part of my life."

Josef sighed.

"Alright. I will tell you all I know. The family Klassen left what was then Prussia and settled near the German and Netherlands border. They were a deeply religious family and well respected by the neighboring farmers. My father's name was Isaiah and my mother Marijke. They had three sons. Franz was the oldest, then there was Isaac and I followed later in life. Franz died a number of years ago. The life of the Klassens was typical of any Mennonite family at that time. They participated in church events and assisted the others in the farming community. Life for them, while difficult, was much simpler than today. The temptations were less. There was no machinery to replace the horse and plow.

Harvesting was done by hand. The family lived a simple and honest life."

"Did Isaiah have brothers or sisters?"

"No. I never heard of any other family other than Isaiah and Marijke. Franz and Isaac were born several years apart. I am told they were the best of friends. Where one went, the other would follow. They fished the local stream and walked to church school together. They were inseparable. Franz took ill early in his life and was no longer able to play with the same energies he had once possessed. Isaac stayed by his side when he was ill and read scripture and simple approved stories to him. At one point the congregation expected Franz would die. Many prayers were offered. Franz recovered and continued to live life on the farm."

"I do not understand why the others who I met with did not want to share this. It seems as if it was a life lived in accordance with the church teachings."

"Jakob there is more to the story. As Franz and Isaac grew older some differences began to appear. The boys were invited to functions held at the church and neighboring farms which they attended. Franz was becoming more religious and considered joining the church. Isaac was more inclined to be social and accept his life. He was the jovial one whereas Franz became more serious. Then it happened. An event happened that caused the family to fall apart.

At one of the church socials Isaac was introduced to Inge. Franz had been seeing Inge and had secretly planned on marrying her. When Isaac found this out he convinced Inge not to marry Franz.

They saw each other without the families knowing. Franz continued to see Inge not aware of the friendship that had developed between Isaac and Inge.

It was late in the harvest season when Franz found Inge and Isaac together in the barn. They were sitting and talking of farm life and their dreams. Franz overheard some of the conversation. He burst into the barn and confronted them. There was a terrible fight. Isaac stabbed Franz several times with a pair of hand shears that were used to shear the sheep.

The next week was miserable for both Isaac and Inge. The church Elders visited them separately. They were to be publicly shamed.

Isaac was angry. He did not believe they should be punished. He argued with the Elders that Franz did not own Inge's life. The Elders were angry and preached scripture.

Finally Isaac crept to Inge's home one evening. He took Inge from her home and told her of his plan. Later that week they ran away to America. Isaac never contacted family or any relatives again. That is the secret being kept from you."

Chapter 83

Jakob sat absorbing the details that Josef had just told him. Finally he started to understand the reasons for the lack of discussion on the family's past. He reviewed the information in his head. Since Isaac and Inge had eloped and been scorned by the church he wondered how they could have been accepted into the congregation in Kitchener. He further wondered why they would have continued with the church and its beliefs since they had been shamed.

As he and Josef continued talking there was a soft tap at the door. Josef scowled. He walked to the door.

"Sabine, I asked we not be disturbed."

"I am sorry Josef. There are two SS Officers at the door. They refuse to leave or set up a later appointment. They are very loud and neighbors are watching. I think you should come now. "

Josef cursed. "Jakob please go with Sabine. I will show these men into the house .

Sabine guided Jakob from the study. They walked past the dining room and into a small alcove in the kitchen. They heard Josef escorting the men to his office. The door slammed shut. Sitting in the kitchen they heard raised voices in the conversation. There was occasional shouting then quiet.

As afternoon wore on there was more urgent knocking at the front door. Sabine went to the door. Several uniformed Officers from the Wehrmacht stood waiting.

"We are here to see Josef Klassen and the other officers." They marched into the house before Sabine could say anything.

"I will escort you to the study where they are meeting."

One of the Officers was carrying a brown leather portfolio stuffed with papers. At the study door Sabine knocked, opened the door and announced their presence. The Officers walked in and closed the door firmly behind them.

Sabine returned to Jakob.

"Something is wrong. I sense Josef has problems with these men. Their attitude was very unfriendly."

There were more raised voices and loud shouting coming from the study.

Late in the afternoon the Officers emerged looking somber. They walked to the front door. As they were leaving one of the SS Officers called back.

"Josef we will telephone you from our Headquarters in the morning. We will review all the information and plan accordingly."

Josef stood at the front door and watched them depart. He quietly closed the door and joined Jakob and Sabine.

"They are impatient. There is little I can do to make our American suppliers deliver any faster. I will need to travel to Berlin tomorrow afternoon for more meetings. Jakob you are welcome to stay. I will return in the evening tomorrow or the next morning. Sabine should you hear my phones ringing it is important you answer them and take messages."

"Josef I do not understand. What is so important?"

"Jakob come to my study please."

When back in the study and seated Josef continued. "Jakob I have been operating an import business here in Germany for many years. Through connections and when the Nazi Party came into power I was asked to handle some military procurement. This grew and now all my business is sourcing and buying arms and equipment for the military. I also negotiated the supply of aviation gas. This is a special high octane fuel that the Luftwaffe need for the Messerschmitt ME-109 and their Focke-Wulf 190 fighters. That is why I travel to America. At present the German High Command is demanding more equipment and fuel than is available. I fear that there are things planned beyond the recent incursions that Hitler has made into neighboring countries. Tomorrow I must meet with the senior commanders and estimate the demand and then arrange for the purchases. I wish I had never agreed to represent them. They have hundreds of personnel handling the purchases but I played a major part in negotiating the supply contracts and they now want to modify and renegotiate. I have no option but to comply with their demands."

"I will stay with Sabine while you make your trip."

"I will leave very early and catch the first train to Berlin. I hope to return late in the evening but that will depend whether we complete our meetings in time for me to catch the evening train."

"I will wait for you. I cannot travel without my papers and money. Once you have satisfied them I will leave and travel back to Amsterdam."

"Please stay in the house during my absence. As you witness these are not normal times. The streets can be dangerous at night."

"You have my promise. I will stay here and read some of the fine books on display in your study."

They continued to talk until Sabine called them for an early evening dinner. Over dinner the talk was of music and travel. Josef was surprised to learn that Jakob had learned music and played at a club in Amsterdam.

"When I return we must go to a club and hear you play. That would be my delight."

They all retired early that evening. Tomorrow would arrive early with its demands.

Chapter 84

After Josef had departed for Berlin, Sabine performed various chores in the house while Jakob read in the study. The day progressed slowly. Jakob yearned to leave the house and explore the streets of Munich. Without his papers he was stranded at the house.

It was mid afternoon when one of the telephones on Josef's desk started ringing. It startled Jakob. He watched it ring. He had never used a telephone before. Sabine entered the study and answered. It was Josef.

"Good afternoon Sabine. Our meetings are taking much longer than planned. I will not return today. I will be home tomorrow. I will phone again with the train information."

Sabine thanked Josef for the update and hung up. She walked over to Jakob.

"Josef is delayed until tomorrow. Come and join me as I prepare us a dinner."

In the kitchen Jakob asked Sabine about her life.

"I was born when my parents lived in the country. It was near the border with Switzerland. It was a beautiful place. I still miss it. One day my father damaged his leg in an accident on the farm. It was impossible for him to continue to run the farm. He found a job at a factory near Munich that did not require him to stand for long hours. We moved to Munich and lived in a house on the outskirts of the city. My father continued to work at the factory for many years. I attended a school close to our house and my mother stayed at home."

"How did you meet Josef and start working for him?"

"One day at the factory Josef arrived to take a tour. As he was visiting he stopped to speak with my father who was performing the assembly of a machine. Josef was fascinated by the process. My father explained the process to Josef and offered that there was an alternative method that would be faster and require fewer components. My father did not know that Josef was one of the owners of the factory. Josef listened to him and made some notes. Later in the day my father was called to the office where the other owners were waiting. He was asked to explain.

He limped across the office and drew on a large blackboard a diagram of the machine and the components he thought could be used instead of the present ones. The owners talked amongst themselves. Josef finally spoke and asked my father to try his suggested changes. The next day the owners watched and timed my father as he performed the assembly. They were impressed. The changes were adopted.

Josef would visit the factory and on occasion go and speak with my father. He noticed that his leg was causing him problems and offered my father a position to help run and maintain this house. We moved into the house within weeks. The change made us all happy. Josef was generous and helped us a great deal."

"I never knew that Josef existed until several weeks ago. My father, Isaac was his brother but never spoke of him."

"I often wonder why there is no Mrs. Josef. He has always been kind and caring. He would have been a good husband I am sure."

Jakob shrugged. "I do not know and cannot guess."

They continued talking about their respective lives while Sabine fussed around preparing a meal for them. She selected a roast of pork. Soon the house was filled with the aroma of the roast. She selected vegetables to add to the roast. Jakob watched her every move.

From their first encounter he had felt some strange attraction to Sabine. He thought of Anke. It was different. He had never experienced the same degree of attraction for Anke though he thought he loved her.

Sabine was aware of Jakob watching her. She moved slowly in front of him on purpose enjoying the attention. "If only things were different" she thought.

Chapter 85

After the dinner Sabine and Jakob retired to their rooms. Jakob fell asleep dreaming of the farm back in Canada. He awoke late in the morning to the sound of ringing bells. He quickly bathed and dressed and ran downstairs. Sabine was in the study speaking on the phone.

After she was finished and hung up she spoke to Jakob. "That was Josef. He is leaving Berlin now and expects to be here late this afternoon. He said there are things he needs to tell us."

"I have slept too long. What time of day is it?"

Sabine glanced at the clock on Josef's desk. "It is noon. Come, I have made a lunch. I am sure you are hungry. I must leave for the market to buy meat and vegetables for dinner this evening. I wish to leave soon while there is good produce still for sale."

"I will join you. I need to be outside. I like the house but feel trapped here. I need to walk and breathe the cool air."

"No, Jakob. Josef told you that to do so would be dangerous. Please stay. You promised him."

"I will take that risk. I will either go with you to the market or I will go and walk alone. My wish is to go with you."

Sabine smiled. Secretly she had hoped he would go with her.

They dressed for the cooler day and Sabine fetched a wicker basket from the pantry. They set off walking at a brisk pace. As they continued along, they encountered a German patrol coming toward them.

"Jakob be quiet. Let me deal with this if necessary."

The lead soldier of the patrol stopped and spoke to Sabine.

"Good morning. It is a nice morning to walk to the market. Do you and your husband live near here? I have not seen you before. I would remember any pretty woman I encountered on our patrol here."

Sabine smiled her most engaging smile. "Good sir, you flatter me. Yes my husband is with me this morning. He has been ill with a contagious flu. I think the worse is over and it should not spread to others now."

The soldier stepped back and looked over at Jakob. He spoke to the other soldiers. They all moved further away from Jakob.

The lead soldier spoke. "Have a good walk Fraulein. You must not exhaust him. He does look pale. I hope he is not too weak for the walk. Go and enjoy the market."

Jakob could barely suppress his laughter. "I am ill? I look pale? Where did you get that story?"

Sabine laughed. "I have my ways of getting what I want. None of those cowards wants anything bad to befall them. They are really very ignorant. Now, walk like an ill man who is recovering from sickness in case they watch us."

They continued to the market and selected their foods from the many stalls. The market was busy. Once in a while a soldier on a bike rode by.

Jakob had enjoyed the walk and Sabine's company. "Let us stop at that café for a coffee. It is cold and we should stop for a minute. After all, I am ill, remember?"

Sabine laughed. "Yes. We will stop for a while. I must get back though to prepare for Josef's return."

They stopped into the café and were seated at a table in the window area. They watched the people hurrying by. Jakob played a game of guessing what each person did or where they were going. Sabine played along.

Back in the house Sabine changed into her domestic duty clothes. Jakob helped her put the foods away in the pantry and selected some for the dinner Sabine was about to make.

Late afternoon the front door opened and Josef entered. He went straight to his study after calling out a greeting. He closed the door. Jakob and Sabine heard his low voice coming from the study as he made several phone calls. He emerged from the study and joined them.

"I have some news for you. Tomorrow I must return to New York. There is urgent business that I must attend to. I pleaded with the Officers to send someone else. They would not. Jakob, I tried to get your papers. They refused. I must complete this work in order for them to be returned to you. I will be back in about a week. I will now go and pack a case to take with me. I will take a flight in the afternoon and arrive in New York the next morning. I will leave details of my hotel on my desk should you need to contact me."

Jakob was not convinced. "Josef, what is it exactly the Nazis are requesting from you?"

"Jakob, I have a number of business interests. One of those is armaments. I deal weapons to them. They have threatened severe measures if I do not deliver certain goods soon."

Jakob was shocked. Sabine turned and stared at Josef. "Josef, how could you assist these monsters? I am sure you know of the rumors about what they are doing to the Jews and others."

"I am not proud, just trapped because of my own greed for profit."

Josef left the room and proceeded upstairs to prepare and pack his clothing for the flight.

Sabine stared at Jakob. "I am worried. I never knew this. We are now in some danger. As long as Josef satisfies them we will be safe."

That night all 3 sat in the dining room with little to say. They ate the roasted pork and vegetables.

"Sabine, this is a delicious meal you made us. I think one of your best." Josef proclaimed.

Sabine thanked him. She left the table and cleared the dishes. Jakob helped her clean up the kitchen.

Jakob sat with Josef in the study when all was finished. Josef poured them some Cognac. He handed a large glass to Jakob who was developing a taste for the drink. He gulped down the drink. Josef arose and poured him another.

"When I started to do business with them it was different. They were the workers party. They had ideals that seemed good and reasonable. The leadership of Hitler changed that. He has overridden those ideals. The nation has been swept into a series of beliefs that are evil and probably unable to be attained. I regret having to deal with them. I have often thought of disappearing."

Chapter 86

With Josef gone to New York, Sabine and Jakob were alone in the house. Jakob was wondering what he could do to fill in his time. He found it difficult without some task to perform. He was reluctant to venture outside again. He did not want another encounter with the patrol. He passed the day reading the books that lined the shelves of Josef's study. He found himself tired and bored by the time night fell.

"Sabine I am going to bed early tonight. Will you be fine alone?"

Sabine looked at him and smiled "Yes. I think I will soon go to bed as well"

Jakob lay awake trying to plan a scheme to get back to Amsterdam and Anke. He lay there for hours preparing plans in his head only to discover a flaw and then prepare another. While tired he could not sleep.

He heard the softest knock on his bedroom door. He frowned. "Yes" he called out.

The door cracked open. Sabine stood in her long white nightgown. She had combed out her hair. It hung long down her back and over her shoulder. Jakob looked at her in amazement. Her transformation stunned him.

"Sabine why are you here? Is there a problem? Come in."

She walked over to Jakob's bed and gently sat on the edge.

Jakob looked at her and realised she had been previously crying.

"What is wrong?"

"Jakob I am scared and worried. Recently the things that have happened are not good. I fear for my life here. I do not think Josef can help anymore."

She sniffled back a tear. Jakob reached for her. He stood and wrapped his long arms around her. She rested her head against his chest. After several minutes she raised her head and looked up at his craggy face. It was lined from the sun and weathered from the constant work he had done outside on the farm. She was drawn to him. She hugged him back. Jakob was confused.

She stood and reached behind his neck. Sabine pulled him down to her and proceeded to kiss him. She held him tight and kissed for the longest time. Jakob responded. He slid his hand down her back. She pushed hard against him. They continued to hug and kiss passionately. She moved her hands down his chest and reached into his pajamas. She found his erect penis. Jakob gasped and pulled her to the bed. He unfastened her gown. Sabine lay naked beside him. He marveled at her perfectly white and beautiful body. He stroked her breasts and the flat of her stomach. Sabine groaned in pleasure. She threw her leg over him and raised herself on him. Her full breasts hung above his chest. She reached for his penis and slid it into her. They stayed locked together for the longest while. She rocked back and forth slowly and finally cried out in passion.

Throughout the night they made love often and then fell asleep.

Jakob awoke and looked over at her. She was sleeping. Her long auburn hair had fallen to the front and partially covered one of her breasts. Jakob marveled at the beauty of it all.

He fell back into a deep sleep. It was hours later when they arose. Sabine gathered her clothing and ran to her room. Jakob drew a long bath and relaxed for the longest time. Now he had a real problem to solve. Any remaining beliefs he had in his religion were now shattered. He lay wondering whether he would stay with Sabine. He thought of Anke. He had never been unfaithful until now. He resolved that he was finished as a Mennonite. He would return and tell Anke of his decision. He knew inside that she would not accept it.

As he lay there Sabine returned. She had brought him a coffee. She leaned over and kissed his forehead.

It wasn't long before Sabine was in the bath with Jakob. They laughed and explored each other. Finally Jakob was happy. Decisions had been made.

Chapter 87

A full week had passed since Josef had left for New York. The week had passed peacefully for Jakob. He had enjoyed many pleasurable moments with Sabine.

It was August 31, 1939. Jakob was concerned. He needed to return to Amsterdam and from there travel home to Canada. Faced with no papers and little money he was trapped. On a daily basis he hoped to hear something from Josef. Each day passed by with no word from him. Jakob was becoming worried. There was no one he could turn to in Munich for help.

As he sat worrying in Josef's study, Sabine entered. She crossed over to him and stroked his hair.

"Jakob I am going to get some supplies we need. It is too dangerous for you to accompany me. I will be a while as I need to visit several stores that are far apart. I will need to take a tram to some of the stores. I will be away for some time."

Sabine pulled on her heavy coat. In her hand she held a thick book and a shopping bag. Jakob watched as she left the house and walked up the street to where the tram stopped. He had become increasingly curious over the last few days. Sabine would disappear in the house. Sometimes she would lock herself in her room for hours.

As he stood at the windows, Josef's personal phone rang. Jakob looked at it. He had seen Sabine use the phone on several occasions. He went to the desk and removed the handset. As he held it to his ear Josef's voice crackled through.

"Jakob. I cannot explain now. Are you alone?"

"Yes, Sabine has left to go and buy some supplies for the house."

"I will come now. I am here in Munich. We have much to speak of. Do not answer my door. No one is to enter my home."

Some 15 minutes later Josef opened the door. He had 2 large files in his hand and carried a travel bag.

"Come quickly. We must not delay."

Josef ripped off his coat and threw it at one of the chairs in the foyer. As he spun to run to his study the flap of his suit jacket opened. Jakob looked in astonishment. Josef was wearing a holster with a pistol. Josef saw the look on Jakob's face.

"Jakob we are in extreme danger. I returned to Munich yesterday. I have friends who are in positions with access to certain information. They have told me some very disturbing things. I hope they are wrong."

Josef went to his desk and systematically opened the drawers of his bureau. He slowly examined the contents of each. He closed the drawers without removing anything. He looked at Jakob.

"I must ask you this question. Did you open or take anything from these   drawers?"
Jakob was stunned. "No. I would never do such a thing. Why do you ask?"

"My contacts within the Nazis have told me of certain confidential matters that are contained in the papers that are always locked in my desk. Has there been anyone here?"

Jakob thought of the long walks he and Sabine had been on together. He told Josef of these.

"They have been watching and gained entry when the house was empty. Jakob you had promised me that you would never leave the house while I was away. The Nazis will now have records of dealings and the identity of other businessmen who oppose them. This is a disaster."

Josef slumped into one of the leather chairs to think.

"I need to deal with this matter. It was not a coincidence that they accosted you on the train and took your papers. They knew the name Klassen. I have some contacts that are not with the party. I will speak with some and attempt to get you away from here. I am afraid I have been told of other things that are most devastating. We will talk of those later. Now we must destroy all these documents. If the house is raided I will be seen as a traitor and executed."

Jakob and Josef filled several boxes with the documents. I will take them in my car. There is a location where I can destroy them. You must stay here and make it seem normal when Sabine returns. Do not say a word of this to her. She must not know. That is critical."

Josef dragged the boxes to the rear door that opened into the yard where his cars were garaged. Jakob helped him to load the car. Josef looked around and started the car.

"Remember Jakob. Do not speak to Sabine of this."

Jakob agreed and walked back to the house. In the study he took some books and spread them around him on the floor to make it appear he was deep in research on some topic. It was several hours before Sabine returned. She carried some boxes containing cleaning supplies and other utensils.

"Jakob you look so studious. What are you reading?'

Jakob had not expected that question.

"I am reading about the days of early Germany. So much has happened here."

Sabine smiled and seemed satisfied with Jakob's feeble answer.

After removing her coat she turned away to leave. As she did so, Jakob observed a slight pause as she looked at the desk. He wondered if it just his imagination.

"Sabine, are you alright. I thought you seemed to hesitate. Are you feeling faint?"

"No. I am just a little tired from the shopping."

As she walked away from Jakob he noticed something was different with her dress. She had been wearing stockings when she left. Now she had none.

Chapter 88

Jakob and Sabine were in the Dining room. They had eaten and were making small talk. Suddenly the silence was broken. There was a loud ringing of Josef's business line. Sabine rose and went to answer.

"Hello Sabine. This is Josef. I am calling to tell you I will return tomorrow afternoon. Good bye I will see you then."

Before Sabine could respond there was a click and Josef was gone. She turned to Jakob "That call was from Josef. He will return tomorrow afternoon."

Jakob nodded. "He will be tired after such a long journey."

"Yes, tomorrow morning I will go to the market and get fresh foods to make a nice dinner with him. It will take longer tomorrow as I am meeting friends for lunch after we shop. I will prepare you a lunch meal before I leave."

Jakob was growing suspicious. Why was Josef deceiving her? Was it Josef's plan not to be at home when Sabine returned? Who had been in Josef's desk? His thoughts ran wild.

Sabine looked at Jakob. "You seem troubled. I have not seen you so quiet. What is wrong?"

She went to him and bent over him and kissed his forehead. Jakob pulled back.

"Sabine I am not feeling well tonight. I think I have a cold developing. My arms and legs ache and I feel weak"

Sabine nodded and stood watching. Within minutes Jakob slumped forward in a deep sleep. Sabine had drugged him.

There was an urgent knock at the door. She went and opened it. To her surprise it was not the visitor she expected. It was Josef. He rushed in before she could close the door.

Sabine shouted for help. There was none to be summoned.

"Sabine. How could you betray me? After all that I did for you and your family. I have found out that you are a Nazi informant and have given them my confidential files. Many lives are now in peril because of you. Why did you do this?"

Sabine did not answer him. She stood with her arms folded.

"Very soon we will have a visit from certain members of the Gestapo. They will take over and answer your questions I am sure" she said.

Josef sprung forward to grab her wrist. She twisted away and reached into the deep pocket of her gown. She pulled her hand from the pocket. In her hand was a 9mm Luger pistol.

"Josef, I will be kind in appreciation of those things you did for me and my family. Leave now. I will not shoot nor will I tell them of your return. I suggest you find a way to take Jakob with you. They will be here in minutes."

Josef ran to his desk. He took a sheaf of papers and money from the bottom drawer. He then ran to Jakob and shook him.

"Jakob, wake up. We must hurry."

He slapped Jakob's face. Jakob opened his eyes and groggily attempted to talk. Josef pulled him to his feet. Josef grabbed the money and papers. He dragged Jakob to the door and across the yard to his car. He opened the rear door and shoved Jakob onto the seat.

They sped from the driveway and headed away from the city.

It was dark and with very little traffic. They drove on until Josef recognized a farm in the distance. He slowed and examined the surrounding land. It was quiet and there was no sign of any cars or military presence. He switched off the car's lights and slowed the car to a crawl. When he was about a kilometer from the house he stopped the car. The house was in total darkness. Josef sat in the car watching for any movements. After about 30 minutes he left the car. Jakob was still sleeping heavily as a result of the drugs. Josef approached the house. He took a stone and threw it against the back window. He crouched down behind some shrubs and waited. The door was finally opened and a burly man in a singlet and shorts stood in the doorway. He looked around. Josef let out a low whistle. The man looked in his direction. He raised his hand ever so slightly and returned inside, leaving the door open behind him.

Josef crawled from behind the shrubs and made his way to the door. He entered.

"Jurgen. We have been betrayed to the Nazis. I need to escape. I have a relative with me in my car. He is my nephew. He has been drugged. I need help and shelter tonight until I can work out a plan."

"Do not turn on any lights. We have seen many troops and vehicles here in the past days. You can stay but no one must see you. Where is your car? We must make that disappear I am afraid.

I will come with you and assist you with your nephew. You will rest and in the morning we will speak and plan."

They left to carry Jakob from the car to the house. Josef picked up the papers he had brought from the house. They carried Jakob to the house and placed him in a low iron truckle bed and covered him with a light blanket. Jurgen took Josef into his room.

"I have no other beds here. You will sleep with me in my bed. We will manage."

Josef awoke in the morning to find Jurgen listening intently to a radio. Through the crackling static an announcer was shouting a news item. Josef tried to listen but the static broke up the announcer's voice.

Jurgen turned to Josef. "The broadcast claims that last night Polish soldiers attempted to invade Germany. There are casualties. German soldiers have been killed. Hitler is furious."

"This is not a good development. I fear that this will create hostilities with others. I must plan an escape from Germany. I must do this quickly before the border patrols are advised of my name and arrest me. I will take the car and leave immediately. Here is money for your help and some for Jakob. I cannot take him. He is known to them and will be arrested. Please assist him. Talk with our comrades and try to get him out of Germany."

Jurgen started to protest. It was useless. Josef had taken his coat and the files from the table. He walked to the door.

"Good bye Jurgen. Until we meet. I will send you information soon. I will travel to Britain if I can get to a port in France."

Josef ran to his car. Within minutes he sped from the dirt track to the road. He drove eastward toward France. Outside of Stuttgart he came upon several large military convoys. He followed behind them for many kilometers and was relieved when they turned north toward Frankfurt. He drove on and eventually turned south and took the road that lead to the crossing into Strasbourg. When he reached the French-German border he was surprised at the heavy presence of German troops. There were several cars ahead of him. Josef sat quietly and watched as each car cleared. Finally it was his turn. He drove up to the barrier. A young lieutenant approached the car. Josef handed his identity papers to him. The lieutenant took them and went into a small kiosk. An older man emerged and looked at Josef. He was one of Josef's informants. Josef looked at him. The older man spoke to the lieutenant who then walked back to the car.

"What is your business in France?"

"I am on business for The Wehrmacht in Berlin. Your superior there knows of my business. You should go and ask him."

The young lieutenant stood back and signaled for the barrier to be raised. Josef drove through to the safety of France.

Upon entering France he was stopped by the French officials.

"What is your business here? How long will you stay in France?"

"I am travelling through France in order to take a ship to Britain. I expect I will be only one day."

The French official nodded and waved him on. Josef was free of Nazi Germany.

Chapter 89

Jakob awoke with a fierce headache. He stumbled from the small low bed and slowly found his way to the kitchen where Jurgen sat still listening to the radio. Jurgen's face was serious. Upon hearing Jakob enter he turned and motioned to him to sit at the table. Jurgen stood and went to the old stove and removed a pot of coffee and took a chipped mug from the shelf. He returned to the table and poured Jakob a cup of the strong brew.

"You have slept long. It is afternoon all ready. Josef has left."

Jurgen filled him in on the events of the morning. As they talked there was a blaring of trumpets from the radio. Jurgen raised his finger to silence their conversation. He walked to the radio and increased the volume.

Over the static they listened to a ranting speech from Hitler. He announced that because of the attack by Poland he had ordered German soldiers to invade Poland.

Jurgen spoke first. "Jakob we must get you out of Germany quickly. I have some contacts that will help. I will need to visit them and devise some way to get you to Amsterdam. Without your papers it will not be an easy."

Jurgen took a couple of enamel plates from the cupboard and some blood sausage. He found a loaf of somewhat stale bread.

They sat discussing the ways for Jakob to get back to Amsterdam. As they searched various options, the radio again blared. The announcer came on speaking very fast. Britain and France had announced an ultimatum to Hitler. Withdraw all military presence from Poland by noon of September 3rd or face the consequences.

Jurgen looked sad. "I fear that we will soon be at war. Hitler has violated every agreement and promise he has made. These countries will try to stop him. We must get you away from here. Stay hidden at the house. I am going to fetch a friend."

Several hours later Jurgen returned with another man. They entered. Introductions were made. A black case was placed on the table and opened. Inside there was a camera and a number of inks and pens.

"We are going to make you some papers. Your name will be Jakob Baumann on these papers. You live on the Dutch German border. Tomorrow the photo of you will be ready and my friend will complete the forgery. I have paid him with some of the money that Josef left for you. When the papers are done you must leave immediately."

The man took several photos of Jakob. He measured him and guessed his weight.

"I will bring you your papers tomorrow in the early afternoon."

Jurgen walked to the door and the man left without any further discussion.

After he had gone, Jurgen and Jakob explored the options to get Jakob back to Amsterdam.

"Jakob, it is my belief that it would be best for you to find your way to Hamburg. It will be easier for you to get to Amsterdam from there. The Nazis have announced that Holland is part of the Aryan Nation. They are less strict at the border with The

Netherlands. Your crossing should not be challenged. Besides, Hamburg is a port city. There are many underground activities there. You should be safe."

"How will I get there?"

"I will ask if anyone is travelling to the North. My neighbors often take trips there for family reasons. This may take several days. You can stay here until we have things arranged."

Jakob accepted the invitation and decision. He thought back over the past weeks. His life had been changed forever.

Chapter 90

Jurgen left the next morning and did not return until late afternoon. He found Jakob studying a map of Germany. He handed a thick brown envelope to Jakob and grinned.

"Welcome Jakob Baumann."

Jakob opened the envelope and removed identity papers and a Dutch Passport. He studied the photo and seal. It was a brilliant forgery. Unless examined by an expert the documents appeared to be genuine.

"Tomorrow there is a truck that travels to Hamburg. The owners drive there often to purchase mechanical parts for the repair shop they operate. They have agreed to take you with them for a small payment. I have made the payment. They do not know you as Jakob Klassen. They do not know the situation with you and Josef. You are Jakob Baumann to them, a Dutch farmer who came to visit Munich and travel. You came to my house because you had met friends of mine. They recommended you to stay with me while you toured our country. You must remember this. Do not slip up. I do not know of their loyalty. They may be with the Nazi Party. They do not know that I, like many in Germany do not believe or accept the Nazi ideology and we await the days when we can promote other political parties. Be very careful. Do not deceive me or Josef or the hundreds of other members that Josef has gathered since 1933. We are waiting and hope one day to form the new German Government,"

Now Jakob understood Josef's anxiety over the loss of information from his desk in the study. Jakob now realized what the thick folder of documents that Josef had taken with him when they fled the house contained.

"When will I leave for Hamburg?"

"Tomorrow is Sunday. It is September 3rd. I imagine they will leave late in the afternoon. They have family in Hamburg and often stay with them."

Jakob thanked Jurgen and again made a promise that he was not sure he could keep.

"What will I do when I reach Hamburg? I will need somewhere to stay."

"There are many rooming houses near the docks. There are many workers there who are employed in ship building. I suggest you stop there until you can travel to Amsterdam. It should be a short stay in Hamburg. You must be cautious. Hamburg has a side that is rough and crime is known. Be careful of who you befriend."

Jakob returned to the table where he had spread out the map of Germany. He pointed his finger at Hamburg.

"I am sure there is some train or bus from Hamburg to Amsterdam. I should only need to spend a night or 2 in Hamburg. I will be back to Amsterdam in time for us to leave for our ship."

Jurgen looked at Jakob with a penetrating glare.

"Jakob, I am not sure about you. You will never tell anybody of your stay here or of Josef. I am not without friends in many places. I will hear if you betray us and we will take appropriate actions. Do I make myself clear to you?"

Jakob realized that even though Jurgen was assisting him, he was still in a situation of some danger. If tipped off, the SS would not hesitate in hunting him down. They had his papers and by now knew all of Josef's plans. He would be accused of being an accomplice. The retribution would be violent and swift.

"I do not want any troubles. I wish to return to my farm in Canada and be away from all this upheaval here in Europe. I will not do anything that could destroy my plans."

Jurgen looked at him for the longest time. "I believe you are serious. It is your life to protect. You make a mistake and you will be dead."

Jakob paled. He knew that either Jurgen or the SS would kill him if he failed and was discovered.

Chapter 91

Jakob had packed his few possessions into a canvas bag. He placed the bag at the front door and returned to find Jurgen hunched over the kitchen table listening to the radio. It was a news broadcast. The announcer spoke quickly. His delivery was occasionally interrupted and an English voice would be heard.

Jurgen looked at Jakob. "It will be more difficult for you now. Britain and France have declared war on Germany. Hitler has refused to accept their demands and withdraw over 1.5 million soldiers he has ordered into Poland. "

"I will leave Hamburg as quickly as I can find transportation."

As they spoke an old truck with an open cargo deck ground its way toward Jurgen's house.

"Jakob go now. Remember our talk. You must keep all that we have spoken of and done a secret. Be careful."

Jakob carried his bag to the passenger side of the truck. The driver and his wife introduced themselves. Jakob climbed up onto the front seat. The old truck slowly ground its way back to the road. At the road they made a right hand turn and started the trip to Hamburg.

The driver spoke. "We will be travelling for almost 9 hours. This morning there were many military vehicles. We will be slowed by this. Do you know what is happening?"

Jakob relayed the information he had heard on the radio. The driver shook his head and spoke to his wife.

"If this means a war then tomorrow we must increase our order of parts. There will probably be shortages like the last war. This will delay our return."

She agreed with him.

"Jakob. Where will you stay in Hamburg?"

"I am just staying for a day or so until I arrange transportation back to Amsterdam. I do not have anywhere to stay yet."

"When we make these trips we stay at a boarding house near the ship building yards. The rooms are clean and the price is good. If you do not have anywhere I suggest you stay there the night. It will be late when we reach Hamburg."

Jakob thanked him and affirmed that he would stay there.

They drove on making the occasional stop for gas and some light foods.

It was close to midnight when they finally pulled up outside the large grey-white house that was the boarding house. The driver jumped down and ran up the stairs and rang the doorbell. The door opened and he entered. Soon he emerged and waved his wife and Jakob up to join him.

It was obvious to Jakob that the couple was well known here. The woman produced a book for them to sign as guests. She then took some keys from a rack and handed one to Jakob and the other to the couple.

They returned to the truck and retrieved their bags and returned to the boarding house.

Jakob entered his room. It was small and basic. He walked to the bed and placed his bag at the end of the bed. The air in the room smelled bad and stale. Jakob opened the windows. He sat on the bed. It was not long before he fell into a deep sleep.

He awoke in the morning confused. It took him several minutes to remember where he was. Since being drugged by Sabine his memory was hazy. He went to the sink and splashed water over his face.

He returned to the bed to take some clothing from his bag. He reached down for it. It was not there. With his memory being poor he looked under the bed and in the closet in case he had stowed it there. It was not. Jakob had been robbed. His bag, money and papers were all gone.

Chapter 92

Jakob slumped onto the bed and sat trying to devise a plan. After some time had passed he went to the reception desk. The woman who had greeted them had been replaced by a tall man in his 30's. He looked up as Jakob approached. He had a nasty scar on his cheek and lanky greasy hair.

"Yes. Can I help you?"

"Last night we checked in late. During the night my room was robbed. I have lost everything. My papers, my money and some clothing are all gone."

Jakob mentioned the couple he had travelled with and asked the tall man to contact them. He reached for the guest register and scanned it.

"I am sorry but they have already left. Should I call the police?"

Jakob thought of the situation back in Munich. He was convinced that if the police became involved they would become aware of the situation with Jakob Klassen.

"No. I will have to replace my papers."

"How will you pay your account with us?"

"I have travelled from Amsterdam where my wife is waiting for me. I can try to contact her and have money sent. I will need to stay somewhere until the money arrives here."

The tall man thought about this. He left the desk and went through the door behind the desk. After several minutes he emerged with the woman who had greeted Jakob upon his arrival.

"Gunther has told me your story. How do we know this is the truth? I should call the police now to investigate."

"I do not need trouble. I will stay here until the money arrives. Please help me with this."

"You are not the only guest who was robbed last night. I believe your story. What work do you do?"

Jakob advised her that he was a farmer and of the farm in Canada. She seemed disappointed with this.

"Well, there are no farms here for you to earn some money while you wait."

Jakob offered that he had played saxophone at a café in Amsterdam and had made some money.

Gunther and woman exchanged looks. Gunther spoke. "We have a cousin who owns a club in St. Pauli. I will take you there. She may be able to offer you work. The area is not the best in Hamburg."

Jakob went with Gunther in an old Citroen car to St Pauli. They parked on a side street and walked. Jakob was astonished. Sitting in windows, like those of a store, were women in various states of undress.

Gunther saw Jakob's surprised look and laughed. "This is Hamburg's red light district. The Nazi Party has declared prostitution illegal but it seems the main clients here are German soldiers. They have also tried to stop jazz and certain music but again they are the main patrons. Their hypocrisy is astounding."

They walked on until they reached a dingy looking building that was located between 2 of the windows in which women sat. Gunther rapped hard on the door. It was eventually opened by a raven haired woman of Jakob's age.

"Gunther. What brings you here to my establishment so early in the day? Come in and tell me."

Gunther and Jakob entered the building. It was decorated with dim lighting and heavy drapes. Velvet couches were arranged at different positions on the main floor. To the left was an area set up as a dance floor with a stage behind it. There were drums and cases containing a variety if instruments scattered about on the stage. Across the room was a long bar. In front of the bar there were several tables with wooden chairs. Many of the tables were stained or had cigarette burns on them.

"Gunther who is your friend here?" she said and pointed for them to sit on one of the couches.

"His name is Jakob. He stayed at our hotel last night and during the night he was robbed of all his possessions including his money and his papers. He is travelling back to Canada through Amsterdam. He tells us he has played saxophone in clubs and cafes. He will be here waiting while money is sent to him. We wondered if you need a musician like this in your club?"

She looked at Jakob. "My name is Ilsa. I own this little operation. What type of music do you play?"

Jakob answered and told her he had a natural musical ability but he had mainly played jazz at the café in Amsterdam. This caused her to smile.

"Gunther your timing in bringing Jakob here is excellent. As you can see, the stage is a mess. There was a brawl between some soldiers last night. The instruments are everywhere. One of the musicians was taken to hospital. Yes, I can use you Jakob. Can you start tonight? We start at 9:00pm and the club stays open until the last person leaves. Assuming that person is spending money. I will pay you for each hour. You will get to keep tips you are given."

Jakob could not believe that his luck might be changing. He accepted the offer immediately.

"I will be here earlier than 9:00pm. Is there a saxophone I can try please?"

Ilsa pointed to the far side of the stage where a blue case stood propped against the wall. Jakob went and took out the saxophone. He started playing a soft tune.

Ilsa and Gunther looked on in amazement and listened to the music Jakob was producing alone. It was clear that he had a great musical talent."

Chapter 93

Jakob and Gunther left the club and returned to the Hotel. On the way they stopped at a restaurant named Brauhaus Erika for a late breakfast. Over a meal of eel soup and black bread, Gunther and Jakob discussed the events that were happening in Germany. When they were finished, Gunther gave Jakob directions to walk back to the Hotel and left. Jakob asked directions to a post office from where he could send a telegram to Anke. At the post office he realized he did not have an address to which the telegram could be delivered.

For the rest of the morning and early afternoon he wandered around looking at Hamburg's buildings and finally found himself in the port and ship building area. Mid afternoon he returned to the hotel. Gunther was nowhere to be seen. The woman greeted Jakob.

"Gunther had business. He will be back soon."

Jakob went to the room and tried to sleep. It would be a long night.

When he awoke it was dark outside. He freshened up and went back to the desk. The woman was still there.

"Gunther told me that he will go to Ilsa's club with you tonight. He has left again."

Jakob wondered what other business Gunther had that took him away from the Hotel. In their talk at the restaurant, Gunther has alluded to certain things. Jakob was curious. As he stayed making small talk with the woman, Gunther burst through the door and immediately ran through the door behind the desk. He slammed the door. Within minutes 2 police entered the Hotel.

Jakob was terrified. They looked at him and then turned to the woman.

"Where did he run?"

"He passed by the desk and ran to the back. I believe he went out the exit at the back. "

The police ran to the rear exit. They pushed the door open and surveyed the area. Not seeing anything they pulled the door closed.

"If he returns you must call us. Who is he?"

"I have never seen him here before."

The police shrugged and left. Jakob was relieved. He watched the woman as she tidied up the desk. Finally he spoke. "What is happening here? Why were they chasing him? Why did you mislead them?"

"A long while back, Gunther was suspected of a crime that he did not commit. There are some police who want to give him their form of justice. They are not to be trusted. They do not know he lives here with me. He is going to need to be cautious now. "

Gunther appeared in the entrance of the doorway. He looked around.

"They are gone. You must be more careful in future. Those police are nothing more than thugs. You should avoid the areas they patrol."

It was 8:00pm when Jakob and Gunther left for the club. It was located off the Reeperbahn where Hamburg's nightlife was centered. Gunther parked the old Citroen some distance from the area. They walked through the district as the clubs and brothels came alive for the night. Soon they were at the door of Club Henri. Gunther pushed open the door and walked in. Behind the bar the bartender was dressed in dark trousers and wore a bright red vest. On seeing them enter he waved. Gunther walked over to him. He ordered 2 beers for himself and Jakob. The bartender sat 2 large steins in front of them. Jakob was about to protest but instead took the stein and swallowed a large gulp of the pale colored beer. It was much better than beers he had previously drunk. Gunther introduced Jakob as the new saxophone player and told the bartender of the music he and Ilsa had heard Jakob play that morning.

Jakob looked around the dimly lit club. Already the air was heavy with cigarette smoke. Soldiers in uniform and some civilians sat at the tables drinking and smoking. When he finished his beer, Jakob went to the stage. There were several others unpacking instruments. Jakob introduced himself and a discussed the type of music he had played. The leader, a young blonde haired youth laid out the plan for the night. Jakob took an immediate liking to him. He was enthusiastic and loved playing music.

At 9:00 the quartet stated playing. The more they played the more that Jakob found himself adapting and fitting in as if he had played with them for years. He was a natural.

Soon girls started drifting down the dark wooden stairway and took up positions on the various couches. Between breaks Jakob listened to the voices as they argued and laughed. Within an hour there were no seats left at the bar or tables. The place was crowded. They seemed to be oblivious to the war Germany had started.

As he played Jakob observed the action in the club. Every now and then the bartender would take a large pitcher of beer to one of the tables for the soldiers. The level of noise in the club increased. As Jakob watched, two of the soldiers started a loud argument. It degenerated into a fight. Within minutes Gunther was there pulling them apart. He spread his arms apart to separate them. He twisted one of the soldier's arms behind his back and pushed him to the door. Jakob now understood Gunther's role in the club.

After they had played for 30 minutes the bartender approached with a tray of drinks.

"These were bought for you by those soldiers over there." He pointed to some smartly uniformed officers sitting at a table a long way from the bar. One of the officers had undone his jacket and was leaning back against the wall.

Jakob reached for the glass of amber liquid. He drank the contents in seconds. His taste for strong alcoholic drinks was developing.

The group continued playing through the night. As they did so, Jakob observed the girls disappearing upstairs with their clients. They would return some 15—20 minutes later and reposition themselves on the couch.

By the time the quartet stopped playing, Jakob had consumed many drinks. The impact of those drinks was taking its toll. Jakob felt light headed and his balance was off.

At 3:00am, there were only a few drunken soldiers left in the club. Ilsa appeared from upstairs. She walked over to Jakob and smiled at him.

"Jakob you make that instrument come alive. I hope we can convince you to stay and play with us for a while. It will not be so bad here. You will make good money and have a lot of fun here."

She went to the bar and spoke with the bartender. He reached into the till and handed her a large amount of cash. Several minutes later she returned to the group. She handed each of them cash. Jakob took the cash and counted it. He was amazed. The amount was large. He pocketed the cash.

Gunther called across the room to him. "Jakob, I will soon leave to drive back to the Hotel. Do you wish me to drive you?"

Jakob nodded and packed his instrument in the blue case. He bid goodnight to his fellow band members and jumped off the stage to join Gunther. Unfortunately the effects of all those drinks caused him to misjudge. He fell heavily, splitting open a cut to his forehead. Ilsa had seen him fall and rushed to him. She called for one of the girls to get a towel and cold water.

 She bathed the cut and applied a dressing then managed to get Jakob to a couch. She made him sit straight upright. Gunther joined them and after 10 minutes assisted Jakob to his feet.

"Ilsa, I will take Jakob with me back to the Hotel."

As he started to shuffle Jakob across to the door, Jakob vomited the evenings cocktails.

Chapter 94

The walls of the room looked strange to Jakob. His head pounded from both the bruising and gash in his forehead and the consumption of drinks the previous night. He looked around. He did not recognize his surroundings.

He lay in a bed with pink satin sheets. The room smelled of scented oils and stale perfume. Jakob attempted to raise himself from the bed. His head was spinning and the ferocious headache caused him to fall back onto the bed. He lay there. He could not understand where he was.

It was some while later when Ilsa entered the room. She looked at Jakob and shook her head."You have slept many hours. Jakob you took a bad fall. You were very drunk. Gunther and I decided it was not wise to take you back to the Hotel. You have stayed here in the club. It is now afternoon. We must get you up. Gunther will be here soon. Go to the bathroom at the end of the corridor and wash then meet me downstairs."

Jakob clumsily went and cleaned himself. When finished he stumbled his way downstairs. Ilsa was sitting at a table near the bar.

"We will get you some food and that should help you feel better."

Jakob raised his hand in protest. Ilsa ignored him and left to arrange food for him. Shortly after that she returned.

"Jakob I have asked for some food which will help you recover from all that drink."

As they sat there; Jakob felt waves of nausea passing over him. He felt as death was visiting.

A young kitchen hand emerged with a large white plate that he sat down in front of Jakob.

Jakob looked at the food and felt the need to vomit. Ilsa looked at him.

"Jakob. In Germany this is what we do. You need to eat something solid with grease. It will help. We have prepared kippered herring and fried eggs. There is much grease and oil in the kippers. They will help you."

Jakob gingerly picked at the kippers. He placed a forkful into his mouth. As he did so the smoky sharp taste of the herring removed the fuzzy and dry taste from the alcohol of the previous night. He ate slowly. As he did the feeling of nausea diminished.

Jakob was finishing his meal when Gunther arrived. He looked at Jakob and laughed.

"Now you are one of us. You must stay for a while and play. The patrons loved you. Don't worry about last night. We all have bad nights."

"I still feel ill. I need to sleep some more."

Ilsa asked Gunther to assist Jakob back to the room. Before he left, Ilsa withdrew another wad of cash and handed it to Jakob.

"Your stay here will be very profitable. I can promise you that."

Gunther assisted Jakob to the room. Once inside he spoke "Jakob, they like you here. Do not leave too soon. I have spoken to friends in the shipyards and docks. It will only be a matter of time before I can have forged papers made for you. You will need money. You can make that money here at the club."

"I need to reach Amsterdam soon. I must take my wife and leave for our ship to Canada."

"Jakob things are changing. With this war that has been declared, some trains will no longer run, ships have been cancelled and many restrictions are in place. I will help you but it will not be easy."

Jakob sat quietly digesting Gunther's words.

"I have a wife who awaits me. There are workers on my farm who need us back. I cannot stay."

"I suggest you take time and think about the situation. With Britain now at war with Germany, your Canada is also now at war. You will not be returning to the life you left. It is best we find a way to get you to The Netherlands. Again they have declared their neutrality. You and your wife should be safe there. To take a ship across the Atlantic will be dangerous even though the British Navy provides escorts."

"How soon can I get papers?"

"It is not easy to arrange. I will make contact with my friends. I must be discreet. I need to avoid being seen by those police again. Now I suggest you sleep here and wait until it is time to perform with the group."

Jakob lay there reflecting on Gunther's words. The more he thought about his life and experiences he realized he no longer wished to return to his former life. He had totally rejected the

Mennonite ways and beliefs and he did not wish to return to farming.

That night at the club Jakob asked Gunther about sending money to Anke in Amsterdam. Gunther replied that he would ask.

"The Netherlands are not at war with Germany. I will ask someone I know who travels there on business if he will help. He will want a good part of that money though."

Jakob agreed.

That night the crowd at the club was loud and business was brisk. There was a mood of happiness. Jakob found this strange for peoples who were at war. The group played till late. Throughout the night they were requested to play certain songs. Often when they obliged, the soldiers would break into song and sing along with them.

Jakob was finding nightlife in the club both bizarre and interesting.

Chapter 95

Days passed. Jakob now knew that he and Anke would not be on the ship back to Canada. Gunther was still trying to arrange for someone to carry money to Anke.

The colder weather was setting in. Jakob had arrived at an agreement with Gunther and his wife for a rent to stay at the Hotel until he could leave.

Late in the afternoon Gunther announced he had business at the docks. He grabbed a long coat and cap which he donned and left.

Jakob decided to go out and eat before going to the club later that night.

Jakob wandered through the streets alone. He was cautious not to arouse anyone's suspicions. He was concerned so he chose to go to the club early.

At the club he found Ilsa sitting and talking to the bartender. They beckoned Jakob to join them. Ilsa looked at Jakob's forehead and then reached across to lift the dressing. The bruise was bright blue and the cut had started to heal over.

"I will get some fresh dressing for that cut. Come. We will go upstairs where I can change it for you."

Jakob followed Ilsa up 2 flights of stairs. At the top of the staircase was a landing and a short passageway. She went to the end and opened a door that lead into a large bedroom. In the room there was a bath and a sink. A small toilet was off to the side. These were Ilsa's private quarters. Jakob followed her into the room.

As Ilsa was changing the bandaged cut, Jakob watched her intently. Previously in the dim lit club he had not noticed how beautiful she was. Her raven hair was swept back revealing a long neck. She wore a gold chain with a locket. He wondered what was in the locket.

When she was finished they left together to return downstairs to the club. She looked at the old clock that hung behind the bar.

"Gunther should be here soon. When you arrived I was speaking with the bartender about my concerns. We are getting more soldiers every night. While this is good for my business, and the girls are happy, the soldiers are becoming difficult. I fear we may have trouble."

The door to the club opened and several drunken soldiers almost fell into the club. They made their way to a table and crashed down. Within minutes they were shouting for beer and some of the prostitutes to join them.

Jakob watched from the stage as he set up his instrument. "May be Ilsa is right. Trouble could be coming" he thought.

The club filled with more soldiers. Ilsa was walking around monitoring the action. She went to the bar and leaned over, cupped her hand and whispered loudly.

"I do not see Gunther. Tonight we will need him. This group looks like they will create problems."

The bartender nodded.

As the band started to play, a group of sailors entered the club. There was a drop in the roar of conversation. It was clear the soldiers did not want sailors in the club. Shouting broke out. It was not long before chairs were being thrown and bottles and steins flew across the room. Fists were flying. Soldiers were fighting both other soldiers and the sailors. There was shouting and swearing.

Ilsa ran into the group screaming at them to stop. It was not long before the doors burst open and a number of police moved in to break up the melee. Truncheons were drawn and heads cracked. Calm was restored after some 10 minutes. The police summoned Ilsa to the door. They demanded she close the club for the night. She had no other option.

Jakob left and returned to the Hotel. When he entered the hotel Gunther's wife ran from the desk.

"Did Gunther join you at the club? He has been gone for over 7 hours. It is not like him. He always tells me where he goes. His car is still here. I suspect something bad has happened."

"He was going to speak to some people about getting me some papers so I can leave Germany. He was also taking money to a businessman who travels to Amsterdam. The money was for my wife Anke to travel back to Canada."

"The people you speak of operate in a dangerous area in the shipyards. There is a lot of crime there. I will not go there. I must speak to my brother. He works in the yards. He can ask if Gunther was there."

She went to the desk and picked up the phone to call her brother. She spoke for several minutes before hanging up and returning to Jakob.

"He is going there now. He will phone if he has any information."

A couple of hours later, Jakob heard the faint ringing of the phone. It was followed by a loud scream. Jakob ran to the reception area. Gunther's wife had her head between her hands and was crying out. Jakob went to her and placed his hand on her back to comfort her.

"What has happened?"

"Those police who chased Gunther the other night caught him. They have beaten him so bad he will probably die. His arms and legs are broken. His head is split open. His nose and teeth are smashed. They are not police. They are thugs."

Jakob attempted to calm her down. He helped her into her room behind the desk and sat with her.

"What can I do? I cannot be much help as I am in hiding."

She looked at him. "Gunther's brother is coming here now. He will help me. These police will be punished. They have made Gunther's life difficult for years. I am sure the brother can obtain identity papers that will allow you to return to your wife."

Jakob stayed with her until he heard the door open and the brother arrived.

Chapter 96

Jakob left them and returned to his room. A short while later there was a knock at the door. He opened it to find the brother standing there dressed in his coat and wearing a dark beret. Jakob invited him in. The brother shook his head.

"No. It is safer for us to talk outside. Come, even though it is late I know a café where we can get a coffee and talk safely."

Jakob dressed quickly and left the Hotel with the brother. When they were outside and walking the brother introduced himself.

"My name is Heinrich. It is not safe to speak inside. I fear the rooms have listening devices. There have been strange things that happened to some who have stayed there. We will speak in detail when we get to the café."

They strolled on for some distance and finally arrived at a very small café. The lights were dim. Jakob looked in through the window. There were only two other men sitting and smoking. Heinrich opened the door and ushered Jakob in.

They sat in a cubicle in the rear out of sight. Heinrich ordered coffees. He fixed Jakob with a detailed look.

"I know who you are and what you have been doing. You are Jakob Klassen from Canada. You were in Munich with Josef Klassen. Before that you travelled around The Netherlands to find relatives. I must warn you that after your narrow escape from the SS in Munich both you and Josef are high on the list of people they are looking for. You are believed to be an operative for the British and were helping Josef with his plans."

Jakob did not know how to respond.

"I have never been involved in politics. All that information is wrong. How do I know you are telling me the truth?"

"I am a foreman at the ship building yards. The German SS visit often to check us. Not everyone there likes Hitler or the Nazi Party. We have workers from many different countries...French, Italian, Poles and Russians. When they visit they show us their file of people they are desperate to find. You and Josef are in that file. They have your photo which I suppose they took from the identity papers they confiscated."

"But I am innocent. All I have done is visit. I just want to go back to my country."

"That will not be possible. Every border point and dock will have this list. You will surely be caught. We must make it so that you will not be apprehended. Here is what I suggest. We cannot have a photo taken until that large bruise is gone. Before that we will make you look more Dutch. I will get some hydrogen peroxide and we will make your hair blonde. After which we will cut it short, like that of a laborer. I will arrange for a job for you on the docks or in the yard. You look strong and fit. I will pair you with a friendly crane operator. We will put you into the team that prepares the materials that he lifts for the building process. It is heavy work. You will be paid 75Marks every two weeks of which you will be required to pay 25 to the Party. That is their rule and not a rule of our union. We will have your papers prepared as those of a Dutchman. You must be careful. I suggest you stay at the Hotel during the day. I understand you have been playing with a band at Ilsa Wolfe's club. Until you have your new papers I suggest you do not do this. I will contact Ilsa and give her an explanation. It will not be the truth. We will now go back to the Hotel."

Saying nothing more they started the walk back.

"Do you have money to pay for the papers? I will need to pay for the photographer and the forger."

"What will it cost?'

"I need 200Marks. That will ensure an excellent set of documents."

Jakob thought. He had earned that and more at the club.

"Yes. Do I pay you now?"

"No. I will return tomorrow after my shift and we will start the process."

Heinrich turned away and drifted into the late autumn fog that had developed and shrouded the streets. Mist swirled around the street lamps.. Jakob reached the old Hotel and climbed the entranceway stairs and went to the room. Upon entering he could see his few possessions had been moved. He went to the table beside the bed and reached underneath. The envelope with his money was still glued there. He was relieved. Within minutes he collapsed into a deep sleep. He slept soundly until mid morning when he heard loud noises. He went to the front door and observed a platoon of Storm Troopers marching and Goose stepping their way down the street in front of the Hotel. There were thousands marching. Some men and women had stopped and stood along the sidewalk watching the display of military force.

Jakob recalled Heinrich's recommendation to stay out of sight. As he was returning to his room he knocked at the door of Gunther's wife.

"Is there any information about Gunther?"

"Yes. He is in hospital. It is unlikely he will live."

"I am sorry. I don't know what I can do to help."

"You can do nothing. You must stay hidden. Heinrich has contacted me. I will give you some books and newspapers to take with you to your room."

Jakob thanked her and returned for a long day of captivity in the dingy room.

He read and napped throughout the day. Late in the afternoon there was a knock at the door. He opened it and found a tray of food had been placed at the bottom of the door. He took the tray of food into his room. He selected some items and ate.

When darkness had descended, Heinrich returned with a package. He went to Jakob's room. Jakob let him in.

"I have the hydrogen peroxide. Let us start to make you Dutch."

At the old stained sink Heinrich soaked Jakob's head with the stinging liquid.

Chapter 97

The following Sunday evening Heinrich returned to the Hotel with the photographer. They walked in as 2 guests and went to the reception desk. For anyone watching it would appear that they were looking for a room. Heinrich was handed a key. He looked around at some others waiting in the lobby area. There were a couple of men who seemed to be observing those who came and went. Heinrich had seen them before at the docks.

Heinrich walked to Jakob's room and knocked. Jakob cracked the door open. Heinrich quickly looked around before entering the room with the photographer.

"Jakob we must hurry with this. I noticed some men in the, lobby who I do not trust and suspect they are spying on the Hotel's occupants."

The photographer went to the bed and stripped off a sheet. He asked Heinrich to help him hang it on the wall. He explained it was to serve both the purpose of providing a blank background and also to cover up anything that could identify the location.

The camera was set up and a series of photos taken. Heinrich and the photographer left within minutes after dropping the key they had been given at the reception desk. It looked like a harmless visit of someone who had just arrived, checked the room and was leaving for a visit to a local restaurant. As they left Heinrich looked around the lobby. The men were gone. This worried him. He told the photographer to leave without him.

When the photographer was gone Heinrich ran back to Jakob's room. He knocked furiously on the door.

"Jakob I sense things are wrong. Take all your possessions now. I will drive you to Ilsa's club now. I believe you identity has been discovered. Quickly, let us leave."

Jakob snatched up the few clothing items he had and reached under the bedside table for the envelope with the money.

They ran from the rear exit of the Hotel to the old Citroen of Gunther's. Heinrich searched his pockets for the key.

"I must go back for it."

Heinrich ran to the exit door and returned a minute later clasping the key in his hand.

The Citroen started immediately and they sped off in the direction of the club.

Outside the club were piles of broken furniture and boxes of broken items awaiting removal. Jakob and Heinrich knocked and were admitted to the club. Inside was empty. Most of the furniture was gone.

Ilsa soon joined them. "It was probably a good thing. Most of the chairs were finished. Tomorrow we have a delivery of new furniture. Tonight we will be closed."

Heinrich spoke to Ilsa and advised her of the developments. She reached up and pulled off the cap that Jakob had been wearing. She laughed uncontrollably at his white blond hair.

"Jakob you look better as a blonde."

Together they shared a laugh. Ilsa went behind the bar and poured each of them a whiskey. It was strong. Jakob found it made him calm.

"Ilsa I ask you to provide a bed for Jakob this night. I do not think he will be safe at the Hotel."

He had no sooner spoken than the phone at the end of the bar rang. Ilsa moved toward it and answered. She listened and hung up. She turned to Heinrich.

"You are right. The Gestapo just visited the Hotel and searched Jakob's room. He can stay but there will be rules. He must not leave during the day. He must avoid contact with the German soldiers. We will watch and see how effective his new identity is."

Heinrich spoke. "I will return on Tuesday night. I will have his new papers then. On Wednesday I will start him working on the docks. He will become known to the other workers and the German guards as a Dutch laborer. He will pay you and find lodging with you. We will find a way to get him out of Germany and back to Holland. At present it is too dangerous to attempt this."

Jakob had listened to the conversation in silence.

"I need to get a message to my wife in Amsterdam. We have now missed our return voyage. It is October and I am sure she is worried."

Ilsa gave him a look of disdain.

"Why is she there and you are here? If you were a real husband you would have stayed with her in these times."

Jakob went to answer. Heinrich raised his hand to silence him.

"Ilsa that is not important. There are things that are best left not discussed. This is one of them. The men at the yard have supported you and your business over years. Now it is your turn to help us."

Ilsa blushed. Her cheeks went red. She had never been admonished by her cousin Heinrich. She had always looked up to him as a father.

"I apologize. It was wrong of me to say that. I am sorry. Will you stay and eat with us Heinrich?"

Heinrich shook his head. "I have other business tonight. I must leave. Keep Jakob quiet and safe. He will be able to go into the club and walk around outside after he gets the papers on Tuesday."

Ilsa nodded her head in agreement. "I will make sure he behaves."

Chapter 98

When Heinrich left, Ilsa and Jakob sat on one of the remaining velvet couches. Ilsa went back to the bar and returned with the whiskey bottle. She poured two glasses for them. They sat and talked. Finally Ilsa suggested they go to the club's kitchen and find some food.

After a light meal they returned to the main room and continued to drink and talk. Once in a while there was pounding on the club's door as someone wanted entry. They ignored the interruptions.

It was late when they decided to retire for the night. Ilsa lead Jakob up the stairs. Instead of stopping at the 2nd floor she continued up to where her private room was. She showed Jakob into what appeared to be a guest room. It was very small. The bed looked as if it had been built for a child.

Jakob lowered himself onto the bed and sat looking at Ilsa. He was curious. She sensed his mood.

"Is something bothering you, Jakob?"

"I wonder why you are in this business. You are a Madam. This is a bordello. From speaking with you I do not understand why you have this business."

"Jakob, we grew up poor after the first war. My father never recovered from injuries he received. Other members of my family starved. Some died from sickness due to their weak condition. I worked the streets and was very good at it. I saw this opportunity.

I promised I would never be poor or hungry again. If this is what it took to achieve that, then this was fine with me."

Jakob watched her as she moved toward the door. He wasn't sure but thought he detected her voice breaking and a wetness in her eyes.

"Ilsa come back. I meant no criticism of you. You just seem too intelligent and decent to be in this business."

Ilsa stood at the door with her hand on the handle. She made no move to leave.

Jakob crossed over to her and reached for her hands. They became locked in an embrace. Passionate kisses were exchanged. Their hands searched each other. Ilsa whispered in Jakob's ear "Come to my room. We will be totally alone there. No one is allowed in that room. They know better than to interrupt."

Jakob and Ilsa spent the next hours enjoying the sex. Jakob had never experienced sex like this before. They stayed awake for most of the night. Jakob was exhausted by dawn.

They slept until around 10:00am Monday. Ilsa left the bed to bathe and dress.

"I must go down to the club. The deliveries are due this morning. I need to have the club back in business tonight."

Jakob extended his hand to her. She returned and took his. He pulled her hard. She fell back onto the bed. Jakob stripped off her clothes. She laughed. Jakob was also naked. He engaged her again with a passion he did not know he had. She cried out in ecstasy. They lay spent for a while.

"Jakob, now I must go. The men will be here soon. You can stay here and rest. It is probably better no one sees you yet."

Ilsa dressed and left Jakob resting.

"I will return with some breakfast for you. Please stay hidden here. I do not want any more problems."

Jakob fell back to sleep. Ilsa woke him later in the morning with a plate of pastries and some dark coffee.

"The furniture has arrived. It is now being placed in the lounge area. I think you will be able to join is in about an hour. We are almost finished."

She kissed Jakob's ear and left. Jakob lay and reflected on all that had happened since he and Anke had left the farm. He had never expected a life like this.

Chapter 99

In the meanwhile life continued normally in the Netherlands. While Germany was at war, The Netherlands had declared neutrality; Germany respected this and in fact they were sympathetic to the Dutch. They saw the Dutch as fellow members of the Aryan race.

Anke had developed a routine and was still enjoying life. While frustrated and concerned about Jakob, she did not give up believing he would be back. As a dedicated and faithful wife she prayed each day for his safe return.

Anke had realized that Jakob was probably trapped in Germany due to some event, though she could not decide what that could be. It had been over two months since Jakob left. She had written to the Munich address of Josef, not knowing he had fled to France and then on to an undisclosed destination. Within weeks the letter was returned unopened.

It was early November. Julia called to Anke to accompany her as she was going to visit friends. Anke willingly agreed and quickly put on a light coat.

The weather over the past weeks had been pleasing. During the day the sun shone in a bright blue sky. There was a slight chill to the air and the evenings were cool. It reminded Anke of her days back at home with Johannes when they would go to their orchard and pick the late crop of apples.

Anke smiled to herself at these memories. She recalled making the pastry for the apple and cinnamon pies that she would bake. They would eat them warm with fresh cream.

They walked on until they reached a large red brick home. Julia went to the door and rang the bell. They were admitted by an elderly lady wearing some type of uniform.

Anke realized it was a nurses uniform and that the friends they were visiting were in a small hospital.

Julia was greeted by a cheerful nurse and they were taken to a lounge area where some older people sat with books or just looking off into space. This was a scene familiar to Anke.

Julia went to visit with two women. She sat and held their hands and talked. Anke watched and saw that the women relaxed and smiled when Julia spoke with them.

Anke stayed back and was standing by herself when the cheerful nurse approached her. They became engaged in a long conversation. Anke told her of days in Canada at the farm and of the nursing career she had pursued. She remembered the horrors of the injuries to the returning soldiers of the earlier war. The cheerful nurse asked her to join her at the cafeteria for a tea and cake. Anke agreed. They sat and talked some more.

Eventually the cheerful nurse told Anke of the shortage of nurses to care for the elderly and sick. She was worried that this would get worse due to the war next door in Germany.

Anke made a decision.

"I would like to offer my services. I will volunteer. My husband is in Germany. I do not yet know when he will return. Until then I could assist here for a day or two each week."

The cheerful nurse beamed. "We need nurses with special training. Some of our patients are very ill. They are on a ward upstairs away from the other patients."

"I was trained in many areas. I believe I can help there."

The cheerful nurse excused herself. After a while she returned with a tall woman in uniform.

"This is Claudette. She is the Head nurse for that section of our Hospital."

Claudette took Anke's hand.

"I am pleased to meet you. My friend here, Geraldine, has told me about you and your offer. We accept it kindly. When can you start with us?"

Anke advised them that she needed to speak with Julia before advising them of a date. Anke did not want to interrupt Julia. She was in deep conversation and the women emitted the occasional laugh.

Finally Julia headed back to Anke. Anke told her of the decision she had made to assist. Julia was thrilled.

"A worthy cause and this is the accepted thing to do as a devout Mennonite. I am happy you are doing this."

Anke spoke to Geraldine and Claudette and arranged a date.

Julia and Anke returned to the house happy and full of chatter.

Chapter 100

The winter rolled into Holland with a roar. Anke continued to work at the Hospital. She enjoyed the work and the company of both the staff and the patients. Soon she was working 5 days a week. She loved the work and was loved by the patients.

When not working the care ward, Anke would sit and talk with some of the elderly patients. She found their stories fascinating. They had tales of the past in The Netherlands. She loved to hear them recall events and customs of those years.

Anke was continuing to learn and liked The Netherlands more each day.

In early January, Anke awoke during the night. She was sweating and had a sore throat. She coughed up small globules of blood. She got up from her bed and tried to walk to her wash basin. She was weak and fell back to the bed. She lay like this for the rest of the night.

When she did not join the others for breakfast Julia knocked on her door and called her. There was no answer. Julia opened the door to Anke's room. Anke lay drenched in sweat. Julia had seen this before. She rushed downstairs and prepared cold cloths for Anke's face and neck.

She placed the cloths and returned to find Wilhelm sitting and writing .

"Wilhelm. We have a serious problem. Anke is ill. I think she has the tuberculosis like you suffered with. We must get a doctor immediately. I will go to the Hospital where Anke has been working. Maybe I can get help there."

Julia dressed and left without any delay. She arrived at the Hospital out of breath and perspiring heavily even though it was bitterly cold. On entering she noticed Geraldine leaving with some trays in her hands.

"Geraldine. We must talk."

Geraldine looked at Julia and saw the panicked look on her face.

"What has happened? What is wrong?"

Julia explained. Geraldine took Julia into an office and sat her down.

"Yesterday we found 2 cases of tuberculosis in the care ward. I believe Anke may have come in contact with it there. We have several excellent doctors here. I will call one now."

Geraldine left the office and shortly thereafter returned with a doctor.

"Julia this is Dr. Wall. He is here from England. He specializes in certain diseases including tuberculosis."

Dr. Wall shook Julia's hand and enquired "Where is Anke now?"

"She is still in bed. She is very weak and her clothing is soaked with sweat."

"I will gather my bag and the necessary items and we will go to her immediately."

Julia started to sob. Geraldine placed a hand on her shoulder and attempted to calm her.

"Julia, if anyone can cure her it will be Dr. Wall. He is brilliant. I know he liked Anke very much. I watched them joking and having fun together. I believe if Anke was not married they may have courted."

Julia gave a small smile. "Anke has been such good company and so kind. I am saddened by this. I will pray for her recovery."

Dr. Wall returned with a box like attaché case. He had put a winter coat on. He sat his case down and assisted Julia into her coat for the walk back to the house.

Upon arriving the doctor went straight to Anke's room. He placed a mask on his face. He took her temperature and then opened her mouth to inspect her throat. He took a large syringe from his case and injected a clear fluid into the top of her arm. Anke murmured something in her delirious state.

The doctor continued his examination. After some time he came out of Anke's room and joined Julia and Wilhelm. He removed his mask. His look was serious.

"Yes, Anke has tuberculosis. It is in the very early stage of the infection. I believe it can be treated. She will need constant care and medical attention. I can advise you of the process."

Wilhelm raised his hand to speak. "Doctor, we have some knowledge. I recently had this disease and recovered. We understand the amount of care Anke will need."

"I can arrange to have her sent to a hospital."

"No. We would rather care for her here. I looked after Wilhelm and I believe I can provide the help Anke will need."

"At this early stage, Anke will need intense care. I will return this afternoon and then each day I will visit twice. I may bring a colleague with me. Try to keep her cool with the wet cloths. I have given her an injection to make her a little more comfortable and to reduce the temperature. I will return between 4:00 and 5:00pm. If possible try to give her some fluids. I advise you to keep any cup or plate that she uses isolated. We do not want to spread the bacteria. This is important. Wilhelm you must stay away from Anke completely. Your system has already been weakened."

The doctor collected his equipment and placed it in his case. He then left to return to the Hospital.

Chapter 101

The doctors returned in the afternoon. Dr. Wall was accompanied by another specialist. They checked Anke and administered more medications. When they were finished Dr. Wall entered the living room where Wilhelm and Julia waited.

"My colleague and I must wash our hands with a special soap. Where can we do this?"

Julia directed them to a guest bathroom. The doctors returned and spoke to Wilhelm.

"This is Dr. Schwarz. He is a research specialist. There are studies to find a new and better vaccine for treatment of this horrible disease. Dr. Schwarz leads a project in this area. We would like to have Anke participate. Medical treatments and costs are covered by the project. We will need her husband's consent. There are some legal issues that require him to agree and sign some forms."

Julia looked at Wilhelm. She was unsure how to proceed.

"Doctors, Anke is a devout Mennonite. I will need to ask our Elders about this. Anke's husband is in Germany. We have not been able to contact him. I don't know what we should do."

"The symptoms that Anke displays are very serious. It could be life and death. The treatments we would administer have proven effective in the past. She will need to be quarantined for a 4 to 6 month period though. She will not be able to travel nor will she be able to go outside into any public area."

"We will go and see our Deacon tonight. We will seek their permission for this."

""Tomorrow morning we will be here at 9:00am. We can discuss then. Anke will need to be watched tonight. I have brought some masks for you. Use them every time you enter her room. Goodnight."

Wilhelm and Julia left Anke in the care of their son, Aaron. They travelled by tram to the Deacon's residence. They rang the brass bell on his front door. They were ushered inside to a library of the entrance hallway. The Deacon asked them to be seated.

"What is so important that you visit at this hour?"

Julia told of the situation with Anke. The Deacon listened and after some thought nodded.

"Yes. You must allow the treatments. I will speak to the other Elders and advise them of this. I am sure they will all agree. Now we shall offer prayer."

Julia and Wilhelm were relieved and returned. Anke's condition had worsened. Julia was worried. She made herself a comfortable seating arrangement and settled in to keep watch on Anke throughout the night. She placed cold cloths on Anke several times throughout the night.

The Doctors returned early in the morning. Wearing their masks they checked Anke. When finished they repeated the same hand washing procedure. They had left the special anti bacterial soaps for Julia, Wilhelm and Aaron to use.

They went to the living room to update the family on Anke.

"I am pleased to tell you that the temperature has come down a little. This is a good sign. It appears Anke will react well to treatment. What are we to do about the research project?"

Wilhelm spoke. "Last night we visited the Deacon. He listened and approved. We cannot contact Jakob her husband. We do not even know if he is alive or in Germany at this point. What are we to do?"

"As family it is possible for you to accept responsibility and sign the documents. I have them with me. I will explain each one to you. They are very simple and provide details of the treatment and that you agree with this treatment."

After many minutes of reading and discussion, Wilhelm signed the documents.

Chapter 102

In Hamburg, Jakob had established a pattern for his life. During the day he worked as part of a crew at the ship building yards and at night he happily played with the quartet at the club. It wasn't long before he made friends. He was cautious in what he said to any of these new friends. He always introduced himself with the new name in his forged papers. Jakob Baumann.

The ship yards were busy. New ships were under construction and several new U-Boats had been laid down. There was no shortage of work. Jakob found additional overtime work. The cold winter days passed. At 10:00am each morning Jakob and his crew would stop working and enter a heated tin shed that served as a rest area and canteen. They would sit and talk amongst the other crews. Talk was often in low tones and sometimes whispers as there was no trust amongst the men. Any topic dealing with the Nazis or politics was especially guarded.

One morning Jakob was sitting with his crew. His friend, the crane operator was in particularly low spirits. The rest of the crew was curious but no one wished to intrude into his thoughts and mood. As they sat smoking and talking a hush fell over the men at the tables.

The door swung open and an SS Officer dressed in his long SS provided long black leather coat walked in. His hat was pulled tightly toward the front of his head. It was an officer well known in the yards. It was SS Officer Kurt Gunner.

Gunner was despised. He was a sadistic, power hungry man who would betray anyone to better his position with those in authority. He was greatly feared in the community and by his peers. He was known to inflict no end of suffering and harassment on those he suspected of lacking loyalty to the Nazi cause.

Kurt Gunner had been assigned to enforce security at the yards. He did so brutally. He had seen to the arrest and deportation of workers he personally disliked or he believed were in any way subversives.

Gunner stared at Jakob with his short cropped blonde hair. Something did not seem correct. Gunner marched to the table at which Jakob was seated.

"Papers. I need them now" he barked.

The other men sat in silence as Jakob removed them from the pocket inside his jacket. He handed them to Gunner.

"Stand up when you are dealing with an Officer of the SS. You will address me as Sir and not speak until I ask you to. Your name is Jakob Baumann? I will check on this. I am taking your papers with me to the SS Commandants' office to have them checked. You will not leave the yards today until this is done. You will come to claim your papers at the end of your shift."

Kurt Gunner started away from the table. He stopped and addressed Jakob's friend, the crane operator.

"I understand you have been drafted to serve at the front with the glorious Storm Troopers. You are privileged and should take great pride in this."

Now the men knew the reason for his dejected manner. After Gunner left, questions were asked.

"When will you leave? Where will you be posted? How were you selected?"

The questions went on. Finally the crane operator stood and left. After he left for the day, he was never seen again by the workers. Later, close friends who knew where he lived went to visit. The home was empty. He and his family were gone.

Jakob tried not to panic. The forgery was one of the best. His photo showed a very different image than that of Jakob Klassen. At the end of the day he trudged to the office and presented himself. He was kept waiting for hours. SS Officer Kurt Gunner appeared holding his papers which he held up to examine.

"Where were these issued?" he demanded.

Jakob froze. He was not sure. He would guess. "I applied in Amsterdam."

"They were not issued in Amsterdam. Why would that be the case?"

"I applied before my trip here in search of work. I do not know why."

Kurt Gunner went through each paper. He looked at the application stub and then at the ID. He noticed the stamp of the Amsterdam office and an additional stamp of the office in Den Haag.

"It seems the Dutch continue to do things in their own way. Here take your papers. I tell you now Jakob Baumann that I do not like you or trust you. If you create any trouble I will have you conscripted regardless of your nationality. I will do it just as I did to that crane operator friend of yours. He thought he was smart and could gather others with him who wanting Hitler to fail. Remember, we have eyes and ears in many places. We will be watching you Jakob Baumann."

Jakob left the office shaken. What had tipped them off? He was just a worker. He thought back to the day he started. He had never spoken of the Nazi Party, politics or any military event.

Jakob returned to the Club Henri in a somber mood. He entered the club late. Ilsa was in the dimly lit lounge area. On seeing him enter she hurried over to him. Jakob stopped at the bar and asked for a large whiskey which he drank in seconds. He ordered another. Ilsa watched and realized there was a problem.

"We will go to my room. We will talk there. Come."

They climbed the stairs to her room. Jakob told her of the day's events. Ilsa thought for a long while before she spoke.

"Jakob, I have grown very fond of you. In fact I suspect that this may be what many call love. I do not want you to be in danger. I will make enquiries with a good and loyal friend of our family. He owns a club near the docks. I will ask him if he has work for you in the band there. It will be safer for all of us. Gunther has died. Please do not try to go to the funeral. I do not want you seen with me, Heinrich or any of our family. There is a traitor somewhere. They searched your room at the Hotel and now this. Someone knows something about you and will turn you in."

Chapter 103

During the week, Jakob noticed that the other workers on his crew remained quiet and avoided contact with him. He ate alone and at the breaks their conversations were marginal. Without the crane operator, the group seemed to lack the life and atmosphere it had.

Jakob continued to work as before. He noticed an increase in the visits from the guards. Previously they would patrol a couple of times each day. Now the patrols were hourly. What had the SS been told? Was someone else planning sabotage at the yards or was it just a prudent increase in security as the war deepened?

Jakob was at the club playing when he noticed a man standing at the bar speaking to Ilsa and the bartender. As he continued playing he watched as the three of them looked in his direction. Ilsa and the man took drinks and went to one of the couches and sat.

The quartet stopped for a quick break. Ilsa and the man approached.

"Jakob, I introduce you to Richard van Ryder. Richard owns a club in the docks. Richard and I have been friends for many years. We were just kids at school when we first met. We have maintained our friendship over the years. I have explained to Richard your situation. Richard is no friend of the Party. They have attempted to close his club several times. They claim it is the music he allows to be played that contravenes the Nazi policy. He is interested in assisting you."

"When you finish for tonight we will speak further."

It was late when the last patrons drunkenly left the club. Ilsa beckoned Jakob to join her and Richard at a table close to the bar.

Richard spoke. "I would like you to join our group. We can use a good saxophone player. Tonight I heard one of the best. Our club is small and very busy. We will be able to pay you the same amount as you are making here I am sure. Here is the address. Can you start tomorrow night?"

"Where will I stay? I have been staying here at the club. I cannot return to the Hotel."

"We will arrange that for you temporarily. If it is true that someone is tipping off the SS it is better for Ilsa and all her family to be away from you. You must understand this. Don't worry. We will help you until you can leave and go back to Amsterdam."

"I will come after the shift tomorrow. Can I give you my case and the few possessions I have for you to take with you? I cannot take things into the yard."

Richard agreed. Jakob left to fetch his personal items. He returned with the small battered suitcase. Richard took the case and wished them goodbye.

"You will be better off with Richard. His club is frequented by those who may be able to assist you get out of Germany. Do not be foolish and try to cross the border with your papers. It is obvious they know something and are watching you. It will be a while before they find you at that club; I suggest you disappear from the yards if Richard can find you an escape."

That night Jakob lay and thought about the events that had happened. He thought of all the people he had contact with. He lay for hours thinking about each person. Finally he realized the one person with whom he had little direct contact but who was aware of his situation and the others who had helped him.

He continued to lay and think about this person and the times he had contact. There were times with Ilsa, times with Gunther. He thought it was strange that this person had vanished when the brawl had broken out in the club.

He would tell Ilsa his suspicions in the morning.

He ran the thoughts through his head and eventually fell off to sleep.

In the morning he went downstairs to join Ilsa.

Chapter 104

Jakob was surprised to find the club empty. Ilsa was not in the club. Jakob returned upstairs and knocked at her door. There was no answer. After several minutes, he opened the door. Ilsa's bed was made and the room was tidy. He was confused. Ilsa had not mentioned leaving the club.

Jakob went back downstairs. As he did, the door to the club opened and Ilsa walked in. She was wearing a heavy winter coat. There was fresh snow on her head and shoulders. Her boots were soaked. Jakob frowned. It appeared that Ilsa had walked some distance. She carried a brown paper bag in her gloved hand.

She saw Jakob. "Jakob, I needed to deliver a payment to one of our suppliers this morning so I decided to walk. On the way back I stopped at the bakery. I have brought us some strudel and croissants. Let us get some coffee and have them. They are still warm."

She looked at Jakob. "Jakob, you seem troubled. Is something wrong?"

"I will tell you while we eat those treats."

Ilsa smiled. She had found herself being attracted to Jakob more and more each day. Even the thought of him moving to Richard's club caused her to experience a feeling of loss. She did not understand the feeling. It was strong.

As they sat Jakob told her of his suspicions. She listened in silence and thought about what he had just told her. She cast her mind back to the several observations he had made to support his suspicions. Finally she nodded in agreement.

"You might be correct. I hired that bartender just prior to your coming here and joining the quartet. What you say is correct. I took him into my confidence too easily. He has knowledge of many things that happen here. He does not start work until late in the day. I do not know what he does during the day. I have seen him in deep conversation with some of the soldiers. I have never seen him challenged. You are correct. He has disappeared at times when there has been trouble in the club. He stays away from all the girls. They have told me that he is cold and rude to them. I will contact Heinrich. He must be told."

She finished her strudel and slowly went to the phone at the bar. She called the Hotel and finally got to speak to Heinrich.

"Heinrich, can you come to the club. I need to speak with you. Please come now. It is important. I will not say anymore over the phone."

Heinrich reluctantly agreed and arrived at the club some 30 minutes later.

"What is so important that you need me here?"

Ilsa repeated Jakob's thoughts regarding the bartender and the fact that things that had been discussed privately had been leaked.

"We were careless and spoke too openly in front of him. I believe Jakob is correct. He is the source of the leaks."

Heinrich thought long and hard. Jakob and Ilsa sat in silence. Finally Heinrich spoke.

"What you say does make sense. I have a plan. I will serve the bar tonight. When he shows up for work you will tell him his job is finished and that you have hired me. Tell him it is because of financial problems. Also tell him that Jakob has been told he is finished with the band for the same reason. Tell him that Jakob was fine with the decision and that he had already planned to return to Munich this weekend. We will give him false information to leak back to them. This will help Jakob. They will stop looking here in Hamburg and start looking in Munich again. Tell them he had a message from Josef and has gone to join him. In the meanwhile Jakob will be at Richard's. I will now go and visit Richard and tell him of this development. I want you to keep Jakob here tonight. He must play and find some way to have a conversation with the bartender and hint that he has plans to travel. We will distract Kurt Gunner and his gang."

Chapter 105

Late in the afternoon the bartender arrived and set himself up behind the long wooden bar. He took steins from the shelves behind him and arranged them at one end of the bar. A few early customers came in from the cold snowy weather. They sat at one of the tables. The bartender pulled some draft beer into the steins and delivered them to the table.

Ilsa was on one of the couches ostensibly talking with one of the girls, but in fact watching the actions of the bartender closely. She realized that the patrons who he just served had frequented the club often in the past week. She found it interesting that they were also the only ones that the bartender served at the table. Everyone else had to go to the bar or wait to be served by one of the girls.

Ilsa waited until later when the club started to fill with customers. Jakob had already played and the band was taking a rest. Ilsa signaled him to join her at the bar. Jakob wandered over to the bar and joined her. They stood at a quiet part of the bar to make sure their conversation could be overheard by the bartender.

"Jakob, I am sorry but since the brawl the club has lost a lot of money. I paid for repairs and the new furniture. I cannot afford to keep you here."

Jakob feigned surprise and pleaded with her to keep him. It was a great act.

The bartender glanced over at them listening all the time.

Jakob walked back to the band with an exaggerated dejected posture and look. To anyone who did not know better, his act was genuine.

Within minutes Heinrich walked into the club and headed to the bar. He ordered a beer and stood making small talk to the bartender. Ilsa joined him. In a voice loud enough for the bartender to hear she told Heinrich of having to "let go" Jakob. She went on about the financial problems. The bartender moved closer pretending to gather some items from the counter below and behind the bar.

She called the bartender over.

"I am sorry to have to tell you this. Tonight will be your last night. The club is losing money. I need to let you go. Heinrich my cousin will tend bar and since he is family we will not be paying him for his services. You can leave now. I will calculate the money we owe you and you can take it with you."

Heinrich positioned himself behind the bar and stood in a menacing stance. The bartender looked at him, shrugged and pulled off the stripped apron he was wearing. Ilsa had prepared an envelope that she handed him. The envelope contained his wages and a little extra money.

"I am sorry we must do this. I am sorry for Jakob to. He is going to go back to Munich. I understand he has some family there."

The bartender opened the envelope and quickly counted the contents. He thanked Ilsa and placed it in his trouser pocket. He went back to the bar and took his hat and coat. He threw on his coat and left the club. As he did, the customers whom he had served left the table and prepared to leave. The wheels had started to turn.

Jakob had watched the whole act unfold from his position on the stage.

The band played until late. Heinrich served behind the bar. The club seemed to be operating normally.

It was late when the club closed. Heinrich told Jakob to gather whatever he had at the club. He was driving him to Richard's.

They left the club amid a major snowstorm. There were very few people out in the storm at that hour of the morning.

Heinrich whispered to Jakob "There are two men standing in that entranceway across from the club. They are in the darkened area at the back. They are watching the club. We will walk away from the car to distract them in case they follow us."

Jakob and Heinrich tramped through the heavy snow until they were convinced they had not been followed. They found the car and Heinrich drove to Richard's club.

Chapter 106

Jakob settled in quickly at Richard's. It was a noisy and boisterous club compared with Ilsa's Club Henri. Each night dock workers, sailors and the girls would drink, sing and dance. The girls would hook their customers and discreetly fade to the rooms on the first floor. Fewer soldiers patronized this club.

Jakob had just vanished from his job at the ship yard. Now he helped Richard at the club during the day and played at night. It had been several weeks since he had started.

It was early on a Monday afternoon while Jakob was stocking the bar with bottles that a familiar face that he recognized from the evenings entered the bar.

"Is Richard here?" he asked. He seemed friendly and had an infectious grin.

"He is working in his office on the accounts. I will go get him. What is your name? He will want to know who it is."

"He knows me well. Tell him Jan Zelder is here."

Jakob left to advise Richard of his visitor. Richard was delighted. He rose from his desk and rapidly walked to the bar where Jan was waiting.

"Jan, what brings you here at this time of day. I thought you would be busy at the ship."

"I will be sailing on Friday. I have heard through mutual friends that you wish to help someone to leave Germany. For a price I may be able to assist. I need to know the circumstances."

Richard told Jan the story as he knew it. Jan nodded. Richard continued.

"It is Jakob who you met you and came to get me. He is a good worker and musician."

"Tell him to come and join us."

Richard called Jakob to join them. He explained that Jan was the 1st Officer on a merchant marine ship. Jan then took over the conversation.

"This Friday we sail to the neutral waters of Venezuela to deliver some oil drilling machinery and then on to Aruba to deliver a shipment of pipes and equipment for the refinery in San Nicolaas. I can arrange to hire you on as a crew member. On the way to Venezuela it is likely we will stop at other ports. Do you have papers? "

Jakob produced his identity papers for Jan who then looked at them in detail.

"So you are Dutch? Then this may work well for you. Aruba is part of the Dutch West Indies and neutral. When we arrive in Aruba I will assign you to the dock crew that will assist in off loading the cargo. There may be an opportunity for you to desert the ship. I cannot be seen to help you with that."

"Today is Wednesday. Can this be arranged for Friday?' asked Jakob.

"Yes. I must warn you though that there are some strange things about this sailing. Instead of our normal crew size of fourteen, the crew for this voyage has been increased to forty five. The Captain is Frederick Heinz. I do not understand why he is in command of a ship in the German Merchant Marine. He was one of the most respected and top Officer Graduates at the German Naval Academy. I would have expected him to have command of a destroyer or a U-Boat. I find it strange. The Captain is also a ferociously loyal Nazi. He has a reputation for hard drinking and is rumored to have multiple lady friends in the different ports. The crew laughs at the little game he plays with these lady friends. It seems when he is bored with them he arranges for them to meet. He enjoys seeing them argue with jealousy. I warn you to stay away from the Captain. He is also a good friend with Kurt Gunner. Richard tells me you have already had experiences with him."

"How am I to get signed on board and join the ship without having to be checked by the various authorities?"

"I will personally escort you onto the ship. We will not be challenged. You must be alert to the dangers of this trip. I do not know all the men. I am sure there are SS men planted amongst us. We are also carrying a cargo that is not destined to either port. It is packed in long wooden crates. It is not on the ship's manifest. Now that you are aware of this, do you wish to try to make your escape this way? There are very few options for you. The ports of Canada are closed to all German shipping. The Americans are diligently watching all German marine movements and have increased searches. If you are successful in deserting in Aruba, it will be possible for you to travel the short distance to Miami and from there back to Canada."

Jakob thought of this. There was nothing to keep him in Germany. He could eventually get back to Canada and send for Anke. It seemed a good plan.

"Yes. I would like to do this. When will we board the ship?"

"I will come for you on Thursday night. Be ready."

Jakob thanked Jan and left to complete the tasks he had started at the bar.

Richard spoke. "Jan I thank you. I am helping Jakob as he is related to one of our friends who oppose what Hitler has dragged us into. Jakob is a fine musician and has worked hard since he has been here. I will make sure he is ready for tomorrow night. "

Jan stood to leave. "Tomorrow night. What time does the band finish?"

"I will have them stop around 11:00pm."

"I will be here then before that. I will have some drinks and make it appear that I am just one of your regular patrons."

"Jan how much will all this cost? I will advise Jakob of the costs."

"I may need to pay a couple of crew to remain quiet. I will need 100 marks."

Richard went to the bar and opened the cash drawer. He took 100 marks and paid them to Jan.

"I will see you tomorrow night then. Goodnight." Jan turned and left.

Chapter 107

That night at the club it was extremely busy and rowdy. The club was packed with German Navy sailors in uniform. Many were very young and excited at the prospect of adventures at sea.

Seated in the middle of the club were a group of German soldiers.

The drinks were served continually. The level of conversation and laughter increased as the night wore on.

The band was taking a break when the German soldiers threw their right arms in a Heil Hitler salute and loudly sang the opening words "Die Fahne hoch" of the "Horst-Wessel-Lied", Nazi Germany's National Anthem. The band stayed quiet. It seemed the whole club joined in the loud singing. Jakob looked across to the bar where Richard stood with a stone look on his face and was not singing. When they finished, conversations bubbled back to life.

Standing at the railing on the first floor was a sultry dark haired woman watching the band. She had become enraptured with the blonde haired Jakob since his arrival. She loved his saxophone playing and had watched him for hours as he played.

As she stood there she was approached by a German Officer in the uniform of a Captain. She froze.

"Good evening Madam. I would like your services tonight."

She looked at him. She had heard many things about him from the other girls. He was brutal and cruel. He had abused many of the other girls. She searched for a way to reject him. She did not want to be subjected to his abuse. The thought of him naked with his psoriasis wracked body on hers repulsed her.

"I cannot tonight. I am unable to. It's a woman thing. My fiancé is here as well tonight. I am sorry you will need to find someone else. She spun and went down the stairs and up to Jakob. She took his arm and invited him for a drink. The crowd at the club started to thin out now that the music had stopped. Richard brought them both drinks. She had a white wine and Jakob drank a large stein of beer. They talked and drank for hours. The club emptied and they were alone. She put her arm around Jakob's waist and her lay her head on his shoulder. They kissed. Jakob was aroused. She felt his arousal.

"Come. We will go to a room."

She went to the bar and removed a key for one of the upstairs rooms. It was not long before they were engaged in aggressive sex. Throughout the remainder of the night they repeatedly exhausted each other.

Jakob awoke to find that she was gone. He quickly got up and went to his own room. He bathed and dressed for the day ahead. It would be a long day. Tonight he was to leave with Jan to the ship and hopefully flee from Germany.

Downstairs he met Richard who was totaling the money from the previous night.

"Jakob, I paid 100marks to Jan for the services he will provide. I need you to pay me. I owe you money for your work here. Should I take it off what is owed?"

Jakob agreed. "Richard, I would also like to buy that saxophone to take with me. Will you sell it to me?"

Richard looked over to the stage and at the saxophone sitting in its blue case.

"I have no idea what it is worth. It will just sit there unused. Take it."

Jakob offered 25 Marks. Richard declined the payment.

Mid-morning there was a knock at the club's front door. Richard went to the door and upon opening it was surprised to find Ilsa there.

"Come in. Come in" he laughed. "What brings a beautiful young lady like you here in this cold snowy weather?"

"I came to see Jakob. I have some news for him."

"Then come in. I will go and tell Jakob you are here. He is in the back."

Richard showed Ilsa to a couch and left to find Jakob.

Jakob arrived in minutes and went directly to Ilsa. "Ilsa, I am pleased to see you. Why have you risked coming here?"

"Jakob we need to talk. I have found out I am pregnant and with baby. It is about 3 months. I have been with no other man. This baby is from you."

Jakob's jaw dropped open. He was in shock. He thought about the nights at Club Henri he had spent with Ilsa. He wondered what he should do. He was to sail from Germany tomorrow. He did not expect anything like this.

"Ilsa I need time to think about this. Are you sure that the baby is ours?"

"Yes Jakob. I had even wished that one day we would live together as man and wife. I do not want to give this baby up or have an abortion."

Jakob put his head down in his hands and thought. This was one more crisis he had created.

"I understand you. I will take today and decide what we should do. I will come to Club Henri late on Saturday afternoon and we will make plans for the future."

Ilsa smiled. "Thank you Jakob. I knew you would be a gentleman."

She arose and Jakob walked her to the door.

"I will take a taxi back to the club. I will see you on Saturday"

Jakob waved her farewell and closed the door. He walked to the bar and poured a strong drink. Richard joined him.

"Why did Ilsa come here at this hour and in such bad weather?"

"She had a message of some importance to me."

Jakob thought about the situation. He would sail away on Friday. He had no intention of seeing her on Saturday.

Chapter 108

Jakob was ready Thursday night when Jan arrived at the club. He had his little battered suitcase and the saxophone in its blue case.

Jan was confused. "Why are you bringing a saxophone?"

"You have told me it will be about 12 days before we reach the Caribbean. I will practice and play to pass the time. I am sure the crew will enjoy some entertainment."

"I am not sure the Captain will. Remember he is a loyal Nazi and their stated policy on jazz is well known. Be careful with what you play."

They took a taxi to the dock where the ship was moored. The ship's deck lights were lit. The taxi stopped in front of the high iron gates. It was after mid night and there was a lot of activity on the wharf. Jan paid the driver and they exited the cab. Jan went ahead of Jakob and headed to a gate at the left. There was a grey painted guard post. Jan went in while Jakob waited outside.

He addressed a guard seated behind an old desk painted to match the grey of the guard post.

"I am the 1st Officer of the ship. I have been to pick up a crew member. Here are my papers and those of the crew member Jakob Baumann."

The guard lazily took the papers from Jan and looked at them. He was not too interested. He handed them back to Jan and waved them through.

They crossed over the dock to the side of the ship where a long gangway descended from the deck. There was no one around. Jan and Jakob carried their gear up to the deck. When on board Jan turned to Jakob "I will take you to the crew quarters."

They walked the length of the deck to a white steel hatchway door that opened into the ship. As they entered Jakob could smell the diesel fuel and hear the hum of engines running. They crossed a narrow bridge and came to another steel door. Upon opening it Jakob saw a row of doors for each crew member's cabin. He had been assigned the furthest from the entrance. Jan went first and opened the cabin door. He waved Jakob into the cabin. There was a bunk bed, a small stand with some draws and a wash basin. On the exterior wall was a large porthole.

Jakob swung the saxophone onto the bunk and then placed his case on top of the stand.

Jan turned to go. "We will be sailing in the morning. Our schedule was changed for reasons I do not know. I will stop by early. I will introduce you to the rest of the crew at the canteen where breakfast is served. Sleep well until then."

It was 6:00am when Jan knocked at the cabin door. Jakob arose and went to join him. They exited to the outside and walked back to yet another door. As they approached, Jakob could smell bacon cooking. He realized how hungry he was.

Entering the canteen Jakob was surprised. He had expected a group of young men. Instead the men were of all ages from 18 to 60. As Jan had told him earlier there was a large crew. Some were standing. The cook was busy behind a metal counter upon which a large pile of plates stood. He called to Jan "Good morning sir. With this large a crew we will be serving in 2 sittings. We will need you to help work out the details and advise who will be in each sitting."

"I will turn my attention to this once we are underway."

He turned to the seated men who were devouring their breakfasts. "Gentlemen, I would like to introduce Jakob Baumann from Holland. He has recently joined our company. I leave him with you as I must now meet with the Captain and prepare for our voyage."

"A Dutchy eh?" one of the crew called out good naturedly.

Jakob smiled and responded "Yep."

Chapter 109

At 10:00am 2 tugboats steamed to the stern of the ship. The mooring lines were dropped and winched aboard the tugs. Black smoke billowed from the single funnel as the ship gave a series of vibrations and slowly pulled back from the wharf. One of the tugs slipped in at the rear of the ship while the other proceeded to the bow and took a line. They worked together to turn the freighter. With the task complete they guided the ship up the shipping canal and out to the sea.

Jakob stood with several of the crew and watched as they left Hamburg. They passed a number of naval vessels and the U-Boats that were penned there.

The cool air was filled with smoke and the fumes of the ships.

The ship proceeded at a slow pace until they reached the opening into the ocean. The tugs turned away. Finally Jakob was leaving Germany.

Once free of the harbor, the ship increased speed. Jan joined the crew on deck and spoke to one of the older members.

"I would like you to add Jakob to the maintenance group. He has worked on farm machinery and can be of great assistance with cleaning and maintaining our ship."

The older man grunted and nodded. Jakob was again introduced. The old man shook Jakob's hand and beckoned him to follow him below.

In the engine room they entered into an office. The roar of the engines dropped almost completely when the door was closed. The older man introduced himself as Ralph. He pointed to a chair for Jakob to take a seat and reached into the cupboard beside his desk and took out a thermos of coffee. He poured them both a mug.

"Jakob, this should be an easy crossing. Even though it is winter we will not be in the Atlantic for long. We are headed south. It is better at this time of year. No hurricanes to worry about. Our main worry will be the British and French destroyers that are patrolling. I believe the Captain has decided to stay out of the main shipping lanes. He will stay close to the shore of the United States. Their Navy will provide escort services as we are not at war with the States. We will be accompanied into their territorial waters until we reach the Caribbean. It will be relatively safe until them. This old girl can gather some real speed. We can probably outrun anything the British or French throw at us. It is important we keep this ship running in top condition in case that needs to happen."

Jakob had never been in a ship's engine room before. He looked at the engines and gauges and tubes. He was amazed at the cleanliness. Brass fittings were polished and gleaming. The faces of the dials were spotless.

Ralph noticed Jakob looking around. "Part of your job is to clean those gauges and polish every morning. If you detect any leak or problem you must tell me immediately. I will introduce you to Alex our electrician later. He is with the Captain on the bridge repairing something at present."

Ralph took Jakob around the engine room pointing out the things that needed to be checked constantly. The room was warm and smelled of the oils used to lubricate the many components. It was not an unpleasant smell. Jakob felt good in this environment. He felt secure.

At a little before noon the ship started a gentle rolling motion. Jakob started to feel a little ill. Ralph looked at him and advised him to go up on deck in the cold fresh air.

Jakob held the ships railing as it rolled from side to side in the ocean swell. Within minutes Jakob was vomiting his bacon and eggs overboard for the fish.

He stayed at the railing for almost an hour before Jan joined him. Jan laughed.

"It happens to us all when we first start on the ships. There is nothing to be ashamed of. By dinner you will be feeling great and very hungry."

Jakob looked at him with a very white face.

Jan walked away laughing and laughing.

Chapter 110

Amsterdam

In Amsterdam the March weather had been mild. The days were grey with lots of rain and cold winds. Anke's recovery had progressed well. She was still quarantined and the doctors visited daily.

A sure sign of Anke's improvement was her impatience at being confined to her bed and the house. She yearned to be outside and visiting the stores and marketplace. She missed visiting the other women she had made friends with.

That afternoon the doctors visited late in the day. Julia opened the door and let them enter. They removed their coats and Julia hung them on hooks near the door. She showed them into Anke's room. Anke was sitting up and reading. She put the book down and scowled at them. They laughed.

"It is good to see you are doing so well that you now give us a look of annoyance."

"I want to go outside. I feel like a bird trapped in a cage."

"It pleases us that you have this fight back in you. You have made a good recovery. I think that in a couple of weeks you will be able to leave the house. It will be spring then and you will be able to enjoy all the flowers and new growth on the trees."

"I still feel very weak. What can I do?"

"Anke, the weakness will go with time. We will give you some medicines that will help, but it is best for you to eat well. I know this has been very hard until now. You must try to eat at least twice a day. When you are ready to go out you will be very weak and will only get strength by eating."

"I will get fat."

They all laughed.

"Anke, which might be a good thing. Now rest. We will see you tomorrow."

Chapter 111

Jakob stayed on deck for as long as he could bear the cold. The Atlantic was in the throes of a small storm. Wind lashed at the ship. A combination of rain and seawater froze on the railings. Icicles hung from the lifeboats and exterior of the ship's superstructure. The ship continued to roll heavily throughout the afternoon.

Jan returned to the engine room to find Jakob with Ralph. They had a manual open on the desk and were studying a schematic. Ralph looked concerned.

"Jan we may have a small problem here. When checking the fuel readings and the rate of consumption, we noticed that the readings are wrong. I double checked the fuel we took on in Hamburg. It is impossible for us to have used the amount the gauges show. I suspect that with the rolling of the ship the measurement sensors in the tanks may have been damaged."

Jan asked to be taken to the fuel monitors. After viewing the problem he asked Ralph whether the problem could be fixed at sea.

"No. The floats for the monitors are inside the sealed fuel tanks. We need to be stopped and in still waters to attempt that. I recommend you advise the Captain. It would be wise to stop at a port and take on more fuel as we cannot see the rate of consumption."

"I will go and advise Captain Fredericks. He will not be happy with this news. He has been in a foul mood ever since we left

Hamburg. He is aggravated with the route we need to take. I will go now and return to advise you of his decision and plans."

Jan left Ralph and Jakob in the engine room office and proceeded to the bridge to meet Captain Fredericks.

He entered the bridge. Two of the crew were steering and manning the various instruments. Captain Fredericks saw Jan enter.

"I thought you had left to take an early dinner. It will soon be your turn to man the bridge. Is there a problem?"

"Yes." Jan relayed the information he had learned from Ralph.

The Captain swore and kicked against the wall. "Why do these things happen on my command?"

He reached for a phone and summoned the ship's navigator who arrived on the bridge within minutes. The Captain explained the situation. The navigator went to a shelving unit and unlocked the protective door. He slid out a roll of maps and laid them out on the long flat surface of glass under which various gauges displayed information. He selected one particular nautical chart of the south eastern United States and Caribbean. Using calipers he measured off distances to various ports and using tables he calculated the required amount of fuel need to reach these destinations. When he was finished he turned to the captain.

"I have calculated that we have enough fuel to possibly reach Maracaibo in Venezuela. However, if we continue south and then east we will have more than adequate fuel to reach Cartagena in Colombia. There we can fully refuel. This will be enough fuel for us to visit the ports in Venezuela and Aruba and still have enough fuel for the return to Hamburg. This will delay our arrival in Venezuela by several days. This is my recommendation."

The Captain looked at the charted route the navigator had prepared. He asked Jan his opinion. A decision was made.

"We will proceed on a southerly route and to Cartagena for fuel. Radio operator could you please send the following message to headquarters. Tell them of our predicament and our planned detour. We do not want to stop at any of the American ports. I fear that we could have trouble or delays if we did this."

Jan returned to the engine room and delivered the news of the change in the destination. Ralph listened and frowned. There was a concern.

"If the gauges are in fact correct, then we must reduce speed to conserve what fuel we have,"

Jan took the intercom phone and signaled the bridge. He gave Ralph's advice to the Captain. There was considerable cursing from the Captain. He summoned both Ralph and Jan to the bridge. He called the navigator to return.

The three looked at the chart. The navigator listened to Ralph who provided a speed and fuel consumption estimation. The navigator estimated the daily distance the ship would travel at that speed.

"Captain, I calculate that instead of 12 days we will need 17 days to reach Cartagena."

The captain was furious. Is there an alternative? Should we go to Aruba first?"

"If we do that and we are unable to purchase fuel in Aruba, then we will not be able to reach Venezuela or make our return voyage to Germany."

The Captain considered this and the ordered everyone except Jan to leave the bridge. The two crew who were manning the bridge expressed concern.

"You will wait outside the door while I speak with Officer Jan. We will only be a few minutes. Please obey."

Everyone except Jan left the bridge and waited in the narrow passageway outside the entrance. The Captain looked sternly at Jan.

"As you know, we are carrying an unspecified cargo. That cargo was loaded onto the ship so it could be offloaded using the ship's derrick after we visited Venezuela where we were to off load the freight that was stored above it and before we reached Aruba. I have instructions in a sealed envelope from Headquarters about where and when to unload this cargo. This delay and rerouting creates problems. Those long wooden crates contain secret arms. We are to be met by one of our German destroyers to offload while in neutral waters. We cannot divert from our planned route until we receive communication from Hamburg."

Jan listened but did not offer any advice.

"I will check with the radio operator. He will be instructed to attempt coded messages and to remain at his station and await the response." Jan left the bridge and found the sailor responsible for radio communication. He gave him his instructions.

Almost an hour later contact was acknowledged. New sailing instructions were provided that would cover the next 12 hours.

The ship was to sail to a pre determined location and rendezvous with a German cruiser.

The Captain looked at the chart. He issued the command to steer to the location.

The weather cleared but remained cold with a strong wind. They arrived at the location shortly before dawn. The Captain had slept and returned to the bridge with a hot drink. Jan was tired but offered to stay until they rendezvoused with the cruiser. He did not have to wait long. On the horizon, an estimated 5 Miles away, they saw the flashing of a mirror lamp signaling them. The message identified the cruiser and requested radio silence. It went on to advise of British and French ships in the area.

The Captain ordered the ship to stop. They drifted and watched as the large camouflaged cruiser closed in on them. It pulled alongside. A rope was secured between the two ships. When lines were secured a boat was dispatched from the cruiser with several uniformed sailors in it. The Captain ordered the gang way ladder to be lowered. After several attempts the sailors were able to attach their boat and board the ship.

The Captain greeted them. The Officer from the cruiser requested a meeting in private.

"We need to remove the cargo you carry. It will be a little dangerous with these conditions, but those are our orders."

"What is in those crates that require this secrecy? Why is there urgency to transfer this cargo now?"

"We are at war. Those crates contain a new type of torpedo. We will soon be joined by a U-Boat. They will take several. The rest we will take on board"

The Captain dressed into a heavy winter coat and proceeded down to the deck.

Chapter 112

In the grey light of dawn, Jakob stood watching as the ship's derricks swung the long wooden crates out of the forward hold and across to the cruiser. The weather had co-operated. There was a gentle swell and the 2 ships rose and fell with it. The transfer of the cargo was completed within an hour.

Jakob was surprised to see another small zodiac type craft lowered into the water by the cruiser. As it made its way across the water to the ship, the Captain ordered the gangway lowered. There were 3 men in the craft. They secured the boat at the base of the gangway and waited.

A number of the crew members who had been invisible throughout the voyage appeared at the gangway entrance dressed in dark navy commando like gear. They wore woolen pull down coverings on their heads. As the craft bobbed up and down at the foot of the gangway, these "crew" descended and took positions in the boat.

Jakob was joined by Jan. Jan rubbed his hand over the stubble that had grown over the past days. "Now I know why we were required to carry such a large crew. Those men are members of the commando squad. I noticed at meals in the canteen that they did not mix with the regular crew."

With the transfer of the freight and the commandos complete, the ship pulled away. As they did, Jan and Jakob viewed a U-Boat sitting on the surface about a quarter mile away from the cruiser. There was a gun crew at the ready on the forward gun. They were obviously standing guard during the operation.

Jakob now realized he was on a German supply ship. This was not just a freighter plying trade in the Caribbean and between Germany. He wondered if Jan Zelder had known this.

They sailed further south throughout the day. It was an uneventful day. That evening Jakob took his saxophone to the canteen where some of the men were playing cards or dominoes. He started to play quietly. Soon the men were asking him to play different tunes. If he knew the music he would play. It was not long before an angry Captain entered.

"What is going on here? Jazz and music is greatly frowned on by the Party. You must cease playing."

There was uproar from the men who were crowded around Jakob.

The Captain quickly assessed the situation. "If this is going to keep these men happy during the voyage then I should allow it" he thought.

"I will permit this if the music played reflects that of the German Fatherland."

The Captain stormed out slamming the door.

Several of the men came and slapped Jakob on his back. They were happy to have the distraction.

They stayed in the canteen and Jakob played every once and a while until it was late. Jakob took the saxophone and retired shortly before midnight. He was finding life on the ship interesting but somewhat boring.

Chapter 113

The next few days became monotonous. Jakob performed the routine tasks he had been assigned in the engine room. Meal times broke the boredom.

The further south they sailed the warmer the weather became. They were entering the Caribbean. The Captain placed additional lookouts on the bridge. He was aware that these waters were now patrolled by both the British and French with heavily armed and fast destroyers. While the destroyers' goals were to protect allied merchant shipping, especially oil tankers, they would be prepared to take an offensive role if German ships were identified.

The Captain called for the ship's navigator and requested an update on their exact location and estimated sailing time to Cartagena, Colombia. The navigator took sextant readings and consulted his charts. After spending sometime calculating he advised the Captain that they should reach Cartagena in a day and a half.

Jakob spent more and more time on the deck each day as the temperatures rose.

The ship reached Cartagena ahead of the estimated time. Jakob and the crew stood on deck admiring the port with its old buildings as they were slowly escorted by a Pilot boat and the Coast Guard to the area of Manga where they would dock.

Finally they were tied up at the Industrial Docks. The area was grey, dull and uninviting.

The Captain spent some time speaking with the Pilot and summoned Ralph to join the conversation. The Captain described the problem with obtaining accurate readings on their fuel supply. The Pilot listened and agreed to contact an engineer.

That afternoon Ralph and Jakob started stripping the fuel line from the main tanks. Ralph did not want to take on more fuel until the problem was found. Together they worked in the oppressive heat of the engine room. The main engines were shutdown and only a small engine ran to power the generator for the ships electrical needs. The air was heavy and stale with the fumes from the fuel.

Each section of the fuel line was flushed and reinstalled. As they removed a crossover valve, the heavy fuel sprayed back from the line. Ralph quickly threw a lever to stop the fuel spilling. On examining the valve, a blockage of a heavy sludge was found. Jakob and Ralph removed the valve and installed a replacement. When the job was complete, Ralph advised the Captain that he intended to start the engines and test the system.

Within 10 minutes, the testing was completed and the system registered the correct fuel readings.

The Captain made arrangements for refueling the next morning and contacted the Harbormaster's office to arrange to sail from Cartagena the next afternoon.

Jakob and Ralph returned to the crew's quarters to shower and clean up after the dirty job they had just completed. Afterwards, they went into the mess and sat quietly. Jan Zelder arrived and joined them.

"We will sail tomorrow afternoon. Since we have been at sea so long, I will ask the Captain for permission for some shore leave for this afternoon and evening. I look forward to a good South American spicy meal and some entertainment. Do both want to join me? I know of some places here in Cartagena from earlier trips I made here."

Jakob and Ralph exchanged looks.

Ralph spoke first. "Of course we will join you. Maybe we can visit a club where Jakob can enjoy some of that exciting Latin music and so we don't have to listen to his saxophone."

They all laughed and Jan Zelder left to get approval from the Captain for their shore visit.

Chapter 114

It was late afternoon when the trio left the ship. They walked through an area of industrial buildings in the heat that still lingered from the sweltering day. The smell of the baked dirt between the stones of the cobbled streets arose and added to their discomfort. Sweat ran from their foreheads. After sometime they entered into the walled section of old Cartagena. The streets were narrow and lined with houses that were a myriad of colors. Some had open windows with decorative bars that allowed passersby to look in.

As they continued to walk, the sound of live music sounded from the distance. Jan Zelder smiled and spoke. "Soon we will be at my favorite little cantina, El Tropico. You will enjoy good Spanish food there and real Spanish music. I have been here many times in the past."

The entrance was through an archway in a stone wall. On either side were old iron gates that were pulled back when the cantina was open. They walked through the archway and into the cantina through a dark wooden doorway. The music was loud and the interior dimly lit. It took several minutes for them to adapt to the change in light after walking in from the bright sunlight.

A large long thick dark wooden bar extended along the back wall. Arranged around a dance floor were a number of tables and off to the side a band of five musicians was playing.

The trio were approached by a young woman and taken to a table that was right beside the dance floor. They sat and ordered cold beer.

"I will order some food for us" said Jan Zelder. He signaled to the young woman who returned to their table. Jan spoke to her in Spanish. He spoke quickly and both Jakob and Ralph were amazed at his proficiency.

When the girl left Jakob asked Jan where he had learned Spanish.

"I studied languages when I was young. I found I had an ability to learn them quickly."

Several minutes later the girl arrived back at the table accompanied by an older woman dressed in an apron. She recognized Jan. They placed several large trays on the table. Each tray contained plates upon which were a number of small but different items. Jan stood and hugged the older woman. They spoke rapidly in Spanish for a while, and then she returned to a door beside the bar and into a kitchen.

Jan looked at Jakob and Ralph. They were looking at the plates with confused expressions.

"These are tapas. I ordered us a selection of hot and cold tapas. There are olives, spicy meats and pastry wrapped sea foods. I know you will enjoy them."

Jakob was looking at a table behind them where three Colombian men were seated. On their table was an odd shaped bottle. His curiosity rose.

"Jan, what are they drinking?"

"I do not know. I will go and ask them what they are drinking."

Jan got up and walked over to them. As he approached, the men went quiet as if expecting trouble. Jan smiled and greeted them in

Spanish. He asked them about the bottle. The oldest in the group smiled a toothless smile and responded. He spoke for some while and then gestured to the barman to bring a bottle to Jan. The barman took a bottle from the shelf behind him and carried it over to Jan. He opened the bottle and poured some of the liquor into a small glass and handed it to Jan, who gulped it back. His throat burned and his eyes watered. The Colombians rolled in their chairs with laughter. Jan thanked them and returned to Jakob and Ralph who had watched the whole thing.

Jakob was eager to find out what the drink was.

"Jakob, this is a traditional Colombian drink. It is called Aguardiente. That is Spanish for firewater. The drink is mainly drunk inland and not so much on the coast. Those men are from farms inland. They have been trading at the market.

Jakob took one of the glasses and poured a drink for Ralph and then for himself. They lifted the glasses and toasted. Jakob threw the drink back and swallowed in a single gulp. For several minutes he felt on fire. The Colombians were watching and joking and laughing at the trio.

It wasn't long before both the food and the Aguardiente were gone. Jan ordered more food and another bottle. The strong alcohol content of the drink was starting to have its effect on them.

Jakob watched as several couples got onto the dance floor and swayed to the Latin beat. He was enjoying the food and the drink. Little did he realise his judgement was becoming poor as he drank more. Soon he staggered to the dance floor and mimicked some of the dance moves.

As they sat talking, another young Colombian joined the others. He was accompanied by a beautiful woman in a revealing flame red dress. Jakob caught her attention and smiled at her. She returned the smile and continued to look at him from time to time. Her partner looked over at Jakob. The look was not friendly. Jakob shrugged and turned back to Jan and Ralph and continued eating and drinking.

As the afternoon faded into the evening, more couples entered the cantina. Soon it was nearly full. Men stood at the bar and groups sat around the tables engaged in various conversations.

The band had paused and after a long break they returned and started playing more Latin music. Jakob was intrigued. He did not know this music. He watched as couples went to the dance floor and engaged in different and suggestive dancing. He watched and tried to memorise their movements. He was eager to try one of these dances. Finally, with his courage inflated by the alcohol, he approached the woman in the red dress with the Colombians. He nodded a greeting and extended his hand to request she join him. She shook her head and her partner glowered at Jakob. Jakob realized it was useless and returned to sit with Jan and Ralph.

Chapter 115

In the cantina the air was filled with cigarette smoke and the aroma of the spicy foods. Loud bursts of conversation erupted at the tables. The music grew louder as the evening progressed.

Jakob cast the occasional glance at the Colombians and the beautiful woman. He knew that the young Colombian woman was watching him.

The band started playing a local tune. The crowd clapped and cheered. It was obviously a favorite of these customers. The young Colombian man stood and pulled the woman to her feet. He looked directly at Jakob and sneered as the couple walked to the dance floor. Jakob looked on in amazement as they started dancing a provocative Salsa. Many of the other dancers stopped and stood cheering them on. They moved slowly and deliberately. She shook her body and flirted with the crowd of onlookers. As the tune progressed, the dance moves became even riskier. Her dress spun and opened as they twirled and bent in suggestive moves. Jakob was mesmerized. Finally the music ended and the couple returned and joined the older Colombian men. Drinks were poured and toasts were made.

After several minutes the young Colombian left the table and exited the cantina. Jakob watched him leave. The woman sat alone and every so often looked toward Jakob. It seemed an eternity and the young Colombian did not return.

Jakob mustered up his courage and went to sit with the woman. He introduced himself. She was radiant.

"My name is Maria. Yes, I speak English well as I work for an American company and need to speak with their offices in America every day. One day I will go there. Tonight I am celebrating my birthday with Carlos my boyfriend. He has left to attend to some business. I am not sure when he will return."

Jakob sat and made small talk with her. He spoke of his travels and Europe. She was fascinated. Gradually the conversation drifted to the salsa dance she had performed with Carlos.

"Yes. I took lessons to learn all the moves. Here in Colombia we have different steps. In other countries the dance is different."

"I would really like to learn that dance."

She reached across the table and took Jakob's hand.

"I will teach you some basic moves. Wait and I will speak to the band. I will ask them to play something that will be easy for you to dance to."

She crossed the dance floor and spoke to one of the band members. When she returned to Jakob she held out her hand and took his to lead them to the dance floor. The music started. She placed her arm low down his side and her hand on his lower back. He held her and she lead him into several steps. He soon was picking up the steps and led her. She bent backwards with her long hair flowing back to the floor. She shimmied and spun. Jakob was totally enraptured and did not see Carlos return to the cantina.

Carlos stood at the table with the older Colombian men. Suddenly he lunged forward onto the dance floor. He pulled a switchblade knife from his pocket and started slashing at the air in front of Jakob. He roughly pushed Maria back. She stumbled and fell.

Carlos was quick. He sprung in front of Jakob and raised his knife. Jakob threw up his hands to protect himself. Carlos slashed the knife across Jakob's chest cutting a large hole across his shirt. He spun back on Jakob and slashed again. This time the knife found home. Carlos cut a large gash down Jakob's right cheek. Blood spurted from the wound.

Jan Zelder and Ralph ran to Jakob's assistance. Carlos menaced the knife at them. Within minutes the older Colombian men were also in the fracas swinging at Jan and Ralph though the Aguardiente had greatly diminished the accuracy with which they could throw punches. Other men joined in and soon the cantina was in chaos.

Jan grabbed Jakob and pulled him to the door. Ralph positioned himself behind Jan to protect them. They stumbled and tried to run down the narrow cobbled street. The street had a lane running off it and several buildings with doorways offered them some shelter.

Jan looked at Jakob's face. It was white and he was losing a lot of blood. Jan thought hard. He remembered that there was a main street that headed back to the docks. He asked Ralph to stay with Jakob and left at speed to try and get a taxi to take them back to the ship.

15 minutes went by until Jan returned in an old Ford taxi. He jumped out of the taxi and opened the rear door. He and Ralph pushed Jakob's inert body into the taxi. Jakob had fainted from the loss of blood and too much liquor. The taxi driver started to complain loudly. Jan responded in Spanish and took a wad of pesos from his jacket. He pushed them into the driver's hand. The

driver grudgingly accepted them and they sped off to the dock where their ship was moored.

When they arrived at the dock a night watchman approached and stopped them. Jan showed him papers and told him they needed to get Jakob onto the ship immediately. The watchman offered to help and they carried Jakob back and onto the ship.

Jan laid Jakob on the bed in Jakob's cabin. He left Ralph to hold a wet cloth on Jakob's face and went to get a medicine kit.

When he returned, he examined the cut. It was deep but clean. The knife had nicked the cheekbone but had not cut through the inside of the cheek. Jan removed some ointments from the kit and dressed the wound. As he was finishing there was a loud banging on the cabin door. The Captain stormed in with two Colombian National Police officers.

"What the hell happened? These police tell me you started a major fight in town. They were looking for you and it seems the taxi driver told them where to find you. You have no friends in this port now. You must accompany these policemen. There is damage to pay for. We cannot depart until this mess is sorted out. After that I will deal with the three of you."

"You can take them." He said to the police.

Chapter 116

The Captain turned to leave. As he did, one of the police called to him.

"Captain. There is no need for us to arrest your men and take them with us. Is there a private area we can sit with them and discuss this matter?"

"I will take you to the canteen. At this time it will be empty. Will you leave this one, known as Jakob here while you deal with those two?"

"Yes"

He escorted them to the dark and empty canteen. He switched on the glaring overhead lights. Ralph and Jan sat at a stained table. The police officers remained standing until the Captain departed. When he was gone, the police turned their attention to Jan and Ralph.

Jan looked at them closely. One was stocky and wore an ill fitting uniform. His hair and skin were greasy. His olive complexion still showed the scaring of acne he had suffered during his youth. The other policeman was tall, with a narrow and mean face. His eyes were black and cold.

The swarthy one took off his cap and threw it down onto the table. He stood in front of Jan and Ralph and addressed them in Spanish. Jan pretended that he could not understand. In exasperation the stocky policeman continued.

"We do not speak German. We will use English. Do you understand?"

Both Ralph and Jan nodded. The police started to talk to each other in Spanish. Jan listened quietly to their conversation. He made a small gesture to Ralph that went unseen by the cops. Ralph subtly acknowledged Jan.

Jan listened to the police. The spoke loudly and clearly, believing that neither Jan nor Ralph understood Spanish.

The swarthy cop spoke to his partner in Spanish. "We are lucky. Since they do not understand us our job is going to be easy. We will play out a game and convince them to pay us the money. You start with them and I will stand back here and watch."

Long face started. "My Name is Juan Rojas. My partner here is Ignacio Del Grande. We are assigned to solve the problems that you and your friend created at El Tropico tonight. If we cannot solve the matter here, then we must take you to the jail until a judge is available to hear a trial. All of you, including your injured friend will be jailed. It will be days and maybe weeks before a trial can be held. The jail is not a nice place for you. There are murderers, thieves, drug addicts, rapists and many other criminals. You will be in a holding cell with many of these prisoners. I fear it will not be a pleasant experience for you. It is better we try to solve this matter now."

The police then sat at the table. They asked for identification papers and hastily made notes in official looking notebooks with a gold embossed seal on the front cover.

The cop, Ignacio stood and walked back from the table. He called to his partner to join him. Again they started speaking in Spanish.

"That was good Juan. You have given them something to think about. We will let them sweat for a while and then I will take over."

They stood and leaned against a wall while they watched Jan and Ralph. No one spoke for at least ten minutes. Finally Ignacio walked back to the table. He scrapped a chair back from the table and sat his heavy frame down with a thump. He stared into Jan's eyes.

"You, my friend I do not trust. Maybe we should just arrest all of you now and call for a police wagon to have you taken to the jail. I feel we will be wasting our time with you here."

Jan shrugged his shoulders.

"What is it you want?"

"The owner of El Tropico wants you to pay for the damage to the cantina. She knows who you are. The customers say your friend started the fight and so you must now pay. If you will not then you will be jailed."

Jan looked at Ignacio's face. He did not believe what was being asked of them.

"What is it you are asking for? How much money is needed to solve this?"

Ignacio looked back at Juan his partner, who gestured for him to join him. Ignacio pushed himself back from the table and shuffled across to Juan. Juan took out his notebook and started pointing to different pages, while again speaking to Ignacio in Spanish.

"This is proving to be too easy. We will ask them for $500US dollars. You and I will take $200 each and we will give our taxi driver partner $100. Here look in my notes. We will pretend and claim they detail the damage and are reports from the customers and our friends at El Tropico."

The cops made a credible act out of pretending to decipher the information in the Notebook.

Juan finally spoke. "I will need to go and telephone the owner of El Tropico. I need more information and the amount she wants."

Jan Zelder sat in silence. They were being manipulated by a couple of Colombia's many corrupt cops. He thought of his options. There were few.

With Ferret face Juan gone from the room, Ignacio returned and sat across from Jan. His breath reeked of garlic, mixed with the body odor from the stale sweat that had been caused by the blistering hot day.

The door opened and Juan walked in with a serious look on his face. He spoke first to Ignacio.

"Now we will try to finish this and get out of here. The Captain is making some calls to other German ships here and trying to raise the Harbormaster. We must get this done and get away."

He then turned to Jan and Ralph.

"I have spoken to the owner. She says the damage is serious. She will not be able to operate her business for days and maybe weeks. Also, the Colombians you attacked want money for their trip back to the interior. They say you stole it. The amount they ask is $500."

Jan looked at him in disbelief. "Pesos?"

"No. She wants to be paid in American dollars. She will then pay the Colombian men in Pesos."

Ralph finally spoke. "We do not carry money like that with us on the ship."

The police remained leaning against the wall. Ignacio spoke. "I will call for the other officers to come and arrest you. There is no other way."

Jan spoke loudly to them in Spanish. They were startled and became angry. There game was exposed.

"We will pay you some money but not the amount you are trying to extort. I will go to the Captain and have him take $50 from the ship's safe."

The police officers looked at each other. Ignacio started to argue with Jan. Juan put his hands on Ignacio's shoulders and restrained him.

Jan left the dining area and proceeded to the Captain's quarters. He knocked and waited until he was admitted. When inside the cabin he quickly told the Captain of the events with the police. The Captain scowled and swore. He called to several crew members to join him at his cabin.

Soon six burly crew members were in the cabin with Jan and The Captain. Jan briefed them on the situation.

The group descended on the canteen and burst into the room. The police were startled. Ignacio reached for his pistol. He never made it. A huge arm crashed down on his neck. He fell heavily to the floor. Two of the crew members grabbed Juan and held his arms behind his back. They carried in some heavy rope that they had fetched on the way. The policemen were then tied together.

The Captain looked at the police and spat on them.

"You will pay for this. Ralph, have them taken to the engine room and have them locked in there until we sail."

Ralph smiled. "It will be my pleasure and duty"

The burly crew members roughly pulled the police from the room and to the engine room. They stripped them of their uniforms and firearms. They left them in shabby underwear and tied them tightly to the heavy piping that carried the ship's water. With their hands and feet bound and several ropes tying each down, the policemen were unable to move.

The crew left them there and returned to the canteen. Coffee was brewed and they all sat to discuss what to do with the cops.

Chapter 117

Jan and Ralph returned to Jakob's cabin. He was lying on his back in a semi conscious state. Jan removed the blood soaked bandages from Jakob's face. The gash was clean and some bruising was starting around the edges of the cut. Jan went to the sink in the cabin and soaked a cotton towel with cold water. He returned and cleaned off the cut. From the medicine case he removed a tube of ointment and spread a layer over the cut. He covered the ointment with an adhesive bandage and stuck it down on Jakob's face.

Jakob stirred and opened his eyes. His head ached from the copious drinks he had consumed and he felt ill. He touched his face.

"What happened? Why am I bandaged? Why are you both here with me?"

Jan shook his head and recalled the events of the night. Jakob groaned.

Jan looked at him and sarcastically said "The next time you want a souvenir of Colombia I recommend you buy one from one of the street sellers."

"What will happen now?"

"The Captain has detained those policemen. I am not sure of his plans. He is furious about the incident. He has been contacting certain parties here. He wants to leave Cartagena as quickly as he can. We are refueling at 7:00am and he has requested Pilot assistance to leave the harbor at 9:00am. We will sail directly to Aruba."

Jakob attempted to sit up. His head spun and he was light headed. Ralph caught him as he started to fall from the bed.

"I suggest you sleep this off. We will return early in the morning."

Jakob fell back on the bed and into a deep sleep.

Jan said good night to Ralph and went to find the Captain.

The Captain was on the bridge with the ship's navigator. He was swearing and smashing his fist down on the chart table. As Jan entered he raised his arm and pointed at him while shouting.

"This whole mess is your fault. You should have got him out of that cantina. I only took him on as a crew member at your request. His papers are false. This has been nothing but trouble. He has drawn the attention of certain German Naval Officers who are onboard with us. I fear we are all to be questioned upon our return to Germany. Keep him out of sight for the rest of the trip. Take him food and drink. Do not let him back into the mess. I have already had communication from Germany. This news has reached there already. There are German agents here in Colombia. They have requested to come aboard. I will stall this off and we will sail before more harm can be done."

Jan stood silently carefully thinking of his response.

"Captain, what will you do with those policemen in the engine room?"

"I am thinking about that. If I let them go our ship will be impounded. I cannot let that happen. I will deal with them just as we are leaving. May be I will send them back with the Pilot after we clear the harbor."

"I will think if that is wise. We can speak further about this in the morning. If there is nothing more I am going to retire for the night."

"There will be more, but in the morning. It will be much, much more. This incident is not going to go unpunished. You have imperiled our ship, our mission and certain individuals on board. Colombia proclaims to be neutral but has done things that show it is not aligned with Hitler's Third Reich plans. We will speak further in the morning. Please bring the other two to my cabin after we are underway tomorrow and clear of the harbor traffic."

Jan bid goodnight and left the bridge to return to his private cabin. He sat for awhile thinking of what to do with the imprisoned policemen. To release them too soon could mean pursuit and capture by the Colombians. The Captain was right. The Colombians had no love of the Germans.

Chapter 118

At 8:30am the next morning the Pilot launch pulled alongside their ship. The gangway was lowered and the Pilot climbed the stairway to the deck. Jan was there to greet him and take him to the Captain.

On the bridge, pleasantries were exchanged. The Captain had already instructed Ralph to have the ship's engines started and ready for a quick departure.

The Pilot was young and eager. "Where is it you are heading to?"

"Today we will start our 4 -5 day trip to Aruba. We have cargo to unload for the refinery at San Nicolaas."

"The weather forecast for the next few days is excellent. You should have a good trip."

The radio on the bridge crackled. The Pilot looked to the port side and saw the harbor tugboat waiting to attach lines to pull the ship away from the dock.

The Captain gave the order and the lines were thrown from the forward deck to waiting hands on the tug. Within minutes they were nudged away from the dock and turning for their escorted trip up the harbor and out to the Caribbean Sea.

Jan beckoned the Captain aside.

"Captain, do not release those policemen to the Pilot. I have given this a lot of thought. I have a plan that I will implement. You must trust me with this. It is better you do not know the details. I assure you it will resolve the problem without any complications."

The Captain frowned and thought about Jan's comment.

"It will be on your head if anything goes wrong. I will not support you. Remember that you, Ralph and Jakob still have a meeting with me when we are clear of shipping and safely underway."

Jan nodded. "We are ready to meet with you. Again, I assure you that the plan I have will work in our favor."

The ship proceeded up the harbor and out to sea without any problems. The Captain was relaxed. Outside the harbor entrance, the Pilot wished them well and prepared to climb down the gangway and back onto the pilot launch.

Within fifteen minutes the ship was clear and the Captain ordered Ralph to increase speed. They cruised on for another hour and saw less shipping the further out they sailed.

The Captain handed control of the ship over to his officers.

"I will be in my cabin. I have a meeting that cannot be interrupted unless it is an emergency. Do you all understand?"

He left the bridge and walked briskly to his cabin. Upon his arrival he found Jakob, Ralph and Jan awaiting him. He unlocked his door and ushered them in. There was a desk and several chairs in front of it. He gestured for them to sit.

"All of you put this ship, her crew and our mission in jeopardy. I have considered the matter. It cannot go without reprimand. Upon arrival in Aruba none of you are to leave this ship. I estimate we will be there for 2 days. We will be meeting with a naval frigate on our way to Aruba. There is some cargo to be off loaded and we will take on several "passengers". Jakob, for the rest of the journey to Aruba you are to stay in your cabin unless you are working with Ralph in the engine room. I will reconsider my position after we depart Aruba. Jan you will stay a few minutes to speak with me. Ralph and Jakob you are dismissed."

With Jakob and Ralph's departure, the Captain asked Jan.

"How safe is this plan of yours for those policemen?"

"I can assure you that we will not encounter any problems. Again it is best I do not tell you of the details yet. You must trust me. Captain, we have sailed together for many years now. You should be able to trust me by now."

"Yes but the antics of last night have caused me some doubt."

Chapter 119

The ship heaved and yawed in the heavy swell. The cloudless sky was a bright Caribbean blue. The sun beat down but its heat was countered by the steady and endless eastern trade winds that blew over the ship.

Jan joined Ralph in the engine room after his meeting with the Captain.

"We have business in here to look after with those two" he said, looking toward the shackled Colombians.

He addressed them in Spanish. "Stand up. You will remove everything except for your underwear."

Jan stepped forward and released one of them. Ralph stood guard clumsily pointing one of the policemen's pistols at the released man.

The men started to object. Ralph stepped closer and brandished the pistol as if to strike the released man. Jan grabbed the stocky police officer by the shoulders and pushed him toward Ralph. After a brief struggle the captured men relented and agreed. Jan took the uniforms that had been stripped from them when they were captured. He searched through the pockets and removed wads of pesos and American dollars. In addition he took their badges and identification, and then on second thought he placed the identification back in the tunic's breast pocket and pinned the badges back on. Ralph was puzzled. "Why return those items?"

"Ralph, I am not returning them. I am going to throw their uniforms overboard. They will drift and eventually be found. We are still close to the Colombian coast. The uniforms will probably be found by fishermen. People do go missing in Colombia. They will assume that these 2 were taken to sea and killed by one of the street gangs from Cartagena. We will keep their weapons in the safe here in the engine room. I will arrange for food and drink to be brought here for them. When we are further into the trip I will spread the rumor that we have stowaways on board. This should stop any suspicions about why Jakob has been absent. We will say that he is assisting you in keeping them under guard."

Ralph nodded and agreed. He asked Jan to have Jakob join him in the office off the engine room.

Jan exited with the police uniforms. Upon reaching the aft deck he looked around to see if anyone was watching him. When satisfied he was alone he threw the clothes into the churning wake of the ship's propeller. He then walked along the deck until he reached the hatch that opened into the corridor that led to Jakob's cabin.

 He knocked and entered. Jakob was sitting quietly on the edge of his bunk reading. He put down the book when Jan entered. His face was bruised and there was a heavy line of clotted blood covering the bandages over the slash on his face.

"Ralph needs you to help him. He is alone in there with those prisoners of ours. He needs you to be there and keep an eye on them. Ralph has other important duties to complete ahead of our rendezvous with the frigate this evening."

Jakob slid off the bunk and accompanied Jan to the engine room. When they entered Ralph was nowhere to be seen. They searched and found him in the small machine room behind the fuel bunkers. His attention was focused on an assortment of parts laid out on the workbench. A white and blue box with the word "Achtung" stenciled on it in red sat to one side of the workbench.

Jan called to Ralph over the noise of the engines. Ralph came over and joined them. Jan nodded toward the workbench.

"I will have the assembly completed before we rendezvous with our countrymen later. It is intricate work and I will need to pay close attention. It is very dangerous work. One mistake and this ship will be blown out of the water."

Jakob looked at the maze of wires and components. At the end of the bench was a large helmet shaped cone. "What is it you are assembling, Ralph?"

Ralph looked to Jan who nodded. "I guess it is safe for you to know. Shortly before we left Germany, a new and powerful torpedo warhead had been tested. Due to the sensitivity of the components there was concern about damage occurring during shipment. We were summoned by The Naval High Command to transport the unassembled device since we were sailing to the Caribbean. This is where I understand it is to be deployed. I was trained to assemble and arm this device. The design has never been used before. We are to transfer it to the frigate this evening. We were chosen to transport it as they did not want any possibility of the device being captured by the enemy. Our ship was considered unimportant and less likely to be attacked or searched. Now Jakob, I ask you to return to my office and monitor the controls. If anything seems wrong call me immediately. Also, please keep an eye on those Colombians."

Jakob left Ralph to his task and walked past the Colombians and into the office area. He recorded the readings from the various gauges and controls.

In the early afternoon Jan returned with a plate of sandwiches, rice and beans for the prisoners. They took the food and hungrily ate it.

Jan stayed for a while making small talk with Jakob. He sensed a change in Jakob. After discussing the war and how things were changing, Jan finally asked Jakob what was wrong.

"Jan, I am missing many things. My wife is stuck in Holland. My farm in Canada is leased and I miss working the land. I have deserted my religion and my personal beliefs. I have used bad judgment. I seem to have no future if I return to Germany. You helped me to escape from Germany on this ship. In Colombia I created a stupid situation and have made a problem between you and the Captain. I have gone wrong in my life. I don't know if I can put it all back together."

Jan stood silent. He had expected that during this voyage Jakob would experience this remorse. He had experience with many like Jakob who he had previously taken on as crew.

"Tonight after we complete the transfer of the torpedo warhead we will sit and talk. In the meantime keep an eye on those two. We cannot afford to have anything else go wrong."

Jakob thanked Jan. "I will be impatient until we speak tonight."

Jan raised his hand and gave a small wave as he left.

Chapter 120

The afternoon slipped by. The ship settled into a steady rolling pattern. At 6:00pm as the sun was setting, the winds dropped and the seas calmed. Ralph returned to his office area and relieved Jakob of his duty. In spite of the Captain's orders to stay hidden, Jakob walked up onto the forward deck. He stood and looked to the west. A beautiful golden Caribbean sunset was developing. The sun was gliding down toward the horizon and the setting rays shimmered across the expanse of the ocean. As the sun continued to sink, the winds and the ocean swell dropped further. It was almost dead calm.

Jakob stayed on deck enjoying the warm breeze of the early evening and watching as the few clouds were tinged pink from the sun. This was a sunset he would remember. As he watched his thoughts turned to a life in the Caribbean. Fishing, swimming, exotic foods and fruits. A very different life he thought. He shrugged this off realizing he would probably never experience such a life.

Jakob was joined by several other crew members. They stared at Jakob's slashed face.

"We hear there are some stowaways onboard and one attacked you. Is that how that gash on your face happened? We will go and give them something to think about."

Jakob now realized that Jan had spread the stowaway story and embellished it with his own ideas. He shrugged and turned back to face the sunset. The other crew members continued to make threats regarding the punishment they would unleash on the stowaways.

A speck appeared on the horizon. As they stood there, it grew in size until it was recognizable as a warship. On the bridge, the Captain observed the approaching ship through high powered binoculars. He recognized the German Naval flag and gave the order for Ralph to heave to. The ships engines died to a low hum and the ship lazily swayed in the waters. The frigate came close. A rubber zodiac was lowered and two sailors dressed in black wet suits steered it across to the ship. The gangway was lowered. After securing the small craft the sailors came aboard. The Captain and Jan greeted them. They remained on deck talking for some time.

Several crew members released a hatch cover and one of the ship's cranes was lowered. A rope net was dropped down into the hold. Orders were shouted and the white and blue box that had previously been in the Engine room was raised in the rope sling. The crane operator exercised extreme caution. The transfer to the frigate was slow. Finally, the Captain bid the sailors farewell as they descended the gangway on their way back to the zodiac. When they had cleared the ship, the Captain gave the order to resume sailing toward Aruba.

Although it was early evening, the sky was dark. They were near the equator and the sunsets quickly faded to night. Soon the ship's running lights were lit and they continued their slow but steady progress toward Aruba.

Later in the evening Jan visited Jakob's cabin. "Let's go up on deck and chat. The air is warm and it is a nice night to walk."

On deck they walked around the perimeter of the ship several times. Jan was deep in thought. "Jakob, you are troubled. I have seen that. In Hamburg when we spoke you expressed these troubles. My only advice to you is to stop and do the things you want to. Do not try to be someone who does things and pretends to be someone else in order to satisfy other people. It is possible that some may not like your decisions, but it is important for you to live a life of contentment. You have experienced many things in life. You now have enough knowledge to make that decision. Your life will pass by. Do not regret that you sacrificed the most important things. Give up the pursuit of the past and settle with a calm of what you have now. This war will create many enemies. There will be suffering and deceit and starvation. You can reestablish yourself with your wife in a peaceful country. Go back to your farm in Canada. Take your wife. I know she is in The Netherlands and will need special help to leave and return. Jakob, think about what is important to you. Leave the past. Forget those things over which you have no control. Go with your mind and heart."

Chapter 121

That night Jakob lay awake for hours thinking of Jan's comments. He realized that he had ignored his friends and betrayed his wife, Anke. As he laid thinking he felt a sadness develop. He needed to find a way to return to the life he had known while growing up. It was near the breaking of dawn, that Jakob fell into a deep sleep.

Jakob assisted Ralph throughout the day. As they sailed on toward Aruba a monotonous routine developed. The boredom was only broken when the crew gathered for meals and conversations and joking happened.

For the next 3 days, the ship made slow progress.

On the 4th night, Jakob sought out Jan to continue their talk and advise him of the plan he had decided upon. Up on deck they watched the phosphorescence of the ship's wake in the brightly moonlit water.

"Jan, I have made a decision I want you to hear. In Hamburg I told you I wished to escape Germany and return to Canada with Anke. I have made a plan and wish to share it with you as you have helped me and I do not wish to deceive you. I will find some way to get off the ship in Aruba and never return to it. My absence will not be noticed during the unloading of the cargo. It will be when it is time for the ship to sail and Ralph has no one to assist him."

Jan listened in silence and then said "How will this help you to return to Canada with Anke?"

"I have given that a lot of thought. As part of the Dutch West Indies, Aruba is a safe and neutral country. I will find some work and then find a way to travel to Miami and from there up to Canada. Aruba is Dutch. This will make it easy for me to make contact with Anke in Holland and to send money to her so she can join me."

"How will you survive? Aruba is hot and very small. What work will you find? There is not a lot there. Most of the work is at the oil refinery and that is controlled by the Americans."

"I will take my saxophone and few possessions. I will find a place where I can play. I have some money and will rent a room. It will not be easy but I will do this and succeed."

"How do you intend to get off the ship? The Dutch are wary of all German shipping and we will be closely watched."

"I will go ashore with the work crew to assist in the unloading. Can you arrange that for me? I will then quietly slip away during a rest time. If you cannot get me ashore with that crew, then I will probably slip overboard in the night and swim from the ship. If I have to swim I will not be able to take my saxophone and the few items I have."

Jan considered what Jakob had just told him.

"Jakob, I will assist you and put you into the wharf crew for the unloading of the cargo which is for the refinery. I will arrange for a small canvas wrapped package to be included with the goods being unloaded. You will have an opportunity to make your escape as I have a distraction planned during the unloading. This plan of yours must stay between us. Do not tell anyone about this. Not even Ralph. He is a good man but a committed Nazi and will probably turn you in."

Jakob returned to his cabin. He laid out the few possessions he had kept with him. He took his forged passport and papers and wrapped them in a waterproof oiled canvas pouch. He then counted out his money. He had several different currencies...Dutch Guilders, German Reich Marks, French marks, US Dollars and some pesos from his Colombian escapade. He divided the money and placed the Dutch Guilders and US Dollars aside to take with him when he left the ship. The rest he placed in a tin and put it in the saxophone case. He folded several shirts and trousers and made them into a bundle to be included in the package Jan would arrange to get to him on the dock.

Exhausted from the day, Jakob collapsed for his last night's sleep aboard.

Chapter 122

The grey light of the early dawn enveloped the ship as they approached the tiny island of Aruba. Although early in the morning there was already a heat in the air. Jakob joined Ralph in the engine room. Ralph greeted him and spoke.

"We are expected to arrive into Aruba within the next couple of hours. The Captain has been in radio contact. We are sailing to the southern end of the island to San Nicolaas Harbor. The harbor has a number of ships anchored waiting to offload cargo and refuel. We will need to anchor offshore until a berth is available."

As he spoke the intercom phone rang. Ralph picked up the receiver. The Captain ordered a reduction in speed as they were to be escorted into port and had been ordered to slow until the Pilot boat and Dutch authorities boarded.

Jakob offered to go to the canteen and get them both coffees. He looked at their prisoners. They were soiled and looked haggard. Feeling some pity for them he decided to bring them coffee as well. They would have a difficult day ahead given the plan Jan had for them. Jakob chuckled at the thought of it.

Jakob left the engine room and started to walk along the deck to the canteen. As he walked he could smell oil and fuel in the easterly wind that was blowing from Aruba. He looked over toward where he thought Aruba would be. A thin plume of blue-grey smoke arose over the horizon. "This must be from the refinery" Jakob thought. The fumes he smelled were strong even at such a distance from the island.

Jakob entered the canteen and took four large mugs of coffee and placed them in a cardboard container. He made his way back to the engine room and handed Ralph the coffees.

Jakob returned to the deck. The coast of Aruba was visible. The tall smoke stacks of the refinery were silhouetted against the rising morning sun. Black smoke belched from the tallest stacks. Flames licked into the air from other structures. Jakob looked on in amazement. He had never seen an oil refinery in operation. The air was a hazy grey and smelled strongly of fuel. As he watched, a small black craft approached with the word PILOT painted in black against a white superstructure. The boat headed toward them. The Captain ordered the gangway to be lowered. The Pilot climbed the gangway accompanied by several Dutch officials.

After greeting them aboard, the Captain took them to the bridge. He provided them the cargo manifest and crew list. The officials scanned the list and requested to visit the holds where the cargo was stored. They climbed down into the dimly lit hold. The officials checked off the equipment destined for the refinery. When they were satisfied they returned to the bridge.

"The docks are all occupied. You will be anchored in the harbor until space is made available. We estimate you will be able to dock this afternoon after siesta. When do you expect to leave port?"

"We leave for Galveston, Texas tomorrow morning."

The officials, satisfied with the paperwork stayed on the bridge making small talk with the Captain and Jan. They eased their way into the harbor. The Pilot gave the Captain the command to drop anchor.

The Captain called down to Ralph to stop engines. He ordered the anchor be deployed. When all was complete, he surveyed the other ships waiting in the harbor at anchor. Moored off to starboard there were two Esso lake tankers that transported the heavy crude oil from Maracaibo in Venezuela to the refinery. The tankers sat low in the water due to their full load. Closer to the dock was a strange looking ship. The Captain took his binoculars and studied it. He observed it was flying the Norwegian flag. He scanned the hull and realized it was a Norwegian whaling ship that had come into port to refuel. Off to port side were two American freighters waiting to dock. They were worn and rusted. The Captain did not recognize them or their shipping company. Obviously they were tramp steamers, many of which plied trade between the Caribbean Islands. Satisfied, the Captain replaced the binoculars on the shelf above the chart table.

The Pilot handed papers to be signed to the Captain. When the task was completed, the Pilot and officials prepared to leave the ship.

Jakob had remained on deck observing the activity on the docks. He formulated his plan of escape.

With nothing to do but wait until berthed, the crew gathered to eat a lunch. Some played cards to pass the time. It was mid afternoon when the ship was cleared to dock.

With the lines secured, the Captain ordered Jan to start the unloading procedure. The hatch covers were opened and the ship's cranes swung over the deck and into the holds to start the unloading.

Jan was walking with several of the crew toward the gangway. He saw Jakob and called to him. "Jakob, come and join these men. They need another hand to assist dockside."

Jakob knew that this was his signal to go ashore and to be ready for his escape. He joined in with the group and descended down the gangway to the dock. When the crew signaled they were ready, the cranes started lowering the large pipes down onto the dock. The crew positioned them for transporting to the refinery. Jakob studied his surrounds. He noticed a small shed near the front gates to the dock. It was adjacent to what appeared to be an office. Men were entering and leaving the office at regular intervals. As he watched, a uniformed man approached them. He looked at the pipes they were delivering. "I am from the engineering and maintenance section of the refinery. It is my job to inspect these." He walked around and made notes on a clipboard. "I notice that there is a swastika stamped on the pipes. This is irregular but not enough for me to refuse the shipment. I will arrange for it to be transported immediately. We have been awaiting the arrival of these fuel supply pipes for some time. We have new storage tanks that we want to get active and without these we were delayed."

Jakob heard shouting from the deck of the ship and looked up. Jan was at the gangway with the Colombian policemen. They were disheveled and dressed only in their underwear. Jakob recognized this was the signal. He looked at the load of piping being dropped to the dock by the crane. He saw the canvas duffel bag strapped to the pipes. He ran to retrieve it as the pipes came to rest on the surface of the dock. As he did so, Jan was shouting for the authorities. Within minutes the Dutch officials were running up the gangway.

Jan was shouting very loudly so all could hear. "Sirs, we have found these stowaways hiding behind our fuel bunkers. They are Colombian and claim to have no papers. Take them into your custody. We cannot proceed to Galveston with them aboard. We have searched and found no identity papers. They must have climbed aboard during our refueling stop in Cartagena."

The Dutch officials reluctantly arrested the Colombians and escorted them off the ship.

This diversion allowed Jakob to pick up his possessions and carry them to the side of the small shed. It was late in the afternoon. The sun was starting to set. Soon it would be dusk. Jakob needed to find an excuse to get close to the gates. He approached the man from the refinery. "Can you direct me to a toilet? Is there one in that small office building?"

"Yes. Go there and they will let you use it"

Jakob called to the others to advise them he was going to use the toilet. Some were confused why he did not go back onboard but they just shrugged. As the crew continued to work, Jakob went to the office. He entered and requested to use the toilet. The clerk sitting behind the desk pointed to a stained and dirty door. Jakob pushed the door open and walked into the filthy cubicle. He stood and waited for what seemed a reasonable amount of time. He walked out and thanked the clerk. As he exited the office, the man from the refinery was hurrying toward the gate. He swung it open and left. Jakob saw his chance. He grabbed his canvas duffel bag from beside the shed and ran through the gate before it swung shut. He kept running until he was far away from the docks. He turned and found himself in an area with bars and clubs. The area was busy with workers from the refinery who were dressed in overalls emblazoned with the company's name. He decided he had to blend in and escape detection.

In the bars groups of men were drinking beer and laughing. The level of conversation was high. Jakob listened carefully. He could not understand the language they were speaking. He had expected Dutch to be spoken but his language was totally unknown to him.

He turned left and walked away from the refinery. He was entering an area away from the main streets where the bars and clubs were. As he walked, prostitutes called to him from the doorways of the tiny adobe like houses. They called to him in Spanish offering companionship. The area was alive with drunken men stumbling down the streets and trying to negotiate deals. Then a thought struck him. He approached a small group of girls standing on the sidewalk outside a dark entrance to a doorway that was wide open.

The girls looked at him with curiosity. He spoke in Dutch. Several responded in rapidly spoken Spanish which Jakob took to mean they did not understand him. One of the girls pointed to a tall black man standing further down the alley. He was watching Jakob and the girls. The girl pushed Jakob toward the direction of the man. Jakob heaved the canvas duffel over his shoulder and crossed over to speak to him. He greeted him in Dutch. The tall man smiled and exposed a row of rotting teeth. He responded in Dutch.

"I am looking to rent a room. Can you direct me to someone who can assist me?"

"For a couple of Florins I will be happy to help." The smell of stale beer oozed from the man.

Jakob found some change and handed it him. The tall man motioned to Jakob to join him. They walked in the late afternoon's heat and after 5 minutes came to a villa with a large porch and a rusty corrugated iron roof. The man walked in the door without knocking and called out. A large black woman dressed in a colorful costume emerged from the rear of the villa. The tall black man spoke in the language the Jakob could not understand. The woman looked at Jakob and finally nodded. The man spoke to Jakob. "She has a room that you can rent. She wants you to pay for a week now."

Jakob asked the price. It was clear that the tall man was cutting himself into the deal. Jakob agreed to an amount and paid it from his American dollars.

The tall man slunk away from them. The woman beckoned Jakob and they went to the room he had rented. It was basic. A rickety bed was pushed against the wall. A couple of old and discolored sheets covered it. A homemade chair sat beneath a dust and grime encrusted window. He threw down his duffel. The woman then pulled at his arm to follow her. They went down a dark narrow corridor to a bathroom. In the bathroom were a toilet and an ancient bathtub that sat on clawed feet. There was no hot water.

Jakob thanked her and then went back to his newly rented room. "This will work until I get organized and learn more of San Nicolaas and this place."

It was dark when he left the villa. He walked back to the main street with the raucous bars. The bars and clubs were busy. He surveyed the situation. There were some stores that sold food and household goods but it seemed that the majority of the action was at the bars.

He passed a bar named The Kit Kat Club and noticed what appeared to be some sailors drinking and talking. He decided to enter. In Dutch he ordered a beer from a heavyset bartender. The bartender understood and replied to him in Dutch. He sat on a stool at the bar and struck up a conversation with him.

Jakob learned a lot from the bartender that evening.

"The language you are asking me about is called Papiamento. It is spoken on the other islands here in the Dutch West Indies. It is a local Creole dialect. It is a simple language to learn. If you are going to stay in Aruba you will need to learn it. Many of the local people only speak this language. Some speak Dutch and Spanish but all speak Papiamento."

Jakob talked for hours, soaking up as much information as he could about Aruba. He needed to plan for his survival for the next few months until he could save enough money to get to Florida and then back to Canada.

It was late when he left to find his way back to the villa and his rented room.

Chapter 123

Jakob left his rented room at the Villa early the next morning. The sun was yet to rise. As he walked in the grey of dawn he passed some of the girls of the night negotiating and joking with the workers who were coming off shift from the refinery. Several of the girls recognized him and called out to him. He gave a wave back as he continued to walk toward Main Street.

Upon reaching the street, Jakob was surprised at the number of people milling about at that early hour. There were refinery workers in their overalls which were emblazoned with the company's name across their back. Several black women were selling fruits from a stall which was leaning up against the brick wall of a store. Seeing Jakob approach they raised some bananas and coconuts and held them out to him. Jakob declined their offerings and continued. He was walking in the direction of the main gate to the refinery. He reached the end of Main Street and found a café on the right-hand corner. It was filled with workers sitting at large homemade tables. Their conversations were loud and confronted Jakob as he entered. He stood looking for a place to sit. Several of the younger workers saw him and beckoned him to join them. Jakob went to their table and greeted them in Dutch. He was invited to take a seat.

A large busty waitress came to the table. She looked at Jakob and spoke to him. He didn't understand a word. She was speaking Papiamento. He spoke back in Dutch. This prompted the waitress to place her hands on her hips and to break into a deep frown. The young workers laughed.

"She don't speak no Dutch. She from Haiti. Only some strange language called French. She also speak Papiamento. She ask you what you want to eat. We have the goat stew in the morning. Very good. You want a coffee. Also good. From Colombia."

Jakob looked at the young man who had spoken to him. "I just arrived here. I do not speak that language yet. Yes, I will try the goat stew but after a coffee."

The young worker spoke in rapid Papiamento to the waitress. She was obviously not amused with Jakob and gave him a look that enforced her feelings. She stormed off and returned with a large chipped mug of a dark liquid that Jakob assumed was coffee. She banged the mug down in front of Jakob. Some of the contents spilled from the top of the mug onto the table.

Jakob turned to the young man.

"I need milk for my coffee"

This brought on an instant outburst of laughter.

"We don't have much milk here in Aruba. Here take this, its goat milk. That what we use, man."

Jakob's breakfast was quickly turning into a learning experience.

"Where you from?" asked the worker.

"I am from Canada. I was in Holland and Germany and came here yesterday by ship. I will be staying until I can return to Canada and send money for my wife to join me back at our farm there."

"I no know any Canada. Where that? What you make on farm, mister?"

Jakob set about describing his farm and Canada to the group who sat quietly drinking their coffees. They listened intently and were fascinated with story. His goat stew was brought to the table. Jakob was starved. He tried the stew. It was rich and thick. He ate slowly savoring each mouthful. Now he understood why the café was crowded and popular. He decided he would come back.

He spent several hours talking with the group. In the process he learned about life in San Nicolaas and Aruba. The younger man told him of the other places to visit and where he could possibly find work.

It was mid morning when Jakob left the café. His new found friends invited him to join them in the mornings. Jakob was starting to like Arubans. He was finding their acceptance and friendliness very different to the cold emotions he had experienced in Europe. It reminded him a little of the way life had been back in his Mennonite community in Canada.

He sauntered through the streets taking in the sights and smells of a bustling San Nicolaas. All the time the smell of oil and gasoline fumes permeated the air which had a constant bluish haze. The refinery was in full production.

There were women street sellers pushing rickety carts laden with bags of boiled peanuts, fruit and other foods that Jakob could not identify. It was hot and soon he was in need of a drink. He returned to the bar where he had been the previous night. Upon entering, the same barman called out a greeting to him. Jakob went to the bar and pulled up a stool and ordered a Heineken beer.

He gulped down the cold beer. As he worked his way through several more, he found himself in deep conversation with the barman. He discussed his situation. He needed to find a job and make some money immediately. The barman paused and stood in deep thought.

"I have a cousin in Savaneta who has a fishing boat. He always needs help. Savaneta is not far from here. You will be able to walk there. Go and visit. On the beach there will be other fishermen. Savaneta is a small fishing village. When you get there ask for Juan. Tell him his cousin Miguel told you to go and ask for a job with him."

Jakob thanked the barman and after getting some directions set off in the direction of Savaneta.

He walked for over an hour and finally came upon a well worn track down to the beach. Jakob took the track and within minutes was standing on a picturesque beach bordered with palm trees and a tree he did not know. It was a strange looking tree and bent toward the west. He stood taking in the scene. At the water's edge there were several brightly painted wooden boats with names prominently painted on them. He walked toward them. He asked for Juan in Dutch. An old man, his face and arms weathered from years in the sun and the winds pointed to a pale blue skiff at the end of a small pier.

There were two men on the boat unloading some cloth sacks containing fish. Jakob walked up to them.

"I am looking for Juan. His cousin Miguel told me to visit. I am looking for a job."

A strong looking muscular man looked up at him. "I am Juan. Wait there and we will speak when I am finished here with unloading."

Jakob sauntered back to the beach and surveyed his surroundings. There were a number of houses along the shore that were nestled between stands of palms and tropical growth. He was finding Savaneta an appealing place. He returned to the pier and sat on the edge dangling his feet in the warm Caribbean water.

Juan joined him and took out a pack of cigarettes. He offered one to Jakob who resisted.

"What work are you looking for? I need a man to work my nets and lines. We leave early in the mornings and return in the afternoon. The work is hard, hot and the hours are long. Can you handle that?"

Jakob told Juan of the work and hours he had to put in at the farm. They sat together talking for some time. Finally, Juan offered Jakob a job starting the next morning at 4:30am. Jakob stood and shook his hand. Things were working out for him on this strange little island of Aruba.

Jakob walked back into San Nicolaas. He reached the town as the sun was starting to set. He turned into the alleyway that led to his rented room in the villa. As he proceeded through the narrow alleyway he encountered a young girl of around eleven years old sitting on the doorstep of one of the decrepit villas. She was crying and holding onto a small black and white dog. She looked up as Jakob approached and wiped her eyes. Jakob stopped and asked if everything was fine.

The young girl turned and called through the open doorway. A woman in her 30's came to the door. She spoke to Jakob in a hesitant Dutch. She told Jakob that her husband was sent back to Colombia by the Government and she has to leave and join him and they are unable to take the little girl's dog.

Jakob looked at the little dog. It reminded him of his dogs back on the farm. The dog was striking. The coloring was unique as it was black, white, and had some brown markings on the face with small brown dots above the eyes.

"I think I can offer him a nice home. I live alone and need a good friend. I cannot pay you for the dog as I have just arrived here in Aruba and will start working as a fisherman tomorrow."

The woman spoke to her daughter in Spanish. The little girl picked up the dog and hugged it. Large tears welled in her eyes.

Jakob saw the love the little girl had for her dog.

"Please tell her that he will have a good home. He will be taken care of and have a nice life with me."

The little girl looked at Jakob and then stood. She held the dog out in front of her and handed it to Jakob who took the dog. He was surprised at the feel of its soft and silky hair.

"I live just over there in that villa" he said, pointing out his villa with the rented room. "Tell your little girl she can visit and see her dog before you leave."

The woman smiled and thanked Jakob.

With the dog tucked under his arm Jakob walked on home with his new friend. He realized he didn't know the dogs name. He thought back to the dogs on the farm. This dog was unlike any of them. It had large soft black eyes and long floppy ears. Its tail seemed to be constantly wagging. He needed to find out what sort of dog it was. After considering many names he settled on one. The dog would be called Timmy.

That night he washed the dog and looked for any signs of ticks or fleas. He found none. That night the dog quietly settled on the floor beside his bed. Jakob was finding this life even better.

He had retired to bed early and set the old alarm clock he had purchased to wake him at 2:45am.

Chapter 124

The work on the fishing boat was hard. The sun beat down and exhausted them. The ropes were wet and encrusted with salt. Jakob's hands burned and soon became blistered. They caught a sizeable catch of wahoo, snapper and some grouper.

At noon, Juan decided to call it a day. The catch was better than he had expected. They headed inshore where merchants from the stores were waiting to buy the best of the catch. Within 30 minutes their catch was sold. Juan counted out the money and then handed some to Jakob.

"This is how I pay. Each day after the fish is sold. The better the catch the more money you will receive."

Jakob found this an excellent arrangement. He liked Juan more and more as he got to know him.

After the second week, Jakob asked Juan if he knew of anywhere he could rent that was closer. He was finding the walk to and from work to be long and tiring. Juan thought for a while and then responded.

"Jakob, at our home we have a small apartment in the garden. We use it for family. I can rent you this. It is small and very basic. Come and take a look. It is empty and you could start staying there now."

They finished at the boat and went to Juan's home which was on the beachfront. It was a simple home with some large flowering plants at the side. They walked around to the rear of the house to a small white building with a turquoise door. They entered. It was immaculately clean. There was a bedroom, a kitchen with a dining area and a bathroom.

"I will rent this. It is excellent for me and my little pal."

Juan invited Jakob into his home where he introduced his wife Carlita. She was a stunning beauty of a woman. Her Latino features were accentuated by her long dark hair and radiant smile. Juan gestured to Jakob to sit with him on the outside porch overlooking the beach and water. As they sat, Carlita emerged with glasses and a large bottle of rum and joined them. Juan and Jakob sat for hours talking about many things. Juan had a dream of one day owning a restaurant. Carlita laughed and joked that while it was his dream she would be doing all the work. Juan reached out and gave her a friendly pat on her shoulder. It was obvious to Jakob of the affection they had for each other.

The afternoon wore on. The sun was low over the horizon when Carlita stood to go inside.

"Juan, I must go and prepare a meal for our family. Our children will be home from their friends very soon. Jakob will you join us ? Tonight I am making one of Juan's favorite meals. I am preparing Keshi Yena."

Jakob frowned. "I do not know Keshi Yena. What is that?"

Carlita's eyes danced as she described the meal.

"It is chicken baked over a tomato sauce. There are nuts and prunes in with the chicken and then covered with a Gouda cheese. After it is all in the pan I bake it in my oven. It is delicious. I am sure you will enjoy it."

"I would like to stay for the meal. If this is as good as it sounds then I would think Juan's restaurant would do very well. Is this a meal that is Aruban?"

"Yes it is truly an Aruban meal. We did steal the cheese idea from the Dutch and made some changes."

Carlita left them to enjoy the sunset.

"I will advise the woman who owns the villa where I am renting of my decision to leave at the end of the week."

As they sat there, Juan's children returned home. The aroma of the Keshi Yena drifted out onto the porch. Jakob inhaled the delicious smell. He was happy.

Chapter 125

On the following Saturday morning, Jakob gathered his meager possessions and prepared to leave for his new home. He said his farewell to the woman owner and gathered his things from the room.

He slung his saxophone over one shoulder and the canvas duffel bag over his other. He had made a rope leash for Timmy. They walked down the alleyway in the heat. Again the girls recognized him and called some lewd remarks to him in Spanish. He knew enough Spanish to understand and chuckled at their humor. He was going to miss this little area of San Nicolaas.

He continued his walk along the red dusty sidewalk toward Saveneta. Timmy walked ahead of Jakob and pulled at the rope leash. Timmy would spring on guard when an occasional iguana dropped from a bush and ran to seek a safe shelter.

It was early afternoon when he arrived at Juan's. Carlita greeted him and opened the door to the small apartment. She had prepared it in advance for his arrival. There was soap on the sink, some toilet paper and on the table a bowl of fruit. Jakob thanked her and set about placing his few things in the chest of draws.

As he was unpacking, there was a knock at his door. Upon opening the door he was greeted by Juan and Carlita's young children. They wanted to see his little dog and asked to play with it. Jakob agreed.

Tomorrow would be Sunday. They would not fish on a Sunday. This was a day for family and church and was strictly observed.

Jakob decided to go back into San Nicolaas as it was Saturday night and he was curious. He stopped at the café and ordered a meal of sopi mondongo, not sure what it was. His enthusiasm dropped when the dish arrived and he found it was a soup made with tripe. He picked at it and left most of it. He paid and went back to the Kit Kat. His friendly bartender friend, Miguel was working. Jakob went and sat at the bar and ordered a whiskey.

At around 7:30pm several men entered the club with a variety of musical instruments. Jakob watched as they set up a makeshift stage. Soon the music started.

The bartender walked over to where Jakob was sitting and topped up his glass.

"How is the job with Juan? I hear you are renting his apartment. That is good. They are hardworking and honest people."

Jakob nodded and asked "Is there music every night here?"

"No. We only have them play on a Saturday night. The music plays very late until the morning comes. People do not work on Sunday so they can sleep and rest. That is why we do Saturday."

Jakob told Miguel of his experience playing in Europe.

"I will tell my friends here about that. Maybe there is a position for you in their band."

Miguel wandered back and served other thirsty customers. The bar was becoming crowded. Smoke filled the air. There were refinery workers in overalls, men in casual dress and women in flashy gowns. The Kit Kat certainly had atmosphere and personality.

The band played for a long time. After about an hour they stopped for a break. One of the men came up to the bar and ordered iced water. Miguel scooped some ice into a glass pitcher and filled it with water. As he did so, he pointed to Jakob and explained that he was a musician.

Jakob extended his hand. The man took it and shook it hard. He spoke to Jakob but again he could not understand the language. Miguel interrupted and told the man that Jakob did not speak or understand Papiamento. The man nodded and in perfect English spoke to Jakob who was in shock at hearing the English.

The man saw his expression of surprise and laughed. "I worked in Texas at one of the refineries for a number of years. That is where I learned my English."

Miguel leaned on the bar and listened to them talk. After several minutes he spoke to Jakob. "I must tell you that this is my other brother. Let me introduce you correctly. His name is Alejandro. I have told him you are staying with Juan and his family."

Alejandro chuckled. "Perhaps I can come to my brothers and hear you play. In America I greatly enjoyed jazz music and those that included saxophone. I can visit tomorrow afternoon. We will need a long sleep after tonight. If you are good and we can work together then we will hire you and pay you to play with us."

Jakob sat at the bar and drank several whiskeys while watching the crowd and groups at the tables. He listened to the music. After his episode in Colombia he was not interested in meeting and talking to strangers. He fingered the still raw cut on his face. It was a powerful reminder.

It was late in the night when Jakob settled his bill and left the Kit Kat. He walked down Main Street and looked into the different clubs. Each club had music blaring and they were all crowded. The refinery was paying its workers well and they in turn were paying the local bars and clubs with their hefty pay checks.

As Jakob walked down Main Street he stopped and looked at the construction of a new building. It was on a corner and a block away from the wall enclosing the refinery. He had no idea what this building was. It had a large opening for a doorway and on the side there were bricked openings for windows. It was an impressive building. Across from the construction was a store that sold books, clothing and foods. Jakob decided he would return on Monday and purchase some of the clothing that would allow him to blend in and appear as a local.

He strolled through the streets and watched the late night partiers. Finally Jakob started his walk back to Saveneta. He arrived home and found Juan's children playing with his dog on the porch of Juan's house. He was surprised that the children were still awake and up at such a late hour. He called to his little dog before starting to go to his apartment. Carlita came out from the house. She ordered the children into the house and off to their beds. When they were inside and settled she returned and sat with Jakob.

"Juan is sleeping. The work on the boat is becoming too difficult for him. I am pleased you are here to help him. We are saving money and one day soon we will have that restaurant."

Jakob told her of his night and meeting Alejandro and of the planned meeting at the house that afternoon. Carlita smiled.

"I know Alejandro well. If he comes he will bring his big family. I will need to prepare many foods in the morning."

Jakob continued to make small talk for a while then took his dog and retired to his apartment.

Chapter 126

On Sunday Alejandro visited with his large family. The children played together on the beach while Juan and Carlita sat with Alejandro's wife on the porch. They talked and laughed. Their conversation was interrupted by the soulful notes of the saxophone as Jakob played some blues for Alejandro in his apartment. They sat in silence listening to the soft and low notes that drifted from the small apartment. Soon they were joined by Jakob and Alejandro.

"That was beautiful" remarked Carlita. "You play that instrument well."

Jakob smiled at her and lowered himself into an old stuffed chair. Alejandro proudly announced that Jakob would play with the group starting the next Saturday. He needed to arrange a time for the group to rehearse before then. He suggested an afternoon when Jakob would be available and Alejandro could leave the refinery after working his shift. A day was selected. Jakob was happy that he would once again be playing his favorite instrument.

The afternoon drifted by. Carlita announced an early dinner. Juan and Jakob needed to be up and on the boat early. Plates and other items were brought out to a makeshift table they had erected on the beach. Wine was poured and plates heaped with different foods were set on the table.

It was dusk when Alejandro and his family bid farewell. Juan helped Carlita to clean up from the dinner and then retired. The morning would come soon enough. Jakob said Goodnight and went to his apartment.

Jakob lay awake thinking of the recent events in his life. They were so different to his life in Canada and Europe. This was a simpler and happier life. He thought about returning to the farm. It seemed so far away and such a long time since he had been there. He considered this. He wondered if he should arrange for Anke to join him in Aruba. They could surely establish a good life here without the tensions that war and politics had brought to their country. He liked that idea.

In the morning Juan and Jakob took the boat out to the area where they trolled for wahoo. It wasn't long before they had a strike and landed a large wahoo into the boat. Over the next 30 minutes they landed another two large wahoo. Juan was ecstatic. They decided to proceed up the coast toward Oranjestad to put out their nets. The sea was choppy but the fishing conditions were ideal. After several hours they had managed to pull in a huge catch. Juan was pleased.

"Jakob, we have a catch that is far larger than we will be able to sell on the beach at Savaneta. I am going to sail into the market area at Oranjestad. This means we will return later in the day."

Jakob was happy to hear this. He had heard stories about Oranjestad and was eager to visit.

"That is alright with me. I am happy to help you there."

They slowly sailed up and into the Oranjestad harbor area. There were several oil tankers anchored there. In addition several small ships were anchored close in by the shore. Jakob watched with as the ships cranes unloaded rope slings and pallets containing produce and wooden crates. The cranes swung the cargo out onto barges that were attached to teams of horses. The horses stood in the water that rode high up their necks. Jakob watched as the horse drawn barges were pulled into the shore where workers awaited them to offload the goods.

Juan slowly moved amongst the other boats and moored alongside and behind the market stalls. Within minutes curious onlookers and vendors were above them and looking down into the boat at the catch that lay in bins in the boat. Juan reached for the rusty iron ladder that descended from the pavement to the water. He climbed the ladder and had no sooner stepped off when he was hailed by a tall Dutchman who was accompanied by local Aruban youths. He approached Juan.

"I see you have a good fresh catch this morning. I am interested to purchase all of your catch. I have several stores who need this fish."

Juan and the man agreed on a price. Juan returned to the boat and sailed it to the small beach area of Governors Bay. He drove the boat up onto the sand. The young Aruban youth were already there to unload the catch. They had a cart that was drawn by an old beige donkey.

With the catch unloaded Juan decided to leave their boat and find somewhere for lunch.

"Juan, I would like to walk around and see this Oranjestad. It looks like an interesting place."

They walked back into the centre of town. Jakob watched the sellers in the little huts with their sloped roofs selling fresh fruit and meats. The market was busy. He found it strange to see Dutch architecture on a Caribbean Island. He considered it a little bit of Europe on an island.

They walked on and found a street seller offering food. Juan stopped and examined the selection.

"I will pick you another Aruban food. You will like this."

He spoke a burst of Papiamento to the vendor, who took some paper and placed several crescent shaped pastries in it and wrapped it tightly. He handed it to Juan who took some coins from his pocket and dropped them into the man's outstretched palm.

They walked down to the dock and sat on the edge looking out at the Caribbean Sea. Juan then unwrapped the package. He removed one of the pastries and handed it to Jakob who was curious but bit into it. There was a sweet tasting filling of vegetables.

"These are called pastechi. Normally they are served at breakfast. I bought a selection. We have vegetable, spiced meat and some with cheese and ham. Pastechi is one of my favorites. I like them at lunch with a nice cold beer."

Jakob tried the different ones. He decided that the spiced meat was the best.

After they ate, Juan and Jakob stopped into a bar that opened onto the street. They ordered a beer and stood drinking and watching the people passing by. Oranjestad was not as busy as San Nicolaas. When finished drinking, they walked through some of the back streets before heading back to their boat.

Jakob was now more curious to visit other places on the island. His feelings about the island continued to be enhanced.

Chapter 127

Over the next couple of months, Jakob settled into a routine. He worked the boat with Juan each day. In the evenings he would often go to a small Chinese bar and eat the different foods they prepared. On occasion he would join Juan and Carlita for an early meal. After the meal was finished, the family would spend hours trying to teach Jakob the Papiamento language. Initially he had great difficulty, and then within weeks it started to make sense. On Saturdays he would play with Alejandro and the band.

Jakob's savings grew. He investigated the costs of returning to Canada and the amount of money he would need to bring Anke back to Canada. He calculated that within several more months he would be able to do this. Jakob felt a twinge of sadness with this thought. He had not told Juan or anyone of his plan to return. They would be disappointed. Again he knew that he would be betraying those who had helped him and taken him into their families and businesses.

It was an overcast morning in May when dawn broke. Juan and Jakob had sailed south and several miles out from the refinery. The currents there were strong and the waves high. Their small boat pitched and rode the waves to a frightening height only to rapidly drop back down and envelope them in a valley with the sea as its walls. Juan decided to return. The fishing had been slow. They motored back to the beach at Savaneta. Juan took the boat in close to the beach to sell off the fish to the people who waited for his daily arrival. Juan scanned the beach. The beach was almost empty of people.

"Jakob. This is strange. I have never seen it so empty here. There are no buyers. Something must have happened."

They placed the light load of fish into an old stained wooden bin and carried it up the beach to Juan's home. They entered and Juan called out to Carlita. There was no response. Juan was worried. His children would be at school and Carlita should be in the home waiting for their return for the break at lunch. He walked out into the humid and sticky day and crossed over and onto his neighbor's property. He called to his neighbor. Again there was no response. Juan called Jakob. Together they ran to the track that doubled as a road. He saw a large group standing outside the Chinese bar. They were standing in silence. Juan ran to the gathering. The crowd was totally silent. He went to ask what was happening but was silenced immediately. One of the men pointed inside where an old radio was crackling with static and the announcer speaking fast in Dutch. Juan and Jakob listened intently. It was May 10th, 1940. Germany had invaded Holland.

The crowd was somber. Jakob immediately started thinking of Anke. He wanted more details. He wanted to know where the Germans had invaded and whether it was a bloody invasion or had they entered passively and taken control. He looked around and saw Carlita at the edge of the group inside the bar. Juan waved to her and she came out to them.

"This is not good news for us. We are part of the Dutch Kingdom. How will this affect us? Will our men go to fight in this war?"

Nobody had answers to the many questions that were now being shouted. Juan motioned for them to return to their home. When they reached home, Juan sat deep in thought.

"Jakob will you accompany me. I will walk to the Dutch Marines Base here in Savaneta. Maybe they can provide us more information."

Jakob looked down at the floor. He was quiet for several minutes. He wondered how to handle this situation.

"Juan, there is something I must tell you. I am not here legally." Jakob told Juan and Carlita the story of his life, the European trip and finally jumping ship in Aruba. "I cannot join you. My Dutch papers are forged and I may be found out. I cannot risk that."

Juan and Carlita looked at him in disbelief.

"I have contacts that will help correct this situation. We will visit them tomorrow in San Nicolaas. I will go alone and try to get more information."

Chapter 128

Life in Aruba changed that May 10th, 1940. Aruba's relative age of innocence came to an end. The Dutch and Aruban authorities swung into some quick and decisive actions. All Germans or suspected German sympathizers were arrested and detained. They were interned on the island of Bon Aire. The Governor of Aruba had previously ordered the confiscation of the radio transmitters aboard the German ships moored at Malmok.

Tensions between people became apparent.

The refinery became a major consideration and needed protection because of its strategic importance. The water distillation plant was unprotected. It was open to an attack. Aruba was vulnerable. Over the next few months, an increase in military personnel was evident. A battery of shore guns was built high on the hills south east of the area known as the Colony.

While these changes were evident Juan and Jakob went about their daily routine.

The next day, May 11th, Juan and Jakob returned to their fishing. They sailed north toward the area of Eagle Beach. The waters were calm. As they dragged their net, Juan watched a Dutch patrol boat pass him at speed heading north. Dawn was breaking and he followed its progress. He watched as it became a speck in distance in the dim light. He was curious. As he looked north and the dawn lightened, he noticed black smoke billowing into the air.

The reason for the Dutch patrol boat's fast passing was clear. A ship must be in trouble. Juan decided to pull in the nets and speed to the location and offer any assistance needed.

They arrived at Malmok and were shocked to see the German freighter, *"The Antilla"* burning. Flames engulfed the entire ship which was listing badly. A second Dutch patrol boat was circling.

Juan steered the boat toward the shore but slowed quickly when he saw the men on the beach. This was obviously the crew.

Jakob looked on. He was surprised at the number of men standing there. Then he thought back to the crossing he had made and when they had stopped to meet the German frigate to take on more men. He wondered if maybe some of these men were disguised as crew but were on other assignments to infiltrate the island.

It was several weeks after the invasion had taken place that he travelled to Eagle Beach with its long pier protruding out from the point at the end of the beach. Tankers were docked to unload their cargo of oil for the refinery at Eagle Beach. Jakob was impressed by the vast expanse of the sugar white sands and the fact that there were only a few villas scattered along the shore.

As he surveyed the beach his mind wandered back to North America and Europe. He wondered if people from those countries would ever visit Aruba for the beaches and climate once the war ended. It seemed an ideal place to escape the cold and bitter winters of the Northern Hemisphere. The idea struck him and stayed in his mind.

His adventuring took him further north and past Palm Beach to the Malmok area. Here he discovered a large coconut plantation. The beach had virtually no buildings. Behind Malmok the land rose gently and became hilly. Jakob was fascinated at the differences that existed in such a small distance.

Jakob looked out to sea and saw the shape of the bridge of the Antilla poking out of the water. The German ships had been sheltering there after Germany declared war. The waters of Aruba, a Dutch country had been neutral until the invasion of Holland. Now that neutrality was gone.

Jakob walked down to a small cove. He stripped his clothes and entered the water. He swam and relaxed. It was mid afternoon when he decided to return to Savaneta.

Upon arriving back at the apartment he was greeted by Juan.

"Jakob, please come and be with us. Carlita and I have some news we need to discuss with you."

Jakob sensed a problem. He had not known Juan to speak like that. He joined them on the porch.

"Jakob, I have received an offer to take over a restaurant in San Nicolaas. It is a successful business and I have saved enough money to do this. I will be selling my fishing boat and small business. I will try to arrange for you to stay with the business. There are several fishermen I know who are interested in buying my boat."

Jakob absorbed the information and settled back in deep thought.

"Juan, I thank you for telling me this and offering to help me stay with the business. I am ready for a change and will soon be sending money to my wife so that she can travel back safely to Canada. I have an idea. Are you interested in a partner? I have some money that I could invest and we could consider making some changes and add entertainment."

Juan thought about this. Carlita quietly asked Jakob what he would do with the restaurant. Jakob discussed his ideas and told her of the clubs he had visited in Europe. She liked his ideas.

That night they talked for hours. A decision was made. Jakob and Juan would visit a Notary to make an agreement between them. They shook hands and Juan went into the house to fetch some Ponche Crema to celebrate. He poured the yellowish cream liqueur into small glasses. Jakob sipped the sweet liqueur. It was not to his liking but he politely swallowed the drink.

They did not take the boat out fishing that morning. Jakob and Juan dressed in some casual clothing and proceeded into San Nicolaas to visit the Notary. The Notary joined them in a small office that had a giant fan blowing in a feeble attempt to cool the room. It was sweltering.

Juan described the agreement they were looking for and handed the Notary the papers for the takeover of the restaurant. The Notary advised them that they would need to return in two weeks time to review a draft agreement. He could not prepare anything before then.

Until then, Juan and Jakob continued to fish. It seemed every moment they were together they talked about the plans for the restaurant. They were both excited.

It was several days later when Carlita asked Jakob about Anke. It bothered her that Anke was in Holland and meant to return to Canada and yet Jakob wanted to invest and start a business in Aruba.

"Jakob what are you planning for your wife, Anke?"

"I am thinking of bringing her here to Aruba. It is a better life here for us. The restaurant will succeed and then in addition we can look to some other business."

Carlita nodded but had a feeling that Jakob was not being truthful. She put those thoughts to the back of her mind.

That night Carlita expressed her doubts to Juan.

"We have never met her. There could be other problems that we do not know about. I will speak to Jakob about this at the right time."

The weeks passed by and eventually Juan and Jakob visited the Notary office. They reviewed the agreement. Jakob and Juan handed their money to the Notary to establish the banking arrangements.

The deal was complete. They walked to the restaurant and inserted the keys to open the protective metal screens that protected the windows and doors. The restaurant had been closed for several weeks and the air was stale.

Juan was taking an inventory at the bar when there was a shout from outside. He went to the window. Miguel was outside. Juan opened the locked door and let him in.

"Miguel, you should be at the Kit Kat working."

"No my brother I have left the Kit Kat to join you and make this place work. We will all have fun and make it a success."

"Miguel, we will not have money to pay you yet. We are just starting. It will be Jakob and I doing most of the work."

"I am not looking for money now. I have saved a considerable amount over the years. I know how this business works. I will help you run it. I have a chef who wishes to join us. He is from Venezuela and makes meat dishes that are excellent."

Juan thought of this. "Wait here while I get Jakob to join us and discuss."

The three of them sat on stools at the bar and traded ideas. Miguel accepted Jakob's ideas and the group planned the opening and operation of the restaurant.

"I will contact Alejandro. We will get music planned immediately."

Throughout the week they planned, purchased food and the items required for the opening. Carlita made table clothes. Miguel had menus designed and printed. Jakob and Juan painted and freshened up the interior. By week's end they were ready for their opening on Saturday night.

They worked late into Friday night. Curious onlookers peered through the windows as they either walked to or left the other bars and clubs. Some knocked on the windows in an attempt to get into the restaurant.

It was at the end of a long week when they closed the restaurant and left in the early hours of the morning. They were bone tired yet excited about tomorrow's opening.

Chapter 129

The restaurant opening was wildly successful. Over the next couple of months business was steady. Juan and Jakob closely watched as the business grew. They noticed that they had the most customers when there was entertainment. Eventually the number of restaurant customers started to slow. Juan and Jakob were concerned. As the number of customers dwindled the profits shrank to the point that they were unable to cover the expenses of all the staff.

Juan called a meeting of his staff. Suggestions were made but none seemed strong enough to solve the problem. Jakob stood to address the staff.

"I have an idea. We always do a lot of business in the evenings when we have music. There are less people ordering food then. Most customers go to the bar or the front tables and drink. On occasion we see some get up and dance. I think we should convert the restaurant into a club that also serves meals. We will need to redesign the inside."

The staff spoke amongst themselves. Juan looked unhappy. He stood to speak.

"I do not want to run a club and deal with all the problems that a club experiences. My heart is in owning and operating a restaurant. I oppose changing the restaurant to a club."

Jakob went over to Juan and placed an arm around his shoulder.

"Juan, we will not survive if we don't make a change. I have some ideas. Unlike many of the bars here in San Nicolaas we will make this one special. We will attract managers from the refinery. Many only go to the Esso facilities and never leave the Colony. There are no clubs that appeal to the Americans who have come here to run the refinery. Our entertainment will be music and small shows. I saw this in Europe."

Juan was discouraged. He shrugged and looked away from the gathering. He undid his jacket and walked to the kitchen. Jakob followed him.

"Jakob, the truth is I do not have any more money to invest into your idea. I must look after Carlita and my children. I enjoyed running the restaurant and the friendships I made with many who ate here. This is a very sad time for me. I understand your idea and I think it will work. I wish I had the money."

Jakob listened and thought about the situation.

"Juan there may be a possibility I can help you. Will you stay and continue to run the restaurant and help with the changes?"

"I can only stay if I can make money. What are you thinking?"

"I have saved money. I will take a job and contribute from my salary to the cost of running the restaurant. I had met one of the owners and investors for the Kit Kat Club. She is very wealthy. I will arrange for us to meet with her and discuss this with her. It is possible she will invest and become a partner."

Juan was skeptical. He had met the woman once when he had visited Miguel at the Kit Kat. She had impressed him as a tough woman who was only interested in making money. She had seemed removed and did not care for the staff or making friends with the customers. Juan was not sure she would be interested in Jakob's plan, but he was desperate.

"Tell me more. What will you offer her? What job can you possibly get to make good money? Where will you find musicians? What will you do to the restaurant? Will the restaurant portion of the club be open all day?"

Questions flowed from Juan.

"Juan, my friend. I have not prepared an exact plan yet. Tonight we will discuss details. I want you to be a part of the new club. We will make a club in San Nicolaas that the others will envy."

Chapter 130

Throughout the following week, Juan, Miguel and Jakob sat each evening planning the design and operation for the new club. When the final plan was arrived at, Jakob asked Miguel to arrange for a meeting with the owner of the Kit Kat Club.

Several days later, Miguel advised Juan that the owner had agreed to meet early the next Monday morning. Juan fastidiously prepared for the meeting. He extracted what he believed were the elements of the business plan that would interest an investor.

On the Monday morning Jakob and Juan travelled to the Kit Kat Club for the meeting. They were greeted at the door by a young woman and escorted to an office on the second floor. The office was strewn with piles of papers, invoices, newspapers. Each was neatly stacked. The young woman offered them some juices or coffee. They sat quietly and were soon joined by the woman who owned the club.

"Good morning. I understand you have come to discuss a business opportunity with me."

Jakob spoke first. "Good morning. Yes indeed we would like to present our plan to upgrade the restaurant that we own and operate. We wish to open an entertainment club for the evenings and maintain a smaller restaurant for the daytime. The restaurant would be open for breakfast, lunch and early dinner. It is our desire to attract businessmen here in San Nicolaas to a restaurant that offers better food than that available at the other places only catering to the refinery workers. In the evenings we would have music and other entertainment. To start we will only be open 3 nights of the week."

The woman leaned back in deep thought.

"It is interesting. Go on. Tell me more."

For the next few hours, Juan and Jakob described their plans to the woman. She sat stone faced taking in every detail. After a long pause she spoke. "Do you have a copy of the plans and financial information that you can leave with me?"

Jakob looked to Juan, who was nodding his head.

"Good. I will read the plans again and discuss with my other partners and accountant. I will ask Miguel to tell you when we will meet again." With this she rose stiffly and made a quick exit.

Juan and Jakob looked at each other. The same young woman joined them and escorted them back to the entrance. She opened the door to the bright blazing sun. They were temporarily blinded after having been in the darkened room.

Juan and Jakob walked back to the Villa and changed into light casual clothing. They went to the porch. The weather was humid and cloudy. A storm that was raging out at sea was drawing the trade winds away from the Island. There was no breeze at all. The humidity and heat were oppressive.

Juan emerged from the Villa with a couple of cold beers. They sat in silence reflecting upon the meeting. Juan spoke. "Jakob, what do you think? I could not decide if she was interested. Maybe she will steal our plans. I am concerned."

"Juan, do not think that way. She has made businesses work for her. I believe part of the reason she is so successful is due to the fact that she does not allow her emotions to show. There is nothing more we can do now. We must await her decision. "

They sat in silence looking out at the flat sea of the Caribbean. All around was quiet. Heat waves shimmered off the pure white sand. Several children ran back and forth into the ocean. The occasional squeal of delight pierced the silence. In the sky large dark clouds were forming from the east. Claps of thunder sounded and sheets of lightning illuminated the darkened sky. The children ran from the beach to their homes. Torrential rain fell. In front of the porch the ground flooded and water pooled in the small indents in the pathway to the beach.

The storm stopped as quickly as it had started. The sun was shining again. As the sun's rays heated the ground, steam arose. Again the humidity rose.

They heard the slamming of the Villa's front door and soon Carlita joined them. She was wet and bedraggled yet laughing.

"I was walking back with our supplies when the rains came. I kept walking. It was nice to feel the rain on my skin after the heat of this day. I will go and put on new clothes and join you. I shall make us some food. You both look sad. Tell me all when I come back."

Carlita returned carrying a tray of small pastries stuffed with shrimp, spiced vegetable and other delicacies.

"Now, tell me about the meeting. What happened?"

Juan described the meeting with the Kit Kat Club's owner and told her of his concerns. He was not happy.

Carlita listened without interrupting. She stayed quiet after Juan had finished.

"Juan I think you are worrying too much. It is only correct that she will want time to look at the plan and speak with others. I think that is good. If she was not interested she would have told you. Besides, you own the restaurant and are inviting her to join you in a business that is already operating."

Jakob was impressed with Carlita's thinking and attitude. She was a bright woman. It made him think of Anke. He wondered how she would react to the plans. He was missing her. He was starting to feel the old conflict arising again in him. This time it was not about his religion and his selected way of life, but rather about staying in Aruba with Anke or whether he should go back to the farms in Canada. He was unable to reach a decision. The more he thought about this, the worse the conflict tore at him.

Jakob rose from the bench he had been sitting on. "I am going for a walk along the beach. I need to think about all that is happening."

Juan and Carlita watched as Jakob walked down to the shoreline.

Chapter 131

A week passed by before Juan and Jakob heard from Catherine. At her request they were to attend a meeting at her bank in San Nicolaas.

They prepared their plans in advance and travelled to meet with her. Upon arriving at the bank, they were ushered into a plush meeting room. In attendance were her accountant, banker and another of her business partners. Introductions were made and they settled in for the meeting.

"I am the accountant for the investors in the Kit Kat Club, including madam here. I have reviewed the business plan you have presented to her for a possible investment in this venture. While I believe the plan is solid there are some problems. The financial projections may not be met. The possibility of a slower growth than you expect means that the operation will not support the costs of the staff you suggest are needed. You will need to make changes. Without those changes, the investment cannot be made."

Jakob looked over at Juan, who appeared lost. Jakob spoke to the assembled group.

"I will agree to leave my invested money in the club and will not take any wages. My involvement with the club will be reduced. It is my wish to see the club succeed. I will assist Juan and his family with the club. In the future we can look at this again."

The accountant turned to the woman. "With that reduction in cost, I believe the planned club has a strong possibility of succeeding."

The woman handed written notes across to the accountant and banker.

"I am prepared to make an investment but will require that I own at least 51% of the business. If you can agree on that then I will have my lawyer prepare the documents and transfer of funds to the bank."

Juan looked at Jakob and then the rest of the group. "I need to speak with Jakob, my brothers and my wife. This is a decision take affects us all. Can we meet again?"

A meeting was scheduled for the next morning.

That evening Carlita prepared a large meal. She sat with Juan, Miguel, Alejandro and Jakob around the large outdoor table. The talk was all about the planned club. Points were raised and debated. Eventually, and after hours of discussion they all fell silent. Carlita sensed the uncertainty.

"I want you to think. This woman is successful. She does not accept failure. She has had professional people look at the plan. You should all be happy that she will invest. She would not do that unless she felt it would succeed. Be happy for this. I know you have concerns. Don't worry. Look at the future. You all have a chance to make a good business."

When Carlita had finished, Juan agreed.

"Jakob, this was your plan. I do not want you to lose."

"Juan, I am able to find a job here and will stay with you in the business. In the future things will be better."

The next morning Juan and Jakob returned to the bank. The accountant introduced the lawyer. After a brief discussion of the planned operation of the club, they turned to the legal aspect of the investment agreement.

Hours dragged by. Juan and Jakob became exhausted with the lengthy process. It was early in the afternoon that the meeting concluded. The lawyer handed them the final documents reflecting the woman's 51% ownership. They all signed. Upon completion, the lawyer advised the banker to set up an account for the club and to transfer funds into the account.

Juan and Jakob left the bank and proceeded to the restaurant. They called together the staff and announced the plans and new ownership. There was high excitement throughout all of the staff.

Chapter 132

No longer involved in the daily operations of the restaurant and its conversion to a club, Jakob turned his attention to finding a job in San Nicolaas. Jakob had spoken with the friends he had made at the Kit Kat, many who worked at the refinery. They convinced him that the refinery represented his best possibility. They arranged for an interview with the manager responsible for hiring.

The following Monday morning Jakob set off to meet with the manager at the refinery.

The morning was already hot as the summer played out in Aruba. Jakob walked from Savaneta and enjoyed looking into the small adobe houses with the dogs barking and running in the front yards. Children played and sat on the covered front porches. The smell of spicy foods cooking tantalized him. Every now and then men who he had previously met in the clubs would call "Bon Dia" to him. Jakob was content with the life he was enjoying in Aruba.

The air had a smoky blue haze. The strong smell of the distilling oil and gases filled the air. It seemed to Jakob that the smoky air fell to the ground. He wondered if the fumes made it heavier.

He walked down Main Street of Saint Nicolaas and at the end of the street he turned right and walked to the main gates of the refinery. There was a sentry security station at the gate. Jakob walked up to the smartly dressed security guard.

"I am here to meet with Bert Johnson, the hiring manager."

"Please stand over there and wait. I will phone the office and tell them you are here. What is your name?"

Jakob responded and stood in the heat of the sun and waited. Within a few minutes a thin young man in his early 20's arrived to escort him to the personnel office. Along the way they made small talk.

They arrived at a large brownish two storey U-shaped building. Several big American luxury cars belonging to the plants executives were parked near the entrance. They entered the building and took a wide set of stairs to the second floor.

Jakob and the young man walked along a narrow corridor past offices painted with titles indicating their function...accounting, office manager, purchasing and so on. Jakob smiled as he noticed the misspelled names on the doors. They reached one entitled "Personal Manager" at the end of the corridor. They entered the office. There was a waiting area outside of a smaller office. Sitting at a desk in the waiting area was a woman aged 40'ish. Her hair was a light bluish grey and she wore a pair of thick framed horn rim glasses. She clacked away on a black typewriter without glancing up.

The young man asked Jakob to sit and wait. He would advise Bert Johnson of Jakob's arrival.

Jakob sat waiting for what seemed eternity. He looked at the woman and the typewriter. She reminded him of a poster he had once seen outside of a cinema advertising some film.

Finally, the door swung open and Bert Johnson burst into the waiting area. He abruptly stopped and stared at Jakob.

"Damn. Y'all don't know how happy I am to see a white fella looking for a job. Those local boys here are dummr'n than shit. Come on, come on."

He beckoned Jakob towards his office door.

Bert Johnson was a tall Texan of over 6feet. He was heavy set. His large jowls wobbled as he spoke. Perspiration flowed from his armpits like never ending streams.

"Sit down boy" he said motioning Jakob to a matching wooden chair in front of his oak desk.

Jakob was taking an instant dislike to him. He disliked the comment about the locals, many of whom had become friends and helped Jakob since his arrival.

"Tell me. Why are you here? What's your experience working? What sort of job are you looking for?"

Jakob responded with a description of his growing up and work on the farm, including his aptitude for repairing mechanical things. He continued and described his position in the engine room of the ship during the voyage to Aruba.

Bert Johnson reached behind him and removed a thick loose leaf folder and thumbed through it.

"Well, you'all be one lucky son of a bitch. We got a real good job for you here. What you've done before is good. It means this is the job for you. I can hire you as a supervisor for a cleaning crew."

Jakob tried not to look disappointed but Bert Johnson saw the expression that passed on Jakob's face. He started to laugh.

"No. Not that sort of cleaning. Not shitters and urinals. I am talking about cleaning in the plant. Help with the production equipment and plant maintenance. It involves breaking down pipe systems, pumps and other components of the machinery that supply the oils to the refinery. You will work with the maintenance engineers. It is heavy work but you will have a crew of 5 of those lazy local bums. The money is good. The work is dirty. There is plenty of overtime work available."

Jakob quietly considered the offer and then accepted. Bert Johnson discussed the pay and benefits that Jakob would be entitled too. Jakob could not initially believe the huge amount of pay that was discussed. His thoughts turned to Anke. He would be able to send money for her return sooner than he had planned. He would also have money to assist Juan with the club. The Gods were with him.

Bert produced a number of forms and assisted Jakob in completing them. Jakob was assigned a company payroll number.

 When they were completed, Bert took Jakob to the company store where he was provided with overalls and other protective equipment. He was then taken to a locker room to change and be assigned a locker. Jakob hesitated at the door. Hung over the door was a sign reading "Whites Only". Bert saw him looking at the sign.

"We provide separate lockers for the local workers. They prefer that."

Inside the locker room Jakob was assigned a locker and padlock. The number of the key was noted by Bert who requested Jakob to change into the overalls for a visit to the area from which he would work.

They proceeded to a large control room with gauges and instruments recording temperatures and events on graphing machines. Jakob was introduced to the Maintenance Manager, a man in his mid-forties. He shook Jakob's hand and set about describing the position and the work to be done. He described the monitoring of the functions in the refinery. When there was the requirement for maintenance and cleaning, Jakob was advised that one of the engineers would originate a service request. Jakob was advised that there were different engineers for each shift and that they would direct the exact nature of the work to be done.

Jakob was fascinated by the workings of the refinery and even more amazed that he had secured the important job of managing a crew responsible for keeping the operations running.

After he completed the tour, Bert took Jakob across the front yard to a structure that stood alone.

"This is our milk bar. It is a canteen for our men to get milk we bring in from the States and other treats from home. It has candy, ice-cream and other things. You can charge things here to your payroll number and it will be adjusted by the Payroll Group. Later we will go to our club and visit. We have a baseball diamond, dance floor and many other attractions for our workers. You will find people from Scotland, England, Italy and other countries here.

Jakob had never realized the size of the operation of the refinery before.

"How many men are here? Where do they all live?"

"We have about 2000 workers here. Most of the American and foreign workers we bring in live in an area called Lago Colony. We have almost 700 homes there. The refinery is a village by itself. We are proud of this. We are one of the world's largest oil refineries. We have just started to distill special aviation fuels for the British."

"When do I start work here?" Jakob asked.

"You can start tomorrow. I will arrange for you to be met at the gate and escorted around on your first day. Welcome to Lago."

They returned to the locker room and Jakob changed back into his casual clothing. Bert took him to the plant security and had a security form made out for Jakob. When all was finished, Jakob walked back to the main gate. There was a group of about a dozen workers leaving for lunch and probably drinks at one of the local bars. They laughed and called out as they approached the gates. The smartly uniformed guard came out from his post and while joking with them opened the gates.

Jakob was impressed. It seemed to be a friendly but dirty and smelly place to work.

Chapter 133

That evening over their evening meal, Jakob discussed the day's events and his new job. He was excited at the turn of events. Carlita listened intently. Eventually Carlita spoke.

"Jakob. You are taking this job and you have invested in the business here. Instead of preparing to go back to Canada and be with your wife you are becoming more involved in life here. You have made many friends and do not show any desire to return. Have you written to your wife? Is she safe in Holland with the war being fought there? Have you sent money to her? Are her relatives safe? You do not speak of her and seem distant from her situation."

Jakob fell quiet.

"Carlita, there was little I could do while trapped in Germany. When I joined the ship, it was meant to stop in Galveston and I had planned to slip away from the ship there. The plans were changed. It is my plan to save enough money to arrange for her to leave Holland and go back to Canada. We still own the farms there. I will join her and we will again farm."

Carlita gave him a long and somewhat unbelieving look. She got up from the table and busied herself clearing dishes and cleaning in the Kitchen. Juan watched her in silence. He knew when a storm was brewing. It was better to say nothing.

"Jakob, I am going to the porch for a drink. Do you wish to join me?"

Carlita overheard the question. Soon she was crashing pots and plates around in the kitchen. Juan knew how angry she was. He did not know what had upset her so much.

"Let us go for a walk on the beach. I want to check on the new little boat I bought after I sold both the business and my big fishing boat. One evening we will go out and fish together. It will be relaxing for us both."

Jakob and Juan left the porch and in bare feet walked onto the cool sand. With the sun having set, the sand had lost its heat and was refreshingly cool.

They walked along the shore to where Juan's boat was anchored. Juan proudly pointed the boat out. Its dark shape bobbed in the waters. In the early darkness, Juan could make out the sharp point at the bow that rose up above the sides of the boat. Juan guessed at the length of the boat. It could not be more that 15 feet.

"Juan the boat is small. Are you not worried by the swell and the high seas out there?"

"No it rides the water well. It is even better than the big boat that we used for fishing."

After Juan checked the anchor was secure, they walked back to the Villa and resumed their positions outside on the porch. Carlita was nowhere to be seen. The villa was silent.

Jakob stood and explained to Juan that he needed to sleep in advance of his first day working at the refinery. He wished Juan a goodnight and left for his apartment.

Upon opening the door he found Carlita sitting on his bed. She looked directly into his eyes.

"Jakob I do not believe you intend to return to Canada or send for your wife. I had thought of you as a good man. I like you. Please tell me the truth. Are you staying in Aruba? I love my Juan but he has become a boring old man. I will soon leave him."

Jakob was shocked at this sudden outburst.

"Carlita, this is not right. Juan adores you. In meetings about the club he spoke of how you and the family must be safe and protected. Do not think this way. I am sending for my wife and yes I will return to our farms in Canada. You must put away any ideas about us. They will never work out. Now, go to Juan."

Chapter 134

Jakob left early the next morning for his new job at the refinery. He was happy to be away from the villa. He did not want any complications to arise in his friendship with Juan and the family members.

As he walked along the dusty red brown soil pathway that edged the road, he thought of the previous night's conversation with Carlita. As he walked through the early morning activity on the streets of San Nicolaas he was oblivious to all. His life at the villa had taken a serious turn.

Soon he was at the main gates to the refinery. He spoke to the guard, who was a friendly older Aruban man. They joked and another short Aruban man dressed in his overalls joined them.

"Bon Dia. I am Pinto and I was asked to greet you and take you to the maintenance area. We will be working on the oil lines to the pier today. It is good work. We will be outside for a while away from the noise, heat and smell of the plant."

Jakob introduced himself. Pinto chatted on about himself, work and family. He was a pleasant natured man with a ready laugh and smile. Jakob took an immediate liking to him.

Jakob was introduced to the rest of the crew and worked throughout the day with them. They took a break from noon until 1:30pm and continued working until late in the day. Jakob enjoyed the work and especially the jovial crew he was required to manage. At the end of the day he returned to the locker room to change from his overalls back into his casual clothes. He was discouraged that the crews were forced to use another changing facility. He did not like this separation.

As he was walking to the gates and about to start his walk back to the villa, a shout came from behind. He turned to see several of his crew preparing to leave. He stopped and waited.

"Jakob, we are going to a workers bar for a drink. Come and join us."

Jakob thought of last evening and decided an excuse to delay his return to Juan's villa would be welcome. He did not look forward to running into Juan and Carlita at this time. He was angry that the situation had arisen. He had done nothing to encourage it.

"Yes. I will join you."

They bunched together and with jokes and good natured bantering between them as they left the refinery grounds. Instead of proceeding into San Nicolaas, the group walked ahead and after 10 minutes turned right onto the road that lead up to Seroe Colorado. They continued walking for a while and finally came to a pale blue house that fronted onto the street. There was a large opening into a dimly lit interior. The group walked in to shouts of greeting. They were obviously well known at the place.

Jakob was introduced to the tall black man who owned the bar. He reached behind the bar and bottles of beer were produced for all in the group. Conversation continued and the jokes flew. They were a very happy bunch.

Jakob's eyes adjusted to the dim light and he looked around at the others in the bar. Sitting at a table not far away from them were several men that Jakob instantly recognized. They were Marines he had met them before at the Kit Kat Club. They were not wearing uniforms and were engaged in what appeared to be an intense conversation. Without saying anything to the others, Jakob looked away and joined in the good natured banter with his new worker friends.

Jakob felt a hand grasp his shoulder and the others were looking at someone behind him. He turned and found one of the Marines standing there with a huge smile. It was Pieter van Doren. He and Jakob had enjoyed many hours talking at the Kit Kat.

"Jakob what are you doing here? This is where we workers come to relax and drink."

Jakob explained his new job at the refinery and how his friends had invited him for drinks after work.

The Marine slapped him on his back as he was about to rejoin his others.

"Come and join us for a drink before you leave."

Pinto and the other workers started to drift off to their homes. Jakob went across to the table where his Marine friend was still drinking. As he approached the conversation halted.

Pieter van Doren introduced him to the other Marines.

"Pieter. Can we speak together? There is a matter I need to discuss."

Pieter agreed and the two left the table and went to the rear of the bar where it was quiet and there were no other patrons.

The events of the previous night were still foremost in Jakob's mind. He was tormented yet again and wanted to solve them before he made more mistakes in his life. "Jakob what is so important that you can only discuss it with me?"

Jakob smiled at him. "Why are you and your friends here? There are many places in Savaneta and San Nicolaas that are closer to your barracks and I am sure they are more entertaining,"

"Jakob that is true. There are times when we need to escape from the eyes that always seem to be watching us as Marines. It is common knowledge that we are spied upon. Sometimes we need to meet certain people and do not want others to see who we meet. I hope you understand what I am saying."

Jakob reflected on Pieter's words.

"Now Jakob what is it that you wish to discuss."

Jakob sighed and told Pieter his story. He described leaving the farms and his trip through Europe to Holland. He told him of leaving Anke in Holland while he pursued relatives in Germany and became trapped. He ended with the story of his trip to Aruba.

Pieter took it all in and for a while said nothing. "Jakob how can I help you? "

"I have been unable to contact Anke since Holland was invaded. The letters I wrote have been returned or never received a reply. I do not have contacts in Holland to assist me in finding her. I wish to locate her and send money so she can escape from the occupation and get back to Canada where I will go and be with her."

Pieter nodded and said nothing. He left Jakob and went to the bar and ordered two large mugs of beer. When he returned he pushed one toward Jakob.

"Let me consider this. You say she was In Amsterdam? It is difficult to communicate with Holland now, but we Marines do have links still. Give me her address and I will see if anyone can check this for you. There are no promises."

"I will need to find the address. It is in my case at my apartment. I will take it to the Marine's base in Savaneta and leave it in an envelope for you."

By the time Jakob left the bar it was dusk. He felt light headed from the strong beer.

Jakob slowly started back to the villa. He was hoping to avoid another confrontation with Carlita. He felt sad as he had strong feelings for Juan and the family. Jakob idled his way through the busy streets of San Nicolaas. Drunken men staggered outside bars. The girls were working them. Several carts had been set up and served different foods. Jakob discovered how hungry he was. The smell of the cooking food drew him to a colorful bright yellow cart trimmed with pink borders. A Haitian woman stood behind the cart with two young children clasping at the sides of her dress. On top of the cart was a metal container cut from the base of an old oil drum containing glowing embers. Some chicken wire was strung across the top of the embers. Cooking slowly were the largest chicken legs Jakob had ever seen. He purchased two of them. The woman scooped them off the fire and into some newspaper which she wrapped tightly. Jakob left for his walk back to the villa.

Before he reached the villa, he turned sharply left and took an overgrown track down to a little deserted stretch of sand. He sat on a log that had drifted ashore and devoured his chicken.

By the time he reached his apartment it was dark. There was no sign of life. Juan and family had gone to bed for the night.

Chapter 135

Jakob saw less of Juan and Carlita as he worked long overtime hours at the refinery. Each morning he would leave his apartment early in the morning and ride his recently purchased bike to the refinery. Often Juan would return very late at night or in the early morning hours after the club closed. Jakob would be asleep at these times. Jakob missed the time he spent with Juan discussing affairs of the Island or new ideas for the club.

The year slipped by. Jakob became well known at the refinery. His crews liked him and were always eager to work with him. He was fair and often took the workers side in any disputes that arose. The management at the refinery recognized Jakob as a hard, fair and intelligent worker. He was promoted into a management position, yet continued working alongside his crews.

Jakob was working double shifts of 12—16 hours each day when possible, yet did not tire from the work. Within months he had amassed a considerable amount of money. He started to investigate the costs for both him and Anke to return to the farms in Canada. Within a few months he would have enough to cover the costs and also have enough money for them to reestablish their lives.

Jakob knew he would miss the job at the refinery, his worker friends there and the life he had come to know on Aruba. Again he found himself in conflict. This time the conflict was not about his beliefs but rather about his life. The conflict churned in his head often. He knew that he must make a decision.

Jakob had become a part of the refinery. His clothes reeked of the never ending stench of the oils and gases generated by the distilling processes. He found that the food he ordered at the canteen smelled of the fumes. Over time he became unaware of the penetration of the fumes into everything.

While popular with the men at the refinery, Jakob was still lonely. He spent his evening hours thinking of his past life in Canada with Anke and of the fateful trip to Europe.

As he lay on his bed one evening, there was a loud knock at the door. Jakob sprang off the bed and answered. Juan was standing at the door with two glasses and a bottle in his hand.

"Jakob. We spend very little time together now. Come and join Carlita and I on the porch. We will drink and talk. It will be like old times. I am not working for a week. I will stay home and spend time with my family and go out fishing. I miss that. Maybe we can go together one evening. "

Jakob was pleased to have the company and readily accepted Juan's invitation

Carlita was sitting on the porch when they arrived. She had prepared a tray of delicacies. Jakob could smell the shrimp pastries and skewered meat. He was hungry.

The conversation drifted from the club to the refinery to the family. It was a relaxing evening. They sat drinking, talking and laughing. Sitting in the cooler temperature, they watched the large silvery moon as its beams glistened in front of them and reflected off the calm Caribbean. Jakob stood to excuse himself and retire for the night. He needed to sleep for the early morning start.

As he was leaving Jakob spoke to Juan."I am not working this Wednesday. We can go fishing then."

Juan nodded in delight.

Within minutes, Jakob fell into a deep and heavy sleep. His little dog Timmy jumped onto the bed beside him and curled into his back and gave a growl to warn any impending foes that they were not welcome.

Jakob awoke refreshed and happy. He was pleased that he had spent the time with Juan and Carlita. He was also thankful that Carlita had seemed to dismiss any idea of an affair with him. Jakob was unsure he could have resisted for long had she persevered. Jakob dressed and left on his bike for another day at the refinery.

Riding to the refinery, he made up his mind. He would send the money to Anke. He needed to find a way to find her and get the money in her hands.

He rode in silence seemingly oblivious to the barking of the dogs that ran to the fences as he went by. In San Nicolaas he detoured around the back of Main Street. He had made his decision finally. He did not want the distractions of San Nicolaas to detract from his plan.

He arrived at the refinery gate and was welcomed in by the security guard.

He rode across the grounds to the main office building. He dismounted his bike and walked in. He climbed the stairs to the second floor and entered the door to the Office Manager. She was a woman in her early 50's. Jakob had met her on several occasions at social functions. She looked up and invited Jakob to take a seat.

"Hello Jakob. Why are you here? I s there something I can help you with?"

"Yes. I will need to send money to my wife in Europe. I know the refinery handles large amounts and sends and receives money from abroad. I am wondering if you can suggest a safe method for me to do this."

"Jakob it is very difficult now. The war has resulted in many restrictions. I cannot help you. I am sorry."

Jakob thanked her and left the office dejected.

He was determined to find a way. First he must locate Anke and then arrange to transfer the money.

Jakob went to the locker room and changed into his overalls for the day ahead. He met his crew and discussed the maintenance plans he had been given by the engineers. It would be a long day. The job involved shutting off several of the pumps that offloaded the crude from the tankers. It was a job that needed to be finished quickly. They would need to work until it was completed. They would not be able to leave the job and return to it the next day.

Jakob advised his crew that it would be a long day. They were ecstatic at the prospect of the overtime.

Chapter 136

Jakob decided to join some of his crew the next evening for drinks at the workers bar. Upon entering he noticed that several of the Marines he had seen there before were in the bar and huddled in deep conversation.

Jakob went to the bar and ordered drinks for his crew. On the way back to his table Pieter van Doren waved a greeting to him.

At his table, Jakob listened to his men joking and discussing the impossible futures they expected to have. The men accepted the stupidity of the claims and howled with laughter when each described the future they anticipated. One claimed he would be a pilot flying to Miami, another claimed he would become a surgeon while yet another claimed he would become president. Each claim was ludicrous and served to fuel the good humor at the table.

Jakob had an idea. He watched and when Pieter van Doren was leaving Jakob beckoned him to join him. Pieter slowly crossed over the room to Jakob's table. Jakob stood and said to Pieter "I have something private to discuss with you. Can we talk alone?"

They went and sat at the same table in the dark area at the back of the bar.

"What is it that is so important?"

Jakob told Pieter of his dilemma. Pieter listened in silence without commenting. Jakob finished and there was a long pause before either spoke.

Pieter looked around the darkened club. He turned his palms up as he spoke to Jakob.

"What you are asking is very dangerous for me. I will consider what you have told me. Meet me here on Wednesday evening."

Pieter stood to leave. Jakob returned to his worker friends who were also starting to drift off and return to their homes, girlfriends and wives.

When Jakob got back to his apartment, Carlita was sitting out with the children.

"Where is Juan? Is he at the club? I thought he had taken a week off to spend at home."

"No he decided to go out and fish. It is in his blood. He loves to be out there on the water. Please come and join us for a while."

Jakob sat on the bench. Carlita poured him a rum drink. It was strong and burned his throat.

"How long has Juan been out fishing?"

"He left as the sun was setting. It is late now. I think he will be back soon."

Jakob and Carlita sat talking. The children ran back and forth down to the water's edge.

It seemed like hours passed by. Carlita was becoming concerned.

"I wonder if Juan met his friends and went to the little Chinese bar here in Savaneta. I should go and check."

Jakob agreed to go with her for the short walk to the bar. When they got there, loud music was playing to a handful of men. Juan was not amongst them. Carlita asked if anyone had seen him. No one had.

They returned to the villa. Carlita returned to the porch and Jakob retired for the night.

When Jakob left the apartment in the morning, Carlita was still sitting on the porch.

"Carlita, have you been here all night?

"Yes. Juan always returns. Something is wrong. Maybe he has problems with the boat."

"Carlita, today is the day I will not work. I will go down and speak with the other fishermen. I am sure someone will know where he is."

Jakob walked off in the direction where a small group of men were preparing their boats. He called to them and told them in his broken Papiamento of the situation with Juan.

No one had seen him last evening or this morning. The fishermen told Jakob they would search for Juan in the area off Savaneta and further to the south where Juan often fished for wahoo. Juan thanked them and returned to Carlita at the villa.

"Carlita. I will stay with the children. You must go and sleep. I am sure the men will locate Juan. It is probably a simple reason that he has not returned. I suspect he has problems with the engine."

Reluctantly Carlita agreed and went inside to sleep.

The day wore on. Juan observed some of the fishing boats returning. He called to the children to join him. Together they walked down to the shoreline where the men had beached their boats. Nobody has seen any trace of Juan. There were worried looks on the faces of the men. They all knew Juan and respected him as an excellent sailor and fisherman. Jakob thanked them and returned to sit on the porch. Hours passed by and Carlita emerged. She asked Jakob if anyone had seen or heard of Juan.

Jakob shook his head. Carlita sat down heavily on the bench.

"I fear it will not be good." She left Jakob alone and went into the villa to prepare food for the children.

Jakob decide to go to the club and advise both Miguel and Alejandro of the situation.

He rode quickly to the club and took his bike in with him. He did not want it stolen.

Miguel greeted him cheerfully. Jakob beckoned Miguel to join him in the club's kitchen.

"Miguel. Something is wrong. Juan left to go fishing yesterday. He did not return last evening and the fishermen looked for him today. There was no sign. He is missing."

"I must contact Alejandro. We will go to Carlita immediately. This is not good."

Miguel spoke with urgency to the barman. He ran from the club and started on his way to find Alejandro. Jakob needed to meet Pieter van Doren before returning to the villa. He walked at a fast pace through San Nicolaas and found his way to the bar. As he entered he saw Pieter sitting alone near the entrance. Pieter acknowledged him and Jakob went across to join him.

"Jakob I have listened to your situation on two occasions now. I am sorry that I cannot guarantee that I can help you. We do have contact with the Netherlands however. I have sent a message to some who are involved with the Dutch Resistance. We may hear a response. I gave the information you had provided. Be aware that communication is not easy in these times. The communications we have are not always secure. I gave as little information as possible but enough for them to attempt to locate your wife in that general area. We will not hear for days. If we hear she has been found you must have the money available immediately. They will try and assist her to flee to a safer country. There are some who we must pay now to look away. It will not be expensive."

Jakob thanked Pieter and assured him that the payment would be made once Anke was found.

Pieter looked around the bar. "It is no longer advisable for us to meet here. I am afraid we are being watched. I will send a message to you at the refinery when there is some news."

Chapter 137

Jakob returned to the villa. Upon arrival he was met by Miguel and Alejandro. A large group of neighbors and local fishermen stood in the beachfront garden. The atmosphere was somber.

"I believe that we have lost Juan. The fishermen who were out there at the same time have told us that the water was extremely rough. They doubt that the small boat the Juan had bought would be safe in those waters. Tomorrow morning all the fishermen are going out to search the area."

Jakob looked across and into the porch area. Carlita was being comforted by some of the neighboring women. She was deeply upset and had been crying. It was evident to Jakob that she knew that Juan would never return.

As they all stood discussing and reflecting upon the situation, an old Ford truck braked sharply on the loose stones at the street side of the villa. Two men in uniforms jumped from the truck. Jakob recognized them as Marines. They walked around to where everyone was gathered. They called out to inquire whether this was the home of Juan. Miguel went to them. The Marines spoke to him quietly. Miguel dropped his head into his hands and openly wept. Alejandro joined him and was also in tears within minutes. The Marines and the brothers continued to speak in hushed tones. Finally, Miguel joined Carlita. He spoke with her and she cried out loudly. Jakob gathered that the worst had happened.

When those gathered started talking amongst themselves, Jakob approached the Marines.

"What can you tell me? Juan and his family are close friends."

"We cannot tell you much. We received a report of a small fishing boat washed up at Mangel Halto. We investigated. The boat was swamped with water. At the bow there is a large jagged hole. The boat may have hit something in the water, but from my experience it looks like the boat was attacked by a Tiger Shark. It looks like a shark bite. The hole is surrounded by a jagged edge and is high up from the waterline. If it was a log or something floating, the hole would be lower. There were reports of a large shark in the water here in the south end. All of the contents of the boat are gone. It is totally empty. We will arrange to have the boat towed here later."

The Marines went over to Miguel and Carlita. Arrangements to tow the boat were discussed and they left to return to their barracks.

Jakob cast his mind back to the days of mourning he had experienced as a Mennonite. He slowly walked up to Carlita, Miguel and Alejandro. He spoke softly to them and drew upon the teachings he had learnt. They listened to Jakob in silence. When he finished, an awkward silence fell over them.

"Jakob we thank you for your kindness, but here in Aruba we have our customs and death is treated differently. Without Juan's body we will need to ask the priest. I am sure we will have the Ocho Dia ceremony. This is our custom. It is a wake with an eight day period of mourning. All of our family and friends will take part. At the end of the eight days all the chairs are turned upside down and all of the windows will be opened to make sure Juan's spirit can leave the villa. I will need to visit the local priest in San Nicolaas to make arrangements."

Jakob looked around at the assembled friends and neighbors. Miguel spoke with Alejandro and told him of his plan to visit the priest. Alejandro was in agreement.

"When the priest advises us on how we should proceed, I will visit all of our family and invite them."

Miguel returned to Carlita and after some minutes left the porch to make his way into San Nicolaas and meet the priest.

It was becoming dark as Miguel mounted the stairs of the church rectory. He rang the polished brass bell. He waited and the door was opened by a tall Aruban priest. He listened and then invited Miguel into the reception room.

Chapter 138

Word of Juan's "death" spread quickly through the Village of Savaneta and amongst his friends in San Nicolaas. Throughout the mourning period there was a steady flow of visitors to the villa. Carlita maintained her composure and greeted those who came to pay respect with great dignity and finesse.

Juan's boat had been towed back and had been pulled up onto the beach. It lay partially on its side with the damage evident. An occasional walker on the beach would stop and look at the damaged boat.

At the end of the mourning period, a memorial ceremony was held on the beach. It was attended by a large number of people.

Father Claudius Ignatius conducted the service in Papiamento. Dressed in a pure white robe and wearing a violet stole, he led the prayers and hymns. Since Juan's body had not been found, the service was symbolic yet deeply religious.

At one point, Father Claudius halted the service and walked forward to the boat. He took his aspergillium and sprinkled holy water around the large hole, where it was believed Juan's life had ended.

At the end of the service the priest called on the gathered mourners to join in a procession to the cemetery in Savaneta. Carlita linked her arm with the priest. She was joined at the front of the procession by Miguel, Alejandro and her children. The procession was long. The men were dressed in white shirts and many of the women wore dark clothing and large hats. They set off in the direction of the cemetery. As they passed the houses along the way, men and women came to the side of the road and removed their headgear and bowed.

As the procession snaked its way along the road toward the Dutch Marine Corps barracks and the right turn up to the cemetery grounds, cars slowed and stopped behind them. Oncoming cars and trucks pulled off to the side of the road.

Jakob was impressed with the service and now fully understood how popular a man Juan had been with all these people.

At the cemetery a marble headstone had been erected. Inscribed on its face were Juan's full name and years of life. There was no need for a customary mausoleum without a body. Jakob looked at some of the magnificent mausoleums that surrounded them. He had been told the graves dug into the ground were not common in Aruba due to the problem of flooding after the infrequent but heavy rainstorms that could cause a person's remains to be disgorged from the ground.

Jakob was leaving the cemetery at the end of the service when he noticed Catherine, the owner of the Kit Kat and investor in their club staring across at him. She raised her thin white wrist and beckoned Jakob over to her.

As he approached her, he was shocked. It seemed Catherine had aged tremendously since he last saw her.

"Jakob, this is indeed a sad day. Juan worked hard and had an unusual work ethic. He was in many ways a unique person. I am saddened that this has happened to him and his family. We must meet very soon to decide what will happen with his ownership in the club."

"I will speak to Juan's brothers and we can arrange a meeting. They will need to be present. As you may know, in Aruba it is customary for any inheritance to be shared amongst family. I am sure they will want to attend."

Catherine paused. For several minutes she stood quietly in thought.

"Jakob, I am not so well. I would like to complete this soon. I am going to retire from the daily operations of the clubs and my investments here in Aruba. I will travel and live in Miami where I have family. I have already made arrangements for my businesses to be operated by one of my children. She is extremely successful in business."

Jakob was shocked. He had never thought of Catherine as a mother and having family.

"I go into the refinery every day. After I speak with the brothers and Carlita, I will visit your office and we can set a date and time for such a meeting."

Jakob made his way back to his apartment alone. He changed into casual clothes and with his dog Timmy, strolled down to the edge of the water and along the beach. He was deeply immersed in his thoughts. 1941 had been a year of change for him. He too had changed. He had found a purpose in life. It was unlike the life in Canada on the farms or that of Europe. He had found an inner peace.

As he walked the length of the deserted beach he wondered what he should do. The club was making a profit. Should he buy Juan's interest or should he sell his. He pondered the choices. He had made up his mind to return to Canada with Anke. He would contact Pieter van Doren and find out if the contacts in Holland had found Anke. He wondered how long he should wait before contacting Pieter.

Jakob started to return to his apartment. As he was passing the porch, Miguel called him to join them. Jakob turned and went up the stairs and onto the porch. Miguel was sitting with Alejandro and Carlita. Jakob was tempted to mention the discussion he had had with Catherine but decided against it. Together they sat. There were long periods of silence followed by bursts of conversation in which they spoke of Juan.

It was late when Jakob picked up Timmy who was in a deep sleep under a chair and placed him under his arm and then proceeded to his apartment.

"I must sleep as tomorrow I have a busy day at the refinery. I will be training a new crew. These are the boys who study at the school at the refinery. Many are smart so I am hoping it will be an easy day."

He said goodnight to them and left.

Chapter 139

Jakob continued his daily ride to the refinery and each night he returned to the apartment. He found it different without Juan's presence. Carlita was cordial and they spent many hours discussing the future without Juan. Carlita was considering moving back to Colombia to be with her family. She told Jakob how she and Juan had met when she had first come to the island to work as a waitress. He had shown Carlita a better life and now she was worried it would all collapse. Jakob assured her that with all of their friends in Aruba that the future would work out.

The next weekend, Miguel and Alejandro visited. Jakob asked them to join him in his apartment.

"Miguel, I have been asked by Catherine to set up a meeting to discuss the club and what should happen now that Juan is no longer with us. Do you know what you; Alejandro and Carlita want to do with your ownership in it?"

"We have decided we will keep the club. It is doing well and the money will go to Carlita and her family. Alejandro and I make good money other than at the club. Please setup the meeting and we will be there."

When they concluded their small talk, they left to assist Carlita with some repairs that needed to be done to the villa. Jakob admired the brother's devotion to the family.

On Monday morning Jakob cycled to the refinery. As he was entering the main gate, the security guard called to him.

"Jakob. Please wait. I have something here for you. A man came here and left this envelope."

The guard went inside his post and returned with an envelope. He handed it to Jakob who looked at the nondescript manila envelope. It was thin and bore no markings or a return address.

Jakob thanked the guard and placed the envelope in his shirt pocket. In the locker room he was alone. He sat on one of the long benches and opened it. Inside was a note scrawled on light blue paper. It read "On Tuesday night at 7:00pm, meet me at the new bar that just opened in September on Main Street. The bar is called Charlie's. Bring the item we had agreed upon. Your missing item has been found."

Jakob understood. He was ecstatic. Anke had been found. He could barely control his emotions the rest of the day. He returned early to his apartment. He was whistling and happily called to the children and Carlita as he passed them. Carlita was curious. She called Jakob to join her.

Jakob told her of the news but advised her to keep it a secret. It seemed that certain individuals were not aligned with the beliefs of the Dutch and were possibly members of the Dutch Nazi Party. Even though Aruba had interned suspected German sympathizers there was suspicion that some had escaped being apprehended and had concealed their allegiances.

Carlita promised to maintain secrecy. She wished Jakob success in getting Anke out of The Netherlands and back to Canada. Her curiosity arose.

"Jakob does this mean you will leave Aruba to join her?"

Jakob explained his conflict. While Canada was his home and he had friends there, he had established a life in Aruba that he enjoyed more. He told Carlita of his inability to make the decision and therefore he would have to return to Canada. There were responsibilities with the farms and financial affairs to be resolved.

Carlita looked dejected.

"I too am facing a difficult decision. My family in Colombia wants me to return. I have many friends here. My life here has been good. I have come to see Aruba as my home, but I miss my Colombian family. I do not know what I should do. What would I do back in Colombia? I would need to start my life again."

Jakob considered the conversation he just had with Miguel and Alejandro. He wanted to tell her of their decision but decided it would be wrong. The brothers would need to tell her.

Chapter 140

Tuesday dragged. Every hour seemed like a day. Jakob was impatient for the day to end so he could go to Charlie's bar and learn more of the situation with Anke. Throughout the day he made several mistakes. His crew laughingly jumped in and helped correct them.

At the end of the shift, Jakob showered and dressed into the clean clothing he had brought with him from the apartment. It was shortly before 6:00pm when he left the refinery for Charlie's bar.

He walked the short distance from the refinery gates to Main Street. He turned left and found Charlie's on the left hand side of the street. Outside a number of men were standing and drinking. Jakob entered through the wide doorway. In front of him was the large wooden bar. He looked around. Pieter van Doren was nowhere to be found. Dejected Jakob sat at the bar and ordered a beer. Next to him was a group of very loud sailors from one of the tankers that had docked earlier. Jakob listened to their banal argument. He was agitated. After a while he ordered yet another beer. There was still no sign of Pieter. The sailors' argument was becoming heated. Jakob moved to the other end of the bar. He shook his head. The sailors were arguing about which country made the best beer. The red faced burly sailor with the black singlet claimed it was Australia. The blonde Scandinavian insisted it was England. They argued on.

Jakob waited until it was 7:30pm. He rose to leave when he noticed a man watching him from a table near one of the open windows. He raised an envelope as a sign. Jakob walked over to him.

"I am Jakob. Have you seen my friend Pieter?"

"I do not know who you mean, but yes Jakob I need something from you. It is not safe to have a long conversation here. Let us go out to the docks."

The man threw some money on the table and they both exited the bar. Within minutes they were standing on one of the empty piers.

The man turned to Jakob. "We received a message from our brave comrades in Holland. The message claims that Anke has been with others seeking refuge from the war. She is being cared for by members of the Dutch Resistance. I cannot disclose her location to you. We are told she is in good health but deeply affected by the events of the war. I am instructed to ask you for the payment. Money is needed to get her out of The Netherlands and to a safe country from where she can travel."

"I have the money here in this package. How will I know when she has left The Netherlands and is safe?"

"We will contact you. There is nothing you can do. You must be patient. This process can take weeks and sometimes months. Do not discuss this arrangement or meeting with anyone."

Jakob thought of the earlier conversation with Carlita and how much he had already told her. He dismissed the thought that Carlita would break their secrecy."

The man took the package from Jakob and tucked it into his open necked shirt.

"We will be in contact. Stay positive. Remember, that you must not discuss this."

They walked back toward San Nicolaas. The man melted away into the passersby who were looking for their entertainment for the night. He went to the club which was close by. Miguel saw him coming through the entrance and hurriedly went over to him.

"Jakob. It is good to see you here. Can I get you a drink?'

Jakob ordered a beer. "Miguel I need to speak to you and Alejandro. It is about Carlita."

Miguel's face changed. "Is there something wrong? Is she sick? Has she got problems?"

"No Miguel. I was speaking with her. She is trying to make plans for her and the children's future. I have information to share with you and Alejandro."

Miguel looked at Jakob and gave him a look of disbelief. "Jakob, my brother has only been dead for weeks. Are you deciding to take Carlita as yours?" The anger showed.

Jakob laughed. "No Miguel. It is nothing like that. She needs help and advice on what to do. You and Alejandro can help her."

Miguel relaxed and were soon joined by Alejandro.

"Let's go somewhere quiet where we can talk" said Jakob.

They left the club's entertainment area and went to an office at the rear. When they were settled in, Jakob relayed the contents of the conversation he had with Carlita. Miguel and Alejandro listened intently.

"Carlita is thinking of returning to her family in Colombia. She is not happy about that. You must tell her of your plans for the club and to send her money from the profits. She is confused and concerned. The sooner you do this I think she will settle back into her life."

Miguel and Alejandro agreed and planned to visit Carlita in the morning to tell her of their decision.

Jakob cautioned them that they still needed to meet Catherine. He was concerned that Catherine could stop their plans.

Chapter 141

The meeting with Catherine did not go well. Jakob, Miguel and Alejandro had arrived early at her office. They had been seated in the adjacent office and provided with rich Colombian coffee. After a wait of around thirty minutes they were escorted into Catherine's office. She sat at the end of a long oak table with her legal advisor and banker flanking her on either side. Large piles of documents were on the table in front of her. She motioned to them to take a seat. Introductions and pleasantries were exchanged and then the business matters were raised.

Jakob was surprised at how weak she appeared. She seemed to have lost weight and shrunk since he saw her at the memorial for Juan.

"As you are aware, I hold a large ownership position in the Stella Maris Club. The other investors are Jakob here and the deceased Juan. With Juan's death, this means the ownership situation must be reviewed. I assume that you, Miguel and Alejandro, are here to speak for his heirs."

Miguel and Alejandro looked at each other and then across to Jakob.

"No we are not here as Juan's heirs. We are here to speak on behalf of Carlita, his wife. She has asked us to help her at this very difficult time. We have spoken with Jakob and expressed what we wish to have happen."

Catherine focused her watery blue eyes on Jakob and waited some time before speaking.

"Jakob you are an investor and partner in the club. You were an equal partner with Juan. In view of Juan's death what is it you propose?"

Jakob watched her carefully. Even though her physical condition was frail, her mind was razor sharp.

"I am recommending that Juan's ownership be transferred to Carlita. They wish to enter into an agreement to have a portion of the monthly profit sent to Carlita to assist her with the costs of living and looking after her children.

Catherine leaned forward in the high backed chair and reflected on the discussion. She finally spoke.

"Jakob I own and run businesses. I am not given to charity. I am not going to have partners that do nothing for the business, yet I am expected to send money every month to some wife who has no sense of business or desire to help run it. I am not going to do this. It is unfortunate that Juan suffered this fate, but it is not my problem to look after his family. Again, this is business,

Jakob looked to Miguel and Alejandro. Miguel's olive complexion had clouded and a dark crimson was evident on his cheeks. Jakob raised his hand and motioned Miguel to relax.

"Catherine, I need to remind you that Juan and his family took big risks when starting the club. Before that Juan operated a successful fishing business. He and Carlita made significant sacrifices to start and grow the club. You must take that into account when you consider Miguel and Alejandro's request."

"I have never had a partner in any of my businesses who was not active in the operation of that business. I will make no exception here."

The room fell silent.

Miguel stood and with the movement of his hand directed Alejandro to follow. They turned their backs and walked to the door and left.

"Catherine, I think you are making a big mistake. Miguel is a key employee. He alone attracts customers and others who wish to work at the club."

Again there was silence which was broken by Catherine's legal advisor.

"Catherine, by law the heirs can share equally in Juan's estate. I believe it is better for you to arrive at an arrangement than to start a fight over this. The heirs will win some ownership."

Jakob watched and listened to the conversations that erupted between the banker and legal advisor. He considered his position. He wondered if he should disclose his plans to return to Canada or remain quiet about these intentions. As he was considered Catherine's position, he decided to try taking over Juan's shares. After a few moments of reflection he decided against this.

"Catherine and gentlemen. I fear we achieved nothing here this morning. I will now leave. I will spend time and speak with Miguel and Alejandro. I am sure that we, as reasonable people, will find a solution."

Catherine scowled at him. Jakob wondered if her health was the reason for her cantankerous behavior.

The legal advisor stood and accompanied Jakob out of the room.

"I fear that Catherine is fading. Her thoughts are clouded. She is astute but at times that is over shadowed by her unreasonable behavior. I will spend time with her and explain the benefits of passing the ownership to Carlita. Here are my business details. Please contact me in several days. We will get this resolved. Catherine is already planning to leave the island and has arrived at an agreement for a family member to assume the business here. It may be that this will only get resolved after that person arrives and takes over."

Jakob thanked him and walked out of the office and into the vibrant beat of San Nicolaas at mid day. He went back to Charlie's bar and ordered a cold beer. Sitting at the bar he became aware of Pieter van Doren drinking alone. Jakob slid of his chair and went and joined him.

"Pieter. What a nice surprise to see you here at this time of day."

Pieter looked up from the table surface he had been gazing at.

"Jakob, we are in contact with our friends. We are informed that in The Netherlands things are not good. The Germans are exercising more control and those who do not conform are suffering. It is becoming harder for us to maintain contact with family, friends and those who help us. It is very depressing. I have many family members in the South and that is where things are bad. In addition Rotterdam is being destroyed. My country is suffering. I am here in this tropical paradise and my family suffers at the hands of these swine. It depresses me."

Jakob pulled a chair across to the table and seated himself beside Pieter. He was surprised to find Pieter in this frame of mind.

"Pieter, it is the start of 1942. The United States has entered into this war. I am sure the end is near."

They sat and talked for hours. It was dusk when they stumbled from the bar. Pieter immediately encountered other Marines and got a ride back to the Savaneta Barracks. Jakob was tired, partially drunk and angry. The world had gone crazy. He thought back to the principles he had been taught and had grown up with. They all seemed pointless now. He crossed Main Street and entered the alley that lead into the red light district. The prostitutes were ready for the night ahead. They stood in doorways and on the corners of the narrow lanes. They called to the men and chased some while making offers of their services. Jakob saw one of the girls who had originally helped him with finding somewhere to live when he had first arrived in San Nicolaas. Jakob stumbled toward her. She slid her arm around his back to steady him.

"Jakob. Look at you. Why you do this to yourself? You a good man. Not crazy like all those other workers from the refinery and those foul sailors who come here."

Jakob attempted a reply. Words of gibberish flowed from his mouth.

The prostitute waved to her friend across the street.

"I take this one and look after him" she called out. Together they stumbled into the interior of the rancid brothel. She eventually got him to a room in the back and half threw him onto the bed. Jakob passed out as his head hit the dirty pillow and he fell onto the stained sheets. Before he passed out in his drunken stupor his thoughts returned to Anke. He now knew from Pieter how bad things had become in The Netherlands.

Chapter 142

The Netherlands 1942

Anke was despondent. Since May, 1940 her life had been torn apart. The dammed Nazis had invaded Holland and her summer had been a summer of discontent. Jakob, against all of the family advice had gone to Germany in pursuit of seeking out distant family. She couldn't reason why. These were old Mennonite relatives going back generations who had little in common with Jakob and his American roots. Believing that he was stuck in Germany and that the prospects of his escape looked dimmer with each passing day, Anke became further upset.

There was no communication with Jakob. She hated the situation of never knowing whether a neighbor or friend could be trusted. There was no privacy. Suspicion was everywhere. The influence and fear of the occupying Nazis permeated everything.

Not content with just capturing Holland, Hitler's Nazis had set about starving and terrorizing the Dutch people. Food was scarce. Mistrust of even close family members had resulted in increased tensions and fear. Anke longed for a return to her staid and comfortable Mennonite life in Canada. Why had she let herself get into this deplorable situation? What had they really hoped to achieve by undertaking this foolish trip.

As she pondered the situation, her thoughts and opinions of her once esteemed Jakob were fading. If only he had respected her and listened, they would not be facing this crisis. Her emotions were changing. Her religion strongly frowned upon divorce, unless there was abuse or other criminal aspects. She found herself wondering about a life alone or with another lover. Was this situation because of a sin for which she was being punished?

As the months rolled by, so did the cold grey and bleak days of an early Dutch autumn. All around their simple villa there was destruction, darkness and cold. Walls pockmarked with bullet holes. Smashed furniture on the streets. Twisted metal frames of bikes run over by the Nazi tanks. Anke started to cry. This should never have happened to her and the good people in the families she had come to know during her stay in Holland.

With all her worry and the food shortage, Anke had lost an extreme amount of weight. Her once beautiful face with her shining and vivacious eyes was now pale and her eyes looked dead and sunken. Was there any hope in escaping this hell, she wondered.

The villa was cold and drafty. Each evening when dusk fell, she and other members of the family left the villa In search of any furniture or items that could be burned in the small fireplace on the ground floor. There was no other source of heat. Hot water was all but a faded memory.

As she sat huddled in the upstairs room thinking of life, she heard a loud commotion below and voices shouting. The dreaded SS had crashed the front door in and barged into the Villa. She heard her Uncle Wilhelm call out, protesting his innocence and that he was a simple factory worker. Someone had tipped the SS authorities that the house was visited by members of the Dutch Resistance. More shouting was followed by the screaming of Julia, his simple but loving wife. A loud shot rang out and silence followed. Anke stayed quiet.

After some ten minutes during which she heard the Germans talking loudly and smashing things as they searched the kitchen and living area, she heard their heavy footsteps crunching on the pavement outside.

When all was quiet, Anke nervously ventured down the stairs. There on the kitchen floor was the scene of violent carnage. Both of her relatives were lying face up. Wilhelm had been shot in the forehead. Julia lay with her throat slashed open. Anke involuntarily vomited. She had witnessed atrocities since the invasion, but none as brutal as this.

As she stood shocked and trembling, another noise startled her. Anke spun around. There in the broken doorway stood a tall dark skinned man. By the color of his complexion, Anke instinctively knew he was neither a German nor a Dutch man.

In a strange Dutch accent, he called out to her. She did not understand the man. He started to approach and she screamed. He rushed toward her and threw his hand over her mouth. "Do you understand English?" he whispered. She tried to nod yes. He again whispered. "Please be very quiet. There are more German Patrols in the area and we do not want to attract them here. I think that they did not realize you were here. I was sent to try and warn all of you before this attack. I am sorry that I was unable to get here earlier and prevent this."

Anke stared at his face. Was he an American or British? It was possible he was either French or Spanish. "Who are you? Why did you come to this house? How do you know these people? What are you going to do to me?" The questions flowed out of her in a nervous stream.

He loosened his grip on her arm and slowly moved back towards the door. He raised a finger to his lips to be silent. He crouched down and ever so slowly moved out onto the street. After several minutes, satisfied with what he had seen, he re-entered the Villa.

"I am so sorry we meet like this Madame. My name is Nemencio Arends. I came from Aruba to fight with the Dutch Resistance. You see, before the war broke out, I had been in Holland to study and made many friends here. The Hun has killed many of my friends. The least I can do is give my support and fight for the Dutch effort."

Anke looked at the tall and handsome frame of the man. If only in a different time and circumstance she thought.

Chapter 143

Anke stood motionless and watched as Nemencio moved into the kitchen area. He asked for a blanket or other item to cover the bodies of Julia and Wilhelm. Anke returned to the small closet sized room where she had been hiding. There were some old burlap sacks at the rear of a small dresser. She removed these and took them downstairs to Nemencio. He gently removed some jewelry from Julia's wrist and blood soaked neck. He then removed a watch from Wilhelm's wrist.

Looking at Anke he said. "I have done this to prevent the German swine from taking these possessions. Furthermore, out of respect for the family, I think these should be given to them"

Anke nodded. She was still in shock of all that had happened in the last thirty minutes. She was unsure what would happen now or how she would survive. The only family she knew in Holland was dead.

"My family" she cried helplessly."I am all alone now and my husband is trapped in Germany."

"Please find somewhere here in the villa to go and conceal yourself," Nemencio said to her. "I must now leave and get some assistance in order to take your relatives' bodies for a proper service. This will be a dangerous act for us. I may not return immediately, but do not worry. We will not abandon you here in this situation."

Anke started to weep. Her frail body was wracked with the sobbing. Nemencio looked at her with pity. "I do not yet know your name or who you really are. It is too dangerous for you to leave with me. Whoever reported the brave Wilhelm is probably still watching this house. Did Wilhelm have any problems recently with any of the neighbors? I need to know that and where to watch. There is definitely a traitor in our midst."

"My name is Anke. I am here from Canada with my husband to visit relatives from a long ago past. Wilhelm and Julia were members of our ancestral family which goes back hundreds of years. My husband wanted to undertake this project. He has gone to Germany to track down others in his family ancestry and has become trapped there. I fear he may not return. I have heard nothing of his fate there"

"We shall discuss this and your future a little later after we tend to the immediate matters at hand. First, I need to know that you are who you say you are and that you can be trusted. Who here can confirm your identity and story?"

Anke again started sobbing. "When the Germans first came here to the house looking for Jews they took my Passport and Papers. They took them. I have no identification, so I cannot travel or be outside visiting others. I have been trapped in this house."

Nemencio rubbed his chin with a gloved hand. "How long ago did your papers get taken?" he demanded.

Anke thought about this. She was confused. Days had escaped her and she could not accurately remember. She told him this. "I do not know exactly, but possibly about 2 months ago. It was still warm here. It was a still and beautiful summer night when they stormed in wanting to know everything. Why is this important?"

"At the threat of telling you too much, we have an informant in the local Commandants Office. I will try to have your papers located. If all you tell me is true, then we will have a forged copy made and returned to their office. We will get your real papers back for you. Hopefully, we will be able to see if there is the possibility of getting you freed from all these horrors."

Anke was starting to relax somewhat. Her confidence in Nemencio was growing and she instinctively knew he was a man to trust. While not a Mennonite he certainly had displayed some strong character traits. Anke wondered if all men in Aruba were like this. If so, it could be a paradise. All Anke knew of Aruba was that it was in what was called the Dutch West Indies in the Caribbean and that there was no Mennonite community there. The closest community she remembered from her church schooling was in Venezuela and it was small and not of the Old Order.

"Nemencio" she said earnestly. "I have nothing to gain and everything to lose by misleading you. Please. You will find I speak the truth. In fact, there was a small store at the next canal that sold cheeses, flowers and fish before the war started. There was a man and wife who will remember me if they are still alive and in the district. "

"Do you remember their names?' he asked.

Anke thought for a while. "I believe the name was Van den Breckel. They will remember me because they have family in Canada and we talked of this on many occasions."

She saw what she thought to be relief pass on Nemicio's face. A barely imperceptible smile twitched at the corner of his mouth.

"I must now go and attend to these and other matters"

He pulled an old beret from his back pocket and arranged it over his head and face to effectively hide his features. Before leaving the front door, he assumed the stooped position of a broken old man. The transformation amazed Anke.

Soon he was gone and the silence closed in on her. Now she was truly alone. She wondered what she should do if she heard the Nazi patrol approach again. She knew that it would be impossible for her to stay in the house any longer. The small amount of food that they had stored had been taken by the German soldiers. The shelling had destroyed the water supply to the house.

As she leaned against the grimy wall she felt the deep despair engulf her again.

"Oh, Jakob, how could you have been so short sighted and put me in this situation. You are a fool" she sighed.

In the distance she heard heavy machine gun fire. She found herself thinking about Nemencio and worrying. This surprised her. After all, she was a betrothed woman but in these days of turmoil it seemed there were no values.

Chapter 144

Night was falling. Several couples wrapped in heavy coats strolled beside the De Vliet canal. The garbage of war lay strewn on the sidewalks. In the canal the remains of cars and sunken boats littered the former pristine waterways. As occupiers, the Germans had certainly destroyed their conquest. The Dutch were suppressed, but the anger and dislike of all things German permeated the air. Dutch hearts were broken and silently many vowed that this must never happen to Holland again.

Two of those strolling arm in arm were an older couple. He was stooped over and shuffled along slowly. Every few minutes he would stop to regain his strength. He used a broken piece of pipe for a cane. His visible features did not betray the true person.

He was accompanied by a tall and large Dutch woman. She was very heavy set with enormous breasts protruding within her winter coat. She grasped him by the elbow and guided him along the path. His breathing appeared labored and his strength seemed to be sapped by the cold wind.

At the end of the canal there was a lock. The Hoornbrug Lock. She looked at it for some time as if wondering how to get her companion over the footway with the high handrail. After several minutes of surveying the lock gates, the couple moved quickly into the small laneway. Certain they had not been seen by prying eyes, they maneuvered their way through the back lanes until they reached the street where Wilhelm and Julia's house was located.

The large woman reached down and snatched up a piece of rubble that had been blown off a nearby building in the most recent shelling. She looked around. With no one in sight she threw the rubble into the doorway where the door had been smashed down earlier by the SS and the soldiers. She heard it crash into the house. They waited in total silence. She looked up scanning the windows of the neighboring houses that overlooked Wilhelm's house. She was watching for signs of someone watching the house in order to tip off the SS again. How this Dutch Resistance safe house had been discovered was a major concern to all the members of the Resistance. They had vouched certain death to the traitors who had betrayed Wilhelm and Julia. They had been amongst the founding members of the Resistance. Their loss, while sad, was considered as serious enough to compromise many of the recently planned attacks on the Germans. This leak would take many months to repair. As she watched, a shadow moved in the second floor window of an empty house located three down houses the laneway. Was this the traitor who had betrayed a good neighbor?

Inside, Anke heard the crash of the rubble as it landed heavily and skidded across the floor into the kitchen area. Oh God, she thought. Now what is happening to me? Will I be attacked? Will I be raped? Who is coming and why?

Anke was terrified. She strained to listen for any sounds of an approaching party. She could not hear any footsteps. She moved further back into the house, thinking that this would afford her a look and the time to react to any possible attacker.

A low whistle sounded near the door. She stood still, petrified. A whispered call followed. "Anke, are you all right? It is me, Nemencio" She felt the fear drain away from her face and arms. Her heart was pounding.

"I am here" she called quietly.

"We will be coming in, but first we need to deal with some unpleasant business here. Please wait. Do not move. Do not scream, no matter what you may hear"

The moon had risen and moonlight was lighting up the doorframe. As she crouched in the kitchen corridor she saw the shadows of what appeared to be a couple pass by.

Minutes passed by. She heard the sharp crack from a firearm followed by a loud thump outside on the laneway. This was followed by running footsteps. Nemencio burst into the house. "Hurry, Anke. We must leave right now. Leave everything."

Anke started to panic. "But, what about....." Nemencio firmly but politely cut her off. "Trust me. What do you care about most? That you continue your life or some replaceable items? We must go immediately before the patrols find the traitor who has betrayed us all. We have shot him and he has fallen into the street."

"I am cold and tired. Maybe you should just go and leave me to whatever fate the Lord has decided for me."

Nemencio pushed into the house.

"Where are your clothing items?"

She motioned up the stairs. He ascended the stairs, several at a time. He returned with a threadbare coat. He ran to her and wrapped her like a Mummy. She was too fatigued to resist. He turned to his female companion.

"Remove the disguise" he said quietly.

The old woman spun around and dropped the heavy coat and fake breasts. He was a strapping 6 foot athletically built man. He bent down and picked up the coat. Soon Anke was wrapped and they carried her out of the house.

They ran down the narrow lane until they reached a main street. They occasionally took shelter in a store entrance and watched, the occasional patrol walked by. The Germans believed they had the Dutch controlled and had therefore loosened up their attentiveness.

However, it would not be long before the Germans found the traitor Jan Hein who had betrayed Holland and the Dutch people. His fate had been sealed.

As they walked in the main street and to the nondescript house near the canal, shrill whistles sounded. Jan Hein had been discovered. The Germans had lost an ally, but the Dutch had lost an enemy.

Chapter 145

Anke was lost. Nemencio and his accomplice had woven their way through many lanes and crossed over canals. It seemed hours that they had been walking and running since leaving Wilhelm and Julia's house.

Finally they stopped at a rundown house. The paint had peeled away around the front windows and in general the house appeared unoccupied. Nemencio glanced around before approaching the front door. He rapped a series of different knocks on the door. It was definitely a code. After a minute the door was cracked open. They all went into the house.

There was the smell of a coffee brewing and the lingering hint of an earlier meal.

Nemencio and his accomplice lay Anke on a reclining cot in the corner of the main room. About a dozen faces looked at her. Through the haze of her mind she stared back. A young woman approached and touched her forehead and took her pulse.

Anke pulled away. "Please. I am a nurse. Let me check you as you do not seem well. We are worried for you"

The nurse then turned and spoke to a very young man. He gathered his coat and went to the door. Anke heard the door creak and close. When she awoke, she was in a bed with two stern looking women at her side.

"We hope you have not brought trouble to our safe shelter" said the taller of the two.

"Are we to trust you? We have not been able to speak with you and learn your culture and belief" said the diminutive one.

Anke smiled. "I am Anke. I am from Canada. My husband had planned this trip before the war broke out. We are Mennonites and were visiting ancestral family here in Holland and in Germany. My husband went to Germany and is now unable to return to me. I was with relatives. I am sure that you have been told of the horrible fate that we experienced this day. I am now lost. I am an honest person. I ask you to please accept me. I know in these times and circumstances that this may be hard. I will prove to you my honesty and innocence. I will recover and work with you. I have no other family here."

The two women looked at each other.

"For some reason, Nemencio seems to think you are genuine. We will know tomorrow if we get your papers. We hope you are telling us the truth. If you have not told us the truth the consequences will not be nice. In the meanwhile, please get some sleep. We will return with some food for you soon."

With that Anke was left to her own privacy.

She lay there and reflected upon the past few months of her life. She had lost all contact with her Canadian family. Did they still believe that she was alive or had they given up? There was no way to contact them. As Mennonites it was difficult to contact them at the best of times.

Anke drifted off into a particularly deep sleep. She was awakened by the two women who had entered her room again. There was a bluish white light in the window. Anke realized that the first snows had come to Holland. She sat upright in the bed.

"We have good news for you" said the tall one. "My name is Maria and this is my friend Gea. Tonight we had a visit. It appears your story is true. We have your papers downstairs. Nemencio is very pleased that this has all been true. Welcome to our little band. We will do everything we can to assist you."

Anke started to cry. This was the first time in months that a stranger had shown kindness and emotion.

"What is today?" Anke asked. "I need to know, please"

"Today is Wednesday. Why is this so important to you?" Maria asked.

"I must give thanks to my Lord and this will be the day I thank him for."

Maria smiled. "We are not without our beliefs either. One day, Anke, this horrible war will be over and those responsible will be held accountable. We Dutch were too trusting. Now we suffer."

Maria's friend, Gea had been very quiet through all of the conversations. Now she spoke.

" Anke, where is this man of yours? How could he leave you here? Why did he come to such trouble? Did he not know of the clouds of war that were forming over Europe? Does he not care about you? Is he that selfish? He does not sound to be a caring man. Are you married to him? If not, I think you should find a loving man who can care for you."

Anke was surprised.

"I always thought of small women as being timid. They obviously have strong opinions." she thought.

Maria left the room and soon returned with a large jug of rarely available coffee. Anke wanted to ask how they could have coffee but decided it would not be prudent to do so. It is better not to know some things, she thought.

As they sat and talked, Anke could feel a bond developing. All the women had suffered a loss of some sort. There was a common need and hope. For the first time in months, Anke laughed. She was shocked that this happened.

As they sat talking, there was an outburst of loud conversation downstairs. Maria and Gea stood to leave.

"Can I also come to meet the others?" Anke asked. Maria and Gea exchanged looks.

"Well, I guess it will need to happen at some time" Maria said.

As they descended the stairway, a silence cloaked the room. At the bottom of the stairs, Maria stopped and addressed everyone. "We have just spent time with our friend here, who goes by the name Anke. We accept her into our group. She has suffered tremendously and we ask you all too please understand her plight. Kindness is needed for us all and especially for Anke."

Anke stood awkwardly at the base of the stairs. "Hello, everyone. I am Anke. I want to thank you all for allowing me to be here. I would like to meet each of you. My mind now is not good. I would be rude and forget names. I hope that tomorrow I will be able to meet each of you and become a friend of yours. Tonight, I will pray to our God for blessings and good acts to be bestowed upon you."

With that, Nemencio, who was obviously a leader in the group advised that they should retire into the night for fear of having candles and lights seen by unfriendly and prying eyes.

Now, Anke was really confused. What had awoken her emotions in this period of hatred and war? It was becoming clearer in her mind that she needed to make changes in her relationship with Jakob. As devout as she was, certain things needed attention.

Chapter 146

As the days slipped by into weeks and then into months, Anke's health and spirit recovered. She was constantly aware of the sacrifices and suffering of other members in their little clique. Some would sit and talk of their losses and share them with her. Others wanted just to sit and reflect. Anke became a source of comfort to all in the group.

Then the tragedy occurred. The Dutch Resistance cells were poorly organized. News came into the group. A major food convoy was to be shipped in and transported in German Military trucks to the occupying forces. When this news arrived it caused a great deal of excitement amongst the group and the other Dutch Resistance cells. Intelligence information was exchanged and meetings between cells were set up.

The Dutch population and especially the Jews were being starved into submission by the Germans. While Holland was an occupied country, the German captors viewed the Dutch as fellow Aryans. Consequently, the Dutch had more freedom than in other occupied countries. This allowed the Resistance to easily move about and meet.

The information on the food convoy was finally confirmed. Nemencio arranged a meeting with several other Resistance groups in the immediate area. To distract the Germans a disobedience campaign was planned. Doctors would not work. Students would strike. Shop keepers would "disappear" The plan went into action.

Late that day, Anke observed Nemencio preparing weapons and dark clothing items. She approached him. "Nemencio, what is going to happen? I am very worried"

"Do not be concerned, dear Anke. As you know, we have many who are without food and are prohibited from working. Tonight we know that the German trucks will cross over the farms and take food to their bases. We will intercept and capture as much of this food as possible to distribute to those in need. The soldiers on these food convoys are generally very low level soldiers. They get these assignments because the top soldiers are needed for more active duties. This mission of ours will be easy. We will stop the convoy and take the food. Many of our brothers in the other cells will join us. This will be a simple and fast operation. Afterwards the people of our country will have some food. We must not fail at this. We have good information from the inside the German military office. Tomorrow we will all be able to have some food." His optimism was overflowing.

Anke thought it was just too simple. Her experience with the Germans made her think otherwise.

As darkness enveloped the city, the men stole out of the house dressed in dark clothing. Anke dropped to her knees and prayed. As a Mennonite she abhorred violence of any sort.

The night arrived. The hours wore on. There was no word of the attack. The women began to be concerned. In the early morning, the front door burst open. Nemencio entered half dragging a fellow Resistance member who was badly injured. Over the next hour others began returning. A deep pall of despair hung over the group.

"We did not know that the local Commandant was to be on the lead truck. We shot at the truck. He was injured. There was a large gunfight. We have lost some of our members and friends. This was a disaster. The Germans have killed some of our best people.

We did not get any of the food and now they will want retaliation. We must be prepared. Tonight we will leave this house. We are no longer safe."

At dawn, storm troopers advanced through the streets of Voorburg and Rijswijk. They banged on doors and grabbed men and boys. They marched these unfortunates to the town square. Other SS officers went to prisons where they demanded the release of the Dutch prisoners they believed were in defiance of German command.

Within an hour 273 men and boys were machine gunned to death by the Nazis in retaliation for the injuring of their Commandant.

Later that morning, the German military drove through the streets in small wagons equipped with loud speakers. They broadcast the following message.

"We are in control. You will conform to our orders. Any attempt at insurrection will result in the most severe consequences"

The situation appeared hopeless.

Nemencio arranged for Anke to be taken to a farm outside of the city where she stayed in hiding with a large family. She often thought about the others and wondered if they would ever see each other again. After several weeks she received a message to pack quickly as it was no longer safe for to remain with the family. A courier was to take her to an undisclosed location near the Belgian border.

Anke rushed into her small room and hastily packed her few belongings. Late in the afternoon, an old motorcycle pulled up at the front of the farmhouse. Anke was called. She ran down with her small case. She recognized the driver as the "woman" that had accompanied Nemencio when she was rescued. He grunted a greeting. She sat on the rear seat of the bike and they slowly accelerated away from the farm.

As they progressed along the way, the driver was constantly scanning the road and the flat neighboring fields for any activity. If they were seen there were no places to hide in the open terrain. After a trip of over an hour, they pulled into a darkened building.

"We are here. You will wait please"

Anke stood in the darkness looking at the gloomy scene in front of her. Suddenly she heard a familiar voice. Turning, she saw Nemencio crossing in front of a barn toward her. He had his arms outstretched in a greeting. She ran to him. He reached around her and hugged her. They stood there locked in an embrace for what seemed like eternity. Now she knew. The decision as to which man to have in her life had been made. Nemencio had won her over. There was no longer any doubt....or so she thought.

Chapter 147

Anke entered into the old farmhouse. She noticed that it was not as dark and gloomy on the inside as she had expected. The windows and doors had been cleverly blacked out so that their lights would not show.

As she looked around, she saw a number of familiar faces from the other house in which she had previously been hidden. Several people came up to her and greeted her with hugs and kind words. This was now her new family.

Maria came across to her.

"You must eat to stay fit for what lies ahead" she said.

Anke was confused. What did Maria know that she didn't? She then noticed that a number of the group was casting glances in her direction. This seemed strange. She gave it no more thought.

There was a loud knocking on the rear door. Two of the men went to the door. One stood back and behind the door on guard while the other slowly opened it. Standing in the door frame was a slight professorial looking man with small wire framed glasses. "Come in Doctor" one of the men said. The timid looking doctor entered and made an attempt to avoid eye contact with the others in the room.

"Please excuse me if I seem not to acknowledge you. I think it is best for us not to know who we all are. They do have a way to extract information from us. Let me just say to you all that I, as a proud Dutch man, appreciate the efforts of you all. When these horrible days pass, and if we are all together, then we will celebrate our cause. Until that time, anyone in need of medical assistance, please come and see me in the room upstairs. Of course there will be no charges. I do need some help soon to continue to buy the medicines on the Black Market."

The little Doctor started to walk to the stairs. He reached into his pocket and took out a yellow piece of paper. He looked up at Nemencio.

"I believe this may be of importance. A message has been received for you from a friend in the remaining Dutch military."

Nemencio looked at the paper and scowled. Whatever was on the paper did not make him happy. The other men looked at him.

"What is the message" they asked.

"It is very personal and of no interest to anyone here" he shouted. Anke watched. He was very aggravated. He slammed the door on his way out. Something was very wrong. She had never witnessed his behavior like this before.

Upon his exit the room fell quiet. There was a general feeling of discomfort.

Not to be deterred Anke thought of the entire trauma she had recently experienced. She wrapped a coat around her, opened the rear door and walked out. She could see the silhouette of Nemencio sitting in the pale night light. She walked up to him and softly called his name. He turned and she saw that his eyes were wet with tears. This was the last thing she expected from this rock of a man. What was all this tenderness and hostility about? She walked up to him and placed her hand on his shoulder. He looked up and then away into the distance.

"Anke" he said. "In my beloved Aruba, I had but one girl whom I deeply loved. She was killed in an accident several years ago. She slipped on the wet floor and fell into a meat grinder at the local abattoir where she worked. I never thought I would ever find anyone as beautiful and as charming as she was. I was wrong. The true love of my life is standing here in front of me. I truly have fallen for you. And, I have never been able to eat ground pork since."

"Nemencio, I am confused. I am here and speaking with you. We have never been more than friends. Why are you now acting so depressed? Surely, we can still remain friends. I do not have a meat grinder."

Nemencio turned to her."Anke, it has taken me many years and I thought I could never find another woman to replace my love of Hermosa. I was wrong. It is you who I want."

"Again I am confused. Why are you acting this way?"

Nemencio reached into the pocket of his shirt and withdrew the yellow paper. " I have received a message through our underground. Your Jakob is alive and is looking for you. He is now living in Aruba in the Caribbean. My comrades there tell me he has enjoyed a great life in Germany with many women and participated in all things that are not of Mennonite belief. I have learned that some Germans arranged for him to become a crew member on a ship that headed to the Caribbean. He has sent money for you to go back to Canada and be with him. I should never have allowed our friendship to develop this far, especially in this time of war."

"Nemencio, I have had a lot of time to think. The events here have allowed me to focus on the positive aspects of life and also to see the dark and Satanic. I believe you are a good man. In fact, had I known you in Canada, I think we would be living a good and holy life."

With those words, Nemencio again teared up. It was obvious that his love of Anke had grown into proportions that would be hard for them to contain.

Anke contemplated the situation. What was she to do as a devout and God fearing Mennonite woman? Furthermore, could she believe the story that Nemencio had just told her about Jakob?

She pressed him.

"Nemencio, why are you so upset? You knew I had a partner."

He looked at her forlornly.

"My dear Anke, I must respond to him. I will find out where he is and you must return to your husband."

"No" she replied

"I will not go back to a man like that. He has shown no regard or respect for me or my family. He is selfish. He has betrayed me and family. I will not go back"

She stood and walked in front of him. "Nemencio, it is you that I have fallen in love with as well. You are strong. You have morals. You are kind. I will go back to him, but only to end this relationship with him directly. I will not abandon him without that. Do you understand this?"

Nemencio looked at her.

"What are you saying?"

"I am saying that we will be together if you wish and that when this war eventually ends we will have a life of happiness"

Nemencio smiled. His white teeth flashed in the moonlight. His dark complexion accented his statuesque looks. She had never seen such beauty in a man. No Mennonite man could ever measure up to this. How would she be able to take him back to her congregation? For a few minutes she thought about this. There really was no reason to do so. Her decision was becoming easier.

She walked up close to him and touched his chest. He sighed and looked into her soul. Together they walked back to the farmhouse.

Chapter 148

As they slowly walked back to the old farmhouse, Anke looked up at Nemencio's face. He was deep in thought. She leaned her head against his arm. He was distant. She did not want to push. It was obvious to her that this man had many reasons for being in Holland and fighting for the liberation of the Dutch. She resigned herself to accepting the fact that she may never know the true answers and that she would have to live with that fact.

They entered into the rear vestibule of the old farmhouse. Anke turned to go to the stairs leading up to her room. As she was leaving, she partially turned back to smile at Nemencio and wish him a goodnight. As she did so, it struck her that the events of war could take them apart at any moment. She was tormented. This was a man she had fallen deeply in love with. She had affections for this man that she had never felt for any other, including Jakob. What would she have to do to repent in her religion to accept such love from this man?

Nemencio smiled at her. It was a heart melting smile. There was no way that she could leave him tonight. She thought about the small room she shared with Gea. There was no way for them to be together there.

Anke turned back to Nemencio and put her arms under his armpits. "I cannot take you into my room. It is too small and also Gea is there."

Nemencio laughed.

"My dear Anke. In my home country we do not allow such small things to stop us. I think that you now know of my love for you. I would never have taken advantage of you. I suggest we find somewhere we can be alone and in love"

Anke thought hard. She remembered that Maria and her partner had travelled to Eindhoven and would be gone for several days. She turned to Nemencio.

"I know where we can be alone and safe"

Nemencio sighed and asked if she was sure. Anke took his hand and led him into the room that Maria shared with her partner. Anke was not sure if Maria was married or just had a good friend.

With no lights shining, Anke undressed and slipped into the bed. She knew what lay ahead. She was fully expecting a night of sex and passion.

Through the window, the pale moonlight shone in casting a pallid color on everything in the room. Anke herself appeared milk white.

She heard a noise and turned to see Nemencio entering the room. He was totally naked.

In Church class, Anke had learned about reproduction and men. The lessons taught her that most Mennonite men had a penis about 8" long. Anke stared at the menacing object dangling between Nemenicio's legs. This did not belong on a man. This belonged to a barn animal. Were all the men in Aruba like this she wondered? Again, she began to think of this place Aruba as a paradise for women.

Nemencio slid into the bed. He reached across and soon the passions broke. Anke wondered why life had never been so good.

Her curiosity was soon satisfied and she wondered aloud whether she should kneel and praise the Lord.

That night was without sleep. Every thirty minutes either Nemencio or Anke needed and craved more of each other.

Finally, the soft light of dawn started to light up the dull sky. While they were miles from the city, the reflections of light that lit the sky, faded as the dawn broke.

Anke got up from the bed. She was unsure how to proceed. She decided to go to the kitchen and start the coffee and breakfast servings. As she walked down the stairs into the kitchen, she became aware of another person. She stopped on the stairs. Maria had returned and was sitting drinking coffee. Anke stood there embarrassed and unable to speak. Maria came across to her.

"My dear Anke. Do not be ashamed to possess a love in these times. We all need something. I think you are blessed to have the interest of a man like Nemencio. He is indeed a special man. We are lucky to have him here with us. There are few who have his intelligence and strength to achieve what he has for us. Please do not be ashamed that he has decided upon you as his lover. In fact, we girls had joked that his would probably happen. I am pleased you have found love in these terrible times. I am pleased that my room was there for you."

Anke blushed. She had never had an affair like this and was unsure how to speak of it.

Anke sat at the table and drank some of the water from the large pitcher. It was too early for coffee, and besides others appreciated it more than her.

It was now that she realized that a decision must be made. Last night she thought she knew. This morning she was confused. Jakob or Nemencio? Each had their own qualities. The more that Anke thought about this, the more Nemencio came into her mind. Finally, the decision was made.

Chapter 149

Throughout the day Anke spent time assisting with chores at the farmhouse. She had noticed that the others had been treating her somewhat differently in the past day. The treatment was not mean or cruel, but it seemed like they had a feeling of sadness for her. As Anke went about helping the others she wondered why. She did not want to ask anyone.

Late in the afternoon, several men arrived at the house. Anke had not seen them before. They entered and asked for Nemencio. One of the women recognized them and took them into a room at the front of the house that was used as a common room. They all entered and the door was closed.

Anke could hear the sound of low voices. The woman emerged from the room.

"Anke, do not be concerned. They are from an area in the South. They have come here on business with Nemencio. He is not here and will only be returning tonight. We must make them comfortable while they wait for him."

Anke gave it no more thought and went to help the women in the kitchen who were stating to prepare dinner. With so many to cook for it was a challenge.

Anke spoke to the woman who had taken charge of the cooking.

"I would like to assist and make a rich soup. It is an easy meal to make and will satisfy the men I am sure. I have made this many times before in Canada for the farmhands."

They busied themselves for the next few hours preparing dinner. Evening was falling when Nemencio returned accompanied by two men. Anke recognized them. She had met them when she first arrived at the other house.

Nemencio was carrying a package that was wrapped in a heavy brown paper. On learning of the men waiting to see him, he placed the package on a chair, removed his coat and went through to meet them.

There was an instant rise in the sound of the voices as he was welcomed.

The men stayed in the room talking for a long time. Finally, Anke was asked to interrupt them and announce the dinner was ready. The men thanked her and filed from the room.

Over dinner, which was served at several tables, the talk was of the war and how different regions of Holland were coping. It seemed that the northern area had escaped most of the severe damages that had been inflicted elsewhere.

After the dinner, the men arose to leave the house. Nemencio went to the door with them. One of the men was staying behind.

It was late in the evening when Nemencio asked Anke to join him for a walk outside. They wrapped themselves warmly and stepped out into the cool night.

"Anke you are probably wondering who those men were. They came from the area near the Belgian border. I have paid for them to take you over the border and escape. They will arrange to get you to Britain. They will take you tomorrow night. The man who stayed will be the one who will travel and escort you."

Anke froze on the spot. She was stunned. In shock she turned to Nemencio.

"Nemencio, I am not going to leave you. How could you do this? I will not leave here. You are my love. I cannot leave you now."

Nemencio threw back his head in laughter.

"Anke, please calm yourself. I have decided it is time for me to return to my country. There are family matters that I must attend to. My mother is aging and my brothers and sister need help. I will be going with you. You wish to resolve the problem with Jakob. Maybe you should travel with me all the way to Aruba. I would like that. Once there you can finish your relationship with Jakob and we can be together."

Anke dropped her head down and walked ahead slowly. This was all a surprise. She was scared and excited at the same time. Her emotions were jumbled and confused. She did not know how to answer Nemencio or whether to agree.

Chapter 150

"Anke, you must return. Jakob has sent the money in good faith. I promised my contacts in the Resistance that I would arrange for you to return. Plans have already been made. We will leave tomorrow. The plan is to cross the border tomorrow night. There will be no moon and the conditions are right. The weather is good. We should cross without much difficulty. Many who have paid this group have made this crossing. I have also been across once before. Do not be afraid. Come and let us return to the house."

They returned and Anke again observed the looks as the others would glance at her. They knew of the plans for Anke to leave.

Nemencio called everyone together and addressed them.

"I have something to tell you all. This will be my last night here. I will be going with Anke on a short trip tomorrow. We will leave early in the morning."

It was clear that the others did not know of the plan to cross the border. They had assumed Anke was being moved to a different safe house. One by one they went up to Anke and Nemencio. Anke was hugged and some cried after learning she would be leaving. The men surrounded Nemencio and peppered him with many questions. Nemencio deflected the questions where he could. He did not want his plan known too widely.

After the news of their departure and farewells made, Nemencio and Anke sat quietly alone.

"I do not know what I should take with me."

Nemencio nodded. "Take your papers and a change of clothes. In Belgium we will be given some clothes to make the trip to Britain."

"We should now go and sleep. Tomorrow will be a long day for us. We must be alert and ready for those who will take us to the border."

Anke went to the room she was sharing. Maria and Gea were in the room waiting for her.

"Here Anke. You must take this."

Gea pushed a small silver medal into Anke's hand. "It is a Saint Christopher Medal. He is our Saint and we believe in him for protection from dangers when travelling. He is our protector."

Anke looked at Gea. "But I am a Mennonite."

Gea smiled back. "I don't think he will mind that you are not a Catholic. I think he looks after everyone." She laughed and closed Anke's fingers around the medal.

Maria unclasped a thin gold chain that hung around her neck and removed it. She walked up to Anke and placed it on her.

"Maria, I cannot accept that. It is yours and personal."

Maria responded. "Anke take it. When this war is over you will return and bring it back to me. We will then have a reason to celebrate and be friends in a better time."

Anke did not know how to thank her. She hugged them both. When they left Anke found her small case and packed some clothing and shoes into it.

It seemed that Anke had just fallen asleep when she was awakened by a soft knocking at her door. She rose in silence so as to not awake the others who shared her room. She had slept fully clothed. She reached for her little case and quietly slipped from the room without waking anyone.

Downstairs in the kitchen Nemencio was waiting with a small band of men she had never seen before except for the one she had already meet. This was the one who would take them across. Nemencio handed her a mug of steaming coffee.

"I will not introduce these men by their names. They are here to take us close to the border. There we will be met by our friends from the Belgian side. We must leave now."

Chapter 151

The progress to the border was slow. They had split into two groups. Anke travelled in one and Nemencio with the other. The old farm trucks rattled along the rutted road. All the while, the men scanned for signs of any danger. They had observed some military vehicles off in the distance and so detoured around that location. This added a large amount of time to their trip.

An old grey farmhouse loomed large in the distance. There were trees surrounding the house and a forest ran behind it for a distance. As a safety measure they drove by the farmhouse for almost a mile constantly scanning the fields and the edge of the forest before turning back to the house.

Anke's driver stopped at the entrance to the barn. He jumped from the cab and went through the motion of removing some equipment and taking it into the barn. It was a ploy to distract unwelcome eyes.

Dressed as a farmhand in men's clothes, Anke left the old truck and assisted in taking some empty boxes into the barn. She did not re emerge.

The driver jumped back into the truck and turned it back in the direction they had come from. He had no sooner left when the second truck stopped at the farmhouse front yard. Nemencio jumped from the truck and went to the door. The truck pulled away. He knocked and waited. The door was opened by a tall blonde haired man dressed in working clothes. They talked for a while and then walked to the barn. Minutes later they left the barn carrying some tools and walked to the fields. The farmer and

Nemencio started working at the base of a windmill used for pumping up water for the irrigation of the fields of vegetables.

At the end of the day, Nemencio returned the tools to the barn and spent some time with Anke.

"We will be leaving soon. I will bring you some food. We will eat in here and then it will be time to leave."

They were sitting at the rear of the barn when several men dressed totally in black entered the barn. They beckoned to Anke and Nemencio. The men looked at them both.

"We need you to remove anything that is shiny and could reflect light. We will need you to put this black dye on your faces. We need to camouflage you as much as we can."

Anke and Nemencio smeared the camouflage paint on the faces and hands. They looked at each other and laughed nervously.

The man who Anke had met at the safe house beckoned them. He was obviously the leader.

It was dark when they started their trek to the forest. They moved slowly in a crouched position toward the tall pine trees. Anke breathed in the smell of the fresh pines. It was a scent she had always loved.

Within minutes they were in the thickly wooded forest. They crept closer and closer to the border. Under the canopy of the trees, and without any moon the darkness obscured everything. Occasionally a twig would crack as one of the party mistakenly stood on it. In the total darkness the sound seemed amplified and they would all freeze.

After several hours, they reached the other side of the forest and the trees started to thin out. The leader raised his finger to his lips and motioned for complete silence. He left them and crawled forward to survey the situation. It appeared that there were no guards patrolling along the open border. He returned and spoke at a whisper.

"It is dark I did not see any patrols. We shall now go."

They stood and stated to move forward quickly. As they did so a blinding light caught them in its beam. They were caught.

As they huddled together there was shouting and German soldiers ran from the forest. They had been waiting.

The group was surrounded by soldiers, some with snarling German Sheppard dogs restrained with heavy leather leashes.

Anke and Nemencio stood together. Anke sheltered in Nemencio's chest. She was terrified. Nemencio placed his hand on her arm.

"Stay quiet. Say nothing. They will try to find out about us. They will listen for an accent and try to determine your nationality. Give nothing away."

As they stood there, a Gestapo officer walked toward them. He had others with him. He was dressed in his black uniform and high black boots with his hat displaying the menacing skull and cross bone insignia. He stopped in front of Nemencio.

In near perfect English he spoke

"Now I have the pleasure of capturing the famous Nemencio Arends, arch enemy of Germany and the Third Reich. I have longed for this day. There have been many attacks and problems for which you are accountable. You were responsible for the death of my brother in that attack on the food convoy."

Nemencio took his hand from Anke's arm. As he did this the officer pulled a Luger pistol from his holster and levied it at Nemencio. Anke spun herself in front of Nemencio to shield him. As she did so, the officer fired the Luger. The sounds of the gunshots echoed through the night.

The bullets passed through Anke's back and into Nemencio's chest. They fell to the ground gasping. The officer walked up to them and fired more shots.

Anke tried to place her arms around Nemencio. It was no use. She did not have the strength. Nemencio was bleeding from his mouth and chest.

Together they lay in a strange embrace as Nemencio died.

Chapter 152

Aruba

Jakob was excited. The arrangements had been made for Anke's escape from occupied Holland back to Canada. He went about his work at the refinery while planning his trip back to Canada and then returning to Aruba with his wife.

Finally, Jakob had arrived at a decision. He now knew the life he wanted and where he wished to live. In his mind he started to plan where they would live. Jakob was ready to buy a home in the hilly area behind Savaneta.

Jakob stopped at the Stella Maris club on his way back to his apartment after a long week at the refinery. The usual Friday evening customers were milling about the bar. The tables were occupied by couples and friends. The atmosphere was friendly and there was a continual buzz of conversation. It was still early and the music and entertainment had yet to start.

Jakob went to the bar and found Miguel assisting the new barman. Miguel was pleased to see Jakob. He poured him a large mug of beer and slid it across the bar to him.

Jakob looked around the club. He recognized some of the people but there were none of his good friends there. He elected to remain standing at the bar and finish his beer after which he would take his bike and ride back to the apartment. He was happy but tired. Now that he had made his decision he found himself tired mentally. He was continually playing thoughts and ideas of the new life he and Anke would enjoy in Aruba.

Jakob left the club and took a slow ride back to the apartment. He was in no hurry. He looked into the gardens and yards of the homes he passed along the way. On occasion he would stop and talk with some of the owners he knew.

He arrived at his apartment and made his way to the front porch where he found Carlita sitting alone.

"Bon Noche Carlita. It is a nice evening to sit out. May I join you? It is a little too early for me to go to my bed."

"Yes of course. Can I get you a drink?"

"Yes. A nice rum drink would be nice."

Carlita arose to go inside for the drink. Jakob went to his apartment door and opened it for Timmy to run out. Timmy ran to the nearest cactus and without any shame raised his leg and quenched the cactus' thirst.

Carlita returned to the porch with her children. Seeing Timmy the children called him and ran down onto the beach to play with the dog. They threw a stick and Timmy obliged in fetching and returning it to the one who threw it.

"It is nice to sit here in peace and watch. I just wish my Juan was here as well."

Jakob looked over to Carlita and noticed she had been crying. Her dark eyes were reddened. Jakob was unsure of what to say.

"Carlita, I am sure time will heal your sorrow. The memories of Juan will still be with you. You must stay strong for you and the children. There will be new things to look forward to."

Carlita looked into Jakob's eyes and her look softened.

"Thank you Jakob. You have really helped us. Miguel and Alejandro often say this."

They sat together in silence. The sounds of the children playing and the crash of the surf on the shore were the only sounds to punctuate the still air of the night.

The sky was clear and dotted with hundreds of stars. It was a perfect night.

It was late when Jakob left to go to his apartment. He called Timmy in for the night.

Chapter 153

Over the next few weeks, Jakob awaited news of Anke's escape from The Netherlands. He would stop at the bars to look for Pieter van Doren. He was unable to get any news. Jakob assumed this to mean that all had gone well and that Anke was on her way to safety.

Jakob was at home in his apartment when Miguel arrived accompanied by Pieter van Doren. Pieter bore a worried look on his face. Jakob welcomed them into his small apartment.

"Jakob, I have brought Pieter here as he came by the club looking for you. He insisted we find you."

Jakob looked at Pieter intensely. "What is it? Do you have news?"

"I am sorry Jakob. The Germans intercepted their escape. They executed several of those attempting the crossing into Belgium. Anke was shot. She is dead."

Jakob collapsed back onto his bed in shock. He was unable to grasp the words Pieter had delivered.

"How is this possible? I thought this was to be a safe escape. I was told that this was where many crossed safely. What am I to do now?"

Jakob sat deep in thought. Pieter and Miguel stood by in silence. There was nothing they could say to comfort Jakob. Miguel left the apartment and went to the house where he knocked on the door. Carlita appeared. Miguel asked her to come and join him on the front porch. Miguel then relayed the news. Carlita gasped and placed her hand across her mouth.

"How is Jakob? How is he dealing with this news? In the past weeks he was making plans to join her and then return to Aruba with her to start a new life. He will be destroyed."

"Jakob is sad. He is with Pieter from the Marines. Jakob is strong and will be able to cope with this."

Carlita rose and ran across to the apartment to offer support and comfort to the grieving Jakob.

"Jakob I am sorry to hear this news. I want to assist. What can I do at this time?"

Jakob looked up at her. His face showed some sorrow but Carlita was surprised he was not more upset.

"I need some time alone. I have to think about the future and what I will do without my Anke."

They looked to each other and finally left Jakob alone in his apartment.

Carlita found the situation very strange. She wondered if Jakob had really loved Anke as he did not seem to be too upset by her death. She returned to the house and later lay in bed thinking about his reactions.

In the morning Carlita called on Jakob to join the family for breakfast, but he had already left the apartment, destined to meet with Catherine to discuss his future business dealings in Aruba. The long walk helped Jakob to focus his mind on all that was happening. Without Anke his whole life had now changed.

Jakob proceeded to the bar over which was Catherine's office. He requested a meeting with her. The assistant asked him to wait in the area outside of her office. After several minutes he was ushered into the Office. Catherine sat at her desk. Her illness showed. She had aged further.

"Yes Jakob. What can I help with?"

Jakob told Catherine of his loss and the impact it had on his earlier plans. He advised her he wanted to increase his ownership in the club. He would leave his job at the refinery, sell the farms in Canada and stay in Aruba where he would look at starting businesses. He told her of the vision he had for hotels and tourism once the war in Europe was over. He spoke of the changes in the world that the war had brought about.

Catherine sat and listened with great interest to Jakob's views. Silently she agreed with his assessment of the growth of tourism, especially from the United States.

"Jakob I will be leaving for Miami a few weeks. I cannot deal with this. My daughter Solange is arriving to take over my business operations here in Aruba. She will arrive tomorrow. I will discuss this with her and arrange for you to meet. She will have final decisions on all my business affairs. I am putting her in charge of everything. I am old and ill. It is time to leave all of this and enjoy what remains of my life. I have worked long and hard. Now I will try to stop and enjoy."

Jakob thanked her and left the office. He proceeded to the refinery and started late on his shift. He did not discuss his plans with anyone at the refinery.

The crew had been working on the replacement of several pipelines from the dock to the crude oil storage tanks. The progress of the job had been delayed due to the continual breakages of equipment that occurred as they worked. The decision was made that it would be necessary to work throughout the night to complete the important job.

Jakob's mind was running. It was February 16, 1942. He had not expected to be away from his farm in Canada that long.

It was during the early morning hours as the crew struggled with the repairs, when loud explosion from the water occurred off from the end of the dock. The crew immediately jumped and stared out into the still dark waters of San Nicolaas harbor. They watched in horror as the oiler *S.S Perdenales* burst into flames. They could make out the silhouette of a submarine. A second oiler, the *S.S. Oranjestad,* realizing an attack was in progress raised anchor and attempted an escape. Too late to escape, the torpedoes hit the *Oranjestad* and it too was engulfed with flames as it started to sink. Men ran to launch some small boats that were moored at the docks of the refinery and raced to the stricken ships in an attempt to rescue crew members from the water.

As Jakob and his crew watched the submarine slipped away. It was shortly afterwards that they heard more explosions and saw the sky lit up by flames. They did not know that Aruba's other refinery at Eagle Beach was also under attack where the American tanker *SS Arkansas* was docked. The U-boat torpedoed the *SS Arkansas* but only caused minor damage.

Jakob and his crew did not know what to do. The work was incomplete. The refinery operations would be impacted if the work was not completed before the early shift started.

As they stood talking and trying to assist those plucked from the waters, they heard another explosion and ran to the dock to see the U-boat had returned. Flashes illuminated from the submarines deck as gunfire rattled. They heard bullets hitting the tanks and the equipment around them. They ran to seek shelter. Suddenly, all went quiet. Jakob looked out to the submarine. In the poor light, he made out what he thought were sailors pulling some men from the water. Aruba had been attacked by the German U-boat U156. The war had arrived on its shores.

The men in the crew were terrified. Although Jakob pleaded, they refused to complete the work. Jakob went to the Engineering office to meet with the engineer on duty. They discussed the attacks. He told the engineer that the men would not complete the work in the darkness and with the destruction of the attack. He suggested a new crew take over. Reluctantly the engineer agreed.

Jakob was growing tired of the refinery and the long hours. The continual smell of the oil that permeated his clothing, hair and skin annoyed him. Now, with the attack on the refinery, Jakob was concerned for this life.

Jakob changed out of his work clothes and walked to the main gate of the refinery along with the other members of his crew. The men were nervous and spoke of their fear that the war would soon burst into their peaceful lives in Aruba. They were dejected.

As Jakob started his walk back to the apartment the skies lightened and people emerged from their small houses that lined the street.

It was on this walk that he had made yet another decision. Jakob realized that the refinery had become a strategic target due to its importance in producing aviation fuel for the war in Europe. He decided to leave the refinery.

He walked on thinking of the options he had available to him. His desire to return to the farm in Canada had waned with the death of Anke.

Chapter 154

Over the next two weeks, Jakob continued to work his daily shifts at the refinery. News of the U-boat attack had spread throughout the refinery and the island. There was a constant tension present. The relaxed atmosphere was gone. The men were worried. On the island there was an increase in the number of armed soldiers from different countries. It was evident that they were there to protect the refinery at all costs.

The extent of the damage done by the U-boat was now known and widely discussed.

Jakob's resolve to resign from the refinery was strengthened by all of this.

It was toward the end of February when he returned to his apartment and was met by Carlita. She held an envelope that was addressed to him in neatly scripted handwriting. Carlita was curious. She handed the envelope to Jakob and he carefully opened it. It was an invitation for him and a partner to attend a function to welcome Solange, Catherine's daughter. The function was also to bid farewell to Catherine in recognition of the work she had done and the jobs she had created in San Nicolaas.

Jakob looked at the date. It was to be held in two nights. He handed the invitation to Carlita. Since Solange was taking over the business, Jakob decided it was imperative to attend.

"Would you care to accompany me? You have not been out very often since Juan's death. With the present atmosphere of fear and possible war, it will be good for you. "

"Jakob, I do not have clothing to wear to an event like this."

"Then tomorrow we will go into San Nicolaas and we will find you some. I have the day off from the refinery. I will not hear anymore from you about this. You must come and enjoy."

Carlita blushed. She was unsure of what to say. She looked at Jakob and smiled.

"Yes. This will be good for both of us. We have both suffered recently. I will be happy to go with you."

The next morning, Jakob and Carlita set off for the fashion store in San Nicolaas. They arrived at the store mid-morning

Upon entering the store, Jakob noticed the strong smell from the bales of dress fabric and the brightly colored clothing on display. Carlita gasped at the display and placed her hand over her mouth. She had never been in a store like this.

Carlita walked through the displays and was soon assisted by a friendly saleswoman. Jakob was quickly becoming bored. Sensing his boredom, the saleswoman left Carlita and returned with a cold beer in her hand which she gave to Jakob. She then gestured to a small table with a chair near the front window. Jakob accepted the beer and thanked her before seating himself at the little table.

As Carlita slowly examined the dresses, Jakob sat by idly watching the activity in the street. There were many troops walking by. The majority were US but he did not recognize some of the uniforms. It was obvious that the troops were here to guard the island and the refineries.

Carlita continued to look at different dresses. The saleswoman had selected several for her to try. Jakob laughed at some of the selections. They transformed Carlita into different apparitions. Jakob was thinking that this was becoming a futile exercise when Carlita emerged wearing a dress in stunning peacock blue. The dress lit up her Latin features. Jakob marveled at the change in her appearance.

The decision was made and they left the store to visit Miguel at the club. It was still early afternoon so they decided to have a lunch at the club. Miguel was surprised to see them enter and welcomed them into the club. They sat together and Carlita excitedly chatted about her purchases and the upcoming event to which Jakob had invited her.

"I am pleased that you have decided to go with Jakob. I too, and Alejandro are invited. Since we are all going, I will stop at your home and drive you. I have just bought a new car."

Miguel sat with them during the lunch. They spoke of the changes that were happening. Miguel wondered aloud what would change now that Catherine was handing the business over to Solange. The talk centered on the changes that Aruba would make now that the island had been attacked. Miguel saw great opportunity with the influx of the foreign troops. They sat and talked for hours.

It was late afternoon when they got up to leave. Miguel jumped to his feet, his pride in his new car bursting.

"I will drive you now. You will be home in minutes, relaxed and able to enjoy the sunset. Let us go."

They exited the club and walked to the rear where a shiny new Chevrolet was parked. Miguel ran to the passenger door and opened it. He helped Carlita into the front seat and Jakob crawled into the back seat. Within minutes they pulled onto the small patch of burnt grass at the front of Carlita's Villa.

Again, Miguel jumped from the car and ran to assist Carlita down from the car. Carlita thanked him and leaned forward to kiss him on both cheeks. She was truly happy for the first time since the incident that had taken Juan.

Jakob thanked Miguel and turned to walk to his apartment.

Carlita called to him. "Jakob, please come back later and join me on the porch for dinner and drinks. I want to thank you for this day. We will enjoy drinks and watch the sun set over the sea."

Jakob accepted the invitation and went into his apartment to wash and rest for a while.

After an hour or so had passed he arose from his bed and left to join Carlita.

She was already on the porch. Jakob joined her and she mixed some rum based drinks. Jakob felt a strange relaxation that he had not experienced since his days back at the farm in Canada.

They sat in silence watching as the sun dipped below the horizon painting the fluffy clouds a brilliant shade of orange and pink.

When the sun had set, Carlita went into her house. She emerged with a large tureen of soup and sat it on the table. Jakob had never tried the Iguana soup before. He was unsure but politely accepted the bowl that Carlita passed him. When they were both seated Jakob plunged his spoon into the pale creamy soup. He gingerly raised the spoon to his lips. The soup tasted salty and reminded him of either chicken or rabbit. He enjoyed the taste. Carlita warned him to be careful of the many small bones.

With the soup finished, Carlita left and returned with plates of a goat stew with potatoes. She placed the meal in front of Jakob and then poured him a glass of heavy red wine.

They sat eating and talking for a long while. Jakob excused himself as he had an early shift to manage at the refinery.

He returned to his apartment and after taking his little dog Timmy out for a brief walk, he returned to sleep for the night.

Chapter 155

Miguel arrived on the day of Catherine's reception in his new car. It was sparkling clean. He went to fetch Carlita and Jakob. He gasped in shock when Carlita walked out in her bright peacock blue dress. Her hair was swept up and she wore some drop earrings.

"Carlita, is that you? You look so beautiful."

Jakob stood and walked down to where Miguel was standing on the sandy soil. He was dressed in linen trousers and a casual white shirt that showed off his tanned features.

They drove the short distance from Savaneta to Reception Hall in San Nicolaas and parked in an adjacent area. At the main door they were greeted by an usher who checked off their names against a typed list. After verifying they were indeed invited, the trio was then escorted upstairs to the large conference room. The room was decorated for the reception. There was a stage upon which a small ensemble quietly played some popular musical tunes. Jakob looked around and recognized many business owners and some he did not know. He took Carlita's hand and made his way through the assembled guests to where Catherine was seated.

"Jacob I thank you for coming. Who is the lovely lady with you?"

"Good evening, Catherine. This is Carlita, Juan's beautiful wife. You met before when we were determining how to proceed with the club."

Catherine stared at Carlita. "I would never have recognized you. Let me introduce you to my daughter Solange."

Sitting to the right of Catherine was a young auburn haired woman. She held her hand out to shake Jakob's, while all the time looking at Carlita.

"I am Solange and I am pleased to meet you and your wife."

The greeting was cool and dismissive.

"No this is not my wife, but a good friend and the wife of a friend who has gone missing."

Solange continued to look at Carlita without a smile or expression of welcome. It was obvious that Solange did not want to be anything less than the focus of the evening. Jakob picked up on the interaction and offered to speak with Solange later and guided Carlita away from where Catherine and Solange were seated. As he turned to move away, he noticed what appeared to be a cane on the floor behind Solange.

He moved around the room and was greeted by some store owners with whom he had done business when setting up the club. Carlita was the centre of attention and a small group gathered around her. Jakob left to get them both glasses of wine from the bar at the end of the room.

As he was returning, Solange motioned him over to her.

"I wanted to speak just with you. My mother has told me of some ideas you have for developing a tourist business here. I would like to explore this with you. I have always been intrigued by the situation in Cuba. They have built a strong business there with hotels, casinos and other businesses to support the main tourism. When can we meet and explore this further? I need a week or two to settle in and understand how things are working here."

"I will come and see you in a couple of weeks. I am in San Nicolaas often."

"That will be fine. I will advise my staff that you will be coming. I look forward to speaking further." Solange made no attempt to get up from her chair, yet gave Jakob a provocative smile.

Jakob was somewhat confused and drifted back to the group who had gathered around Carlita. Miguel and Alejandro had joined her.

The talk centered on the impact of the war and the consequences for Aruba now that it had been attacked.

Chapter 156

The evening function saw the arrival of Aruba's business leaders. Jakob knew many of them through his dealings with the club. He was introduced to some who were recent arrivals on the island.

After an hour one of Catherine's trusted advisors rose and went to a microphone to address the guests.

"Good evening. Thank you for attending this farewell for Catherine this evening. It is my pleasure to also welcome her daughter, Solange who will be taking over for Catherine.

Catherine has decided it is time for her to retire from the daily demands of business and enjoy her life. Unfortunately, Catherine has decided to leave us and live in Miami. We sincerely hope that she will grace us with her company and not stay away too long. Maybe she will change her mind and return."

The farewell speech continued for a long while. Her accomplishments and involvement in the community were highlighted. Finally, Solange was introduced.

Solange motioned to the speaker that she wished to introduce herself and speak. She reached down to the floor and picked up the thin cane and used it to steady herself as she stood. Jakob watched her movements closely. She seemed to be using the cane for support as she stood, after which she left the cane and walked to the microphone unaided.

"Good evening. I thank all of you for coming here this evening and making this a great farewell for my mother, Catherine. The achievements that Catherine has had here have already been addressed. It is my desire to continue to build on these and grow our businesses here. Over the next few weeks I am hoping to personally meet many of you. I look forward to visiting and getting to know you better and the type of businesses you run. I will be looking for new possibilities to expand the business that Catherine has so successfully built."

There was a prolonged round of applause. Solange acknowledged this with a slight bow and then returned to her seat. Jakob watched her carefully. Solange was classically beautiful in a different way. She was unlike the many Latino women and her looks were neither European nor North American. He wondered about this and her ancestry. She differed in looks and nature to that of Catherine.

Jakob continued to watch as Solange gently lowered herself back into her chair. He was puzzled. Her mobility seemed fine and she did not use her cane for this. Solange looked up and saw Jakob staring at her. She gave him a direct look and locked her eyes with his. A faint whisper of a smile could be detected on her lips. Jakob decided it was time for him to leave the function. He found Carlita, along with Miguel and Alejandro speaking with some Venezuelan men. The Spanish was spoken fast and he was unable to comprehend most of it. He gently placed his hand on Carlita's arm. "It is time for me to leave. Will you stay with Miguel and Alejandro or leave with me?"

"Jakob I am truly enjoying myself here. I would like to stay longer. It has been many years since I attended any parties or gatherings like this. Will you be offended if I stay?

"No, please stay. I am happy to see you laughing and meeting new people."

Jakob said goodbye to the group and went across the smoke filled room to where Solange sat. There were several local men chatting with her and Catherine. Upon seeing Jakob standing behind them, she raised her hand and waved Jakob forward.

"I have come to thank you and wish both you and Catherine goodnight. Catherine, I want to tell you that I have enjoyed the times we have done business together. If Solange is like you then I believe we will continue to have success."

Solange blushed and Catherine thanked him for being a good business partner with her.

Jakob left the noisy and smoky room and walked down the stairs and out into the warm but refreshing air. He was looking forward to the walk back to his apartment.

Chapter 157

The next two weeks passed by quickly for Jakob. Now that he had decided to stay and pursue his dream and vision in Aruba, there were many matters to attend to. Jakob wrote a letter to the Elders of his church in Canada explaining his decision and the loss of Anke. In the letter Jakob advised them that he wished to sell off the farms as he would not be returning. He inquired whether the family who had leased the farm would be interested and named the selling price.

At the refinery, Jakob resigned his position. After the attack on the refinery and the fact that Aruba was now at war, he had decided that working at the refinery was too dangerous. The refinery was now a key target for the Germans as it was producing most of the aviation fuel for the war in Europe. His belief was confirmed by the active U-Boat campaign and the sinking of many tankers attempting to transport the fuel to and from Aruba.

With the presence of the troops from America, Britain and France, Jakob saw more opportunities for the expansion of the Stella Maris Club. He asked Miguel to arrange to visit with Alejandro and Carlita to listen to his plans. The next Sunday afternoon they lunched on Carlita's porch and chatted. Finally, Jakob spoke.

"I have made decisions I wish to share with you. I will not be leaving Aruba. I have decided to sell my interests in Canada and with that money I will start some new business here. I have been watching how things have changed in San Nicolaas since the arrival of the troops. The club has been doing extremely well. Often we are unable to serve many and turn customers away. I have a plan to change that."

Jakob continued and for the next hour laid out his plan. He was peppered with questions and suggestions from the trio. There was great excitement at the prospect of expanding the club.

The afternoon started to slip into early evening. Carlita insisted they all stay and enjoy an early dinner. Over the meal, the discussion continued. Miguel was a little worried.

"Jakob how do we finance this plan of yours? I do not have the money that this will require."

"Miguel, I am awaiting to meet with Catherine's daughter Solange. I will present this to her. I will also provide some money from the sale of my farm."

Jakob watched the trio as they sat quietly thinking about this. It was obvious that they were unhappy to see their interest in the club diminishing as Jakob and Solange increased theirs. Carlita was the first to speak.

"Jakob I understand the need to finance the expansion. Instead of selling our interest, maybe we can set up a loan that can be repaid over time."

Jakob had not considered this option. He sat and thought hard about this.

"I am prepared to do this with my money. I will present this to Solange. I think she will make very hard demands and probably want to be in a position to take over the club if the loan is not paid."

They continued to discuss different alternatives and came to the conclusion that a loan would be best.

"I will meet with Solange and determine if she is interested. I will await a response from Canada to learn whether the farm will sell at the price I have requested. I hope to hear from the Elders within a week or two. In the meanwhile, Miguel can you have the accountants prepare fresh financials for me to take to the meeting."

It was around nine at night when they finished. Jakob decided to take a stroll on the beach before retiring for the night. He went to his apartment to fetch Timmy for his nightly walk. Upon entering he was greeted by the little dog with great enthusiasm. He wondered how the little dog didn't hurt his tail as it wagged nonstop.

Jakob strolled along the beach. His bare feet sunk into the cool soft white sand. He was pleased that he had made these decisions. Finally the conflicts he had previously fought seemed to be resolved.

At the far end of the beach he found a log that had been washed ashore. He sat on the log throwing a piece of wood for Timmy to excitedly run and fetch. He sat thinking of the future and watching the reflection of the large full moon and stars on the calm waters of the Caribbean.

Chapter 158

Jakob received the letter from Canada containing the response to his question of selling the farm to the family who were presently leasing from him. The response was positive but with an unusual condition. With the death of Anke and her father, the two farms were owned by Jakob. The offer was to purchase one and continue to lease the other. For this arrangement, an offer had been made. Contained with the letter and offer were legal documents that had been drawn up on the assumption that Jakob would accept the deal. Jakob examined the offer and did numerous calculations. It was a fair offer. In order to close the sale he would need to have the enclosed documents witnessed and legally processed.

Jakob visited the banker who dealt with the club's banking matters. The bank was in an old Cunucu style home. It had been converted to function as a bank. The walls had small cracks in them. The slow turning overhead fans did very little to lessen the stifling heat. Several people were standing in a line to conduct their business with one of three tellers at the huge counter that ran the length of the building. Jakob walked past the line and reached an office where a receptionist sat working on a large file of papers. She looked up and saw Jakob.

"Mr. Jakob, welcome. What are you here for today? Can I help you?"

"Yes. I need to speak to the manager. I am selling some land and need advice."

"I will go and tell him. Please just wait a minute" and with this she disappeared into the office, only to emerge some moments later. "Mr. van der Heyden will see you immediately." She ushered Jakob into the office.

"Jakob, bon tardi. It is good to see you." The tall Dutchman spoke in heavily accented English. "What can I help you with?"

Jakob explained his need for legal help and the plans he had for the future. The manager kept his fingers pressed together as if in prayer and pursed to his lips. When Jakob had finished, he spoke.

"For this matter you will need a Notary or Attorney here on the island who can work in English. I am aware of an attorney who is excellent and handles many matters in English for the refinery. I will draft you a letter of introduction."

Mr. van der Heyden reached across his desk and removed an ink pen and stated writing out the letter on the bank stationery with its grossly exaggerated graphic letterhead.

When completed he turned the letter over on the green blotter and placed it down to dry and remove the excess ink. He took the letter and read it through and then handed it to Jakob. It was an excellent letter of introduction and reference. The letter contained a glowing account of the relationship that Jakob had with the bank and his involvement with the club and other businesses. Jakob looked at the address. It was within minutes of the bank. He decided to visit. He thanked the manager and left to walk the short distance to the Attorney's office. As he casually walked through the streets a female voice called out his name. Jakob looked around and saw Solange across the street. He waved and crossed over to speak with her.

"Solange. I am surprised to see you here walking around at this time of day. I thought you would be busy with matters at your office. Are you well? How are you finding your new position here in Aruba? Are you enjoying it?"

"Thank you. Yes I am well and enjoying the new challenge very much. I find that business here is so different to what I am used to in the States. To answer your question as to why I am here at this time of day, I have decided to find somewhere to have lunch away from the office."

"Solange, then I will invite you to join me at the club. It is open for lunch. I will introduce you to some fine Aruban cuisine. In fact, I was planning on meeting with you to review some plans. We can talk over lunch."

"I would be delighted and accept your kind invitation."

As they started walking, Jakob noticed her slight limp yet she did not have her cane with her. He decided to ignore this fact and they slowly proceeded to the club.

At the club, Miguel greeted them and fussed over seating them at a private booth. Within minutes a large pitcher of water was delivered to their table. To Jakob's amazement, Solange ordered a Manhattan. He decided to accompany her and ordered a beer. After the drinks were delivered they sat making small talk. Miguel returned to tell them of the special lunch that day. Jakob listened and advised Solange to order the special of Keshi Yena. Solange was puzzled and asked Jakob to explain what Keshi Yena was.

Jakob explained that it was a chicken casserole made with peanuts and raisins in it and served over a base of tomato sauce and sealed with Gouda cheese. He elaborated further on its preparation and method of serving.

"It sounds delicious" she said after Jakob had provided the meticulous description.

As they awaited their meals, talk drifted to business. Jakob detailed his plans for the sale of the farm and his desire to start new businesses in Aruba. Solange leaned forward in deep concentration.

"Jakob, my mother told me somewhat of your vision to build accommodations here. Please tell me more."

"Solange, here in Aruba there are very few places for visiting dignitaries and others to stay. In fact when leaders or other important officials come here on business, they are often required to stay in the homes of other senior government officials. Now that Aruba has so many troops from other countries stationed here I see that things will change. I expect that when the war is over. Many of those men will return to their homes and tell of this place. It is my firm belief a large number will want to return with wives or family for a holiday here or to live. There is nowhere for them to stay. The opportunity I see is to buy land on or near the beaches from the government. I will buy more land than I need. I will start with one hotel and if it is successful I will then build another. I will build the second hotel at a different location. I hope to buy land in three areas of the Island. Those areas I am interested in are Palm Beach, Oranjestad and here in San Nicolaas. I will also build small houses for the families who will move here."

"How will you pay for this adventure you are planning?"

"I intend to use monies from the farm and to seek partners here. I will also ask the bank. First I need to meet with the government and determine if the lands can be purchased."

Solange quietly ate her Keshi Yena. "Jakob you were correct about this food. It is delicious. I will have to try this again."

Jakob was quiet. He wondered if he had told Solange too much of his plans. Finally they had finished their meals.

"Jakob there is no reason for you to request a meeting to present your vision. I am interested in a partner arrangement. We will, however, meet to discuss details. I will request assistance from the professional firms in which we have investments. The project will be sworn to secrecy until we are ready to announce the start of the building. We will be able to prepare estimates for the building and land purchase."

Jakob was delighted. He had not expected Solange to readily agree with his ideas. They continued talking and hours passed by. In late afternoon, Solange attempted to stand in order to leave. As Jakob watched he saw her stumble and grasp the edge of the table to prevent falling. He quickly jumped to his feet and reached across to support her.

"Are you alright? Please let me help you sit for a minute. "

Jakob called to Miguel to bring some water. He guided Solange onto the red leather seat of the chair.

"Jakob I am sorry. I am embarrassed. I will be alright. I should have brought my stupid cane. I hate people seeing me with it. I guess I am too vain and need to suffer events like this."

"Solange, may I be bold and ask you what the problem is? Will you need medical assistance? Is it a condition that may worsen?" Jakob was concerned. After all, this was his new partner.

"No Jakob. It is something I will need to live with the rest of my life. It will not worsen. "

"What is it? What happened?"

"When I was a little girl of three years old, I had a mild polio infection. It was miraculously cured. I have weakened muscle in my legs. I need my cane to support me when standing up and at times when I am required to stand for a period of time."

"I shall assist you stand and walk you back to your office."

Solange looked up at Jakob and smiled an affectionate and warm smile. Jakob wondered if he had seen this correctly. Yet there was no mistaking that Solange had developed an interest in Jakob.

Chapter 159

Over the next three months Jakob attended at Solange's office. They met with government officials to discuss the land purchases. The meetings were long and difficult. It seemed no one wanted to make any decisions for such a bold project. Matters were referred back to the Dutch government in exile for consultation. Briefs were made by Jakob to senior Dutch representatives on the Island.

After almost a year, agreements were reached.

Architects and engineers were hired and the process was started. It was decided to build the first hotel in a location between Dakota Airport and Oranjestad. Work was commenced on a small hotel that overlooked the bay and the Caribbean.

While Jakob continued to be absorbed by the project, things were changing. The war in Europe was ending, Aruba was slowly developing as the importance and capability of the refineries became known internationally. Small companies grew overnight to provide services to the refinery and the military presence on the Island.

The relationship between Jakob and Solange also changed. The feelings Solange had developed toward Jakob were strong and he found himself intrigued and drawn to her. It was not long before the affair blossomed and they feel into love. Jakob eagerly yearned to see Solange each day as he travelled from his apartment to the office.

It was late one evening at the office when the others had left. Jakob was exhausted. Solange suggested he have a dinner with her before Jakob made his way home to the small apartment. Jakob expressed that he was too tired and would just leave. Though the distance to Savaneta was not far, Jakob told Solange he would take a taxi. Solange walked around the desk at the centre of the room and put her arms up around his neck and drew him to her.

"Jakob we will go and eat at the Stella Maris and after you will come back and sleep at my house."

Jakob looked at her in astonishment. He realized that the relationship was now far more than just business and had become a love interest. He considered his options.

"Solange we will go to the club, but I must return home as I have some matters to attend to. Timmy needs to be looked after and I have documents I need to complete and send back to Canada."

Solange released Jakob from her embrace and with a pout looked deep into his eyes. "Jakob there are times I do not understand you and this is one of them. Come now; let us walk down to the club. After we eat you will be free to do what you wish. I will be disappointed if you reject me."

Jakob nodded and together they left the office and started in the direction of the Stella Maris. The club was busy. Men in uniforms stood drinking near the bar. Jakob spotted Alejandro rushing from table to table. They entered and were immediately escorted to a table that overlooked the busy street.

Solange ordered a bottle of fine Spanish wine. Together they sat in silence sipping the wine. Solange would occasionally look at Jakob's face and the scar from his altercation in Colombia. She wondered about this man's life and past adventures. She was determined to find out all she could about Jakob Klassen.

Chapter 160

Munich, Germany early 1947

Josef Klassen surveyed the damage that the Allied bombing raids had caused as he drove his old Citroen slowly through those streets that were passable. He was saddened to see many landmarks destroyed. Gangs of men and women were working to clear away bricks and debris. Many of the workers had only gloved hands while others used garden spades and equipment. Munich had been devastated. Josef was silently angry that the vision of one man, Adolf Hitler, had resulted in so much destruction of the once proud Germany.

Josef had fled through France at the beginning of the war. He had stored his precious Citroen with a friend in Paris and continued on to Britain where he had assisted the British intelligence with his knowledge of the Nazi war machine. He was now returning to Germany and hopefully his home in Munich which he understood had only minor damage.

Josef, who had been a successful businessman before the war, had been asked to work with the occupying forces and assist in the rebuilding efforts.

Josef pulled onto the street where his home was located. He drove by the former beautiful homes that were now reduced to rubble. He wondered how any of this could ever be rebuilt. He drove slowly observing each home. Finally he rounded the large curve and arrived at his home. The gardens were destroyed. The large trees that had sheltered his lawn and the front of his house were now no more than shattered stumps from which grotesque arms of broken branches protruded. Josef parked on the street and walked up to the front of his home. Some of the large glass windows were broken. He continued and walked around the outside. The roof at the rear of the house had caved in and the exterior brickwork was badly damaged. Josef returned to the front and climbed the stairs to enter the house. The front door was unlocked. He swung the door open. As he did so, he heard voices from inside. Josef was scared and stood still listening for several minutes. The voices appeared to be those of a child, several women and a male voice. Josef cautiously walked to the kitchen area at the rear of the house where the voices originated. Upon entering the kitchen he startled the occupants. The kitchen had been stripped of its furniture. There was makeshift bedding on the floor. The occupants were dressed in rags. Josef strode across to the man amongst them.

"Who are you and what are you doing in my house?"

The man displayed nervousness. "This is my wife and her sister. These are my children. Our house was bombed. We tried to get into one of the shelters but could not. We saw your house and found it empty. We have been taking shelter here for several months. During the day we join the work crews cleaning up the destruction. We have nowhere else to take shelter. We do not like what we have been forced to do by entering and living like this in your house. I am sorry."

Josef listened in silence and said nothing. He turned and walked through the house examining each room. Other than at the rear of the house, most rooms seemed intact except for the fact they had been looted. Josef considered the situation. The damage could have been much worse. He assessed that repairs were possible. To furnish the house again would be difficult as many items were not available in Germany.

Josef returned to the kitchen. The little group were huddled together and watched Josef intently.

"Who are you and what did you do before and during the war?"

"I was a carpenter and my wife a cook at The Excelsior Hotel. We had an apartment nearby the Hotel. It was totally destroyed in the bombings. I lost my tools and my job. I have been unable to find work as a carpenter. Now that you are here to take back your home will you throw us onto the streets?"

"It is my intention to repair and restore my home. I do understand your situation. Please tell me more about yourselves. I will make a decision about this when I know more about you."

The man spoke of their life before the war, his love of the work he had done, his wife's outstanding cooking skills. Josef probed further. He wanted to know if the man had belonged to and was sympathetic to the Third Reich. The man spat on the floor and loudly denounced the policies that had lead Germany into war and the consequences that had resulted. Josef continued to interrogate them. After an hour had passed Josef decided and took the man aside to speak.

"I will allow you to stay. You must move from the kitchen. We will select two rooms and set them up for you. In return, I will ask you to assist with the restoration of my home where you can use your skills. Your wife can cook and assist in the house. That is all I am prepared to do. You must continue to look for work."

The wife ran forward to Josef. There were tears in her eyes. She hugged Josef.

"Thank you. Thank you. We have nothing and nowhere to go. We will work hard for you. You will be pleased."

Josef nodded and proceeded to set out the living arrangements.

The man was curious.

"There is very little to buy. You will need lumber, masonry and furnishings. How will you get these things?"

"Before the war, I had successful businesses. In anticipation of the war, I moved my collection of art and securities to a bank in Switzerland. They remain there safely. I will travel there and arrange for the things I will need to reestablish my home. I will need some time to prepare a plan. Do you have food? I am working with the authorities for the rebuild of Munich and am entitled to food."

The wife's sister spoke. She looked pale and broken. "We have very little food here. I am not proud but most of what we have I have had to steal."

Josef looked at the woman. He realized that at some point she had been a beautiful woman but the ravages of war had usurped her beauty.

"Please tell me your name what you did before and during the war."

The women dropped her eyes to the floor. Her cheeks reddened. She fidgeted and very quietly spoke. The child held the side of her tattered skirt and glared at Josef.

"My name is Ilsa Wolfe. I worked in Hamburg in the clubs and bars. Work became very difficult as the war continued. I came to

Munich with my son as there was work in the factories. I was able to get a factory job."

"What happened to your husband, your son's father?"

"He has no father. The man who is his father ran away to sea and left me with Hans. It has been very hard. He is an angry boy and sometimes very difficult. I love him but at times cannot understand his behavior."

Ilsa continued to speak to Josef of her past struggles and her desire to find a better life for her and Hans in Munich.

Josef was impressed by her. She expressed a hope and desire he had not seen in a long while.

"I will now leave and obtain some food for us from the store operated by the authorities. I will return and we will set up the house so we can all live properly. I will arrange for some bedding and clothing from Switzerland tomorrow. We will set up an account. You will repay these things through the work you will do. We will set this up when I return."

The man accompanied Josef to the front door.

"You are kind to help us like this. You have shown us such trust. We will not let you down."

Josef and the man shook hands and Josef walked off to his Citroen.

Chapter 161

Josef found himself immersed in the reconstruction efforts. He worked night and day with the engineers and advisers from the British and American Forces. There was a sense of urgency to restore services and provide shelter for those who had lost homes and been displaced by the war.

At Josef's home, progress was being made at a rapid pace. Franz took charge of supervising and assisting the workers who he had been able to hire to repair the home. A team of masons had been found at a significant cost to fix the damaged stonework and bricks. Josef had travelled to Switzerland with Franz to order special building materials and select furniture to replace that which had been looted.

The bond between Josef and Franz grew stronger each day. Josef found he could confidently trust Franz to make decisions regarding the restoration. Franz's wife, Gertrude organized the kitchen and was soon preparing splendid Bavarian dishes with what food she could find. Ilsa found work in a factory that was reopening. Life started to feel normal for them, although the wreckage and destruction of war surrounded them. Ilsa's son Hans continued to be a challenge. He was constantly in fights and had been caught on several occasions stealing food and items from stores. He ignored all warnings and rejected Josef's reprimands. It seemed Hans was an uncontrollable child. Ilsa worried and discussed her fears with Josef. Together they were unable to find a way to satisfy Hans and pacify his continual rebellious spirit.

As the rooms of the home were completed, Josef returned to Switzerland to arrange for the return of his valuable artwork. There were contemporary paintings and some work by the masters. It was an extensive and expensive collection. When the arrangements were completed Josef scheduled an appointment with his Swiss Bankers the next day. He had transferred his vast fortune from Germany in 1938 and the securities he owned in various companies. At the meeting he arranged for the withdrawal of significant funds for the completion of the work on his home and to allow him to start up his business again.

It was in the autumn of 1947 when the majority of the work was completed on the home. Josef, Franz, Gertrude and Ilsa had transformed the home and their relationship into one of a family. Almost weekly they despaired as Hans continued to create problems.

It was late in October when Hans was escorted home by two US Military Police. He had been caught stealing liquor from the US PAX store. This was a serious offence. The policing by the occupation forces called for imprisonment of anyone caught stealing or looting. Ilsa was distraught. Josef sat in with her and the Military Police to discuss Hans and try to arrive at a solution. Josef had an idea. He asked the Military Police to excuse them while he spoke with Ilsa.

"Ilsa this situation cannot be easily controlled by us. The city is still a shambles. There are many who are taking advantage. Hans is exposed to this and probably associating with these criminals. He is crafty and old before his time. He has seen and experienced some horrible situations. I feel he is young enough that he can be corrected. The situation here will not provide for that. He sees the chaos that has been created by the war and has no structure or morals regarding how people have treated each other. I do have an idea but you will need to be the one to make the decision. I can only offer this but it will be up to you as his mother."

"Josef I am unable to find any way to control him. If you have something that might work I would be happy to consider it. Please tell me. Do not be offended as I fear there is really very little more I can do and he will grow into a nasty and horrible person."

"Ilsa I have friends in Britain. I propose we contact them. I will ask them to assist in having him placed into a strict Boarding School. It will not be a particularly pleasant time at the beginning. I imagine that Hans will rebel. The school is well equipped to handle such behavior."

"Josef I like your suggestion. I am afraid it is not possible. The cost of sending him to England and the school costs are far beyond my financial means."

"Ilsa I will pay these costs. You have done a lot here. I am sympathetic for the suffering you have experienced. Will you allow this?"

"I am not comfortable to accept your money. Maybe it would be a lesson for him if he was incarcerated by the military."

"I fear that would only cause him to rebel even further and maybe run off. No, that is not an option."

They sat in silence for several minutes.

"Josef you are a good man. Yes, I will agree. Let us return to the Military Police and advise them of our solution."

They returned to find the two officers waiting for them. Josef explained the plan and decision. After some discussion it was agreed that the Police would release Hans to them. The Military Police set a condition. The travel documents and enrollment confirmation needed to be provided to them within the next two weeks. Josef agreed.

"Josef there is no way that I can repay you for this. Hans is such a disappointment to me, yet, there are days when he is the sweetest person. I sense he experiences a great conflict in his life."

That comment caused Josef to stop and think. He thought back to the time he had spent with his nephew Jakob. He too had been conflicted. He shrugged off the thought and yet something nagged at him. There had been days when he saw a likeness of Jakob in Hans features. He recalled Jakob leaving for Hamburg and wondered what had become of him. He resolved that he would write to the Elders of the Mennonite church in Canada and find out what had happened tom Jakob.

"Ilsa, do you know who Hans' father is or what became of him?"

"No, we had arranged to talk about the pregnancy and the future but he disappeared. I was told he left on a German ship headed for the United States. I know no more than that. For weeks I debated having an abortion. Now I think that would have been best. The war has resulted in the loss of my friends and family and the destruction of my home. It has all been too much. There have been times when I contemplated suicide. Had it not been for Hans I would have killed myself."

Chapter 162

Throughout the next day, Josef reflected upon his conversation with Ilsa. He had decided to contact Dr. Bernard J. Walsh whom he had met and befriended during the war years he was London. Dr. Walsh had gone to London from his home country of New Zealand to continue his studies into child behavior. Josef and Bernard had become good friends during that time. They had discussed many things including Bernard's studies into the area of delinquency and crime. He recalled Bernard's arguments that in some cases the behavior was a result of a medical condition, whereas in others it was a mental situation often developed over time as a result of exposure to the constant struggle and negative events in life. Josef wondered which category Hans would be considered.

That evening Josef stopped Ilsa as she returned to the house with a small bag of rationed goods.

"Ilsa, when you are able, please join me in my study. There are things I need to speak to you about."

Ilsa sensed a certain formality. She immediately assumed that something serious had happened.

"I can come now."

"No. Finish what you are doing and then come and join me."

Josef went to his newly rebuilt study and seated himself on the large leather couch he had recently found. It was not long before there was a knock at the door and Ilsa entered. Josef motioned to a chair near the sofa.

"Herr Klassen is something wrong?" Ilsa was distraught and nervous. She withdrew a cloth that she had fashioned into a handkerchief from her dress and dabbed at her eyes.

"Ilsa please be calm. I am about to write to Dr. Walsh. I will be asking him to accept Hans as a boarding pupil. There are things I know he will ask. I do not have the information I will need to provide him. He is a friend and the Vice Principal of the County Kildare Reform School for Boys in Ireland. He is well respected and acknowledged as an expert in assisting reform troubled boys. I believe he can help Hans. In order to explain the situation and background I must ask you some personal questions. You have now been here in my home for a long while. I have never asked for any explanations before, but now I must if I am to succeed in getting Hans accepted."

"I understand. Please ask the questions."

"Please tell me about Hamburg, what you did and also about Hans's father. Was he a soldier? Did he get killed in the war?"

"I am not proud of my past in Hamburg. In 1937 I moved from a small country village to Hamburg as I understood it would be easy to make money. I was employed as an office worker. The job was boring and did not pay well. I changed jobs and worked as a sales clerk in a clothing store. It too became boring. I was only 19 years old and one night went with friends to a club for drinks. During that night my friends and I were joined by some men who entertained us. One of the men said he owned another club and could set us up as hostesses where we could make money. It sounded good. I quit my job and accepted a job at a club that was not far from the shipyards. Soon my hostess role changed. I became a prostitute. I had many men. There were sailors, workers from the shipyards, travelling businessmen in Hamburg, government officials and lastly members of the Nazi Party. What hypocrites they were. It was in 1939 that I was introduced to Hans' father. We spent time together and yet I never found out his real name. He was a Canadian and had travelled to Germany from the Netherlands. He was in hiding and his papers were forged. We spoke of the future and had made plans to meet when I became pregnant. I never saw him again. I only know his first name was Jakob."

The mention of the name Jakob and the information hit Josef like a bolt of lightning. Now he was sure that the one Jakob Klassen was indeed Hans's

father. He pondered the situation and decided against revealing this to Ilsa. He needed to find out more regarding Jakob. He now understood that the disobedience and arrogance he had detected in Jakob had been passed on to the son.

"I came to Munich from Hamburg as I had heard that some factories would open and there would be work. Now that you know my past I will leave your house. You are a fine man and I do not wish to bring you disrespect."

"Ilsa I am sorry to ask you these questions and drag you back into that past. I do not wish for you to leave. These last years have caused many to do shameful things. You are welcome to stay. Besides I enjoy your company. I will write to Dr. Walsh if you permit. I will do this tonight."

"Yes please write to him. Now that you know my background will you tell Hans or the others? I will be deeply ashamed."

"No. That is private and confidential between us. Now please leave me to compose the letter."

Josef sat to pen his letter.

Dr.Bernard J. Walsh

Vice Principal

County Kildare Reform School for Boys

Leinster, Ireland

Dear Bernard,

I hope this letter finds you well and in good health. I have returned to Munich, Germany to assist in the reconstruction effort after that horrible war. I have been busy reopening one of my factories and assisting the occupying forces. I will be travelling to London in the near future and hope we can meet. This time I will pay for the beers. Coming from New Zealand I know how much you appreciate a good beer. Now to a serious matter

I have living in my home a young lady who has suffered terribly during the war. I found her and her two friends sheltering in my home. They had no other place to go. I took pity on them and they have been great company and helped in restoring my home from the damage it suffered. She was working in Hamburg at the outbreak of war. She has an almost 10year old boy. His father ran away when he found out she was pregnant. The boy has grown up on the streets and witnessed to destruction and inhumanity of war. I fear that this has affected him tremendously. He is a very difficult child. He is negative, defiant, disobedient and hostile to those in any authority. There are days when he seems perfectly normal and can be quite charming.

I am writing to see if you will accept this boy at your school. You will be doing me a personal favor. I will be responsible to all expenses associated with this.

I look forward to hearing from you

Yours Truly

Josef Klassen

Josef reread the letter several times before folding it carefully and putting it into an envelope engraved with his company's logo and address. He addressed the letter to Bernard and marked it Private and Confidential.

With the task complete, Josef poured himself a large scotch and sat to contemplate the information he had recently learned about Hans and Jakob. Was it really possible that Hans was Jakob's son. It seemed too coincidental. Why had Franz, Gertrude and Ilsa ended up in his home? Josef sipped at the Scotch. If what he believed was true then what should he do? The more he thought about the situation, the more questions he had.

It was too late to write an intelligent letter to the Elders of the Mennonite Church in Canada where Jakob had been a member. Josef had kept the addresses for Jakob's farm and the Church in safekeeping.

Tomorrow he would write.

Chapter 163

Several weeks passed by before Josef received replies to his letters. He opened the manila envelope which had the County Kildare School address printed boldly on the front upper left corner. He read it quickly. Dr. Walsh had accepted his request to accept Hans at the school. In the letter Dr. Walsh requested more information pertaining to Hans. Josef decided he would leave his office early that afternoon and take the letter to Ilsa. She would need to provide the information.

The second letter was in a plain white envelope. Josef's name and address were handwritten and the envelope had a Dominion of Canada stamp attached. Josef slit the letter open and read it with great interest.

Dear Josef Klassen,

Thank you for your recent correspondence. We have very little information to share with you regarding our former church member, Jakob Klassen. We received a letter from Jakob some while ago requesting assistance in the sale of one of his farms. His wife has been killed in the war. Jakob inherited his neighbors farm and has leased it to a family here who are working the land.

Jakob has settled in Aruba in the Dutch West Indies. He is no longer a practicing member of our faith. In his letter to us he has advised that he will stay in Aruba and has started a business. The only address we have for Jakob is

Poste Restante

San Nicolaas

Aruba,

The Dutch West Indies.

We are providing this information to you since you are a family member. Beyond this we have no further information to provide you. I hope this assists you in finding Jakob

Yours with blessings

Pastor Ludwig Friensland

Josef read the letter through again and then filed it with his personal documents in the large grey filing cabinet behind his office desk.

It was mid afternoon and a pleasant day. Josef decided to walk back to his home. He gathered up some papers that he would work on later that night. He told his small staff he was leaving until the following morning.

Josef started his long walk back. He began to regret his decision to walk as he passed by the bombed ruins of some of Munich's historical and magnificent buildings. Many were reduced to piles of brick and timbers. There were many poorly dressed workers hauling away debris and loading it onto trucks. A sense of despair seemed to hang over each of the destroyed buildings. The air was filled with dust that blew in the winds that swirled around the ruins. Josef was approached by men, children and women begging for money or food. He was depressed by all the destruction around him. As he walked on he wondered how it was possible to rebuild Munich to its former grandeur.

Josef reached his home in the early evening. He walked up the front stairs and into his study. He called out to Ilsa to join him. Ilsa ran to his study. He took the letter from Dr. Walsh and handed it to her. Ilsa looked at Josef in bewilderment. Josef then became aware that Ilsa could not read English. He sat her down and read the letter to her, interpreting some of it into German. When he had finished, Ilsa jumped up and hugged him.

"Ilsa, we must prepare now to send Hans to Ireland. I suggest we do not tell him of this yet. We will wait until he has one of his calm periods. It is important that we make it so he will want to go. It must be presented to him as an adventure with new friends, a different country and things to learn."

"Yes I agree. We must make it exciting for him. When will he leave and how long will he be gone?"

"Dr.Walsh wants him to stay a full year at a time. I respect his recommendation. He is an expert and we must take his advice."

Josef and Ilsa spent hours talking and planning to send Hans to the reform School.

Chapter 164

Josef was encouraged. Hans temper fits had become less frequent and his attitude toward Ilsa and others seemed more subdued. Josef sensed that this was the ideal time to tell Hans of the plans for his upcoming trip and schooling. Josef left his study and found Hans playing with a model plane.

"Hans can you do something for me?"

Hans looked up and was eager to find out what task Josef had in store for him.

"I need some letters to be mailed urgently. Can you take them and do this please."

Hans jumped at the opportunity to get away from the house and out into the streets. He hoped he would meet some of his friends. As soon as he departed, Josef looked for Ilsa and found her tending to some plants she had grown in the yard.

"Ilsa come back inside. I need to speak with you."

Ilsa laid down her gardening tools and went inside. She fetched herself a large glass of water before joining Josef.

"Ilsa it is time to tell Hans of the plans. He has been very calm and I believe now is the best time. I have sent him on an errand. He should return shortly. I suggest we sit down with him then and tell him of the adventure ahead. We must tell him in a way that will excite him. You must start the talk. I have some ideas that I think will excite him, but you must start. Hans must think that this is your idea."

Almost an hour went by before Hans returned. He was in a cheerful mood and skipped his way through the house and into the kitchen.

"Hans" Ilsa called. "Please come to me. I have some big news for you."

Curious, Hans ran to his mother. Ilsa tousled his fair hair. She felt guilty knowing what lay ahead. She told Hans to take a place at the table and she placed a glass of juice in front of him. As she was getting herself a coffee, Josef arrived in the room.

"Hans did you mail my letters?"

Hans nodded. He was starting to become impatient. "What is the news? I want to know. Is it good news? Am I going to get something new?"

Ilsa looked at Josef. "Josef, why don't you stay and join us. I am about to tell Hans some great news. I know you will have some things to say as well." At this comment, Hans frowned and looked at Josef. It was not a good look.

"Hans, Josef and I have been able to enroll you for schooling. You will be going on a long trip to Ireland. Josef knows the man who runs the school and he has agreed to accept you. It will be fun. You will be in a safe country that has not been torn apart in the war. You will eat good foods and meet new friends. It will all be new. You will learn a new language and see many things."

Hans looked from Ilsa to Josef and back. "I don't want to go anywhere. I am staying here. I don't need to go to any stupid school."

Josef raised his hand up off the table. "Hans it will be an adventure. You will travel on a plane, take a train and also cross the English Channel in a large ship. Together we will make these plans. You will help and we will go and get the tickets together. You will be able to choose the ship. It will be fun. You will have a real adventure to tell the other boys about."

Hans thought about this. After several minutes many questions flowed from him. Josef told him of Dr. Bernard Walsh and his friendship with him. He described the school and what he knew about Ireland. Hans started to become excited. Josef looked over at Ilsa and smiled.

"Hans join me in my study. We will look at some brochures and start the plans."

Hans went with Josef. They spent hours with maps and brochures planning the "adventure".

Chapter 165

San Nicolaas, Aruba

At the Stella Maris Club, Solange and Jakob dined on a meal of freshly caught fish. When finished they walked out of the club. Solange looped her arm through Jakobs.

"Jakob you look tired and worried. I want to you come and stay with me tonight. In the morning you can go to your apartment. There are more things I want to learn from you."

She smiled as she looked into Jakob's hazel eyes. The night was young and there were indeed many things she wanted to learn.

"I will walk you to your home. Maybe I will join you for a drink, but then I must go home."

"I would like that. I have some fine imported wines from France at my house. We will be alone and quiet. That will be different. At the office we are always surrounded by people and being asked questions. I like the club but it is busy and again we do not have time to ourselves. I am looking forward to spending time alone with you."

They walked through the town. The warm evening air gently caressed them. The night seemed extraordinarily quiet, even the girls who worked the streets were absent. Jakob found it a strange night.

They arrived at the small Cunucu that Solange had rented. There was a fenced yard at the front with a sparse growth of grass. Near the gate was a tall Bonairean plant with a profuse display of white blooms. The path to the front door was lined with flowering Bougainvillea.

Solange opened the unlocked door and walked in leading Jakob by his hand. She turned on a dimly lit lamp in the front room and went to get some wine and glasses. Jakob sat on a large plum colored couch. Solange returned and sat close beside him. She placed the glasses on the low table and poured the wine. She took a glass and handed it to Jakob and then raised hers in a toast.

"I toast to us Jakob and to our plans. We shall succeed and build that dream of yours."

She moved closer to Jakob and he felt her breasts pressing against his arm. He looked directly at her. She seemed to be distant. He moved to the end of the couch and immediately felt some relief. Solange followed his every movement. She dropped her head onto his lap. Jakob pushed her back and attempted to stand. Solange reached up and grabbed his belt and pulled him back. She placed her hand into the front of his trousers. Jakob was becoming aroused. Solange sat up and started to unbutton the neck of the white blouse she was wearing exposing her feminine beauty. Jakob placed his hand on hers.

"Solange. Tomorrow we must work together. I cannot continue with this. It is not right."

"Jakob you are a fool. Don't you see that I want this to happen with you.. I want you for everything. It is not just tonight. I want to make love but I also want to develop a love with you and one day we will live together. You intrigue me. I want to hear of your life and the times you have had."

Jakob lay back on the couch and wondered at Solange's sudden outburst. As he lay back Solange tore off her blouse and crawled on top of him.

The lovemaking was furious. Solange was insatiable. Jakob had never experienced a woman so passionate. He wondered how this was possible.

They collapsed together and fell into a deep sleep. Jakob was awakened by shouting outside on the street. Quietly and gently he arose. He looked through the window and saw two drunken soldiers stumbling along the road.

Jakob felt refreshed and alive. He decided to leave and return to his apartment. He would return to the office tomorrow and face Solange .

Jakob dressed and left the house for his walk home.

Chapter 166

The relationship between Jakob and Solange grew quickly and within months they married. Within a year Solange presented Jakob with a son. Jakob decided to name the boy after his father, Isaac. Shortly after the birth of Isaac Junior, Catherine, the mother of Solange passed away. Solange inherited the vast wealth and control of the family companies.

Jakob buried himself in the affairs of the company and was respected in the community and seen as a visionary. The plans for developing a tourist industry yielded encouraging results. The hotels were constantly booked. Jakob worked feverishly for 6 days of each week. On Sundays he religiously devoted to time with Isaac Junior. He would take Isaac Junior to the beach or go fishing with him in the nearby Spaans Lagoon.

As Isaac Junior grew, he exhibited many of the same fine attributes that Jakob had displayed as a young boy. Isaac Junior excelled at school. He had a particular way of solving problems and was extremely well liked by the other children. It seemed impossible to Solange that he could know and remember all his friends and their likes and dislikes.

As the years passed, Jakob oversaw the acquisition of more land for the company's development plans. Isaac Junior started to display an interest in the company and worked on small tasks in the afternoons after school. At age 18, Isaac Junior took a full time role in managing projects. He was smart and structured deals that were both fair and profitable. Jakob confided in Isaac Junior on the deals and partnerships that were often presented to him. There was one occasion that Jakob was particularly proud of. A group of Venezuelan investors had approached Jakob with an offer to buy some land that the company owned. They wished to build an entertainment complex with a casino. The proposal was sound but the land they wanted was already set aside for the building of another hotel. The offer to purchase the land was excellent and the financial return would have been huge. Jakob and Solange were in a quandary. It was an offer that was too good to walk away from. Finally, Isaac Junior came up with a solution.

"Jakob instead of selling all the land, why not take a lesser amount of money and become a partner with them. The company will still make money on the land sale and will have a new interest in the casino. With the tourism business growing a casino makes sense for the Island. Look at Cuba and the impact that casinos have had on their tourism. Now that Fidel Castro has seized control, the tourism and casino business there is uncertain. We can offer the American tourists an alternative."

Jakob and Solange prepared a counter proposal to the investors. There were meetings yet no decision was made. The investors requested time to speak with others in their group. Weeks later they returned to the Island and agreed to the proposed deal with some minor changes.

Construction began within months. The hotel with its vast entertainment venue and the sparkling new casino were heavily promoted in Miami and New York. Headline entertainers were hired. Aruba was starting its serious effort to become a Caribbean tourist destination.

Jakob and Solange hired in trusted manager to operate the companies. They wished to spend more time pursuing other interests in life. Together they had decided that the control would soon be passed to Isaac Junior. He had continually demonstrated keen business acumen. Jakob was a little concerned. He saw in Isaac Junior some of the same character traits that he had possessed as a boy. Jakob hoped he would not falter and make the same mistakes in life that he had.

Chapter 167

Munich, Germany. 1956.

Hans returned from his schooling in Ireland. While he was not an outstanding student he did well. His grades were above average and he dominated in certain sports, including football. The School had an arrangement with a marina on a lake not far from the grounds. Hans showed strong interest in sailing and proved to be a force to be reckoned with in sailing competitions. Hans took every opportunity to be involved with anything related to the sailing program.

It was with some regret that he returned to Munich. Every Christmas Hans had returned. Upon his final return he found that much of the city had been restored. He found work at a local construction company. The job boring and again he started to rebel against the supervisors. Within six months on the job, Hans was fired.

Josef was aging and no longer as active as he wished. His legs had become weak and often he could not stand without help. He cursed his body for letting him down. Josef had thought about trying to teach Hans the business. He had some severe reservations. While Hans had matured at the reform school, Josef still had some serious concerns. On several occasions he had observed Hans associating with some youths who already had criminal records. Hans started to spend large amounts of cash. Josef had no idea where this money came from and upon confronting Hans he was threatened with a beating. Josef resigned himself to the fact that Hans would never fully change.

The autumn arrived with a blast of cold air and snow. Josef found himself restricted to the house. He was irritable. He missed the days when he could visit friends at the parks and drink coffees in the intimate cafes.

Ilsa had stayed with Josef and assisted to run the house. Josef was happy with this arrangement. They had remained friends with no romantic attachment. Franz and Gertrude had moved into a house not far from Josef's. Franz had started a carpentry business and had more work than he could handle. Gertrude ran the administration of the business. They had two daughters whom they admired.

The winter months arrived and Josef's health continued to deteriorate. The end came quickly and quietly.

Ilsa had prepared the normal breakfast of sausage, egg, toast and coffee. She retrieved the morning newspaper and waited in the kitchen. Josef had been late in the past but this morning was the latest he had ever come down for his breakfast and read of the paper. Ilsa climbed the stairs to his room and knocked at his door.

"Josef are you awake? Are you alright?"

There was no reply. Ilsa edged the door open and found Josef lying in a crumpled manner beside his bed. She ran to him and touched him. His body was cold. Josef was dead. Ilsa started to sob and ran back down the stairs. She called for Hans. He did not respond. She quickly threw on a coat and boots and ran out onto the street. A uniformed police officer stood under the awning of the local grocery store sheltering from the blowing snow. Ilsa ran up to him.

"Sir, Herr Josef Klassen has died. Come with me I need help. He is in his home. He has fallen from his bed. I don't know what to do."

The police officer followed Ilsa back to the house. He viewed the situation and after covering Josef's body with a sheet he left to get assistance.

Later that morning Josef's body was removed. Ilsa contacted the law firm who dealt with Josef's affairs. The senior partner of the firm expressed his regrets and advised Ilsa he would stop at the house to pay his respects.

The news of Josef's passing spread. A steady stream of people came by the house offering help and condolences. In the afternoon the lawyer arrived. He was dressed in a black suit and carried a small folded over briefcase. He expressed sympathy to Ilsa but also told her he had an envelope addressed to her that Josef had entrusted to him. When all the other mourners had left when he handed the envelope to Ilsa.

Chapter 168

Ilsa stood alone with the lawyer. The house was empty of the visitors who had come to pay their respects. Ilsa asked the lawyer to join her in the living room while she read the contents of the letter. As they sat in silence, Ilsa started to read the letter. It was a brief note to which there were sheets of legal documents attached.

"I do not understand all of this paper. What do these documents say?"

"The note that is handwritten was prepared by Josef just a few weeks ago. He has left the house, the art collection and the vast investments in Switzerland to you. The companies are to be sold and the proceeds of the sales are to be directed to his nephew, Jakob who he had found in the Caribbean. You are a very rich woman, Ilsa. The attached legal papers are the formal documents that must be executed for the inheritances. I will leave them here and when you are ready you can visit at our offices and my partners and I will ensure all is done correctly. Josef was both a client and a good friend for many years. I will miss him. He taught me things that I will never forget. He never forgave Hitler and remained despondent over the destruction that the war brought on Germany."

Ilsa was in shock. She had not expected this. She was an emotional mess. Her benefactor and the guide in life was now gone. She was nervous at the thought of the immense amount of money and the responsibility she now had. Why had Josef never discussed this with her?

"Today has been a hard day. I will need some time to think about this. I have many things to prepare ahead of the funeral services for Josef. I will contact you about this in the coming weeks."

"Ilsa you will not need to take on the arduous tasks of preparing the funeral."

The lawyer reached back into the briefcase and took out another letter which he also handed to her.

Ilsa read the note

Dear Ilsa,

You will be reading this after I have passed. I thank you for all you did for me. You have been kind and understanding. I could not have rebuilt my home, businesses and life if you had not been there to support me. As a small appreciation I have left my fortune to you. In addition I have set up a trust fund for Hans. The fund will be administered by the law firm. Hans is not to have the money directly and there are stipulations regarding the use of the money.

For my funeral I have already made the arrangements. My trusted legal advisors have all the instructions. They are responsible for the matters to be performed.

Goodbye my true and loyal friend

Josef A Klassen

Ilsa dropped her hand containing the note to her lap. She sobbed heavily and tears splashed down her blouse leaving large wet areas. The lawyer went across to her and held her. It was apparent to the lawyer how deep the bond between Ilsa and Josef had been. He wondered why they had never married. He assumed that Hans was the problem. He asked if there was anyone that could spend the night and next day with her. The only friends she thought would assist her at this difficult time were Franz and Gertrude. She gave the lawyer their address.

"I will contact them immediately. Here is my card. I have a telephone at my home. I have written the number on the back of my card. If you need any help please call me. It will be my pleasure to help with any of Josef's matters. He spoke fondly of you. I am here to help you."

Several hours passed. There was a knock and Franz and Gertrude pushed through the front door. Gertrude ran to Ilsa and embraced her. The two women sobbed and recalled how their lives had been enhanced by Josef.

They all sat that evening recalling the good that Josef had done for them.

Chapter 169

The funeral was held in the rebuilt Church of Our Lady, an iconic presence in Munich and famed for its two dome-topped brick towers. Construction of the cathedral began in the latter part of the 15th century and had been finally completed some 20 years later. The cathedral had almost been destroyed in the bombings of World War II. In attendance at the funeral were politicians, business leaders, representatives from the charities that Josef had supported and some military members who had worked with Jakob in the reconstruction efforts for Germany.

Ilsa, Franz and Gertrude sat in the front pew. The service was conducted with dignity and ceremony. It was only now that Ilsa realised the huge impact that Josef had upon the community. The service was complete and the funeral procession to Bogenhausen Cemetery left the church. Many followed for the burial service.

Ilsa watched in despair as Hans stood at the stairs to the church entrance. He drew long on a cigarette before flicking it onto the church stairs and smothering it with his black boot. Unlike the other mourners, Hans had not dressed for the funeral. He wore an old tan coat, worn trousers and an open neck blue shirt. He stood in contrast to the others in their more somber attire. At that moment she realised the burden he had been to Josef and the attention and help that Josef had given. Hans glared over at Ilsa and turned away. She watched him walk from the church. He met with a small group of youths. A young girl wrapped her arms around him. Laughter broke out from the youths as they started walking away from the church and the cars gathered for the trip to the cemetery. Ilsa was sad. As she continued to watch, Hans turned his head back toward the church and spat on the ground. Ilsa started to cry again. Franz was with her and witnessed the behavior of Hans.

"Ilsa, he will never amount to much. He is scarred from all the violence and destruction he has witnessed. Do not blame yourself for his actions."

The mood was decidedly depressed and intensified by the dark grey clouds and winds.

Franz assisted Ilsa and Gertrude to the lead car behind the hearse. The procession wound its way through the streets of Munich to the graveyard. At the graveyard the pallbearers slid the mahogany casket with imposing silver handles from the hearse. As the casket was removed, a Bishop blessed it. The pallbearers took the casket to the fresh;ly dug grave where it was slowly lowered into the ground. The Bishop loudly recited Psalm 23 and several amongst the gathered joined him. The service was brief.

After the service, many returned to Josef's house where a reception was to be held to celebrate the life Joseph had lead and remember his contributions to the life of many.

Upon arriving back at the house Ilsa was shocked to find Hans in Josef's study. The youths she had seen him with at the church were sprawled out on the couch and chairs. Open bottles of beer littered the desk. The air was filled with smoke and the pungent smell of marijuana. Franz bristled. He went to Hans and snatched the cigarette from his mouth. Franz was a powerful man. His carpentry work kept him fit and strong. He grabbed Hans arm and twisted it behind his back. He frog marched Hans to the front door and threw him down the steps. He slammed the door and returned to deal with the others in the study. He need not have bothered that had grabbed coats and bags and were heading for the door.

Franz temper remained high. He excused himself and discreetly let himself out into the back garden. He sat and composed himself before returning into the house. He would speak with Ilsa about Hans in the coming days. Today was not the day.

Chapter 170

Oranjestad, Aruba. 1965

Isaac Junior had done well in managing and growing the company. He had decided that the company needed to invest in businesses other than tourism. He and Jakob would sit for hours exploring new possibilities. Jakob was convinced that there was a need for tourist activities. He strongly believed that the tourists would grow bored with just the beaches. After many discussions, Jakob convinced Isaac Junior that the company should establish an operation that took tourists out sailing and fishing. Initially Isaac Junior was not convinced. He wanted to make the hotels' restaurant larger and more sophisticated. Jakob agreed and a compromise was arrived at. Before proceeding though they wanted to obtain opinions from Solange.

Solange had missed the restaurants of Miami since her arrival in Aruba so was partial to Isaac Junior's plan. She talked of building a restaurant that would be over the water. Jakob thought this would be a wonderful venture and embraced it wholeheartedly. Solange was skeptical of the sailing operation. She suggested they start a small operation and monitor it closely. No one in the company had sailing experience or that of running a water sports company. They agreed on both ventures and targeted to have them in business before the end of the year.

Solange was excited with the prospect of building a first class restaurant in Aruba. When she had lived in Miami, Solange had enjoyed conducting business and casual dining with friends in some of the top rated restaurants. She convinced Jakob to agree for Isaac Junior and her to fly to Miami and meet with architects to start the design. This project had reinvigorated her. She loved Isaac Junior deeply and was highly supportive of his project.

Jakob was intrigued as he researched the starting of a water sports company. He had received information to his many inquiries looking for yachts and boats that would be suitable. Jakob visited with government officials and presented his ideas. He needed a location and a pier from which the company could operate. He soon became frustrated at the slow progress and indecision of the officials. For months Jakob visited the offices and each time received excuses and reasons for the delays. The project seemed destined for failure.

Solange and Isaac Junior returned from Miami excited and accompanied by the architect they had chosen to design the restaurant. They all arrived at the home and found Jakob fuming after a frustrating day dealing with the officials.

"Jakob you will not solve this by getting angry. You will lose your focus and not think clearly. Leave it alone for a few days and then we can all look at the project."

"Solange I have found the ideal boats in Colombia. The price is excellent. I wish to move quickly and purchase these boats. I will need to go to Colombia and take someone who is knowledgeable to inspect the craft."

Solange had grown to know and understand Jakob's moods. She placed her hand on his forehead and spoke softly to him.

"Jakob things will wait. It is important that you assist with other aspects of our business. I have brought the architect from Miami. I want you to spend time with him and Isaac Junior to review the restaurant plans. Let us get this done and then we can address the situation with the boats."

Jakob smiled. As usual Solange had a way of diffusing the frustration when dealing with difficult situations. He loved her so much and wondered what his life would be without her. He thanked his Lord for bringing them together.

"Solange you are right. I have been working too much on this. I need a distraction and something new. I am sure the restaurant project will help me to approach this differently."

Solange and Isaac Junior introduced the tall lanky architect to Jakob.

"I am pleased to make your acquaintance. I have heard many great things about how you have built a tourism empire here. It must not have been easy. My name is Clyde James. I am looking forward to working with you all to design and build a magnificent restaurant here."

Solange sent for her house servant and ordered drinks and light food for them all. They sat and talked for hours. Clyde spoke of the many projects he had designed. Jakob and Solange spoke of the business in Aruba and the difficulties involved in starting them.

"Clyde, for months I have been trying to get the approval of the officials to allow me to build a pier for the planned water sports company we wish to start. They have delayed and not given any real reasons. I cannot understand why this is the situation. In the past they have always cooperated with us."

Clyde sat back and sunk into the cushions of the oversize couch. He stayed quiet for several minutes and then stood and went to his large art folder. He unzipped the folder and removed some early designs he had prepared for the over water restaurant. He laid them on the floor in front of him and studied them.

"I have an idea for you. It would be possible to include an area to the side of the restaurant where you could dock and operate your boats. It would be basic and it would not interfere with the pedestrian traffic or operations of the restaurant. Here is what I am thinking"

Clyde took a pencil from inside his jacket and roughly sketched an area in front of the entrance walkway. He drew a side extension and placed a moored boat beside it. Jakob was dumbfounded. He was delighted.

"Yes. The officials have already approved this project. I am sure we can convince them to allow this when we show them the plans. Clyde you have solved my dilemma."

Solange and Isaac Junior watched the interaction with both apprehension and then relief. Jakob arose and went to pour them all a drink.

"This calls for our best Champagne."

Chapter 171

Munich, Germany. 1965

Life had changed for Ilsa since the death of Josef. Instead of worrying about chores around the house, she found herself replying to social invitations and dealing with Josef's lawyers on financial matters.

Franz and Gertrude remained steadfast friends. At times Ilsa believed they were the only ones who listened and confided with her. It was late one evening when Franz and Gertrude visited. It was a warm summer night. Ilsa invited them to sit in the garden she had meticulously designed and decorated. The sweet scent of honeysuckle drifted in the evening air. Crickets chirped and the sounds of the city were muted by the growth in her garden.

"Ilsa it has been a while since Josef passed. We remain very concerned about Hans. He is still a very deeply disturbed young man. He has been in trouble with the law here. I fear he will become more involved with the gangs he is associating with. He is headed toward a terrible situation. Those friends of his are no good. Gertrude and I are worried for you and Hans. Do you have any ideas on how we can reach out and stop him before it is too late?"

Ilsa looked down at the ground in embarrassment.

"Franz, while the lawyers and I were sorting through Josef's papers we found some things that Josef had hidden. There were letters that he had concealed from us. They dealt with Hans and his natural father. Josef had found him and written to him about Hans. Hans's father is Jakob Klassen. He is living in the Caribbean on the Dutch West Indies Island of Aruba. He is married with a son and is a successful businessman. In the letters, Josef had pleaded for Jakob to contact his son and try to provide him with some purpose in life. Jakob has steadfastly refused. Josef had told Jakob of the trouble that Hans had caused and the problems with disciplining him. Jakob had written back and refused. Jakob had built his own life and did not want the burden of a delinquent son to deal with at his age."

Franz and Gertrude were shocked at these revelations.

"Ilsa it must be the responsibility of Jakob to help. This is his flesh and blood. Surely he must have some conscience. He left you with this child. You have had to look after Hans and care for both yourselves during the war years. He must owe you some help. It is wrong."

Gertrude, who was generally quiet, spoke. "Ilsa does Hans know about his father and where he is living?"

"No. The lawyers are unsure how to proceed. For all the problems that Hans created, Josef still left an inheritance to him. He was restricted and could not withdraw monies until he was thirty years old. He is thirty and has already withdrawn a significant amount from the inheritance. He has bought imported sport cars and spent money on many girls, many of whom I suspect are criminals. He was arrested on suspicion of financing a large drug dealing operation. I cannot control him. If I speak to him he threatens me. I am scared of him."

The three sat around the cedar table in silence. Ilsa poured them all some wine which they sipped as they thought about Hans and the new information. There was a scratching at the rear gate near the garage. Hans entered with a beautiful young woman. He proceeded directly to the table where they all sat.

"Ilsa, Franz and Gertrude, I wish to introduce you to my friend and hopefully in the future, my wife. This is Greetje. She is from Holland. I have known her for many months. We have become good friends and lovers. I intend to live my life with her."

Ilsa and her friends were shocked. Greetje went to each of them and shook hands. She was not the type of girl they expected Hans to associate with or bring home.

"Grettje, what do you do here in Munich?" asked Franz.

"I am here with the hospital. My training is in helping children who have suffered serious traumatic injuries. It is a job I love but it certainly presents me with many thoughts I find hard to handle."

"Please. Sit with us. Maybe Hans can join us as well." Ilsa was optimistic.

Greetje took a seat beside Ilsa. Hans had gone into the house and returned with a large beer stein in his hand. Franz reached across the table and took Ilsa's hand to reassure her that this was acceptable and to stay quiet.

"Tonight I went with Hans to a play. He told me he has never seen a play before and only saw school plays during his time in Ireland. We both liked the play and hope to go again to another one."

Hans shuffled in beside Greetje. Ilsa watched Hans closely. She saw the same emotions and behavior that Hans displayed as a boy. He was courteous and considerate of Greetje. Ilsa decided that this was a good thing and should be encouraged.

"I will ask Hans, but on Saturday night we are preparing a large traditional Bavarian dinner. Maybe Hans will invite you. We would like you to join us."

Greetje looked at Hans.

"I would like to accept but first Hans must invite me."

They all roared laughing, Hans included.

"Yes my dear Greetje you must come. It has been a long time since I enjoyed an event at home."

They engaged in small talk and around mid night Franz and Gertrude excused themselves to return to their home. As they were leaving, Gertrude spoke to Ilsa.

"I think she is a lovely girl. She is unlike what I expected Hans to want. Let us hope that she can tame and calm his monsters."

Ilsa closed the door and went to return to the garden. As she opened the door she saw Greetje and Hans embraced in a long kiss. She quietly withdrew back into the house. After a few minutes she again opened the door to the garden. She looked at the pair and saw a look on Han's face that she had not seen in years. Ilsa was happy. She would go to bed happy this night knowing that Hans had established a love with someone whom could possibly help him.

Chapter 172

Ilsa was delighted with Hans' relationship with Greetje. She had noticed that Greetje had a calming influence on him. He was staying home more often and even offering to assist with tasks at the house. She wondered if Greetje was using any of the training she had received to assist those traumatically scarred children she treated. It seemed to Ilsa that in many ways, Hans was still a child. He had spent his inheritance to impress his "friends" and buy his way into the underworld where he participated in black-market activities of selling stolen food and items. Ilsa resolved that when the time was appropriate she would have a private talk with Greetje. She did not want to scare her away from Hans. She would need to handle this very carefully. It was her belief that Greetje could help Hans and hopefully stop him from continuing to make mistakes in his life. Even though he was now thirty, his actions were like those of an adolescent.

Months passed by and Greetje visited with Ilsa often. Ilsa decided it was time to tell her of Hans past and the problems he had.

"Greetje there is a sensitive matter for us to speak about. It is Hans. I do not wish to scare or criticize you in any way. I have reflected many times on whether we should even speak about these things but I feel I must as you are now heavily involved with my boy."

Greetje put down the mug of the hot cocoa she had made for them.

"I think I know what you are going to say. I will save you any embarrassment and I will start. I know that Hans has issues and has had some serious problems in the past. I have given him encouragement to pursue the things he loves. I fear he will soon become bored here in Munich and revert to his old ways. He has a passion for sailing but there is no sea close by. This seems to be the one thing he has spoken of consistently and has a passion for. I wish I could help him with this but I cannot. Hans has told me of his days at the school in Ireland and of the friends he had made there. I have asked him to contact them but he will not. I must admit to you that I have seen some recent signs that worry me. There have been occasions when we have been out that he has become violent in confrontations at night clubs and restaurants. I fear it is only time before he explodes. I have warned him that I will not tolerate that and if he continues I will leave him."

Ilsa was dumbfounded. She had no words. Finally she was able to collect her thoughts and speak.

"Greetje, it would be a sad day for both Hans and I if you need to end your friendship. I will miss you and our chats. You have become a good friend to me and part of my family along with Franz and Gertrude. I do understand. It worries me what Hans will do and I worry about your safety. He will not accept the rejection or loss."

"I am hoping that Hans will continue to be calm and then I will not need to leave him. I am not hopeful, however."

As Greetje was preparing to leave Ilsa to start her evening shift at the Hospital, Hans arrived home. He was in a rage. His face was cut and his lips puffy and bleeding. He had been in a fight. He slammed the door shut and shouted at Ilsa and Greetje that it was none of their business and to leave him alone. Greetje looked at

Ilsa and together they knew that the romance between Hans and Greetje was over.

Chapter 173

The breakup with Greetje was acrimonious. Hans made serious threats including one to kill her so no one else could have her. He flew into frequent rages, smashing furniture and throwing kitchen utensils. He was involved in street brawls. The crisis was mounting. In desperation, Ilsa reached out to the lawyer who had dealt with Josef's estate and who had overseen the disbursement of the inheritance to Hans. They arranged a meeting at the law offices.

When Ilsa attended, there were two other lawyers in attendance. They were introduced as solicitors who specialized in crime and domestic violence. They listened to Ilsa's account of Hans' behavior. One of the lawyers had obtained a copy of Hans' criminal record. He spoke crisply.

"From the pattern of Hans' actions it will only be a matter of time before he commits an offence so serious he will be jailed or killed in some gang related violence."

Different scenarios were explored. No one could find a solution or make a recommendation to stop the downward spiral Hans was in. All seemed lost until the senior lawyer who had dealt with Ilsa after Josef's death spoke. They all fell silent and listened to his ideas.

"Ilsa, you will recall that we found those letters between Josef and Jakob. While Jakob wanted nothing to do with Hans I feel it is time we write him and demand his assistance. We will detail the problems that Hans has had. I will also write to Dr. Bernard Walsh at the school in Ireland and request he write a report on Hans. I will enclose this report with the letter. I will be direct. It is the responsibility of the father to provide assistance and care. He is guilty of abandonment. While the period of 1938 and 1939 were difficult years when atrocious crimes were committed, I believe that we can initiate a legal proceeding against Jakob in Aruba, as it is part of The Netherlands. I will check and find what our options are. As I understand it, Jakob had become a very successful businessman with substantial assets. He will probably not want any litigation. I believe we may be able to accomplish something. I will contact the law firm in the Netherlands who we have done some work with. In the meantime, I will write a letter to Jakob Klassen to see whether he will now cooperate.

After more discussion, it was decided that a letter should be sent before taking any further action.

Chapter 174

Oranjestad, Aruba

Jakob went to the office early. He was working through some mundane papers when the secretary walked into his office and handed him an official looking envelope. He looked at it and saw it was from a Munich based law firm. Before opening the letter, Jakob took his favorite mug and went to get a coffee. He returned to his desk and relaxed back in his chair with the letter. He started to read the following

Horst, Horst and Weiner

Solicitors

99 Prannerstrasse

Munich

Dear Mr. Jakob Klassen,

We are the lawyers representing Fr.Ilsa Wolfe. She has requested us to contact regarding the following matter.

Fr.Ilsa Wolfe gave birth to a son, Hans while living in Hamburg, Germany in 1939. Fr. Ilsa Wolfe has sworn that she had an affair with you and later advised you of her pregnancy. She claims that you had agreed to visit with her to discuss this and make appropriate plans. This meeting did not materialize and Fr.Ilsa was left to fend for herself during the difficult years of the war. She worked the little work she could find and begged on the streets for money and food.

After the birth of Hans, Ilsa attempted to find you to no avail. With her dire situation she resorted to a life that was demeaning and dangerous.

Hans is now 30 years of age. Requests to you in the past for some financial assistance have gone ignored or been outright rejected. Hans is in serious need of assistance which we believe you can provide.

We are asking you to reconsider your position on this matter.

We have been instructed to immediately proceed with an action against you and any property you may own wholly or with others.

We, of course, would be pleased if litigation could be avoided.

I await your prompt response.

Govern yourself accordingly,

Herman Horst

Jakob sat the letter down and spun his chair around to look out over the Oranjestad harbor. There were ships anchored off the pier waiting to unload cargoes of fruit, food and goods. The area was busy for that time of morning. Jakob stood and decided to walk while he pondered the legal letter. He crossed over to the stalls where bananas, coconuts, mangoes and other fresh fruits were being sold by the local women in their brightly colored dresses. He bought a banana and sauntered off to the park near the river that flowed out to sea at the south end of Oranjestad. Upon arriving he took a seat on a bench that overlooked the river. Some local boys were playing with makeshift boats. If not for the letter, Jakob would have considered it a perfect morning.

Jakob reflected on his life. He had experienced many things and been fortunate to have achieved so much. He loved Solange and Isaac Junior more than anything material that he owned. He had never told Solange of some of his past indiscretions. He wondered how she would react now. Would she forgive him? It was over 30 years ago and he was young and reckless. He continued to think of the consequences. Would she leave him or leave herself after all this time? What would happen to the business successes they had built together?

He sighed. There was no other way but to tell Solange and Isaac Junior the truth.

Chapter 175

Jakob began his walk back to his office. He was not looking forward to facing the day ahead. He barely acknowledged the waves and greetings that were called to him. Already the day was hot. Jakob felt the need for a strong drink. He continued his walk away from the office building to an old rum shop. It was open at this early hour. As he entered he noticed there were a few other men sitting at the bar. The interior was dark and lit by a single electric bulb hanging on a wire from the ceiling. The bar was old and showed it. Jakob looked down and realized the floor was packed dirt. There were cigarette and cigar butts littering the floor. He made his way up to the bar.

"Bon Dia Moro. What can I get for you?"

"I would like strong local rum. What do you recommend?"

"Sir, we have since 1965 the local Palmera rum. It is very strong and very good."

Jakob nodded and ordered. He drank the clear colored rum in a single gulp. It burned his throat and he felt it slide into his stomach. Not satisfied he ordered another and repeated another gulp. Still not satisfied he ordered a third. This one he sipped. The rum was taking effect. His head was becoming light and his focus was no longer clear. He finished the drink and slapped some money on the bar and left to confront Solange and Isaac Junior with the disclosure of his past.

He reached the office and climbed the stairs up to where he had his private room. He entered and sat on the bench near the window. His thoughts were confused. He thought back to the days on the farm, his school and friends ha had then. He wondered what was inside of him that had made him want to leave. He thought of Anke and became melancholy. He realized how badly he had treated her. She had been there for him, yet he ignored her pleas and requests. He thought of the days in Holland and Germany and of his selfish actions. His mood became more depressed as he now understood how he had hurt and mislead people.

Jakob dropped his head into his hands and for the first time started to weep. He had gained a fortune in Aruba, but had used friendships and the goodwill of others at their expense. He thought of his age and understood he could never repay the many that had helped him.

As he sat in his depressed state, the door opened and Solange entered. She took one look at Jakob and sensed something was terribly wrong.

"Jakob, look at you. What is wrong? Why have you been drinking so early in the morning? This is not the Jakob I know. Why are you like this? What has happened?"

Jakob looked at her. She stood directly in front of him with her arms tightly folded. Her expression was one of concern and not anger.

"Solange there are some things we must discuss. Please find Isaac Junior and later this morning we will go for lunch and I will tell you these things. There are things that Isaac Junior must hear directly from me."

"Jakob you have me very worried. I will send for Isaac immediately. We will stay here until he joins us. You are in no condition to appear in the office in front of our employees. I will go and get some strong coffee. I order you not to leave this room."

Solange returned with a large coffee pot and some mugs. She poured a dark coffee for Jakob and pulled up a chair to sit beside him. She placed a hand on his knee.

"Jakob do not let whatever is worrying you consume you. We experienced good times but we have also experienced some that were very bad. Whatever it is that worries you, we will deal with it. Together we are a very strong team."

"Solange what I need to tell you will probably change all our lives. There are things in the past that I am ashamed of and need to confess to you. It is important for Isaac Junior to hear them as he is the one who will have to carry on the Klassen name and business when I am gone. It is time for me to tell you of all the past things I have done."

Chapter 176

Several hours passed until Isaac Junior was located and taken to the office. Fearing that something had happened to either Jakob or Solange, he rushed into the building and up the stairs to Jakob's private area. He threw the door open and burst in. He was sweating profusely.

"What has happened? Is there an emergency?"

Solange stood and placed a reassuring hand on his arm.

"Isaac please calm down. No there is no emergency. Something is troubling Jakob immensely. He wishes to tell us what this. He insists that you be here.

Isaac relaxed and walked over to Jakob. He stared at Jakob's face. It seemed as if he had grown older overnight. Isaac Junior saw the lines of age, the sagging skin on his neck and the hollow look in his eyes. Isaac wondered how he could not have noticed this before.

"Jakob what is wrong that is troubling you so much. Why is it so urgent we must stop everything to hear your problem?"

"Son, please sit. What I have to say is going to take some time."

Jakob started to tell his life story. Solange and Isaac Junior sat in silence and listened. Every once in a while Jakob would pause and take a long drink of water. They did not interrupt him though they had many questions. Finally, and with a shaking hand Jakob handed the lawyer's letter to Solange. She read it and covered her mouth with her hand as she gasped. She handed the letter to a confused Isaac Junior.

Solange starred ahead. She averted her eyes away from Jakob. Isaac Junior finished reading the letter and swore. Jakob spoke.

"It was at the beginning of the war. I was young and did not think of how my actions were affecting others. What is in the letter is true. Isaac you have a half brother. That is the Hans mentioned in the letter. I have been callous and refused requests for assistance in the past. I am not proud of this or some of the things I have told you happened in my life.

This now affects us all. I will respond to the lawyer and tell him I wish to negotiate. I do not want this matter to become nasty and create problems for you or the business.

Solange, I am sorry I have not told you of these things earlier."

"Jakob I will need some time to think about all you have told me. What do you know of the boy?"

"I have been told that he has been in serious trouble in Germany. There have been occasions when he has threatened his mother. My uncle Josef had made special arrangements for him to attend a school in Ireland for boys in trouble. I will write the lawyer today. I will ask him to send me details of what Ilsa is wanting in this matter."

"I am leaving now. I do not want to continue with this. I will be in my office. When I wish to speak of this further I will let you know." Solange stormed from the room.

Isaac Junior seated himself next to Jakob. "I do not think Solange will forgive you easily. How much more can you tell me about Hans?"

"I understand from Josef that he was a very difficult and destructive boy. He grew up on the streets during the war and therefore his character and values have been affected by all he has seen and experienced. It seems as if no one can control the boy. I have spent many hours considering him and the past requests for assistance. I did not provide this as all I could see was trouble that would result from so. I did not want him to bring troubles for us here in Aruba. I forbid you from ever telling Hans you are his half brother as I fear he will destroy you too. Isaac you must swear that you will never divulge this information."

Chapter 177

It was a lonely afternoon for Jakob. Solange and Isaac Junior had left to visit and monitor the construction progress for the new restaurant and the water sport dock extension. Throughout the trip Solange had remained quiet. When they arrived at the pier, Solange was delighted at the progress. Isaac Junior spotted Clyde James, the architect, standing and gesturing to two of the workmen. Isaac Junior hailed him and went up on the pier to join them.

"Good afternoon, Clyde. It seems that good progress has been made. Is everything satisfactory?"

"There are some small things to change. I am advising the men that we will need to reinforce the footings and add an additional edging to prevent any damage should the boats push too hard against the pier. I am concerned about the high winds and should the boat dock at speed. These are only small changes but very important ones. Is Jakob here with you?"

"No. Jakob had some business that required his attention. He is at the office. Is there something I can help with?"

"No. I just wanted to speak to him about another project our firm has been requested to look at. It may be of interest to him. It is a housing project in the North. There will be a number of houses to be designed and built."

"I will tell him. I am sure he will contact you."

Solange continued her examination of the restaurant. She was thrilled with the interior and the rustic look that the decorative diving and boating items provided. In particular she loved the planked floor. The placement of the kitchen and bar had been designed to allow diners a maximum view of the Caribbean and the gently curved beach. She slipped off her shoes and walked from the restaurant and across the warm silky soft white sand to join Isaac Junior and Clyde.

"I am happy with the restaurant. When will the work be completed? I need to hire staff and select a couple of experienced managers from our other restaurants."

"The work is meant to be completed within the next three weeks. With the speed at which the construction has progressed I believe it will be completed before then. I suggest you start hiring now."

Isaac Junior examined the area that had been added to accommodate the boats.

"When can we moor the boats? They are on shore at present being painted and checked for any minor repairs."

"The job to install the additional footings will be slow. It is a job that must be done perfectly. They will need to dredge and sink in the pilings. I think another month is needed. We must obtain some special equipment for the job and it needs to come from neighboring Curacao."

"That is a little disappointing but since it is for safety I understand."

Solange wandered away from them and paddled in the warm clear water that was gently lapping at the shore. Isaac Junior watched as she walked some distance away. He recognized the signs. She was upset and angry but did not allow her emotions to interfere with business. Isaac Junior decided to just let her walk alone with her thoughts. He returned to the interior of the restaurant and inspected the work that had been done on the kitchen area. He was about to leave when Solange walked in.

"Isaac let us return to the office. I have made some decisions about the situation that Jakob has caused. I am not happy. I understand how at that time Jakob could have behaved badly. It is not the existence of Hans that upsets me. At the moment I am sad and have lost respect and trust in Jakob. He lied to me. What other mistruths has he told me over the years and is he hiding other things? I am lucky to have you. You have made me proud and I know you will continue to be honest and supportive. I have made some decisions already. Tonight I will pack some clothing as I intend to take a flight as soon as possible and stay with family members in Miami. I will stay until I decide whether I wish to return. You will manage the opening of the restaurant."

Chapter 178

Jakob's troubles mounted without Solange being there. Firstly a fire destroyed their Kit Kat club in San Nicolaas and also damaged the adjacent building. The damage was extensive and the club would need to be totally demolished and rebuilt. Jakob was struggling with coordinating the daily tasks of running the company. Solange's assistant left the company. Jakob received devastating news regarding the yacht they had purchased for the planned sailing cruises. During the maintenance and preparation of the yacht, a crack had been found in the hull above the keel. The repairs would be both costly and time consuming.

As the problems continued, Jakob became more despondent. Isaac Junior's attitude to Jakob had changed. Since Jakob had confessed the situation regarding Hans, there had been less contact and no friendly conversation with Isaac Junior. The strong bond of father and son friendship seemed to have been shattered.

Jakob had written to the law firm in Munich in response to the letter he had received regarding Hans. After weeks he received a reply. Included was a report of Hans' achievements and educational standing during his schooling in Ireland. Jakob read them with great interest. A proposal for a financial settlement was enclosed. Jakob felt trapped and unsure how to proceed.

It was late in the night when he heard the front door of the office downstairs open and slam shut. He rose to go down and find out who had entered the building. As he was opening his door, Isaac Junior appeared in his doorway. He had a bottle of rum and two glasses in his hand.

"We have done so much together to build and run the company. I have done a lot of thinking. We must fix that which is wrong between us. The news you gave Solange and I was bad. Solange understands the fact that Hans was the result of your being impulsive and probably scared when you were trapped in Germany. She is not angry about that. It is the fact you lied to her. Now she worries that there are other things you have been dishonest about. I have come here to share a drink with you and we will speak about what we should do. There are too many things that have gone wrong since Solange left."

Isaac Junior sat the glasses down on the desktop and poured two large portions of rum. They sat in silence for several minutes.

"Isaac, my son. There are no more surprises. For years I have tortured myself over Hans. I never expected this to arise. Josef and I had mailed each other on many occasions attempting to find a solution. It seems there are none. Josef left a considerable amount of money to Hans. He also left him a house that was filled with antiques and art. He has squandered that money and sold the house. He has no sense of values and seems to always find trouble. I am getting old and am tired. I wanted to spend more time with Solange away from the business. I had planned a quieter life for us. I have secretly had a home built for us in Malmok that overlooks the Caribbean. This was to be my gift to her. Now it all seems futile. I have made a mess of things."

"No. Things can be fixed. I suggest you write an apology to Solange. I am sure she will be sensible and understand. You must be truthful and sincere. In your letter tell her of the troubles here and what has happened in Germany with Hans and the law firm."

Together they sat and drank. The tension that Jakob had sensed between them was melting away.

"Isaac in the morning I will write. I did think of flying up to Miami to speak with her and ask her to come back."

"You can do that but she may resent your arriving without first telling her. Please send her the letter and maybe if she responds you should go to her."

"Isaac how did you develop this great sense of logic? It must have been from Solange because when I reflect upon my life some of my choices have not been that sensible."

They continued drinking, talking and laughing until dawn.

Chapter 179

Jakob received a fast response to his letter to Solange. She advised Jakob against travelling to Miami to meet her. She continued that she was concerned about the investment the company had made in the water sport and restaurant ventures. She advised Jakob of the date for her return.

On the day of Solange's flight back to Aruba, Isaac Junior drove out to the airport to greet her. Jakob stayed at the house and prepared it for her return.

Isaac Junior waited patiently at the airport. Hour passed by. The plane was late and no one from the airline company had an explanation. Isaac was concerned. Others who were awaiting the arrival of the flight were becoming worried. Isaac Junior noticed a friend who worked at the airport and hailed him. His friend spun around and upon seeing Isaac Junior quickly approached him.

"Isaac it is good to see you. Why are you here?"

Isaac advised his friend of meeting Solange on her return and driving her back to their house. His friend looked grave.

"The plane is very late and we have lost contact with it. The control tower has been in contact with the airport in Miami. The plane was a little late leaving and they have not had any communication. We are trying to establish contact. There is an extremely bad weather system north of us. The winds are almost hurricane force. It is possible the pilots decided to fly around it or land elsewhere until the conditions improve. I will go now and check the latest information with the control tower. Wait here and I will return and advise you of the latest."

Isaac Junior experienced a feeling of despair. He realized that if he lost Solange a huge part of his life would be gone. He became disturbed at the thought. He paced the airport floor until his friend returned.

"There is no new news. The tower is contacting airports in Curacao, Bonaire, Venezuela and Colombia to find out if the plane either landed there or had made contact. The plane has sufficient fuel to continue flying for this length of time. There is hope that they diverted."

Isaac Junior realized his friend was pacifying him. He moved away from the area in which the other passengers were standing and waiting. The level of conversation amongst those waiting was high and Isaac wanted somewhere quiet to phone Jakob. He approached the counter and asked for the use of a phone. The staff recognized Isaac Junior and invited him behind the counter into an office area and handed him a phone. He called Jakob. The phone rang unanswered. Isaac waited a few minutes and tried again. There was still no answer. Isaac presumed that Jakob had gone out on an errand, though he could not imagine what that would be. He decided to make one more call. This time Jakob answered. Isaac Junior explained the situation. Jakob had no words. He was worried and distressed. Jakob advised Isaac Junior to stay at the airport and to phone when he had any information.

Jakob slumped into the couch. "Was this yet another piece of bad luck? Was he being punished for his mistakes and betrayals? If Solange does not return what will I do?" He sat and was startled by the jangling of the phone. He rushed over to answer it.

"Jakob there is still no news. The airport has been trying to contact the other airports but due to the storm, radio contact is poor. There is hope that the plane may have landed to avoid the severe lightning and turbulence. Are you alright?"

Jakob absorbed the information. "Do you want to stay at the airport or return here? I am sure that the airline will telephone us when they find out what has happened."

"No. I will stay here."

Jakob grunted his agreement.

Isaac Junior found a chair and sat watching the other worried families and friends awaiting the arrival.

Chapter 180

After hours of waiting, Isaac Junior returned home. Jakob and Isaac Junior sat quietly. Neither spoke of their fear that the plane may have crashed, but both were thinking this. Shortly before midnight they were startled by the loud ring of the phone. Isaac Junior jumped and ran to answer it. He listened intently as the caller told him of the news. He turned to Jakob and made a gesture of encouragement.

"Jakob the plane made a landing in the Dominican Republic. The plane was struck several times by lightning and lost use of the radio and most of the navigation systems. The passengers are being flown here in the morning in another plane. They are all safe."

Jakob was relieved. The thought of losing Solange had affected him deeply. Tired and mentally exhausted, they both retired for the night.

Isaac phoned the airport early next morning to ask for the time the plane was expected to arrive. He looked at his watch. The plane would arrive in approximately an hour. He went and awoke Jakob and advised him of the information. Jakob sprung from his bed and started dressing. He wanted to be at that airport for Solange's arrival. Within minutes they departed the house for the airport.

There was a crowd at the airport waiting for the arrival of the passengers from Miami. There was a larger crowd of people than the previous evening. Isaac Junior guessed that the situation had caused some to appreciate their friends and family a little more.

Solange walked out into the waiting area. She was dressed casually in a white pants suit and carried several bags. Jakob and Isaac junior hurried over to her and took the bags. Jakob set them down and wrapped his arms around her. They embraced for the longest time. Isaac Junior detected the slightest tear in Solange's eye. He smiled and thought that this was an indication that the past would be dealt with and they could resume their happy life.

As they drove toward their house, Jakob asked Isaac Junior to continue to drive up the coast toward Malmok.

"There is a project there that I wish to show you, Solange."

In the car Solange told Jakob of the time she had spent with her family. She seemed refreshed and in high spirits. They finally arrived at the small bay at Malmok. The surf pounded into the deserted beach. Jakob instructed Isaac to drive a little further around a sharp bend. As they turned the corner a magnificent two story home overlooking the beach and Caribbean came into view.

"Isaac please stop the car."

Jakob got out of the car and reached to take Solange's hand. They walked up to the house. There were still ladders and construction materials lying to the side.

"Jakob this is a beautiful house. Who is it being built for? Do I know the owners?"

Jakob laughed. "Yes you certainly do. They are very close to you. In fact you deal with them every day."

Solange frowned. She was confused.

"Solange, I built this house for you. It is my gift to you for all you have done for Isaac and me."

Her mouth fell open. She walked all around the outside and finally asked to be taken inside. Jakob took some keys and gave them to her. They entered into a foyer and she saw rooms on either side that faced the water. They climbed the stairs to the bedrooms and a room that could be a library or study. They went back downstairs and Solange inspected the kitchen. It was equipped with the most modern appliances.

"Jakob, how did you manage to do this and keep it a secret? You know I generally find out about everything? When will we move here?"

Chapter 181

With Solange's return to the office, things returned to normal. Solange quickly turned her attention to the serious problems that had arisen in her absence. She was happy to rehire her assistant who had left the company during her absence. Jakob, Isaac Junior and Solange visited the remains of the burned out Kit Kat club in San Nicolaas. They all agreed that nothing was salvageable and returned to their office in Oranjestad to decide whether to rebuild the club or instead build an office building or store.

Before returning to their offices, the trio decided to buy a lunch and sit at the nearby beach to eat. The day was warm and pleasant. The stifling heat of the last few weeks had broken. As they sat eating and making small talk, Jakob raised the issues they were facing in the company.

"Solange, we are behind with the restaurant project on the pier. I think we should meet with Clyde James immediately. We are weeks past the planned opening. There have been recent construction problems and I do not see any extra effort by the builders to get the project completed faster. Also, we have been unable to attract local people with the experience and skills to run a restaurant of this nature. Isaac has spoken with many."

"Yes, Jakob. Please contact Clyde James. I want to see him as soon as possible. I reviewed the financial accounting for the building. It is completely beyond what was agreed. Let us try to meet him this afternoon."

They talked about some other business matters that were less important. Solange was determined that the restaurant on the pier would be completed, be first class and be finished quickly.

Upon their return to the office, Solange dispatched one of the clerks to visit Clyde James' business and tell him he was wanted for an immediate and serious meeting with the Klassens.

While waiting for his arrival, Solange asked about the progress of Jakob's water sports operation.

"We have been fortunate that both boats are ready to launch. We have identified several good people to sail the boats. We have decided that the yacht will take tourists on sailing cruises, while the launch had been equipped for fishing. The repairs that were needed to the yacht were less serious than we first thought."

"Then there is some good news. Who is going to manage the operation?"

"Solange there is something I want to talk to you and Isaac about. Let me go and ask Isaac to join us."

Moments later Isaac and Jakob joined Solange in her office.

"I had promised that I would be honest and tell you of any developments with the law firm in Munich and Hans. In your absence Solange, I did receive several letters and a report on Hans'. The report covers the trouble he has been in, but also contains his records of his achievements at the Reform School. I find the section that details his superiority and love of boats and sailing informative. In my correspondence I have asked about the amount they are looking for in a settlement. I received a reply that Ilsa received the majority of Josef's huge estate and that what they seek is not money but acceptance and assistance with

Hans. He does not know I am his father. Ilsa named him with her name. He is known as Hans Wolfe. He has been told that Josef has a nephew, which is me, who lives in the Caribbean. I propose that we take a risk and invite him here to work in the water sports company."

Solange and Isaac sat in silence.

"Jakob that risk is huge. You have never met Hans. How do you plan to control him?"

"I do not have everything worked out. I just wanted to present my idea to you. Let us take time and think about it and then we can discuss it in a few days."

Solange shrugged and looked to Isaac Junior who was expressionless.

Sensing the discomfort, Jakob went to his office and retrieved the dossier on Hans that had been sent to him by the lawyers. He returned and handed the file to Solange.

She opened the binder and carefully read each page. When finished she handed it over to Isaac Junior.

"He has certainly led an interesting life. I wonder if he is too old now to change his ways. I do agree that the report from the school contains information that his whole nature changed when he was involved with the boats and sailing. I find that interesting. Since it is your wish to have the water sport business, I will leave the decision to you and Isaac."

Isaac Junior had finished reading the file. "I believe that there will be enough work to keep him fully occupied. Let us make an offer to him. We could offer him some ownership position if it works out. I recommend we only offer ownership in the water sport business and nothing else. We will limit our risk."

Jakob was pleased. "I will prepare an offer and review it with you both and when we agree I will send it to the lawyers."

Solange turned to Isaac Junior. "Isaac I have been thinking about the restaurant and the problem you are having in finding good staff. I suggest we ask Miguel and Alejandro to manage it. They have no work at present due to the fire at the club. It will be months before it can be rebuilt, should we decide to reopen it."

"That is a brilliant idea. They know the suppliers and have many friends in the restaurant business. Tomorrow morning I will drive to San Nicolaas and meet with them."

Jakob marveled at how Solange could solve problems and generate an atmosphere of calm and confidence.

Chapter 182

Over the next month, Jakob exchanged correspondence with Munich. Finally an agreement was reached. Hans would travel to Aruba as a Captain of the sailing operation for the water sport company. The agreement contained a provision for Hans to become a part owner should the operation perform well and he did not become involved in any criminal or destructive behavior. Jakob sent money and arranged the travel plans. The date for Hans's arrival arrived.

The day was stormy. Heavy black clouds slowly crossed over the island. Lightning flashed and the rolling thunder was deafening. Torrential rain fell for long periods. The roads became flooded as the rain water gathered without adequate drainage. It was late that afternoon when the storms cleared. Isaac made his way to the airport. It was a slow drive. He parked and entered the terminal and joined others awaiting the arrival of passengers from Amsterdam. Hans had travelled from Munich to Amsterdam to connect to the Aruba flight.

The plane touched down on time. Arriving passengers exited and were met by their excited families and friends. Isaac waited patiently, eager to see what his half brother looked like. Eventually, a tall slim man with closely cropped hair and glasses and carrying a duffel bag on his shoulder emerged. He stood looking around. His expression was one of annoyance. Isaac approached him.

"Are you Hans?"

"Yes I am Hans Wolfe. Are you Isaac Junior? Are you to meet me and take me to meet Jakob Klassen?"

"I am indeed Isaac Klassen, Jakob's son. Do you have any other luggage? If not, we will go to my car and I will take you to Jakob's home."

"Before I meet Jakob, can you take me to see the boat I am meant to sail? If it is a poor craft, I will not be sailing it. I will just return to Germany."

Isaac Junior agreed and drove Jakob to the tiny marina where the yacht was moored. Hans left the car and slowly walked around inspecting the yacht. He jumped on board and continued his inspection. After fifteen minutes Hans returned to the car.

"She looks fine. I am impressed. I will need to sail her tomorrow and learn a little of the winds and currents of the sea here. The conditions will be very different to those I have sailed in before. I am looking forward to learning this and the challenge ahead."

Isaac was pleased to see the change in Hans. He seemed to have relaxed and become less hostile. They drove on chatting about Aruba and Germany until they reached Jakob's new house in Malmok. Isaac parked the car and opened the door for Hans to enter. Jakob and Solange stood in the large room that overlooked the sea. Jakob was anxious. Solange stepped forward.

"I am Solange. I am pleased to meet you Hans. This is my husband Jakob."

The two shook hands and Jakob invited Hans to sit. He offered drinks and all of them sat casually talking while each party measured the other. The small talk gravitated to the water sport operation. Hans advised Jakob that he had already looked at the boat and wished to take it out. He asked about a crew. Isaac told Hans of the crew he had hired and their experience. Hans was skeptical.

"Can you arrange for me to meet them tomorrow? I would like to sail the boat and test their skills. I am eager to start. Now I am exhausted and would like to rest. The difference in time and the long flights have made me very tired."

"Come. I will escort you to the guest room where you can stay until we find you an apartment."

Isaac escorted Hans up the stairs to the bedroom. They said good night and Isaac returned to Jakob and Solange. He told them of the change in mood he observed from when he met Hans at the airport and when they stopped at the boat.

"It is like he became a different person. I hope this will work out well for us."

Chapter 183

The next afternoon, Hans returned from sailing the yacht and working with the crew. He was ecstatic.

"That is one fine boat. I very impressed. It handles beautifully. I was able to test it in the high winds and currents near San Nicolaas. It is the ideal boat for taking tourists for pleasure sailing."

Jakob was pleased with Hans' reaction. "That is good. Now we must plan a date to start the business." Together they discussed all that needed to be done before they could launch the business. As they planned, Solange and Isaac Junior returned to the house and joined them. Jakob quickly gave them an update.

"Jakob and Hans, I have been thinking about how to announce this new venture. Isaac and I have come up with a plan. We will be opening the new restaurant on the pier next weekend. We are extending invitations to many who have businesses here on the island. We will be offering complimentary food and drinks. I think you should offer a complimentary short sail. It will be unique and demonstrate the appeal that this will have to tourists and others."

Again Jakob was stunned at how Solange could make things so easy.

"I like that idea. Yes I say we do that. Solange you are brilliant."

Isaac Junior was apprehensive. He had been watching Hans' reaction and observed a distinct lack of enthusiasm. He wondered if this was due to the fact that it was not his idea or if it was the character trait that Hans did not like being told what to do by others. Isaac sensed trouble ahead for them.

Hans spoke. "How will I be paid if you are going to be giving free trips to all your friends? I think it is a stupid idea."

Isaac was incensed. "Hans you will apologize to my mother. If you want this job you will cease with the insubordination. We have made you a very generous offer financially and given you a job doing what you love...sailing."

Hans stood and walked away and out the front door of the house without speaking a word.

Isaac was angry. "Jakob I tell you now that we are going to have some serious problems with Hans. He has only been here for one day and already we see his attitude."

Solange reached out and placed her hand on Isaac's arm to calm him down. "I say we ignore what just happened. Let us continue with our plans. I think that if we make Hans responsible for the water sport business and he is busy then he will be less likely to act like that. I think parts of his actions now are because he is nervous. Let him get involved with the sailing and we will see what happens. Remember we are in control. I suggest that Jakob go on each trip for the first week or two. He can make sure that everything goes smoothly."

Isaac spoke. "I am not at all happy with this. I do not trust him. My instinct tells me that we should stop this now and send him back to Germany."

"Isaac, you and Jakob are used to the business and have worked together for many years now. Hans has just arrived here. He is in a strange new land with people he does not know. Please give him some time to adjust. We will all keep an eye on him. We must give him a chance."

"Mother you are too kind. Please remember this as I am convinced he will hurt us and our company. I will be most happy when we find an apartment for him. Jakob, he may be my half brother but I do not see having a partnership with him or even working with him. There is something in his character that I feel he is unable to control."

"Isaac when I worked at the refinery, I had men like that to manage at times. If you treated them correctly they often worked harder and produced better work than the other men. I say we let him show us if he can behave and succeed."

Chapter 184

The gala opening of the restaurant and launch of the water sport business were a major success and continued to draw customers through the next weeks. Jakob was happy to see the rapport that Hans developed with the tourists. Hans had developed a story he proudly told on each trip. He pointed out highlights and told a yarn about the German ship *"The Antilla"*. The tourists listened intently and asked many questions. Hans spoke like an authority. Jakob was impressed and soon stopped taking the trips.

Jakob decided to spend less time at the office. He spoke with Solange and Isaac of his decision. He was finding that he tired easily and wanted time to himself to go fishing and enjoy a life other than daily business. They agreed with Jakob and agreed with his plan to spend three days each week at the office.

The calm life was soon to be shattered. Several months had passed since the opening of the business and Jakob had paid less attention to the operation. He was satisfied that Hans had settled down and was doing an excellent job. He had no concerns until one afternoon when Isaac came into his office with one of the clerks.

"Jakob there is a matter that we need to discuss. This man has found some problems with the sailing operation. There is a large amount of liquor being used on the boat. I have reviewed the numbers. It is impossible for that amount to be drunk each week by the guests. I suspect someone is stealing from us. Here take a look at the records. Here is the ledger for the supplies provided to the boat each week."

Jakob took the ledger and turned to the beginning. He traced the consumption of the different items....food, soft drinks, fruit and liquor. All seemed correct except for two items. The number of bottles of Vodka and Rum had tripled since the operation started. Jakob asked for the book that contained the number of tickets sold each day. He asked the clerk to analyze the records and report back immediately with the statistics showing the amount used per passenger.

"Jakob I tell you again that I do not trust Hans. I think he is stealing the liquor from us. I have also received some disturbing news about him and what is happening. Hans has been sleeping on the boat at night. He takes the boat from the pier and moors at an anchorage off Palm Beach. He is taking women with him for the night. These are women he meets on the trips. "

"This is serious. How did you learn this information? How long has it been happening?"

"One of the young boys on the crew who is a relative of Miguel's went into the restaurant last week. Hans had beaten the boy who was bleeding and badly cut. He told Miguel that Hans was using the boat at night and that he was taking bottles from the boat in his knapsack. We cannot ignore this. We must catch Hans and deal with him. I will not allow this to continue and I do not want him as a partner in our business."

"Isaac I told you earlier that he must never know that I am his father. He only knows me as Josef's nephew. It must stay like that. He must not find out you are his half brother. You were correct about him in the beginning. I fear that if he finds out the truth he will wreck everything we have built."

"I will speak to Miguel and Alejandro about this. Do I have your blessing to proceed and remove him from our operations?"

"Yes it is best you handle this."

"I must tell you though that Miguel's Latin temper has been fuelled. I asked him not to do anything until we spoke. He is angry and wants to punish Hans for the injuries his nephew suffered."

The clerk returned with a page of hastily scrawled numbers. It was obvious that it was impossible for that amount of liquor to be consumed on each trip. The statistics revealed almost a bottle per passenger.

Isaac laughed. "They would need carts to wheel the passengers back."

Chapter 185

Isaac visited Miguel at the restaurant. The boat was gone from the pier on a trip. Isaac took a stool at the bar. Alejandro served him a cold beer and Miguel pulled up another stool and sat beside him. The three of them huddled in conversation.

That night when the restaurant was closing, Miguel observed Hans attempting to assist a woman onto the deck of the yacht. The woman was laughing and shrieking. She was obviously drunk. Miguel called to Hans who spun around with a look of shock on his face.

"Hans, let her go you bum. You and I have some serious business to settle."

Hans released the woman who stumbled and fell from the yacht into the water. Hans dived into dark water to help her. He wrapped his arm through hers and awkwardly swam back to the beach. His tumble into the water had dampened any desire she may have had to spend more time with Hans. She sensed the danger and watched as Miguel walked menacingly toward them. She started to run up the beach and faded into a stand of palm trees that bordered the sand. Miguel continued onto confront Hans. Within minutes blows were exchanged. The beating was vicious and fierce. Miguel was strong and Hans suffered at his hands. Blood streamed down from cuts above Hans eye. A blow to his face had torn the skin below his right eye. Miguel hit him directly in the face and heard the snap as Hans's nose broke. Hans fell to the ground. Miguel spat on him and delivered a kick to his back before walking off.

Hans lay on the sand for hours. He was in agony and still in a partial drunken state. The faint grey light of dawn was breaking when he finally stumbled off to the room he had rented.

Throughout the day Hans stayed in his room. Occasionally he would vomit from the pain of the beating and the effect of the hangover. He sat and reflected on what he had lost. He decided to find another job sailing for another owner.

It was not an easy task. Hans' reputation had spread in the small community. He finally found a position with a local who was starting to offer rides in his small power boat. Hans was not happy. He preferred to be sailing a yacht but really had no other option.

During the day he would take a few people out and motor from Palm Beach down to the area of Spaans Lagoon. While the guests were content, Hans was bored.

Hans began to consider moving from Aruba to one of the other islands in the Caribbean where tourism was more firmly established. At night he would stop into one of the many dimly lit bars in Oranjestad and drink until he was unable to stand. He would often awake in the mornings to find himself still in the same bar. His idea of leaving Aruba was pointless. Any of the meager money he earned was spent on booze.

He resigned himself to the fact he was probably trapped on Aruba. He wondered if another company would start a sailing and excursion operation. He convinced himself that could happen and then he would have a job. He did not have to wait long. Jakob's sailing venture had been watched closely and soon there was a competitor. Hans went to see the owners who explained that they had purchased a catamaran in Florida. He was hired to sail the boat down to Aruba.

Hans tried to hire his old crew away from Jakob to assist him with the task. Nobody wished to sail with him.

The owners recruited a crew and arranged for them to fly to Miami and take delivery of the boat. It was a fine craft of 45 feet. The sails and gear were all new. Hans suggested to the crew that before leaving for Aruba they take the boat out for several trials. All agreed and they spent the next few days trying the boat and the equipment.

It was a beautiful clear morning with the sun peeping over the horizon when Hans and crew set sail for Aruba.

Chapter 186

Jakob spent less and less time at the office. Solange and Isaac Junior had hired some staff and developed an effective team which allowed them to focus on new projects. Solange worried about Jakob spending so much time alone. She confided this to Isaac. Recently she had noticed signs of Jakob's aging. He was forgetting appointments and frequently misplaced items. She made a decision to spend more time with Jakob outside the office and business. She suggested a trip to Florida and New York which they decided to take. Isaac assumed control of the company and ensured that he consulted Solange on any major decision that needed to be made.

The company continued to progress well under his leadership and became a serious leader in the tourism and hospitality industry. Isaac was invited to participate in other new businesses and developed a reputation as a strong and honest person. He made many friends and took part in sports and social events. Isaac was a person to be seen with or invite to a function.

It was at a party that he was introduced to Janelle. He was enraptured by her charm and personality and within months they were an inseparable pair.

Within a year they married. The wedding was a grand affair by island standards. The restaurant on the pier was specially decorated and the best chefs on the island were hired to prepare a feast. Isaac worshipped Janelle. Solange was happy for him. She and Jakob were happy that Isaac had found someone so special.

Janelle gave birth to twins, a girl and a boy. It was an occasion for much happiness and celebration. Solange was delighted and mothered them more than their own mother. Jakob would sit with the boy and show him tricks or read to him. Together he would take the little boy to the shore to try and catch fish. Even though age had slowed Jakob down, he was enjoying every minute with his family. He now understood what he had missed in his earlier years, still he had no regrets.

They received an invitation from Carlita to visit with her at her home in Savaneta to attend a birthday party for Miguel. In the invitation she enclosed a note for Jakob. In the note she told him that many of his old friends from when he lived in San Nicolaas and some who worked at the refinery would be at the party. Jakob looked forward to meeting them again.

Jakob and Solange drove down to Savaneta the following Saturday afternoon. The party was large and Jakob spent time speaking to his old friends. Eventually, Jakob became tired. He slipped out from the party and walked down to the beach. He found the log he had sat on many times before watching the sunset.

As he sat looking out to the sea he heard the far off sound of a boat motor. He scanned the water and off in the distance saw the dot of a fast approaching boat. As the boat grew closer Jakob could make out figures on board. The motor slowed and the boat ran up onto the sand at the end of the beach. Jakob squinted against the sun and watched as two men jumped from the boat and helped a third man out of the boat. They assisted him up to the sandy beach, left him and ran back to the boat. One jumped into the boat as the other pushed the boat back before also jumping into it. The motor revved and the driver quickly spun the boat around and headed back out to sea.

"Probably dropping off a friend after a day's fishing" thought Jakob. He continued to watch as the man slowly made his way toward him. Jakob squinted against the setting sun. "Is that Juan? He wondered. He gazed at the stooped figure on the beach. "No, I am just an old man thinking crazy thoughts. My eyes are weak and I am tired."

He heard Carlita calling his name. He turned and walked back to the porch where he found Solange and Carlita seated and waiting for him with his rum drink. He glanced back to the beach. Who was the man from the boat? He was sure it was Juan.

FIN

The sequel to Journey of Betrayals is scheduled for release in the summer 2018 with the title

Journey to the Unknown Consequences

Epilogue

The Mennonite and Amish communities of Pennsylvania and South Western Ontario continue to flourish. While Old Order Mennonites still work the land and practice their traditional ways, many others have adapted to new technologies and medicines. Many own cars and travel.

The City of Berlin, Ontario was renamed Kitchener after a long and acrimonious process. Today Kitchener and is home to Insurance, high tech and manufacturing companies.

The grandiose trains of Canadian Pacific have been replaced long ago by sleek modern trains, which while fast and efficient they lack the style and class of their predecessors. CP Ships sailed their last passenger ship in 1970. *"The Empress of Britain"* was sunk by a German U-Boat in October of 1940.

The Netherlands slowly rebuilt after World War II and swore to never be poorly prepared for any future invasion. A strong and modern military force has been built and serves in parts of the Dutch Kingdom today.

Munich, like the rest of Germany was rebuilt with the help of Britain and the United States after the war. Munich was particularly devastated from the Allied bombings. Within ten years many of the damaged churches, cathedrals and landmarks were restored.

In Aruba, life changed drastically after WWII. Today San Nicolaas is a mere shadow of its former self. The oil refinery was closed by Exxon. Several attempts were made to reopen it by other companies. Unemployment spiked and attempts to sell and reopen the refinery have all but failed. With the loss of thousands of jobs, homes were abandoned and stores boarded up. Today the Aruban Government has made effort to revitalize the town but it still remains a desolate and sad place.

Savaneta has remained the same and offers tourists a glimpse of old Aruba.

Oranjestad, the Capital of Aruba is a bustling port into which the cruise ships dock.

Palm Beach has become a tourist hub with major Hotel chains present along with timeshare resorts, restaurants and many water sport companies.

Malmok has developed into a quiet and upscale residential area with the beaches of Boca Catalina and Arashi nearby. The German freighter *"The Antilla"* lies about 400yards offshore in 60feet of water and has become a favorite diving site.

Aruba gained "status aparte" from the Dutch in 1986 but still remains a self governing part of the Dutch Kingdom. Today approximately 1 million tourists visit Aruba annually.

FIN

www.ingramcontent.com/pod-product-compliance
Lightning Source LLC
Chambersburg PA
CBHW022142130726
47905CB00004BA/946